THE Black HEART

By Natalie England

The Black Heart

First Edition April 2025

Published by Natalie England Publishing LLC

Print Cover by Damonza.

To my boys

I love you most!

And to my Savior, Jesus Christ ...

my greatest source of hope.

To my readers,

While I've tried to make this series fun and full of adventure, the root message behind these books is based on depression and the struggles that go with it.

Which means there will be dark moments.

My hope is that you will finish the series to the end when you can.

That is where happiness is discovered.

Chapter 1

I shift quietly behind a berry bush, concealed from the groups of Pepps in front of Petrichor's school. A growing pile of listless berries lies on the ground in front of me, mashed to bits.

My legs ache from sitting, but I ignore their protests.

I need to talk to Flint.

I wipe the sweat off my face before plucking another handful of berries from the branches, then squishing them between my fingers one by one.

Groups of Pepps have been practicing for the Dino Games all morning in front of the large barren mountain that houses the school. Fire must be their greatest resource in the game because that's all they've been doing. For hours, creating fire. The extensive flames have had me sweating profusely since I got here.

I squish another berry, watching the juice ooze out.

It seems like a tremendous waste of time and resources for the Pepps to still hold the games, especially when there are so many other things to be done.

Like find Danny.

I clench my fist, multiple berries juicing in my grip.

But the dinosaurs were brought to Petrichor hundreds of years ago to use as protectors. And after everything that's happened, after everything I've done, the Pepps ... need protecting. The Dino Games will be held to give the trainers a chance to teach the dinosaurs *how* to protect. *How is that even possible?*

I squeeze my eyes shut. I've been fighting to keep my thoughts from drifting down this path for the past hour. I don't want to think about the truth, about *why* they need protecting, or *how* Danny is still missing. If I let my defenses crumble, I'll be bombarded by an endless torrent of memories that might just drown me. So, I fight them.

Regardless of how tightly I shut my eyes though, one bitter thought slips through.

Danny is still missing, and it's all my fault.

I gulp back the threatening tears, pick more berries, and open my eyes, tightly squishing them in my hand. I need to think about something else.

The dino training. I inhale slowly, observing the training in front of me. Each dino trainer is focused on bordering a small area of grass with fire and attempts to keep the flame alive for long periods of time. They're doing this because in the game they'll need to confine their dinosaurs to a bordered area to roam.

If the flame dies, they try again.

But looking at the fire doesn't help. I hate fire. It reminds me of Mitch's death. And being trapped with Mark at Case's hideout, SilverDen—the silver mine where Pepp prisoners had been kept.

I bite my cheek hard, drawing blood. I *really* don't want to think about Mitch. Or Mark. I frantically grab at more berries and clench my jaw, forcing myself to think about *just* the dinosaurs. *Just the game.*

After what happened at SilverDen, the game was postponed for three weeks. But because the dinosaurs are getting dangerously antsy, and because the chief says it's time, the game won't be held off any longer. It'll take place in a week, and Flint is one of those now training for it. If I didn't hate him so much, I'd admit that he's a terribly good shot with the bow and arrow. I've watched him repeatedly take a fire arrow and send it through a bull's-eye target hundreds of feet away.

He's also disturbingly good with power. Unlike me, he seems to be able to control the elements in several different areas. Not only can he command fire, ice, and plant life, I've also seen him heal wounds and morph into an abnormally large crocodile. Not sure why he would choose that animal, but it confirmed that he's also a morpher.

That's why I'm here. I'm hoping that since he's a pureblood—good at everything—he'll be able to do what I ask.

No, be *willing* to do what I ask.

I openly sigh in relief when the mountains of fire die down and the groups begin to disperse. The training must be over.

But then my chest tightens. Flint, with his perfectly cut golden-red hair and deeply tanned skin, starts walking in my direction. This is what I wanted, I remind myself. But when his face gets closer, countless emotions surface.

Fisting my berry-stained hands, I try to ignore the dull ache in my chest and stand. I need Flint to do this for me, something nobody else will. I just hope more than anything he hates me as much as he did the day he threw that rock at me and forced me to morph.

Unfortunately, Flint's not alone. Nadia is with him, the blonde girl who was on my initiation team. Flint was on our team too in the beginning, until he burned me with acid. Then the chief removed him from initiation altogether. Nadia was angry that Flint had been removed, and even though she's matched and moved on, it looks like she's still close to the boy. Which means she probably hates me too.

But I need to do this now, before I chicken out.

I step out of the bushes before he gets too far ahead. He sees me right away, and a flash of anger clouds his face. I hide a smile. Perfect. He still hates me.

Before I can speak, he turns to walk in a different direction, away from me.

I catch up quickly though and tap his arm. He swirls around, his hands fisted. I take a step back, trying to speak calmly.

"Please, I need to ask you something."

"No," Flint spits, turning on his heel once again, taking Nadia with him.

Standing my ground, I shout after him, "I want you to remove my totem."

My words make him stop. He seems to quietly contemplate them before turning around. My skin prickles, knowing I've gotten his attention. I avoid the temptation to fold my arms and hide my shaking hands.

"You want me to *remove* your totem?"

My confidence wavers slightly, but I square my shoulders in an attempt to appear stronger than I feel. "You know how to do it, don't you?"

"Of course I know how to do it. The question is, do you know what will happen *to you* if I try?"

My eyes betray me now, redirecting to the grass.

"Of course you do. That's why you've come to ask *me*." His voice is cruel. "You know that nobody else would be willing to sacrifice your life to remove that defected thing."

It's exactly the response I was hoping to get out of Flint. Yet, standing here now, his reaction hurts me more than I want it to. He's not the only one who would like to be rid of me—he's just the only one brave enough to say it out loud. The words as true as they are, though, don't feel good to hear.

My body sags. I'm tired. Tired of reliving everything. Every. Single. Day. Tired of being constantly reminded of the friends I no longer have because of my choices. And that Danny, an innocent boy, is now being held captive because of the power harnessed in my defected totem. There's only one conclusion I've come to at the end of each day since the morph. That the totem is to blame for everything, and I need to get rid of it. As long as it's still on me, I will never be happy.

Unfortunately, my totem is not easily removed like the normal ones. Because of the fishlike hooks imbedded into my vessels, it's impossible to discharge without extreme pain or even death.

That's why I need Flint.

I nod, confirming his statement. I don't need to say it out loud. If death is the cost of removing the totem, so be it.

At least, I think so be it. My hands begin shaking again, but I hold my head high.

"So, will you help me?"

Flint's cruel smirk slowly fades. "No," he says and stalks away.

Anger and relief both flood me in the same confusing moment, but I'm not ready to give up. Catching him, I grab his arm. "Why not?"

Flint's green eyes tighten before he rips his arm out of my grasp.

"Do you remember the day I threw that rock at you while you were rappelling? The day I got you to morph?"

"Of course."

"That day, the chief threatened that if I ever went near you again, he would personally see to it that all my power generators would be removed from my body, and I would be taken away from Petrichor to live as a *human*." Flint shakes his head in disgust, bringing his bitter face within inches of mine. "I'm sorry, Alena. But as much as I would love to see an end to you, I'm not willing to give up my life as a Pepp *for* you."

I step back, surprised by his words.

The vine, or *totem*, woven through the skin of the usual Pepp is loaded with thousands of tiny Peppate generators. When a Pepp morphs into an eagle, those tiny generators are activated and Peppate seeps out of the skin to be spread. During the process of producing Peppate, the generators also produce a yellowish liquid known as power. This liquid is pushed through the totem until it reaches the heart, where it's collected in a glass sphere. From there the power can be removed and given to other Pepps if needed. With a sphere full of power, a Pepp is able to hear the elements all around and ultimately control them.

But Flint is a pureblood. Unlike normal Pepps, he doesn't need a totem to obtain power. His power generators are imbedded into the vessels all over his body. I never imagined all those generators could be removed.

"The chief couldn't do that to you, could he?"

Flint glowers at me. "Of course, he could. He did it to my uncle. Took his powers away and then sent him to Algor Prison. I don't understand how my mom can stand working beside the chief when he ruined her brother's life." Flint shakes his head. "Now leave me alone."

He walks away with Nadia. This time I don't stop him. He won't help me. I hate how conflicted this makes me feel.

"Oh, Alena." Flint stops and turns back. "If you're really hard up for help, you should go pay a visit to the totem tree at the Post. One touch of the poisonous trunk and you turn to dust. It's painless, really."

Flint's trailing words sting deeper than I ever imagined they could. I should expect nothing less from him, but his comment pricks at something deep inside me. I glance at my totem, new tears swimming in my swollen eyes. He would be happy to see me turn to dust. Everyone would. And now I'm more embarrassed than I've ever been.

My least favorite person in the world knows just how weak I am.

***

I wander through Petrichor, fatigue oozing through my body like tar that threatens to drag me down. My heavy feet move themselves, burdened by Flints words and a hopelessness I can't seem to shake. I'm alone. Completely alone. I keep thinking I need to send a letter to my family. There's a stack of letters they'd sent to me on my nightstand, but I've been unable to open them. I'm guessing they're worried since I haven't responded, but they still don't know about SilverDen. I can't conjure enough energy to tell them about it.

I'm not sure what to do anymore. How am I supposed to live here as a Pepp with the defected totem on my arm scaring everyone, including me?

Amid my thoughts, though, something inches into my mind. Something Flint said about his uncle. The generators that create the power we use to control the elements around us had been removed from him. It had to have been done one by one, right? I'd never thought about it before, but is that something that could be done with my totem? The chief said the totem as a *whole* could not be removed because it would rip apart my blood vessels. But what if each of the generators *within* the totem were removed individually? With power.

Before I realize it, I find myself walking through the tunnels of the Post. Not knowing where the totem room is, I stop a hurried Pepp and ask for directions. I try to ignore the accusing way the man glares at me when I talk to him, grateful when he finally tells me the way.

I find the door to the room down a dark, isolated hallway with a sign that says "Totem Tree Observatory."

Opening the door, I walk into a large open circular cavern at least a hundred feet high and just as wide in diameter. Directly in the middle of the room is a large tree, with a thick mossy-covered trunk that reaches up only a few feet before splitting into several branches. The smaller branches shoot out toward the bright opening in the ceiling, and at the tip of each branch are hundreds of brownish vines that stretch down almost touching the ground. The tree looks like what I've come to know as a Weeping Willow, just without any leaves.

I notice how the Pepps close to the tree shift carefully around it, staying away from the trunk. *Flint had said it was poisonous.*

I look closer. The Pepps are touching the vines, but they have heavy gloves on their hands. Flint must have been right. Touching the tree with bare hands is dangerous.

The rest of the room strongly resembles the chief's office, with various kinds of rocks pushed together to make the walls. Then there's dust. Lots of dust floating in the sun's rays.

A river of water flowing through one cavern wall passes quietly by the tree, feeding its roots before wandering out the other side. The far wall has been removed, bars placed over the opening, allowing sunlight and air to reach the tree. Past the opening, though, the rock drops. It must be part of the cliff that I flew up when I first came to Petrichor.

The Pepps next to the tree talk and laugh freely, making the room overwhelmingly loud.

For the first time, I question why I really came here. Did I come to actually touch the tree trunk? I sigh when I see that I'm not even in the same room as the tree. What I'm standing in is some sort of lookout separated by a thick piece of glass. I guess that's why it's called an observatory. Of course, the tree wouldn't be accessible to everyone, especially someone like me.

I look down at the totem on my arm. The vine starts at my wrist, branching and winding up and around in unique swirls, buried only under the very top layers of my skin. From my shoulder, some of it continues up to my jaw while the rest cuts over to my heart.

Laced around the vine in my upper arm is a bright red ribbon, identifying me as a medic. To anyone it looks like a normal Pepp vine. But, in truth, it's the opposite of normal. It creates Doler instead of Peppate and makes me feel like crap.

"Alena?" I hear a muffled shout through the glass. The voice is familiar, but I can't remember why. I search the room until my eyes land on a face I know and hold back a groan. I didn't come here to talk, but Bapoto, the boy who participated in initiation with me, was never good at sensing bad moods. I should have known he'd be here. At initiation he matched as a totem trainer.

I fake a half-smile and wave politely, hoping he'll just move on with his work, but he doesn't. Turning around, he exits the room, and somehow I know he's coming to find me. I search the walls in the observatory to see if there's another door that leads to the cavern, but the only door I see is the door I used to get in here.

Sure enough, that's the door Bapoto comes through. "Alena!" He grins widely. His black hair is trimmed to perfection, and his dark skin is sweating from the work. Raising a heavily gloved fist, he prods me to bump his hand. His grin widens when I oblige.

"What are you doing here, Alena?" he asks curiously, walking to the glass overlooking the tree.

I immediately hang my head in embarrassment. I don't know why I'm here, and yet I do, and could never admit it to someone. Especially

Bapoto. Balling my fists, I come up with the only socially acceptable excuse for me being here. It isn't entirely false either.

"I was wondering about the totems," I say. "How they're created. I had one question in particular maybe you could answer for me."

"I can answer anything for you, Alena. I know everything there is to know about the tree." Bapoto winks at me, and I try not to feel jealous of his confidence.

"How do the Peppate generators get into the totems?"

Bapoto's expression turns thoughtful, and he places his hands on the glass to observe the tree. "Well, the totems are grown from the branches of the tree, which have the generators woven into them. So, the generators come from the tree. But in order for the generators to get into the tree initially, someone had to have put them in there." Bapoto blinks, then nods, happy with his response.

"They were put in there one by one?"

"Yes. I think power was used to help, but they still had to be put in one by one."

"Do you think the generators could be removed from the totem in the same way? One by one?"

Bapoto turns toward me. "Are you referring to your totem?"

I don't answer.

Bapoto rubs his chin thoughtfully. "You must be. I wonder if Jeter has thought about that. It seems like it would be possible, especially with power. You could give it a try."

I sense no judgment in Bapoto's voice. I don't know why, but that relieves and comforts me, encouraging me to ask another question.

"What do they sound like? The generators. How do I identify them in my totem?"

Bapoto's face falls. "I can tell you what normal generators sound like, but yours are going to be very different. They lack Peppate. Even standing here, the sounds of your totem are unfamiliar to me. I wouldn't know what to listen for. I'm sorry, Alena—I'm afraid I can't help you with that."

I clear my throat. "Can you at least tell me what *Peppate* generators sound like so I have somewhere to start?"

Bapoto's eyes brighten. "Of course. Do you have power in?"

My chest tightens, and I clench my teeth.

"No, I don't have power in." I don't bother telling him that I haven't put power in at all lately. After what happened at SilverDen ... I can't hear the elements. At all. My jaw twitches at the tightness of my teeth. I don't want to talk about this anymore. Just thinking the word *SilverDen* has my heart aching.

"Oh. That's okay. I can at least explain the sounds to you. That way when you have power in you can listen for them."

I wring my hands.

"Peppate generator sounds remind me of ..." He pauses, thinking. "They remind me of turning pages in a book."

I pause and draw back. That's an odd description.

"Have you ever heard someone read a book? The air is quiet, peaceful. Then there's the soft turn of a page. It's quiet again for a bit until another page is turned. That's what Peppate generators are like. Quiet, peaceful, and emitting a pulsing sound only every thirty seconds or so. They're quite different from other elements that have faster, louder beats. You have to be patient to hear them."

I tilt my head. I can't say that I've consciously heard that sort of sound. Suddenly I'm eager to hear the Peppate generators.

"But, hey," he continues. "You should check out some books in the library. Maybe if you study the totem and the generators you can figure out a way to identify yours. You know your totem better than anyone. It has to be possible."

"Books in the library will teach me about the totem?" I ask.

"Alena, you can learn anything from the books in the library."

I stare at the totem tree again. Maybe he's right. I need to check out the library.

Bapoto's ease fades, and the air around us changes. He suddenly shifts uneasily on his feet. I glance at him from the corner of my eye. *What's wrong?*

"How are you, Alena?"

For these few brief moments talking to Bapoto, I had forgotten my struggles. But his comment beckons them all back. I snap my head toward the tree again, trying to hide the sudden tears that spring forward so quickly. *Don't ask me that!*

"I heard about what happened at SilverDen with Mark and Cody. I just want you to know that I ..." His words trail off. I sense the awkwardness he feels. What do you say to someone like me? Someone who's caused so much damage but didn't mean to. Bapoto shuffles from one foot to the other before finishing his sentence. "I'm sorry, Alena. I guess that's all. You didn't deserve to go through that. You didn't ask for the totem on your arm."

I blink through the tears. His genuine words touch me. Ever since the incident, others have shied away from me, scared. But Bapoto is willing to care about how I feel and say something nice to me.

"Thank you," I whisper. "That means a lot."

Bapoto nods seriously before shifting uncomfortably again.

I rub the back of my neck and tap his arm. "You can get back to work now."

With a simple lift of his lips the awkwardness disappears. "I probably *should* get back."

After returning the tap on my shoulder, he moves to leave. But just before he slips through the door, I ask, "Hey, how do you get to the tree?"

Bapoto smiles again. "Sorry, only totem trainers can know that."

I scoff. Probably better that way.

Chapter 2

Standing at the base of a massive green hill, I cross my arms and hide my trembling hands in my armpits, trying to stop them from shaking. It's been difficult distracting myself the past week, due to the embarrassment I feel after talking to Flint. I wipe the sweat off my forehead. I can't believe I actually asked him to remove my totem.

I sigh. Fortunately, distracting my mind won't be too hard today. Leinani, my one medic friend from initiation, kneels on the ground, readying the equipment and beds we might need for injuries induced by the Dino Games.

The Dino Games.

I've heard so much about these games. How the shrunken dinosaurs living in Petrichor are set free and allowed to wander in their semi-normal habitat. When the Pepps first brought the dinosaurs to Petrichor, they shrunk them down to tiny-size, for everyone's safety. But then the dinosaurs started dying off at younger ages. So the Dino Games were invented. Giving them a chance to roam free at their normal sizes extended their lives. Normally the games only last three days, but because the focus has shifted to training the dinosaurs to protect, the games will be extended to ten days.

I'm worried, though. According to Leinani, the dinosaurs are more restless than ever because it's been so long since they've been set free. The number of injuries expected at the beginning of the games is high.

In addition to the chief extending the number of days, and the focus being on protection training, there's another adjustment to this particular game.

Usually, the Dino Games are held outside of Petrichor to give the dinosaurs more space to roam, but because of the incident at SilverDen, the chief decided that we would stay within the protection fog for this game. So all the dinosaurs are going to be forced to stay within the large meadow and trees at the base of Training Mountain. The amount of space for the dinosaurs cut in half.

I look around nervously, shifting restlessly from one leg to the other. I've never seen a Dino Game, let alone participated in one as a medic. Dinosaurs in general make me nervous, but I don't think that's what has me on edge.

I still can't hear the elements.

The sounds of the elements in an injured body tell me what needs to be healed. If I can't hear them, I can't heal. If Danny were here, he would tell me that I'm too full of Doler. I can't hear the sounds when I'm full of Doler, but regardless of my efforts to get rid of it, it won't come out. It's as though it's stuck inside me, heavy and thick.

I'm pretty sure it's because of what happened at SilverDen three weeks ago. In addition to everything else that transpired that night, the experience has taken away my ability to heal. I gulp back threatening tears. It was the one thing I actually enjoyed doing here in Petrichor, the one thing that made me feel like I had a place. And now it's gone.

I try to steady my breath and watch Leinani.

She thinks participating in this game will be good for me. She thinks my mind will correct itself and bring back the sounds the moment I see a body in need of healing. The confidence she has in me should calm my troubled heart, but standing here with a full sphere of power in my totem, I realize this is a mistake. I hear nothing.

A loud blow horn sounds from the top of the green hill, pulling me from my thoughts. It announces to everyone that the game is about to begin.

I scan the crown of the hill. Hundreds of Pepps participating in the game line up, looking like little black lines from the distance. They each get on their vehicles.

Mark is up there. Somewhere. I bet he chose a four-wheeler to be his vehicle, which will help him keep up with the dinosaurs.

I look to the sky, squinting in the light. The rest of the Pepps, who are not medics or accompanying a dinosaur in the game, are flying, their usual eagle feathers shimmering in the sunlight. They're ready to get the injured to the medics. Carlos from initiation is up there.

I stand with the medics, in a large semicircle at the base of the mountain. Leinani and I stand in the middle of that semicircle. The medics on the ends are so far away I can barely see them.

I suck the air in. If I wasn't so weighed down with other things, the sunlight, greenery, warmth, and excitement might almost be ... beautiful.

With her equipment and beds ready, Leinani stands next to me. Today she has a bright pink flower tucked carefully into her ponytail and her thin chestnut-colored face is full of both excitement and worry. Gripping my shoulder, she gives me a comforting look before turning to focus on the start of the game. I continue to pin my hands in my pits.

Two blasts sound, and I watch the games begin.

The hundreds of vehicles atop the hill roar to life. Behind them, dinosaurs quickly expand to their full form, thrashing around wildly. Their roars instantly travel across the area, jumping on my unease. I see from here that the dinosaurs are separated into groups of their own kinds. The largest ones with long necks are easily seen from where I stand and assemble mainly on the right side of the mountain. The smaller dinosaurs are harder to see, but I recognize some of the medium-sized ones with long and dangerous teeth pushed to the left side of the mountain. Mark is probably over there.

Before I can fully analyze the dinosaurs, massive waves of flames begin flowing from each of the Pepp participants.

Of course. Fire.

Unable to contain the dinosaurs any longer, the participants spill down the mountain. I gape in awe. It looks like hundreds of ants overflowing from a jam-packed anthill. The game has been explained to me several times since arriving here in Petrichor, but to see it in person is quite another experience.

The fire emitted from the four-wheelers and motorcycles leaves a trail, confining each dinosaur to their own pathway down the mountain. It seems to keep them from crossing over and attacking the other dinosaurs, ultimately allowing them to only follow their game participant.

The participants are supposed to take each dinosaur to their own designated piece of land and keep the dinosaur there for the full ten days, guarding it.

If each dinosaur learns to protect its land from intruders, then we could potentially use them to protect *all of Petrichor* in the case of an emergency.

Looking at the wild animals now, though ... I wonder how that will ever work.

My eyes search the hill for Mark amid the crowds and fire. I finally use the binoculars Leinani gave me and squint until I find him on the far-left side, riding his four-wheeler. His favorite dinosaur, Dilo, is running beside him, her orange frills slicked back while she runs. Other dangerous dinosaurs are behind him too, particularly a large one with painfully dangerous teeth. I heard he's one of the few trainers who was allowed to be assigned more than one carnivore. I lower the binoculars, feeling a pang of loneliness hit my stomach.

Since our attempt to free the Pepp prisoners from SilverDen we haven't talked. I betrayed him by not telling him about Gabbro's plan, the plan that had me descend into the electrical mine and free the prisoners being held there. Then I injected him with a dinosaur serum that paralyzed him so he wouldn't follow me.

I miss him. I could probably handle everything that's happened if we were still friends. But I'm sure he blames me, just like everyone else.

I miss Danny too. It's been three weeks since he's been gone. The chief has sent out several teams to look for him, but all in vain.

We did get one clue. A communicator's Magbaby came to Petrichor in a panic. Said it was forced to use its tendrils to retrieve a memory from Jax's brain, then deliver that memory to the chief. The memory, of course, consisted of images of Danny being held as a prisoner. It stated that Danny will die if I don't hand over the black power in my totem, the black power that was generated when Mark and I stupidly morphed together to get out of the fire surrounding SilverDen.

When the chief got the message, he immediately ordered the Magbaby to take him to his home. That's where the Magbaby's communicator was found dead.

Jax. He's the one behind everything, isn't he? The one behind taking the Pepp prisoners, the one who now has Danny.

Bile rises in my throat.

Now the chief is scouring the area close to that dead communicator's home. He's hoping that Jax is hiding Danny near there. It's been a grueling week since the chief left. Silently, I plead that he'll come back soon with good news ... or some hope.

"Alena!" Leinani shouts next to me, her dark-brown eyes anxious for me to see what she's seeing. The scene in front of me is what I expected to see during a Dino Game, but I still gasp. The injuries have already started. With the fire fading, the dinosaurs are crossing lines and attacking everything within their reach. The trainers, using special weapons and power, are trying to distract them, control them, but I watch as several get thrown around effortlessly. The eagles from the sky are diving down already, saving the injured. I search the crowd once again for Mark, but I don't see him anywhere.

An eagle drops down next to us, setting our first patient on the grass. I swallow seeing the man with large gashes across his stomach, blood already soaking the green grass beneath him. My body responds without thinking, kneeling at his side, eager to help.

I'm reaching out my hand, when I freeze midair. It's faint, but it's there: the sound of the elements. With wide tear-filled eyes, I stare at Leinani. She grins, immediately knowing what my look means. She was right.

As if I've been handed a precious gift, I carefully press forward to heal the man.

But then I hear a scream behind me. Another eagle has brought a woman burned from the fire, her skin still simmering from the heat.

That's all it takes—my smelling the burnt flesh and hearing her screams—for the sounds of the elements to disappear. Her screams mirror the screams of Mitch, my friend, the night he died. The images of him being eaten to death by the flesh-eating bug, and then burned by Scance, slam into my mind. I'd tried to save him. But I couldn't.

It's like a tender candle glow has been snuffed out inside me. Once again.

I'm unable to move.

"Alena!" Leinani shouts in my ear as she shakes me.

Her face seems so far away. I think she moves around me to help the woman. The one who's burned. The one I can't seem to pull my gaze from. She's yelling at me. *Why is she yelling at me?*

Finally, I blink several times, and the colors and smells all become clear again. I turn my body away from the burned girl and try to focus on the man bleeding to death in front of me. I hold out my hands, but the ringing is gone.

I curse. Taking a deep breath, I try to whisper the shortcuts to healing, guessing what the boy needs, but he only screams louder.

"Alena, stop!" Leinani shouts. I try not to take her reprimand personally, but I stare at her, hurt.

"I'm sorry, Alena. It's not working. Can you go out there and help gather up the injured?" she asks desperately.

I look out into the field and see it littered with injured Pepps. Anger blazes powerfully inside me. I told her I couldn't do this, but she insisted. And now, here I am making things worse. Gritting my teeth, I push away, grab a stretcher, and walk out to the field. I head to the first injured body. As carefully as my frustration will let me, I roll the person onto the stretcher and drag them back to Leinani, before going out for another.

***

The day passes quickly but my anger doesn't. I'm still seething when the injuries slow. Soon the tired dinosaurs head into the trees or run through the meadow looking for food that's been strategically placed by the trainers, giving all the Pepps a much-needed break. There've already been dozens of injuries, but nobody has died, thankfully.

The medics begin gathering in small groups ready to make camp as the sun starts dropping in the sky. Most of the groups talk excitedly around roaring campfires about the day, their voices reaching me. I sit in my camp chair, close to our roaring campfire, but my group remains quiet.

It's because of me. Leinani may still be willing to be my friend, but others are not and seem terribly uncomfortable. A young man with large hands and a small head quietly cooks some food over the campfire, while I sink further into my chair, distracting myself by observing the flames. Fire has always been comforting to me in this form. Small, controlled. I try to summon that comfort now.

A chomping sound draws my attention off to the right as a woman with short brown hair jumps up from her chair screaming in pain. I stand in response, immediately eyeing the blood spurting from the injured hand she's now cradling.

"What's wrong?" Leinani asks.

"It bit me!" The girl gestures to a small creature hiding in the shadows. I stand and move around the chairs until I see it. It's a baby dinosaur, probably a T-Rex, with grayish skin. Its eyes blacker than the night flicker in the firelight. It attempts another nip at Leinani, but she jumps back in time. Then it whimpers and backs away.

"Where's its trainer?" A young man with tan skin and brown hair gazes into the darkness, his eyebrows wrinkling in concern.

"Where's its mother?" someone else asks.

Stupid dinosaur. Drawing my jacket tightly around me, I sit back down. With the dinosaur and bloody finger, the group moves with new purpose, the awkwardness dissipating. I wonder if I should simply slip away to keep the awkwardness from returning.

I'm about to leave and go to my tent without dinner, when I hear someone calling out my name. With a quick glance over my shoulder, I see a messenger running through the camps, his orange totem gleaming in the dark night. *Has the chief returned?* Leaping out of my seat, I only walk a few steps before his searching eyes find mine.

"Alena, the chief wants to see you," he says, catching his breath. I don't miss the urgency in his tone, but he doesn't even give me a chance to respond before turning away.

Surprising him, I run and grab his arm before he can leave.

"Did he find anything? Danny?"

The boy pulls his arm away, a flash of fear running across his face, as if my touch hurt him. He's afraid of me too.

It's like being slapped over and over again, each time I see the fear in others' eyes, constantly reminding me of what I've done, what I am. Dangerous. Unwanted.

After Mark and I destroyed acres of trees and killed Cody's father, Tom, with our simple morph, why wouldn't they be afraid? I should be more sensitive to his fear, but I find myself annoyed with his delayed response, my anger from the day boiling close to the surface. Stepping closer to him, I repeat my question through clenched teeth. "Did he find anything?"

The boy backs away. "No, he didn't."

Turning now, he disappears into the darkness. I stand there, the pang of disappointment more than I can bear. I should have known not to get my hopes up, but each day that goes by without Danny being found, a part of me dies.

A hand touches my shoulder. I know it's Leinani, but I don't even look. Tearing myself away from her, I make my way to the Post.

Chapter 3

Unable to keep the tears from spilling over now, I stumble through the darkness, barely able to see anything through my blurry eyes. My guard has dropped exponentially, and I find myself unable to fight the memories that have longed to bombard me. They callously flood my mind, crashing into me, wave after ocean wave, forcing me to, once again, relive everything that's happened without letting me come up for air.

Of course, they start at the beginning.

The day I was swimming in the hot spring and obtained the vine woven into the skin of my arm. It was the mark of a Pepp, a target of death in my mind because of the Pepps that had been found murdered. When I went looking for others with the same vine in their skins, needing answers to my questions, I found Mark, who told me that my vine, or rather *half-vine*, is defected. A half-totem ... created by an enemy, that produces the opposite of Peppate. Doler. The other half of my defected totem lies in the skin of a man I've come to love but ended up betraying. Mark.

He convinced me to come to Petrichor, where I eventually made friends: Cody, Rusty, Danny. My mind shifts now to Cody's friend,

Abby, the refugee, who was kidnapped and tortured to draw Cody out, in an attempt to draw *me* out for my totem. My stupid defected Doler-filled totem. I still don't understand why someone would want it so bad that they're willing to kill and torture for it. I recall the images of Cody's bruised face and malnourished body. Oh, how I would have gladly turned myself over, given them my totem so Cody and the other prisoners could go free. But I never knew where to find them. Whoever *them* is. The location of where they wanted me to go was always missing from their threats.

My mind tumbles forward. To the night when Pepp prisoners were sent to Petrichor in toboggans besieged by some sort of aggressive flesh-eating bug that took the lives of the prisoners—and anyone who touched them.

Mitch. He was my medic trainer who had grown to be my dear friend. He made the mistake of touching the flesh-eating bug. It moved so fast, all over his body, inside and out. In an attempt to save him, Scance tried to burn the bug. But she only ended up burning him.

I pound my forehead with my fists trying to move past the image of Mitch getting eaten alive, then burned to death. I pound past the horrible smells of simmering flesh and nightmarish screams, but the images don't go away and my lip quivers. He died. I couldn't save him. Tears trail down my cheeks as the memories I've tried to hold back continue to flood freely.

We finally went to SilverDen that night, where the rest of the prisoners were being kept.

I shake my head forcefully.

Mark followed me to SilverDen, even though he wasn't supposed to be there. The last thing we needed was for the other half of my totem to be within reach of our enemy. So I injected him with the paralyzing dinosaur serum he had given me and left him with Rusty.

I clench my fists. Stupid. Stupid. Stupid. The look of betrayal on his face haunts me every moment, making my stomach hurt. *How could I do that to the man I so deeply care for?*

I got the prisoners out, freed a woman hidden in the walls of Silver-Den, and then came out of the mine.

That's when I knew something was wrong. The trees around the mine were on fire. Mark was still there, paralyzed, left by Rusty, strangely changed into human non-Pepp clothes. We were trapped.

I curse myself. *There had to have been another way out. If I had only looked harder, tried to find an opening in the fire.*

My heart rate picks up at the memory, pounding painfully in my chest.

Case was there too, Danny's brother—possibly the one who created my defected totem. It seemed as though he was ready to capture me, but when he saw that woman I brought up from the mine, his demeanor changed completely. He not only let me go, he gave me a toboggan to get myself out. I used it to free Cody.

Instead of looking harder for another escape, though, I decided to morph into eagle form and carry Mark up and out of the fire, except I wasn't strong enough and ended up sending us right *into* the fire. In an attempt to save us both, Mark morphed into his eagle form.

We were always forbidden to morph, especially together, and yet we did so, creating an electrical force that destroyed everything in the area.

Every leaf, branch and tree trunk, turned to dust within miles.

And every human.

My heart sinks.

Tom. That was his name, the Pepp who died at SilverDen. Cody's Pepp father. The one Pepp I killed. Every day I wake up seeing his face in my mind, replaying each little interaction I had with him on the flight to SilverDen. I relive the way his kind expression tried to hide how scared he was. How he quietly listened as Gabbro and I revealed our plan. I can't help but wonder what it felt like to die by my lightning. Did it happen quickly, or was he in pain? I'll never know exactly where he was when he died. And not knowing is creating a gaping hole in my chest that grows with each passing day.

I wipe at the tears on my face.

Our lightning also killed the hundreds of Clan members down in the silver mine. If they didn't turn to dust, they burned with fire.

All for what?

Everything was set up, a trap. It was all done to collect the totem on my arm and Mark's. But not for the deadly electricity like I initially thought. No, someone wanted Mark and I to morph ... together, to create *power* in our totems.

The black power.

It was generated when Mark and I morphed together, killing everything around us with lightning.

I flinch. Now the horrible memories are turning into my never-ending questions.

Who is really behind everything?

At first I thought it was Case, Danny's brother. He's the one who tried to capture me at initiation, and the one who—we believe—created the terrifying defective totem.

But then this other man, Jax, came into the picture asking for my totem too.

And then SilverDen happened. I think Case was supposed to take my power there, but he didn't. He saw that strange woman I had saved from the caves below, then immediately left with her. That's when Jax took Danny.

Ugh, I cradle my pounding head in my hands. So does that mean Case was working for Jax?

And why did Danny have to follow me to the silver mine?

Danny. He had these tracker bugs. Bugs that are terribly attracted to a source called MiraWax. Someone saw him pulling them out that night. MiraWax is a rare wax that just happened to be in the necklace he gave me that day in the meadow. A necklace I was wearing the night I left Petrichor. He apparently gave it to me to be sure he could find me if I somehow disappeared.

So when Jax saw Case fail to obtain the power in my totem, he hopped on the only other leverage available. He knew the best way to get the black power from me was to take another someone who meant the world to me. Danny.

He's missing, and it's all my fault.

I rub my aching head.

Then there's Gabbro, Danny's Magbaby. I clench my teeth. He used me, lied to me. Told me Mark couldn't be there at SilverDen, but then dragged him along anyway.

Why? Gabbro and Trevor are the ones who saved me at initiation from Case. Why would Gabbro save me there, but then hand me over at SilverDen? Did he know Danny would be taken that night? Is Gabbro with Jax and Danny now? He hasn't been seen since.

I kick a rock. *And what about the Clan members?* Were they supposed to be destroyed as part of the plan too? Did they know we would tear apart the ground and expose them? Their deaths haven't hurt me nearly as much as Tom's. Probably because I knew Tom and knew he was a good man. Cody's Pepp father didn't deserve to die.

Ugh. My head pounds from the game of Ring around the Rosie my questions are playing. Will I ever get answers?

I look up, realizing that I'm standing in front of the sign leading to the Post.

But I just stand there, biting my lip.

There's something else that's been bothering me.

Danny. I think about how I led him on, all the while kissing Mark behind his back. I kick myself silently. *How could I be so cruel? So unfeeling?*

Wiping my nose, I move my feet and descend the steps, into the torchlit halls, finding my way to the chief's room.

When I approach the door, I find it open, with murmuring voices bouncing into the hall. Stopping, I almost turn to leave, deciding I'm not in the mood to talk. Unfortunately, the chief calls to me.

"Alena, please come inside."

How in the world did he know I was here?

Unable to ignore his command, I move my legs and force myself into the room. I've only been in this room a couple of times. It's dark, with no windows except for a wood-framed skylight in the ceiling. The ground is made of dirt, and the walls are an odd mixture of different types of stone, mostly covered with bookcases. Candles scattered around the room attempt in vain to provide light. A single large desk sits in the middle, surrounded now by several older Pepps, council members wearing the blue mark on their totems.

If there was such a thing as a death stare, I'd be dead. Their faces are filled with so much hate and distrust it physically hurts.

Many of them wanted to throw Mark and me in Algor after what happened. The Pepps would be safer if we were out of their way, but the chief refuses to blame us for the morph. I don't know why.

One man steps away from the others. "Hey, Alena."

He has dark hair except for the scant gray brushed against his temples. He's wearing a camo shirt that looks like it's stuffed with protective gear underneath. A gun even hangs on his belt—a foreign look here in Petrichor, since Pepps don't use weapons. His face looks young, but he emits a sense of elderly confidence. When he smiles at me with kind blue eyes, I look away.

The chair behind the desk is empty, but it doesn't take me long to locate the chief. My eyes widen when I see his bloody body pressed up against a wall, next to three other very injured men. I step sideways to get a better view. There's blood everywhere, soaking their clothes and puddling beneath them. The gashes in the chief's face have wiped away globs of his beard hair that are now smeared down his neck. There are also burns. I can smell the putrid stench of scorched flesh. I hastily glance at Chief's chest, needing to see the rise and fall of breath. I wring my hands. I can't tell if he's breathing from here, but he did just call out for me, didn't he?

What in the world happened?

My eyes drop to the floor glinting in silver, and I take an unsteady step back. The floor is covered in knives, dozens and dozens of them, all laced in red blood. *Those couldn't be the culprit for the gashes in his skin, could they?*

Fortunately Jeter is right there healing him, the best medic there is.

"Shut the door, Alena," Chief says, his voice heavier and more gurgled than usual.

"I need Alena to be here." He addresses the council members. "If any of you have a problem with that, you can leave." The chief's voice weighs in the air, strong and steady. Even as I stare at the floor, I can feel the hot anger of the council members aimed at me. But nobody says anything. Clearing his throat, the chief draws the attention back to himself, allowing me to slide into a dark corner.

"The message we received a week ago in the communicator's Magbaby was ... well, it was for Mark and Alena. Jax asked that they meet him in a desolate field at SilverDen, where all the prisoners were found."

My head jerks in his direction. He had told me the message was just a threat, reminding us of what Jax wants. He didn't mention that it was addressed to Mark and me specifically, demanding we meet him.

My fists tighten.

He kept this from me? I would have gladly gone and handed myself over if it meant Danny could return home. *How dare he try to do this without me.*

My glares don't faze the chief, though.

"I went to the communicator's home, where you know we found the communicator dead. We searched the area around his home for a couple of days, looking for some sort of footprint or trail that would tell us which direction Jax fled in. But there was nothing. Which makes us wonder if he has more help than we think."

I don't want to listen to him anymore.

"After giving up on that site ..." Unfortunately, he continues. "We went to SilverDen, where the message indicated Alena and Mark should go. We searched it too for any signs of Jax. But it was all ashes. We didn't find anything. No footprints, no life. Nothing."

I bite my cheek. *You should have let* me *go, idiot.*

"But then the ground underneath us blew up." The chief picks up a knife off the floor next to him. "There was explosion after explosion. and quicker than the blink of an eye the air was filled with fire ... and hundreds of these."

"Chauly," someone whispers across the room.

The chief raises his head so Jeter can work on his neck. His voice already seems clearer. "I think so," he says. "Alena, several years ago, there was a Pepp who broke some heavy rules here in Petrichor. I won't go into all the details, but when I found out, I went to get him, to send him to prison. But he just vanished. We weren't able to find him."

I've decided that the Pepp power is good for everything except one thing: finding people. They seem almost powerless when it comes to that.

"His name was Chauly. He was particularly fond of creating explosives loaded with dangerous blades inside that would kill those within its radius. Oddly enough, killing people this way did not affect his power source. The totem couldn't tell whether anyone was hurt or not because it often exploded long after Chauly was gone. I think it was Chauly who set up the explosives at the mine where I was supposed to meet Jax."

No, where I *was supposed to meet Jax.*

"Which means Jax has help. From a Pepp. Unfortunately, we were too injured to continue our search. We barely made it back here alive."

Chauly. Jax has help ... from a Pepp who has power.

"We have to be careful," Chief continues. "Being a Pepp, he can easily enter the safeguards of Petrichor. I hate to do this, but we need to arm every protector at the borders."

"With weapons?" someone asks.

"Yes. Good weapons. And we need the men to know how to use them. Patrick has already started this process." The chief signals to the dark-haired man who is standing beside me. The nice one.

A darkness shrouds my heart. I remember when Jax snuck into Petrichor to deliver his threat to me, then mysteriously disappeared. It was horrible, constantly wondering if I was going to get attacked. That fear returns now in full force, making my whole body ache. It looks as if not even Petrichor can keep me safe.

The chief clears his throat. "This isn't why I've asked you all to come here, though. I've called you here because I received another message since then, from Jax. It was sent by another communicator's Magbaby."

Soft murmurs blanket the room.

My heart plummets. It's been a long time since Danny disappeared. Too long. And now Jax is probably angry since the chief went to Silver-Den instead of Mark and me. I worry that any message at this point is bad news.

I'm not sure I want to be here for this. I contemplate leaving, but then the chief attempts to stand.

"Sit down." Jeter's tone is hard and demanding, but the chief ignores him and uses the wall to help himself up. Then, limping to his desk, leaving bloody footprints in the stone floor, he opens his torn and battered satchel lying there and pulls out a black Magbaby. Suddenly, I can't move.

Does he know the burden he's placing on me by asking me to be here?

"Alena, I need your help. I know this won't be easy for you to watch, but, next to Mark, you knew Danny best."

What's he doing?

Holding the rock in his hand, he walks toward me, Jeter following. I see the Magbaby open up and realize what he's about to do. I back into the wall behind me, trying to get away, but the urgency in the chief's piercing blue eyes freezes me. As much as I don't want to see an image of Danny suffering, I need to know that he's still alive. *Will this memory give me at least that?*

The chief stops in front of me, a chunk of his right ear missing, his hair soaked with blood.

"The message he sent in this Magbaby is a memory. Will you watch it?"

I stare at him mutely. *Please, no.* He raises the rock to my ear and coaxes its tendrils inside. I shiver as the tendrils slither into my head, further than they normally do. I know when it has attached itself to my brain because suddenly my senses are no longer mine.

I *hear* the memory first. Screaming sounds echo through my head, spreading throughout my body, piercing my heart.

It's Danny.

Then I see him, his face disfigured fuzzily in such a gut-wrenching way that I almost don't recognize him.

Did the chief seriously just bring me in here to listen to this? Is he trying to torture me? Tears well up, and I squeeze my eyes shut, wanting it to go away. When it doesn't, I claw at my ear, demanding that he remove the tendrils. The moment they're free, I run. From the room and down the hall.

I don't get very far, though, when a strong arm grabs me, flinging me backward, forcing me to stop. I don't have the strength or willpower to fight. Or the strength to wonder how the chief, an old, frail, and very injured man, could catch up with me so quickly. I yank myself away from him and sink to the floor, sobbing. Leaning against the wall, I cry into my knees.

I hear the chief quietly slide down beside me.

"I'm sorry, Alena," he whispers. "I was selfish. There's something off about the memory. Something different. I was hoping you could help me figure it out. I didn't take into account that you might not be ready to hear it. I shouldn't have asked that of you."

I raise my head and try to wipe away the tears but still don't look at him. I can hear him shifting his body so he's facing me. He probably wants me to do the same, but I don't.

"Alena, how are you?" he whispers.

The knot of emotions living in my chest begins to expand at his gentle words, and a tightening pain in my heart reaches up to my jaw. I clamp my mouth shut, refusing to respond. *Please don't ask me that.*

He waits. I clench my fists and grit my teeth, trying to hold everything in, but he still waits. Finally, after a painfully long time, my body tires and my breathing slows. I know the chief. He won't let me go. Not until I talk.

Finally, I swallow and open my mouth.

"I'm sorry, Chief." I hadn't planned to say those words. I wanted to say something stronger, something to indicate that I'm okay, but the moment my mouth opens, the words slip out, along with more tears.

His strong arm slides around my shoulder, and I reluctantly let him pull me into an awkward side hug. The metallic smell of blood reaches my nostrils, but I don't care. Not within his warm embrace.

"It's okay, Alena."

I shake my head. It's *not* okay. Nothing is okay.

"I want to help out here," I murmur. "I want to heal again. I *need* to find Danny. But I can't. It's like I'm stuck in mud clear up to my neck. I'm unable to move in any direction, unable to get free."

I sigh and wipe my nose. "Danny would tell me to go exercise or something stupid, to get rid of the Doler, but I've tried. I've even tried to recognize the truth, like he told me to. But the truth is, those prisoners died from the flesh-eating bug because of me. Danny is missing because of me. And Tom is *dead* because of …" I can't finish and instead grip my head with my hands.

"Wiggems," the chief quietly says after a while.

The acronym Danny made up comes out of the chief's mouth, sounding like a question. I pull myself up and look at him now.

"Wiggems?" he says again. "That's what Danny calls them? The things you do to get rid of the Doler?"

I wipe my nose again. "Yes." Apparently, the chief knows about Danny's made-up acronym and how it helps remove the Doler that so cruelly plagues my body.

Clearing his throat, the chief nods and rubs his icky wet beard. "Perhaps, right now, the truth you need to see isn't about *what happened*."

I don't want to listen to him. He has this uncanny ability to draw me in, make me see things differently, but I don't want that right now. I want to wallow in my sorrow. I wish he wouldn't talk.

Shifting his tone, he asks, "Alena, how do you *feel*?" His kindness hits something inside me, something that's been waiting to be acknowledged. It bubbles up now, anxious and ready to be released.

I grit my teeth, trying to hold it in, but it escapes anyway.

"I'm angry," I whisper, ashamed.

The chief is not disappointed in my answer but kindly pushes more. "With whom?"

With everyone, I want to scream. *Every. Single. Being!*

But, instead, I gaze at the dirt wall across from us. I can't tell him all the names, but since I know he won't let me go until I give him something, I keep it simple.

"I'm angry with Gabbro," I whisper. "For lying to me and using me to activate the totem." My voice softens. Getting one name out opens the door for others, and since I'm unable to hold it back, the next one comes. "I'm angry with Danny for giving me the tracker so he could follow me. I'm angry with Jax for taking Danny and ..." Now I stop.

The chief doesn't need to know that I'm also angry with Mark for not trusting me enough at SilverDen to let me go. I turn my body further away from him. But he continues to stare at me with that stupid look that tells me he knows I'm not done. That we'll stay here all night if we have to.

I sigh and look down at my hands.

"I'm angry with Mark," I finish. My lip trembles. "But I know I have no right to be. He deserves to be angry with *me* for not telling him about Gabbro's plan and then paralyzing him with that stupid dino serum."

An expression of empathy softens the chief's face as if he understands exactly what I'm saying.

"How long has it been since you've talked to him?" he asks.

"Since the night at SilverDen," I say shamefully.

The chief smiles kindly. "It's okay to be angry, Alena. Even with Mark. The way you feel is just as much truth as is the fact that the sky is blue. If you want to get rid of the Doler, start out by accepting the way you feel as truth. Once you accept how you feel, then it will be easier to do the wiggems you need to do the most." Chief shifts uncomfortably. "Alena, I'm sure Danny explained that friendship is one of the most powerful wiggems. But friendship isn't just about *making* friends. It's about *keeping* them. It's about extending grace. That's one of the wiggems, isn't it?"

I feel a jab. *Grace.* That's probably one of the G's Danny didn't explain. The word sends a jolt through my chest. Chief is asking me to forgive Mark.

Tapping my leg, he changes the subject.

"Before you go see Mark, though, will you run an errand for me?" He extends a folded piece of paper. "Will you get this message to the head guard at the prison? My Magbaby is out on another errand right now, and I should probably let Jeter finish healing me."

I knit my eyebrows together. "The prison?"

I've never been there before, but the idea of going out to the cold, dark area where the prison sits does not sound fun to me. Actually, nothing sounds fun to me. But then I think about going back to GreenGrotto alone, or, even worse, back to the Dino Games. Before I realize it, I'm taking the paper from his hand, agreeing to deliver it.

"Thank you, Alena," he says, standing up. "And when you're done, go see Mark."

Chapter 4

I stop by my room in GreenGrotto. The prison, located just outside Petrichor, stands in the true cold elements of the land. I'll need my winter clothes.

Sitting on my bed, I take out the capsules I needed for the Dino Games and replace them with cold clothes. I shake my head. It still amazes me that every item needed for dropdowns or runs can be collapsed into a tiny bullet-like capsule, then slipped into a satchel for easy carrying.

I pause briefly to study one of the capsules. The jacket, given to me by Mark, the night after initiation. The night he walked me home. The night I couldn't stop shaking. He let me keep it. I bet it still smells like him.

I sigh and lay it away with all the other the supplies I don't need, then leave GreenGrotto. I don't see a single Pepp on my way out. Everyone is at the Dino Games.

I walk around the base of the large mountain. I think I know the way to the prison. Last time I went this direction, I was with Danny and Mark and we went on four-wheelers. Tonight, I don't have a vehicle, or Mark and Danny, so the walk is long. I wander through the hills and then into the mountains. It's dark, the night only lit by a half-moon that casts a silver glow on the leaves of the trees. I let it guide me for a bit, but after tripping several times I decide to light a lantern. Much easier.

As I'm walking, I realize I feel a little better. I feel calmer; the tormenting fire inside me has fizzled out. *Was it the chief? His words that calmed me? Or that I actually admitted to him what I've been trying to hold in?* Maybe it's that he told me to do what I've known I need to do all along—go see Mark. I sigh. Without the anger that's been my constant companion the past few weeks, I suddenly feel exhausted. Too tired to even be angry with the chief for calling me out.

My heavy feet carry me forward. Slowing more and more as I go.

Then I reach it and stop.

It's the meadow, with its purple, blue, and white wildflowers. Danny's meadow. The snow in the distance piles up against Petrichor's fog wall, standing aggressively high and cold.

Deep down inside I knew I would have to walk through Danny's meadow to get to the prison, but I guess I didn't really think about what it would do to me to see it again.

Suddenly I can't move. I can't think. I can't even breathe.

I just see. I see the flowers, the way they stand strong and beautiful, brushed carefully with moonlight. I see the area where Danny, Mark, and I sat, once friends. I'm again painfully aware of the hollow feeling inside me from their absence.

Then I hear.

A gentle melody. I purse my lips. It seems to rise from the flowers, gracefully moving through the air, matching the sadness in my heart.

Then the tune changes to something familiar. A song I've heard only once, but a song that touched me deeply.

Danny's song. The one he wrote and played for me here.

I sink to my knees, too tired to stand now. He's still out there, and I need to help find him.

But how do I help him when I can't even help myself?

I pluck a flower next to me and twist it in my fingers.

"I'm sorry, Danny," I whisper. "I'm so sorry." I don't even have enough energy to cry anymore.

I sit there. For a long time—Danny's tune replaying over and over in my head, while gripping the flower in my hands.

Then, when my knees and back ache from sitting on the ground, my mind slowly comes back to the present.

That's when I realize something is in my ear.

A tendril. Breccia's tendril. I stare at my Magbaby sitting on my shoulder.

I'm about to ask her what she's doing, but I already know. The melody, the song. It wasn't coming from the meadow like my irrational mind had thought. It was coming from Breccia.

"Alena, do you remember the day Danny told you about the wiggems?" she asks.

I nod. Of course I remember. It was one of my favorite days with him, running up Training Mountain, then sitting on a rock. That's when I learned about what Doler and Peppate do.

"Do you remember him mentioning the Magbaby bubbles?"

I nod, vaguely recalling the bumps on Breccia's back that he called Magbaby bubbles.

"There's something I'd like to show you." She points to the small bubbles on her back just before an image appears in my vision. I'm startled at first, but Breccia's calm touch encourages me to just watch. The image clears, and suddenly I see myself through Breccia's eyes, the day I met Danny at GreenGrotto.

I remember Danny telling me about the Magbaby bubbles. He had said that the Magbabies hold on to memories. Good memories. And then they show them back to us.

I watch myself in the image pick up the books Danny had dropped after seeing me walk through the door at GreenGrotto. It's strange, watching myself from an outsider's perspective. And embarrassing. I was dirty that day.

I want to stop watching, but then the image changes to later that night as I sat by Danny's bedside, trying to help him through his panic attack. Unable to resist them, the memories draw me in. I relive every encounter with Danny through Breccia's eyes.

Then I see the day that Danny and Mark brought me here. To this very meadow. It was sunny and bright. As if sensing my particular attachment to this memory, Breccia freezes it in my head. I let myself observe the moment carefully, taking in the grin on Danny's face. I'm smiling too, tucked between the two men who came to mean so much to me. Even though my heart had been weighed down by worries that day, I know I truly felt happy in that moment.

I felt happy.

Suddenly, I remember with new light how difficult it had been after I had obtained the totem. Staying hidden in my home for months with little interaction had left me feeling lost and alone, exactly how I feel now. I had wondered countless times if I could ever be happy again.

But this moment, this memory here in front of me, proves that it *was* possible. That I did find happiness again.

Could that mean that happiness is still possible? Is it always possible, regardless of how much the darkness seems to say otherwise? That hope is always there even when things seem so hopeless?

As much as I want to deny this and convince myself that the experiences from the past few weeks have been far more traumatic than being stuck at home was, deep inside, my heart aches to believe. To want something better. A life full of despair would be a terribly long and lonely life.

But even if I do want to find hope, find a way back to happiness, how do I do that? I think back to the time when Caleb dragged me from my home to find answers after living hopelessly for months. My body sags. It was Caleb. He helped me find my way again. Unfortunately, he's not here to help me now.

But then my mind moves forward to the moment at the cabin with Mark. After learning the truth about the Pepps, and realizing that Mark wanted me to join them, I had to make a choice. I could have gone home with Caleb. Could have continued hiding. But I knew that would not bring happiness.

No, Caleb might have dragged me from my home, but *I* made the choice to join the Pepps. It was terrifying, and I didn't know how I would survive. But that one choice did lead to happiness, because it led me to people, Cody, Danny ... and Mark. It led me to purpose, being a medic. It led me to answers.

Is that what happiness takes sometimes? Redirection? To stop and acknowledge that life is out of balance and something needs to change, and then being willing to take that terrifying step? But, then, how do I know which terrifying step is the right one? There are so many choices I could make. Is it kind of a trial-and-error type of thing? My mind quietly considers all the paths before me.

I could leave Petrichor and go home, be with my family again.

Or I could leave Petrichor on my own and go searching for Danny.

Or I could learn how to get rid of the Doler generators in my totem and live a normal life.

I try to imagine myself going down each of these paths, but my mind repeatedly comes back to one thing.

Mark.

Regardless of which path I choose, I have to talk to him. That's the one thing that feels most right.

I try to cling to the curl of hope swirling inside me, but then something starts eating it away again.

Tom is dead. *Am I even worthy of being happy again?*

I look closer at the image still projected in my mind. At Danny's face. If he was here, he would tell me that I'm absolutely worthy of being happy again. At least I think he would. My own Doler-filled mind tells me that I should suffer for the rest of my life for the things I've done, but I wonder if the truth the Peppate is trying to reach, the truth Danny taught me about, is the exact opposite of that.

That I am still worthy of living a good life.

I feel a soft touch on my neck, and the image in my mind disappears. I wipe the tears on my cheeks and look at Breccia as the chief's words come to me. He's trying to lead me back to Mark, because he knows that that is what will bring true happiness. So, *he* must believe I still deserve to be happy. *Can I believe that?*

Every cell in my body fights the idea. Rejects it as if it's a foreign substance needing to be eradicated. Danny would probably say that that alone is proof enough that I need to cling to it. For dear life.

My knees and feet protest loudly now at the position I'm sitting in. So, I shift to my butt and let the blood fill my limbs.

Suddenly, I'm grateful to Breccia for showing me the memory.

I've been so stuck, so focused on everything I did wrong at SilverDen. So focused on the devastation I've caused to everyone, including Danny, that I've completely forgotten that I *have* felt light in my life. I have had happy moments.

Seeing Danny's smiling face in my head doesn't take away the pain. The guilt of everything I've done to hurt him twinges inside me now.

But the light from the memories Breccia showed me reminds me of how close we were, how much we did together, how much he taught me. And as much as I want to deny it, it also shows me how good I was to him. I showed him how much I cared in every moment I was in his presence.

For the first time in a long time, the few tears slipping through don't stem from remembering what I did wrong but from remembering what I've done right. The darkness around my heart shifts and lightens. Just a tiny bit.

I wipe my tears with new determination. I don't know where Danny is, but I *will* find him. I want to see his face again. I want to beg him for forgiveness.

Carefully tucking the flower into my satchel, I decide it's time to get going. I need to deliver the chief's message so I can get back to Petrichor.

There are a lot of things I need to take care of.

Chapter 5

I stand, a tingling sensation immediately flooding my legs. I relight the fire in my lantern that must have gotten blown out by the gentle breeze and take a few wobbly steps.

I haven't gone too far when the sound of rustling grass reaches my ears. I stop and look behind me, my gaze nervously scanning the dark shadows.

Is something out there? My heart pounds wildly in my chest.

When my eyes find nothing, I turn and frantically move toward the snow wall. I need to get out of here.

Then I stop again. The rustling sound is louder, closer, steps definitely pounding against the ground. I pull out the knife I always hide up my sleeve, then gulp back bile.

"Who's there?" I curse at my shaky voice.

The grass, just ten feet ahead of me moves, and I jump back. *Is it Jax, finally come to get me himself? Forget the knife, I need to run!* I'm ready to bolt, when a small sound chortles through the grass.

That doesn't sound like a human.

I scream out loud and practically pee my pants when a gray creature with black eyes and tiny claws finally pops out of the plants.

It's the baby dinosaur from down below. The one who bit the medic in my group. *Did it follow me?*

It takes me way too long to realize it's not Jax and that I'm not going to die in this moment, at least not from a man. When my rapid heart slows its pace, I realize my knife is extended dangerously toward the animal, and it's eyeing it nervously.

Lowering my hand, I step away from it, my pulse throbbing in my ears. *Why in the world do we have dinosaurs here?*

It takes a step toward me.

I take another step back.

Then it whimpers.

It's the whimper that stops me in my retreat. It whimpered the same way back at our campsite as if trying to communicate something.

I look around. Where *is* your dino trainer?

Every ounce of common sense I have screams at me to stay away from the dinosaur. I don't know anything about this little one, and the last time I underestimated dinosaurs by walking into the dino covert at MossyHollow, I got attacked. Besides, didn't this baby dinosaur nearly bite off the finger of the other medic? It's obviously dangerous.

But then the little creature whimpers again.

I roll my eyes at the ridiculousness of the situation. A baby dinosaur only means trouble, but, slowly, I take a step forward. It stays put. I take another step. Then another until I'm standing right over it. Bringing the lantern up so I can see it better, I slowly bend down.

Its black eyes glow in the light, and its grayish skin is smooth, unlike the stretched and dry skin of other dinosaurs I've seen. Maybe because it's a baby?

"What's wrong?" I ask it. "Where's your mom?"

The baby dinosaur turns, showing me its tail, and I draw in a shallow breath.

"Your tail. It's ... gone." A bloody little stump is all that remains.

"I'm sorry ..." I'm about to apologize for not having power, or rather apologize for having power but not being able to use it, when I hear the ringing sounds in my head. *I can hear the elements?* My hands shake in response. *What changed?*

I can hear the elements!

Anxiously leaning forward on my knees, I immediately go to work listening for the injured elements in the dinosaur's tail. But my heart sinks in disappointment. I can hear the elements around me *except* for the dinosaur. I scoot closer and lean in, no longer worried about getting chomped. I frown. There's no element sounds in the dinosaur. Just hollow silence.

I straighten. *I'm still broken.*

With a sigh, I reach into my satchel and pull out a shirt capsule along with my water canteen.

"I can't heal you," I say, "but I can clean you up a bit." I try to sound as nice as possible, not that the dinosaur can understand me at all. I open my canteen, then inch it toward the dinosaur. It's hesitant but also trusting. *Why does it trust me?* When I pour a little water on its stump it flinches, but then almost sighs in relief.

My lips lift. "Does that feel good?" It dips its head into the steady stream of water and then starts licking at it until the canteen is empty.

"Can I bandage you up?"

I pull out my T-shirt, but then realize it's probably too big for its tiny tail, so I pull out a sock instead. Inching my hands forward again, I move to place it over the stub. This is much harder. The little critter bolts forward several times but then comes back as if it wants the help … but doesn't. Finally, I get the sock over the stub before it can run away.

"Gotcha."

The dinosaur spins around, looking at its tail, then comes to me nuzzling its face into my lap. My hands freeze in the air. It's a simple gesture. It reminds me of a dog licking its owner, or a child wrapping its little hands around a mother's neck. It's a gesture of love.

My eyes fill up. It feels good to be loved. Even if it's received from a silly little dinosaur.

I rub its head. It's scaly yet slimy at the same time, soft yet hard.

"What's your name?" It climbs further into my lap, and I take this opportunity to wrap a hair tie around the sock to keep it from falling off. "Do you even have a name? How old are you?" Hmm. I don't even know if it's a male or a female.

Time ticks heavily in my head. I look up at the moon. It's moved, meaning it's getting late. My spirits fall. As much as I would love to just sit here all night with a baby dinosaur, I should get to the prison.

"Hey, I have to run an errand. You stay here. I'll be back in a bit, and then maybe we can find your mom. How does that sound?"

I pick it up and place it in the tall grass in front of me. It stands there, its short arms hanging in front of it, its head cocked.

"I'll be back." I smile. Smile. What a foreign feeling on my lips. Foreign but good.

I move toward the border of the meadow, and the dinosaur waits.

Chapter 6

The little dinosaur follows me to the edge of the meadow, watches me layer myself in snow clothes, but doesn't follow me any further.

The last time I wore my snow clothes and traveled through the fog separating the safe bounds of Petrichor from the natural cold around it, I was with Mark and the cold weather was calm.

Tonight, it is not.

The moment I step through the fog, wind slaps snow in my face. I shield myself as best as I can with my arms. The cold takes my breath away. *How am I supposed to find the prison in this blizzard, especially when I've never been there before?* I turn around to go back, but Breccia calls out, "I'll get you there; just listen to the sound of my voice. It isn't too far."

I frown. This doesn't sound like a good idea, but Breccia is already humming in front of me, flying in the air and calling out my name. I stomp through the snow in the warm snowshoe-like boots I brought. My mind briefly wanders to the man the chief was talking about earlier.

Chauly. How the borders of Petrichor need to be more protected than ever because he has a totem.

Here I am just beyond the borders of Petrichor without a protector in sight. Are they here? I can't see anything at all. Maybe protectors aren't needed on this side of Petrichor, at least not tonight. Nobody would dare venture into this storm. Well, nobody except me.

The wind whistles in my ear, making it hard for me to hear Breccia, but she makes sure not to get too far ahead of me. I eventually cover my face with my scarf to free my arms and make my way through the snow. My snow boots sink with each step I take, and it takes a lot of energy to heave myself forward. I can't imagine how much worse it would be without the snowshoes.

With my lips trembling from the icy air and my nose screaming out in cold pain, I want to yell out to Breccia, make her take me back, but I bite my tongue. We're probably almost there.

Sure enough, she finally announces our arrival over the roaring wind.

I sigh in relief, ripping the scarf off my face, but immediately hiccup my sigh back in. Standing in front of me is a wall of solid ice.

"Do we have to climb that?" I don't even try to hide the dismay in my voice.

"No, there's a doorway over here, somewhere," she says. "We should be able to just walk in. But once we go in, we can't come back out. At least not without the help of the warden. The blizzard will also get worse inside the wall, so you better cover up your face again."

I obey, and she leads me to an opening in the ice wall. It's so small and blends in with all the white blurriness surrounding us that I would have missed it without Breccia's help. I step into the hole and understand Breccia's warning. I thought the storm was bad before, but now the wind is so strong, it seems to reach in and steal the air right from my lungs.

Turning around briefly, I search for the entrance but only find a solid wall of ice. It must be like the protection fog but in reverse. You can go in, but you can't come back out.

"The warden's hut isn't too far," Breccia shouts. "It sits right at the base of the mountain that makes up the prison. I think I can see the light."

I follow her until we reach a cabin-like structure with snow piled high on its roof and icicles that stretch dangerously low to the ground. There's only one window, but it sheds as much light into the storm as it can, trying not to get swallowed up by the darkness.

Eager to get out of the cold, deliver my message, and get back to Petrichor, I knock loudly on the door, with Breccia on my shoulder. My body quivers uncontrollably as I stand there on the step. I rub my arms, trying to generate some warmth for myself, but then I stop when the door opens.

There, standing in the doorway, is a man that looks unbelievably similar to the chief. I would almost believe it was him if it wasn't for the longer straggly hair and unkempt beard. I gape at him, confused, not sure what to say or do.

A gust of snow dusts the man's body, and an annoyed look flashes across his face.

"Come in, quickly, before you smother all the warmth I've been working for today." His voice is loud and commanding.

I step inside, and he closes the door behind me. Not sure if I should stomp or shake the snow off my body and leave a wet mess here in the cabin, I stand perfectly still and wait for the man to tell me what to do.

"Well? What do you want?" He walks toward a bookcase, then pulls out a bottle of liquid and pours a glass. "This is my only time off this week from securing the prisoners. It's the only time I don't have to be sober, so tell me what you want and be on your way."

His words force me into action, and I reach inside my coat where I had put the chief's message.

"The chief asked me to give this to you," I say, holding out the paper.

Eyeing me curiously, the man rips the parchment out of my hand and opens it. I study his face, wrinkly like the chief's but in a different pattern, more around his eyes and ears. His bushy eyebrows furrow deeply, almost knitting together in the middle. His expression turns from confused to angry.

"The chief gave this to you?" he asks, not bothering to keep his voice down. When I nod, he shakes his head "Who are you?"

"Alena Carlston." My voice shrieks more than I wish it did. I suddenly feel very afraid of this man.

He seems to find my answer amusing ... no, annoying. He scoffs angrily.

"Of course you are." He plops down in the lone chair sitting at his table. "Well, you've delivered your message; now you can go." He waves one hand, shooing me out the door, while drinking the liquid with the other, squinting as it goes down.

I turn to leave, wanting to get away from this place as quickly as possible, but Breccia hovers in the air.

"We can't get out of here without your help."

This draws out a laugh from the man, but it doesn't make me feel happy.

"I've been out in the cold all day with those damn prisoners. I'm not going out again until tomorrow."

I begin to question the chief. Why did he send me here? Did he know this would happen?

I jump when the man slams his hand on the table angrily.

"Why does the chief do these things to me?"

Frozen by his anger, I stand there, wide-eyed, unsure of what to do, when the smell of food reaches my nostrils. The man gets out of his chair and exits the room through a doorway in the back of the cabin, grumbling very loudly.

I dare a glance at Breccia, who looks as confused and frightened as I feel.

I straighten when the man comes stomping back into the room, holding a plate of meat and burnt potatoes in his hands. He sits at the table and begins to eat his food, right in front of me.

"I told you I'm not going out in the cold again until morning, so you might as well get comfortable on that couch. You can sleep here tonight."

My throat closes. I try to swallow but find the way blocked. I try to breathe but am unsuccessful.

Sleep here, at the prison? With this angry man who is apparently trying to get drunk? Will I be safe?

"Don't worry." The man scowls as if my thoughts were loud enough for the world to hear. "I won't hurt you. Just stay out of my way and keep quiet."

I try to read his dangerous expression as he raises a forkful of potatoes to his lips. My stomach growls loudly at the sight of food, reminding me that I denied it dinner tonight, but I hush it quickly. I don't want to make a single sound.

With the man focused on his food now, I send a panicked look to Breccia. *What do I do?* I mouth the words to her, but she just shrugs. Man, I hate this.

Finally, realizing that I should probably remove my snow clothes before sitting on the couch, I carefully take them off and lay them by the door. Keeping my sweater on, I tiptoe across the room, vowing not to speak at all until morning.

I notice dozens of pictures hanging above the couch when I approach it. I examine them only briefly before sitting. Thankfully, the man doesn't acknowledge me for a long time, giving me the chance to observe his cabin.

It's simple, holding only the most basic necessities, similar to our rooms at GreenGrotto. A couch, table, and bookcase are the only furnishings. A thin ladder that seems too delicate to be able to hold such a large man ascends to a loft hovering over the other side of the cabin. The space above doesn't hold much either. All I can see is the side of a mattress on the floor. *Is that where he sleeps?* The opening in the back, I decide, must be a kitchen where he got his food. *Is there a bathroom back there too?* Even if there isn't, or even if I need one, I don't think I'll leave this couch no matter what. I'll hold it.

A fire crackling in a fireplace next to the door is the only source of warmth and light.

When I'm confident the man isn't paying me any attention, I turn my body around to examine the pictures on the wall behind me. They're all face shots of men and women, some looking scary, while others looking clean-cut. My attention is drawn to a particular picture of a man on the far right. I inch my body closer to get a better look. He looks strangely familiar. I almost gasp when realization strikes.

He looks like Flint.

"Ah. Does he seem familiar to you? That's Cal. I believe you were supposed to participate in initiation with his nephew, Flint." How does this man know about Flint and me participating in initiation together? "His sentence here was a tragic one. I think the chief went a little too far, if you ask me. Taking power away from a pureblood Pepp. The chief couldn't have done anything more humiliating."

"What did Cal do?" I find myself asking against my better judgment.

The man stares right through me. "He actively chose to interact with human women even after the chief demanded he stop. He fathered many Mixed Bloods just like a lot of other Pepps before him. It was actually *his* imprisonment that made everyone truly understand how important it was to stay away from the humans."

I recall the bitterness in Flint's voice when he told me the same thing. He believes the sentence was too harsh too.

My gaze now falls to several pictures along the bottom. Across each one is slashed the word *missing*.

"Ah, they're men just like Cal. Made big mistakes, but knowing they'd be thrown in prison chose to stay away from Petrichor. The chief hasn't been able to find them." The man lowers his voice to a whisper, but I catch what he says. "Smart if you ask me. Better to be on the run than in prison here." He huffs.

My eyes land on one picture with the name Chauly written underneath.

Chauly. Wasn't that the man that made the explosives that hurt the chief? His picture makes the hairs on the back of my neck rise. He's unlike any Pepp I've ever seen, his sneer exposing a mouth filled with rotten, crooked teeth, his black hair long and greasy, his skin covered in lots of scars. He almost reminds me of the clan men.

It's odd seeing a Pepp so negligent with self-care. With power, the scars and the rotten teeth can easily be fixed. I've never seen a Pepp *not* fix things like that.

I turn away, hoping to never run into that man, sinking into the couch, trying to be invisible again. The man that looks like the chief, pours another three glasses of strong drink, consuming them each in one swallow. When his food is gone, he leans back into his chair, staring at me.

I focus my attention on the fabrics of the old couch.

"So, you're the one who's caused all the problems." His words sting. He knows who I am. I should be used to this by now—complete strangers being unfairly aware of my mistakes, but I'm not. I straighten, holding my head as high as I can, but still not meeting his gaze.

"Do you want to see the note the chief had you deliver?"

For the first time after sitting down on the couch I really look at him. His face has relaxed, probably from the drink, and he's now smiling.

He crumples the note and throws it at my face.

My skin flushes at his rudeness, and my breathing shallows. I want to ignore the paper, maybe throw it back in his face out of spite, but I'm too curious. Avoiding the cruel man's glare, I pick up the paper and flatten it out on my lap. Then I flip it over.

My heart drops. It's blank.

"I don't understand," I whisper, looking back up at him.

He laughs his bitter laugh again, but this time it's lined with humor. "It turns out the chief thinks you needed to pay me a little visit. Perhaps learn something from me." He pours himself another glass, then lifts it to me in a salute before drinking.

"What do I need to learn from *you*?" My voice drips with disgust ... which he finds funny.

"Well, let's see. You kept your plan to free the prisoners a secret from your boyfriend, and then paralyzed him when he tried to help. You killed a Pepp down in the silver mine by morphing and got your friend Danny kidnapped. Are you feeling a little down lately?"

My fists clench on my legs, and tears sting. *How dare he talk about those things so casually, so heartlessly?* I feel the urge to go punch him in the face. I bet Mark would, if he was here.

"It's okay, Alena. I would feel crappy too, if I were you."

Jutting my jaw, I pull my knees up to my chest on the couch and turn my face away, trying to hide my tears. I hear him gulp down another drink before he becomes quiet.

The air is potently heavy for a while. But, eventually, when my anger has diffused through my entire body, and my jaw is aching from being clenched, I allow myself to glare at the man's face. His smile is gone, and he's staring blankly at his glass. He might look like the chief, but he definitely isn't *like* the chief.

He breaks the silence. "I'm sorry, Alena. That wasn't fair."

I shake my head, refusing to accept his apology.

Placing his elbows on the table, the man leans his forehead onto his hands. After another long silence, he speaks again but much softer this time.

"I used to have a younger sister, many years ago," he says quietly. "She was the middle child, right in between the chief and me."

So he is related to the chief. I scoff. And he's trying to pull me into a story, just like his brother does. I don't want to hear what he has to say. Unfortunately, I don't have much of a choice.

"Our father was the chief before my brother. I was the oldest of the three of us, and at a very young age I was taught to take our father's place.

"When I was nineteen, I went on a run with my sister, Brendy. It was her first run, and she was more than excited to practice all the things she'd learned. It was my responsibility to watch out for her and protect her."

The scary man from only moments ago melts now into something … broken. It's as if the reason for his heartless actions surfaces, allowing me to see him in a unique and vulnerable way.

"During our run we were attacked by some men who knew we were Pepps. They somehow got their hands on Brendy and threatened that if I didn't make them rich, they would kill her. I didn't hesitate. I knew how to make gold and silver and could make them richer than they ever dreamed of. Right there in front of these men, as they held a knife to my sister's throat, I created piles and piles of valuable metals. I expected the men to immediately let her go, having been given what they wanted." His words hang in the air, and I study him, anxious to know what happened.

"But they didn't. They slit her throat. They killed her right there in front of me. Took their gold and ran."

The air is pulled from my lungs, the image painfully clear in my head.

The man's voice is now a whisper. He's talking more to himself than to me. "How do you get over something like that? How do you survive the daily guilt and shame?"

The man raises his head now and leans back into his chair, studying my face.

"I later tracked those men down and killed them. But that didn't help."

He rubs a hand down his face. "This's why the chief sent you to me. To give you a front row seat into my joke of a life where one simple experience made me bitter." His lips press into a hard line. "He says I can either choose to move on and forgive myself, or I can continue to live in anger." Pouring another glass, he frowns deeply. "I choose anger."

Drinking the liquid, he smacks his lips. "So, are you impressed? Do you want to continue on the path you're on and join me?" He picks up the glass bottle that's more than half empty, then holds it out to me.

When I don't move, he scoffs. "How about I leave it right here just in case?"

I still don't move. Instead, I just stare at the floor. The silence is heavy again, stretching on and on. *Maybe the drunk man has fallen asleep.* Maybe I should lie down and rest too.

When the man speaks again, I jump.

"I want to show you something."

His chair grinds against the wooden floor when he stands, and he moves around the table before disappearing down the hallway in the back—where he got his food. *Am I supposed to follow him?*

The man peeks his head around the corner. "Well, come on."

I stand, then walk through the doorway. There's a kitchen on the right, the countertops overflowing with dirty dishes, a potent garbage can full of discarded food. I shake my head, then look to my left. The man is there, in a cold, dark hallway that I couldn't see before.

"I'm Eli, by the way," the man says slowly, having difficulty enunciating his words.

I roll my eyes. *Oh, he's trying to be nice to me now?*

After picking up a lantern sitting on the floor, he wobbles down the hall. I follow behind until we reach a heavy metal door. Eli fishes a chain out of his pocket loaded with keys and works hard to find the right one. He's drunk, which makes the effort almost amusing.

Where are we going? Are we going into the prison? Is it a good idea for him to go in there drunk?

After cursing several times, he finally finds what he's looking for, sticks the key in the lock, and opens the door.

I gasp at the freezing air that escapes. *Holy crap, it's cold!* I see my breath, thick and white as I exhale. I hug my body, wishing I had brought my coat with me.

The hallway extends far beyond the metal door, ice reaching down from the ceiling, spreading across the walls. On both sides of the hallway are rooms. No cells. Dozens and dozens of cells.

This is the prison.

"This way," Eli says.

We walk ... I shiver ... and observe, noting that each cell is blocked off by bars and thick glass. Inside, the prisoners are given cozy accommodations. A bed with blankets and a table for eating. A fireplace, tucked behind another piece of glass, heats each cell, and I notice firewood. Stacks and stacks of firewood, carefully placed just outside the bars, next to me. Eli is probably really busy, keeping those fires going 24/7. *How does he get the firewood in there?*

I look at Eli now. Unlike me, his teeth aren't chattering wildly. He doesn't even have cold goose bumps on his bare arms. *Is it possible to get used to this type of cold?* Maybe the strong drink is keeping him warm. I rub my arms now. He's definitely warmer than I am. The cold bites at my bones, making my whole body ache.

One prisoner looks up as we pass by and walks to the glass separating us. He doesn't look dangerous, but I still sidestep away from him. There's a reason he's in prison.

"The prisoners can stay warm inside their cells," Eli says, "but if they try to escape, they freeze to death. There's no way out with the end doors locked, and the temperature in here is well below zero."

Eli sways when he walks and uses the wall to stay upright, but we only take a few more steps until we reach the cell Eli wants to show me.

"Here." He points into the cell.

I rub my arms rapidly, struggling to generate even a tiny bit of warmth, but then I stop.

The warming fire in the prison cell sends flickering light over the face of a man sleeping on the bed. He's familiar. His dark beard and hair are longer and greasier than before, but it's definitely him—the clan man that attacked me at initiation.

I step back. He tied me up that night and threw me into a toboggan so Case could take me away. Breccia cuddles into my neck. She remembers that night too.

"We've been searching his memories again," Eli says. "The first time we searched his memories we learned what your totem does when you and Mark morph. It produces lightning. Helpful information." Eli hiccups. "Now we're trying to gather any information he has on Jax. He worked with Jax and Case, you know."

I step forward now. "Have you found anything?"

"There are a few memories of Jax talking about a daughter. A daughter he really cares about." Eli leans his forehead on the wall now. "If he had a daughter, that means he had a woman, and knowing Jax and the rebellious man he was, I'm betting that that woman was not a Pepp."

The pieces come together slowly in my frozen brain.

"Which means the daughter is a Mixed Blood."

"Correct. Chief went looking for her in the main Mixed Blood community down in the swamplands."

I lean forward on my toes, waiting for Eli to tell me what was found.

"She *had* been there, but Jax came and got her a couple of months ago."

I rock back, gritting my chattering teeth.

Mixed Blood community? My mind goes back to the night I morphed with Mark. Chief had concluded that everything that night was a set-up, to create the black power for the Mixed Bloods—the sick children conceived in a mixed relationship, by one Pepp and one non-Pepp. We think it was created to heal them since they can't be healed with normal Peppate power. If Jax's daughter is a Mixed Blood, that explains why he's fighting so hard to get the black power.

"Do any of the Mixed Bloods know where he went? Are there other communities out there?" I ask.

"No, there aren't really any other Mixed Blood communities. And they don't know where Jax went. But *I* have a theory. I know someone who works in the Mixed Blood community. She says that Mixed Bloods get really sick when they live around a lot of plants. It's like they're allergic to them." Eli rubs his temples. "You know what I would do if I was allergic to plants?"

I stare at him.

"I'd get the hell away from plants."

At some point in the conversation, my anger toward Eli had fizzled out. He was cruel before, but he's obviously more aware of things going on in my life than I knew. Maybe it's the cold, but I'm not so angry with him now. And he might have a point. Where would Jax have taken his daughter? Danny has to be with him, right?

Eli pushes away from the wall he's leaning on and attempts to stand. I'm stepping forward to keep him from leaning too far back, when my eyes catch on something: a very large map taped to the wall he was leaning against. While holding onto Eli, I step toward it.

"Chief agrees with my idea, if you can believe it. So he's searching for Jax and Danny in the deserts," Eli waves to the world map, his breath coming out in white puffs. "Chief is using that to keep track of where he's looked."

Eli stumbles back to lean on another wall, and I look closer at the map.

It's huge and shows everything: the blue oceans, the southern lands, the northern lands in the west. I touch the high mountains with my fingertips. My home.

My eyes wander to the GreenLands in the east and the big country of Verdure. Even Petrichor is on the map, far north east.

I look for deserts on the map, deserts where the chief could potentially be looking. There are many, but only three seem to be totally barren of life. Three that are circled. And in one of these areas called Dakdete there are pins. I'm guessing those identify where the chief is currently searching.

Hope floods my chest. He's searching for Danny in other places! Why didn't he tell me?

Can *I* help?

Unfortunately, the pins are stuck only in a tiny portion of Dakdete. I exhale. It could take weeks to finish searching. Do we have that kind of time?

I search the remainder of the map. There are two other desolate desert lands: Kalahaki and Namib. Neither of these spots on the map have pins in them. Has the chief even gotten there yet?

"Chief is also building up his power supply," Eli says. "He has Pepps going out on Peppate runs to generate power. When the capsules are full they bring them back, add them to his stash, then head back out. Jax might only be human, but we can't afford to keep getting attacked. When the chief finds him, he's going after him with *all* that power ... without holding back. Jax won't stand a chance."

I shiver violently. Jax might only be human, but he also has Pepp men working for him. At least that's what the chief thinks. Eli is right. We can't afford to hold back.

"Can you get any more information from him?" I point to the still sleeping clan man, hungry for more clues. "Where Jax is?"

Eli sighs and hiccups again. "I think Jeter got all we're going to get out of him. The memory bugs can only find what's *actually* in the memory. I don't think he knows the location of Jax or his daughter."

My shoulders slump.

"Anyway, I just wanted to let you know that we're trying to find Danny. We at least know Jax's motive now. He wants the black power so he can heal his daughter."

The chief is working harder than I thought. And Eli is a part of the effort. I don't know why, but this touches me. This horrible, mean, detestable man is helping. I lean heavily against the wall, my eyes blurry, my body tired.

"Thank you," I whisper. Then I close my eyes and lean my head back.

"Hey, we should get out of here before we freeze," Eli says.

Yeah, we probably should. I'm not even shivering anymore.

Eli reluctantly peels his body away from the wall, then wobbles to me and grabs my elbow, yanking me forward with a strength that doesn't seem possible. I struggle for balance but move my feet and force my eyes open. I know there's a fire ahead. I can't wait to thaw my frozen fingers and nose.

When Eli shuts the heavy metal door behind us, I stand there, making sure he actually locks that lock.

Hypothermia combined with intoxication makes for a very wobbly man. I'm wobbly too. I don't know who holds up whom, but we slug our way down the rest of the hall, round the corner, then head straight to the ladder. Eli grips it and starts climbing. It creaks and bows under his weight, but he gets to the top just fine and plops on the mattress. It isn't too long before he's snoring loudly.

I'm so agonizingly cold that I just want to lie right on top of the fire. But I grab my coat and snowpants by the door and push my trembling limbs into the clothing before sitting right by the flames.

The fire isn't big enough.

I lean over and grab two logs of wood from the pile next to the old couch and drop them on the fire, hissing at the pain this causes in my frozen fingers.

When my body finally starts to warm, and my nose thaws, I look up at the mantle. It's empty except for a single picture of a woman. She has long brown hair, hazel eyes, a thin chin, and a contagious smile.

Breccia whispers to me in the quiet. "I think her name was Mia. I heard Eli loved her. She loved him back too, but he wouldn't accept her love. Said he didn't deserve it, so he pushed her away. She was a communicator down below. I'm not sure how they met, but I hear she was willing to come back to Petrichor to be with him. But he didn't want her to. She eventually gave up trying to convince him they should be together. It hurt too much for her to be so close and yet so far away from him." Breccia crosses her tiny legs, sitting on the floor next to me. "At least that's what I've heard. He's sentenced himself to working in the prison because he believes this is what he deserves." She drops her voice even more. "I even heard that he had a terrible rebellious period, where he went out and did some pretty bad things. Who knows, maybe he does deserve to be here."

Breccia falls silent. I stand and pluck the picture of the woman off the mantel before dropping back to the floor. After staring at it for a while, my eyes slide to the fire.

I watch it crackle, watch the flames lick the bricks around it, feel it's warmth finally spreading through my body. It reminds me of the night

Mark brought me out this way, the night he gave me Dilo. The night he kissed me for the first time.

I look up at the man in the loft. Regardless of the mean person he is, I can't help but relate to him. As an outsider, it's easy for me to determine that his path is an unhappy one, but how can I judge him when I've been making the same choices?

I understand him. He wants to be alone without the woman he loves, to punish himself. But is it a worthy punishment? Or is it just easier? Is it easier to push others away rather than to try to forgive and be forgiven?

I analyze the picture in my lap. Is it fair to the others who *want* to love us?

Am I being fair to Mark by shutting him out and not taking the chance to tell him how sorry I am ... for everything?

I straighten my back. I need to get back to Mark. I need to apologize. I can at least do that. I miss him. I look up at Eli one last time and wipe my nose. I don't want to be a monster anymore.

I curl up on the floor next to the fire and try to get some sleep.

Chapter 7

Sleeping in a cabin next to a prison, on the floor, without a pillow or blanket, makes for a very restless night. I couldn't have been more relieved when Eli angrily told me to get up and get dressed so he could be rid of me. I didn't need to get dressed, though, since I slept in my snow gear.

He looked pleased with my timeliness.

Then he pushed me out the door, without even offering breakfast. I think I like him better when he's drunk. Oh well. The sooner I leave the sooner I get back to Petrichor, away from him.

Finding the opening in the ice wall was easy for Eli. I was standing right in front of it and couldn't even see it. He must have some gift, being the warden. After pointing the way, he gave me only one warning.

To watch out for Miss Wintriness.

He didn't bother to explain before turning away. Fortunately, I have Breccia.

Apparently, Miss Wintriness is the lake that sits right on the border of the warm meadow, but on the frozen side. Regardless of how cold it gets, though, she never freezes all the way through because of how close she is to the warm meadow. She's dangerous though. If you fall in through the thin ice that laces the top of it, you can easily get trapped underneath and drown. And since I still can't command ice or fire, that would be most inconvenient. Under Breccia's guidance, and with much calmer weather, we made our way back to the border. Breccia pointed out the lake when we passed it. With all the snow piled on top, it was almost impossible to tell that it was a lake.

When we passed through the fog back into the warmth of Petrichor, I took off my snow clothes and immediately looked around the meadow. No baby dinosaur in sight. Hopefully, it found its mother.

The wind blows through my hair now as I run. It probably has soot in it from sleeping by the fire and has been flattened by the snow, but I don't have time to shower. I need to see Mark now, before my fear returns and I talk myself out of doing what I need to do.

I still don't know exactly what I'm going to say.

I slow, my lungs protesting the exercise.

What *do* I say?

I'm sorry. That's all.

The snap of a branch echoes behind me and I stop, glancing back and forth between the bushes and trees. I see nothing, but my skin still crawls nervously. *It's probably just an animal. Maybe the baby dinosaur.*

I pick up my pace, occasionally glancing over my shoulder, and race toward GreenGrotto. The corners of my lips lift slightly at the comforting sound of ringing in my ears. I can hear the elements again!

When I approach GreenGrotto, I find it empty. My shoulders droop.

The Dino Games are still going. Mark is probably still below with his dinos. That complicates things.

I stop for a moment to catch my breath, wishing I had a four-wheeler at my disposal to get around. It'll take me at least another hour to get to the bottom of the mountain on foot. But then I remember Cody's stash of capsules still hidden in her closet. She's still being taken care of at the hospital, so she hasn't been to her room since she was kidnapped. She won't mind if I borrow something, will she?

I run up GreenGrotto's stairs, through the tunnels, to our room. I enter her closet and pull out her satchel. Unfortunately, she doesn't have a four-wheeler, but I do find a bike. Clutching it in the palm of my hand, I run back down the stairs and outside. After expanding the bike, I hop on. It's been a while since I've ridden one, but my body easily finds its balance, enjoying the chance to push my feet against the strain of the chains. I ride over the grass, across the bridge by Training Mountain, and down the path.

I round the mountain, pedaling as quickly as my legs will allow, when something slams into my back right between my shoulder blades with a force that makes me lose control of the handles. My front tire hits a rock and sends the bike to the ground, me with it. I skid to a stop, my knees and elbows instantly burning from the fall, and my upper back pulsing as blood rushes to where I was hit.

What in the world?

I roll onto my butt and look back at the path where I just came from and see a man standing there, his head twitching in a way that quickly fills my body with fear. Despair rises sharp and swift. I know him, from the picture on the wall at the prison.

Chauly?

Where the hell did he come from?

He's wearing a red gingham shirt and dirty, holey jeans. His feet are bare, exposing blackened toenails grown out long. And there on his arm is a totem void of any ribbon.

"Well, well, well. What a lucky guy I am."

He takes two oddly jerky steps toward me, a disturbing grin growing on his face. His teeth are even more rotted than in his picture, and a darkness radiates from his being, spreading across the path, clawing out for me.

I scoot toward my bike. I need to get out of here.

"Do you know how long I've been waiting to get you to cross my path ... alone?"

Goose bumps ripple through my skin.

He rubs his hands together. "Jax will be so pleased when I bring you to him. And I get to have a little fun along the way. What a great day."

My hands shake when I reach out to my bike.

"Help!" I scream and rise to my feet as fast as I can. I drape my leg over ready to take off, when another rock slams into my left arm, deadening it painfully.

Dammit! I let my arm hang there, gripping the handle with my right, still determined to get away, when Chauly grabs the neck of my shirt and yanks me back. I stumble, half dragging the bike with me, half twisting my leg. Before I know it, I'm lying on the ground with the horrible man straddling my torso.

"Look what I found in your drawer after you left your room."

Chauly brings his right hand up where I see that he's got my vial of black power in it. *He was in my room? How did I not see him?*

"Now all I need to collect ... is you."

The ringing sounds of power trickle through my brain. I've never used my power to hurt someone because then the power will deplete, disappear. I can't afford to lose the power now. So I reach up and grab his hand with both of mine. I'm not sure why I'm fighting to get the black power back. I hate it, what it represents. But it doesn't seem right being in his slimy grasp.

I feel the glass underneath my fingertips. I'm twisting and pulling, when his hand releases the vial, pulls back, and punches me in the face. My head rolls, and my vision blacks out. I feel immediate blinding pressure behind my left eye that spreads over into my nose and forehead. I groan as little yellow stars prick through the blackness.

"No." I weakly shake my head. I need to get away, but he ties my hands together. *No!*

Then I hear it. I don't know exactly *what* it is. It's like hearing a tiny new baby cry for the first time. Precious, different, a sound that makes total sense.

I force my eyelids to open, then blink several times before zeroing my sight on a baby dinosaur right next to me roaring its biggest roar. The same baby dinosaur I saw last night.

"Oh, aren't you cute." Chauly sneers, then backhands the tiny dinosaur, sending it several feet to the side. I bring my knee up and hit him in the back, but he just cocks his arm again, ready to hit me. I cover my face with my tied hands, and tears sting my eyes. *Please don't punch me again.*

Just then a *real* monstrous roar vibrates through the air, a sound that chills my bones. A large meat-eating dinosaur suddenly breaks through the trees, and the rocks on the path beside me leap in the air in response to the dinosaur's quaking steps. When it comes into my vision, I see that it towers several feet above the trees. Its skin is scaley and dry, with long, wet, and terrifying teeth.

Its yellow eyes quickly fixate on us, there in the middle of the path.

Oh boy.

Chauly pulls me to my feet, placing me in front of him as a shield.

I just cover my face with my hands, not knowing what else to do.

Should we run? No, that seems stupid. But so does standing here. If I could get to the bike quickly ...

It takes another huge step toward us, then roars again, a sound that shakes every cell in my bones. My entire body goes rigid, its saliva raining over my body. I cower, trying to cover my ears, which is hard to do with tied hands.

Dammit!

Then the dinosaur's head hovers over us, its steamy breath reaching my skin. I gulp loudly. *What does it feel like to being eaten by a dinosaur?* I can't even cry, scream, or beg. When death is knocking on your door, it seems the only thing you can do is cower in the corner and hope. Hope that something will make it go away.

The large, hard, scaly head whips sideways with a force that sends us flying through the air. Chauly lands first, keeping me in front of him. I land on my back, the air knocked from my lungs. Before I can catch my breath, Chauly rises to his feet and runs. I hear the pounding of his steps leaving me here all alone. Still unable to breathe, I flip onto my stomach and cover my head with my hands in my best attempt to be invisible.

Then little claws dig into my skin as the baby dinosaur climbs onto my back. It roars and chortles at the larger dinosaur. Without another thought, the giant dino steps over me and chases after Chauly. I look up briefly to see it snapping at an eagle rising in the sky.

I melt into the dirt path, my limbs feeling like rubber. *What in the world just happened?* I remember Mark telling me how the dinosaurs bow to him. How he thought it was because of the Doler he produced. Did the baby dinosaur smell the Doler on me? Is that why it's still following me around? Why it just saved me?

I sit up and grab the baby without any thought of its dangerous teeth, then pull it against my chest. My shoulders shudder, and tears swell but

I choke them back. My eye hurts too much to cry, and blood is dripping out of my nose.

"Thank you," I say. The dino quickly chomps at the ropes tying my hands, and within moments I'm free.

I'm rubbing my wrists, when a man suddenly runs out of the trees, looking tired, dirty, and terribly distressed.

"Have you seen Giggy?"

He must be the dinosaur's trainer. If I hadn't just been almost kidnapped, I would have laughed. *Giggy? What kind of name is that for a terrifying dinosaur?*

Am I in that dinosaur's guarding territory?

Without waiting for a response, he disappears into the same trees Chauly went into.

"Wait," I yell. I need to tell him about Chauly. That he needs to be careful.

But he's gone.

The baby dinosaur in my arms squirms free and runs into the trees too. *Is that giant dinosaur its mother?*

I rise to my feet and contemplate entering the trees too, only to stop after taking a few steps in. I don't see or hear anything. Not even Giggy's roar or pounding steps in the distance. The silence makes me jumpy.

No, I'll let Giggy take care of Chauly. I need to get out of here.

Huffing back to the path, I clench my fists. Only now do I realize that I have the vial of black power. Chauly had let it go before he punched me and tied me up. As much as I hate this power, I'm relieved to know he didn't take it. I carefully place it in my satchel.

"Are you okay?" Breccia has wiggled free from her harness.

"Yes." I pat the skin around my right eye and swipe at my nose, smearing blood across my hand. "Hey, will you go tell the chief that Chauly is here? I need to go find Mark. Chauly might go after him too."

Breccia nods quickly before taking off into the sky.

I grab my bike, drape my leg over, and ride faster than before. That dinosaur might not have wanted to eat me, but others might. And Chauly might come back.

But then my hands squeeze the brake, skidding me to a halt.

Chauly was going to take me to Jax.

And Jax has Danny.

I let out a frustrated yell. *Why did I fight back? Why didn't I just let him take me?* I've been wanting to find Danny, and that man was my ticket.

Yet my shoulders shiver. Maybe I should have gone with him to free Danny, but the thought of going anywhere alone with that man has me choking back a sob. I don't ever want to see him again. Besides, the last time I tried to make things right by myself I ended up making a big mistake.

No, if I'm going to find Danny, I need to do it with the help of someone who is smart. Mark, Rusty, the chief. I can't do this on my own.

Pushing my feet back into the pedals, I ride as quietly as I can, my nerves pouncing on any movement. Occasionally I see walls of fire along the path, marking the boundaries of dinosaurs. Other boundaries seem to be marked with yellow flags only inches off the ground. Those trainers must be good. It doesn't take me long to reach the open hillside where the Dino Games had started yesterday.

I pause for a moment to catch my breath. I had little faith in the Dino Games. Little understanding of what the chief was trying to accomplish with them, but that dinosaur back there just saved my life from an intruder. Perhaps the trainers and dinosaurs are better than I thought.

I look around the empty area. The medics are no longer stationed around the borders like they were before. Leinani mentioned that they move into the trees closer to the dino trainers in case they're needed, which is probably where they are now. I lift my eyes to the sky. There aren't even any Pepps flying above.

I set off in the direction I saw Mark take his four-wheeler yesterday, into the northern trees. The air is quiet except for the infrequent dinosaur roars in the distance. Occasionally, I spot a long neck reaching up above the tree line. *Those* dinosaurs don't make me too nervous.

I reach the other side of the clearing and enter the woods again.

"Mark," I whisper, not wanting the dinosaurs to hear me.

I pass more yellow flags and some smaller dinosaurs. The few trainers I see look confused at my presence but keep their dinosaurs from crossing their borders and coming after me.

I don't realize I'm holding my breath until I miraculously see the familiar orange frills of a dinosaur up ahead. "Dilo!" I exhale too loudly.

She turns at the sound of my voice.

But where is Mark?

I ride closer, looking around. Then my muscles go rigid.

He's there, on the bank of a river, lying facedown in the rocks.

No! Don't let him be hurt.

I hop off the bike and drop down next to him.

"Mark." I gently shake his shoulders trying to wake him, but when my hands touch his skin, my worry deepens. He's hot with fever. I turn him onto his back and reach out for the elements of his body.

I can hear!

I beg the elements to tell me what's wrong with him, but I get a confusing response. All I can hear is that his body is suffering from an infection. But I can't tell what the source of the infection is. I don't sense any viruses or wounds. Not even any foreign objects. It's like a dead wall is blocking the source from me. Kind of like with the baby dinosaur.

Am I still not fully recovered?

But then I see it, in the middle of his neck, right at the site where I injected him with Dilo's dinosaur serum. His skin is swollen, red, and terribly hot. *What's wrong?* Did Jeter not heal Mark when we came back? Why can't I sense the serum?

I cradle his head in my hand and rub the sweat off his face. His cheeks are shadowed with a day's worth of facial hair and his clothes are smudged with dirt. It's been so long since I've been this close to him. I want to soak in the moment, but his burning skin screams at me for help. I look around, hoping to find another Pepp who can give me some answers, but there's no one.

"Mark," I whisper his name, trying to wake him up again, but he doesn't respond.

With his head in my hand, I use my power to heal the infection as best as I can, but without removing the serum still in his neck, the infection will come back. His temperature lowers, and his breathing slows but he still doesn't wake up.

I need to get him to the hospital.

With my free hand, I reach for the ring on my middle finger, the one I was given to help with the Dino Games. It's a one-man toboggan that's only to be used for the worst cases during the games. They're to be sent directly to Jeter at the hospital.

Wiggling it off my trembling finger, I push the button. It expands into a bed made of crisscrossing branches like a bird's nest. I carefully roll Mark on with the help of Dilo.

There are several buttons and levers inside. The lever lets you control the toboggan like a vehicle and go anywhere you want. But I push the blue button. The one programed to go straight to the hospital. Then I shut the cover. It jolts to life, moving Mark away from me into the air. When the flyer disappears from my sight, I speak to Dilo.

"Will you take me to the hospital?"

Chapter 8

Petrichor is buzzing with a different type of urgency. Pepp men are running in all sorts of directions, dressed in heavy protective camo gear, carrying dangerous-looking guns in their hands, a foreign sight here in Petrichor. Dozens of Pepp eagles are flying in the sky, and I don't think they're looking for injured Pepps from the Dino Games. Chief must have gotten my message about Chauly.

As I approach the hospital, I search the honeycombs on the outside—the rooms where the loaded toboggans go so medics can heal the injured. I hope Mark's toboggan took him to the top level where Jeter works. He's the only one, I'm sure, who'll be able to help Mark.

Dilo jumps over a patch of grass, sending me flying into the air. I cling to her bare skin, just barely holding on before my body slams back down onto her rough torso, then I kick her to go faster. Breccia finds me while I'm riding Dilo and hovers along, sensing the urgency.

I practically fall off when Dilo comes to an abrupt halt at the door of the hospital. I grab Breccia, put her in the harness, and go inside, climbing the stairs as fast as my tired body will allow.

As soon as I reach the top floor, I search the hall. The glass windows allow me to see into all the rooms lining the side of the mountain, and when I pass each one, I find the worst victims of the Dino Games there—terrible gashes breaking their bodies—but I don't see Mark.

When I reach the end of the hall, I pound on Jeter's door. He needs to know Mark's condition and help me find him if Mark was taken to another level of the hospital.

"Are you looking for Mark?" A familiar voice interrupts my pounding.

I turn. It's Scance, with her dreadlock hair tied back in a thick, long ponytail. I've always held a respect for this medic, the first one I ever met. She might have tried to strangle me when she first saw the totem on my arm, but she also healed my brother Caleb's broken leg. I'll always appreciate her for that.

Unlike everyone else, Scance doesn't nervously retreat when I turn around. Instead, she stands there, obstinate.

"Yes."

"Jeter took him to GreenGrotto. He thought Mark would be more comfortable there while being healed."

I frown. *That's unusual.*

Grateful for her help, I run down the hall. Fortunately, Dilo's still outside, extending her orange frilled head up a tree, snapping at a squirrel. She's not too happy when I climb on her back and pull her away, but she obeys.

When we reach GreenGrotto, I jump off again and enter the large mountain, then run up to the boys' dorms. When I reach Mark's floor, I slow.

What if Mark is awake? What if he doesn't want to see me?

His door is slightly ajar when I reach it, and I peek inside.

Mark is there, still unconscious on the bed pushed to the left side of the room. I gulp, trying to steel myself for the truth of his condition.

Jeter, his back to me, sits in a chair next to him.

Taking in a deep breath, I place my hand on the wooden door and push it open. It squeaks, splitting the silence. Jeter turns at the sound, his hazel eyes narrowing at the sight of me and my dirty clothes. I groan inwardly. *Why do I always have to look so pathetic?*

"Alena," he greets warily before turning back to Mark. "Was it you that sent him to the hospital in the toboggan?"

"Yes," I say, shutting the door behind me and sliding against the wall. I take special care to stay as far away from Mark and Jeter as I can. "I found him unconscious in the Dino Game. What's wrong with him?"

Jeter doesn't look at me when he responds, but I sense a tightness in his voice.

"It's the dino serum you injected into his neck. It's lodged itself deep in the tissues. His body has recognized it as a foreign substance and is trying to fight it, but unfortunately all it's doing is causing infections and fevers."

I purse my lips. *So, it's my fault.* "Can't you get rid of it? Can't you burn it?"

Jeter shakes his head.

"I tried, but I can't hear the sounds of the serum. Because I can't hear it, I can't burn it. I ended up hurting Mark more when I tried before." Jeter leans back in his chair and crosses his arms over his chest. "I've never seen anything like it. The serum is different, lacking Peppate altogether. It doesn't respond to our power at all."

"So, what do you do?" I ask, my voice rising with worry. *If Jeter can't get the serum out, will Mark suffer its effects for the rest of his life?*

"I've just been treating his symptoms. Getting rid of the infection and telling his white blood cells to go home. It's what I did after you brought him to me a couple weeks ago. Although, it looks like the effects of that have worn off, and his fevers have returned. He'll probably need to be seen every week to make sure the infection isn't too bad."

I scoot closer. Mark's skin is still wet from the heat, but it's not as red. I resist the urge to touch him, to make sure it's cooled.

"Well, I've done all I can for now," Jeter says, standing. "I should get back to the hospital."

As he moves past me to the door, I get a good look at him for the first time and almost gasp at the change in his appearance. I'm surprised I didn't see it before when he had turned around: his thin face, the weary circles under his eyes, his blond hair unkempt. Even his mouth, the feature that used to so easily break into a smile, is now set in a firm, unbudging line.

"Oh," he adds quietly. "Be careful. We've just been informed that we have an intruder here in Petrichor."

I don't bother telling him that I already know that. That I was the one the intruder tried to take.

Without another word, Jeter steps out, shutting the door behind him. My gut tightens. The last three weeks haven't only been hard on me. But what could Jeter possibly be struggling with?

After watching him leave, I teeter. I should leave too. All my confidence from earlier wavers. I don't deserve to be here, and if Mark wakes up, I'll be the last person he wants to see.

But I can't leave.

I stare at the man lying on the bed, let my eyes wander over his face, take in the neat cut of his hair, his dark eyebrows, his straight nose that used to crinkle when he laughed.

Slowly, drawn to his side, I sit in Jeter's chair. The churning in my stomach deepens. I only injected the serum into Mark because I thought it could be easily burned out. But I was so wrong. Not even Jeter can heal him.

How could I do something so stupid? I didn't know anything *about the serum, and I just decided to inject it into Mark?*

Tears break free, sliding down my cheeks. I reach for Mark's hand, suddenly needing to know for sure in this moment that I haven't killed him yet.

I slide my fingers into his callused, cooled palm and grip him selfishly.

"I'm sorry, Mark." My lip quivers. "I'm so sorry."

I cry. For several minutes, letting my tears fall on his quilt.

Then, I feel it. A pressure in my palm. Staring intently at my hand clinging to Mark's, I see the muscles pull in his fingers. He's squeezing my hand.

I blink twice trying to clear my blurry vision, then look at Mark's face. His eyes are open ... and he's looking at me.

"Alena." His voice is filled with an unexpected warmth.

A lump forms in the back of my throat, and I grip his hand tighter, feeling the urgent need to speak before my opportunity slips away.

"Mark." I stare at our hands, my tears slipping off my chin. "I'm sorry. Sorry for everything." There's more in my head, more I should probably say, but suddenly my voice won't work through the sobs. *Sorry for being so angry with you. Sorry for being so heartless to not even know you were sick.*

Mark's body shifts on the bed. He's sitting up. I wipe at my tears, unable to meet those brown eyes. At least not until his fingers grip my chin. Then I have to look at his furrowed expression.

"What happened to your face?" His voice is low, dangerous. My hand rises to my swollen eye. *Crap.* I should have healed it before I came in here. I'm not used to being able to hear the elements around me. I want to tell him it's nothing, but I promised myself I'd never keep anything from Mark again.

I sigh, my shoulders slumping. "Have you heard of a man named Chauly?"

Mark's muscles tense. "Yes."

"Well, he's here in Petrichor."

"Chauly attacked you?" A tortured look passes across his face.

"He said he was going to take me to Jax."

Mark's jaw twitches. "Are you okay?"

I gulp back emotion in my throat. The reality of events floods me now and my pulse quickens. *I'm not sure.*

"Yes," I say instead.

I don't seem to convince Mark, though. "Is he still here?"

"I think so."

Mark unexpectedly jumps to his feet, forcing me to sit back.

"Whoa, Mark, you should probably rest." He ignores my suggestion, immediately pulling a small handgun out of his drawer.

Whoa. What's he doing with that?

"Wait, Mark," I try again. *He can't leave now. I have more to say, don't I?*

Mark moves to his closet. He's not listening.

"Please don't go." The words are barely a whisper.

Mark stops, letting my words hang in the air. I watch his shoulders rise and fall in a deep sigh as he runs his hand through his hair. It hurts—the tearing in my chest, wanting to both move toward him and alienate myself from him at the same time. Battling between what my heart so desperately wants and what my strict mind deems I deserve.

"I'm sorry too, Alena," he finally whispers.

I shake my head, and wipe my nose with the sleeve of my sweater. "You have no reason to be sorry, Mark." *I'm the one who made all the mistakes.*

Slowly turning around, he walks back to me and sits on the edge of the bed. He gently cups my swollen cheek in his hand, rubbing my tears away with his thumb, a gesture that has me tearing up again. I lean into his touch, having missed it so desperately.

"I do have reason to be sorry, Alena. I'm sorry I didn't trust you."

My bottom lip trembles, his words touching me deeply. *How did he know that's exactly why I've been angry with him?*

"I saw you leaving with Rusty," he continues, wiping more tears with his thumb. "I guess I became jealous, wondering what important thing you needed to do with him that I couldn't be a part of. I was so angry that Gabbro chose to put *you* in danger, and not me that I couldn't think properly. Things would have gone a lot better if I had just trusted you and gone back to Petrichor like you asked."

I stare at him, my throat thick with emotion. I had come here needing to apologize to Mark. I needed him to know how sorry I am for everything that happened. But I didn't anticipate him actually forgiving me, at least not this quickly, and that is what his words sound like—forgiveness.

"You had ..." I pause to swallow. "You had every right to react the way you did, Mark. It's okay."

My words are sincere, which both surprises and relieves me.

But Mark's eyebrows furrow hard, his persistent gaze angry at the sight of my battered face. "I should have been keeping a better eye on you. Just like I should have been keeping a better eye on Danny." Sighing, he drops his hand to his lap, an awkward silence hanging in the air. My skin immediately laments the loss of his touch. "I can't believe we still have no idea where he is, even after all this time." He shakes his head again. "The only clues we have are the stupid torture memories Jax keeps sending us."

I cringe, remembering the horrible sounds from the memory the chief tried to show me yesterday.

"Has the chief shown them to you?" Mark asks quietly. I observe the speckled golden color in his brown eyes reflecting in the sunlight. *Have they always been so bright?*

I clear my throat. "He tried," I say, "but Danny's screams ..." My voice trails off. I don't want to think about those screams.

"He showed me the newest one late last night. Alena," Mark murmurs seriously. "There's something off about those screams."

I grimace. *The chief had said the same thing.*

"In the background, there's a very subtle hum. I don't know for sure, but it sounds like Gabbro. It's almost as if he's right there with Danny. The hums are weird, though—high pitched then low, as if he's ... singing."

Gabbro? The traitor? Of course he's right there with Danny. He's working with Jax. My blood boils hearing the black rock's name.

"What if it's a message? A message in a song." Mark's voice rises as the idea occurs to him.

I shake my head. "Mark, Gabbro is working with Jax. If it *is* him humming in the background, we can't trust it. He betrayed us."

"Alena, it's all we've got. Isn't it worth looking into just in case?" He stands, holding out his hand. "Will you go to the Post with me?"

Of course we should be concerned about Danny. Isn't this what I've wanted all along? To make things right with Mark so we could focus on finding our friend? So why do I still feel so … discouraged? Did I have more to say to Mark?

I place my hand in his.

"I want to see those memories again," he whispers when I stand. "If he is humming a song, maybe our Magbabies can help us identify which song it is." Mark lets go of my hand and moves to his nightstand, quickly harnessing his Magbaby, Dacite, around his right arm. I try to ignore the very distracting tightness of his bulging bicep now strapped with his Magbaby.

I guess the Magbabies with their endless knowledge of songs would be a perfect resource for finding music … if that's really what Gabbro is doing, singing us a song.

When Mark is done tying Dacite to his arm, he walks to the door.

I slink after him but practically run into his back when he abruptly halts in the hallway.

Turning around, he looks down at me, his expression changing from determined to something that makes my body warm. His fingers brush against my arm softly, sending shivers up my spine. I try to slow my breathing, thrown off balance by his sudden closeness.

"Thank you, by the way," he says, his breath brushing my face. "Thank you for helping me in the Dino Games. I wasn't feeling well but was too stubborn to leave the game."

"You're welcome," I say.

He's standing right in front of me. I want to close the distance between us, to feel him, to hear him breathe. *Would that make him terribly uncomfortable?*

When Mark doesn't move, I can't help myself. I step into him, bury my face in his chest.

His arms immediately embrace me, pulling me close. The gesture makes my bottom lip tremble, and I raise my arms to grip the back of his shirt.

He's forgiven me. I can feel it. Things aren't perfect, but we're headed in the right direction, right?

"Chief is looking for Danny in the deserts," I murmur into Mark's chest.

"What?" His voice vibrates against my face, his breath stirring my hair. I grip him tighter, feel the muscles beneath his shirt.

"Jax has a Mixed Blood daughter, and since the chief believes the Mixed Bloods are allergic to plants, he thinks Jax is hiding his daughter away from plants ... in a desert, with Danny." I breathe in Mark's scent. He smells like burned wood, and pine. "I wish I could help with the search."

Mark gently weaves his fingers through my messy hair, making me melt in his arms.

"We'll figure out a way to help," he whispers.

Unfortunately, someone runs down the hall toward us in this moment.

"Petrichor is on full alert. Protectors at every post. Keep your eyes open." The man informs us of what I already know, then tries to get past us, forcing Mark and me to move. I step back, and Mark's arms drop. When the boy is gone, so is the moment.

I don't bother meeting Mark's gaze. I just break the awkward silence by saying, "We should go."

Sighing, Mark agrees.

Chapter 9

Our trip to the Post is quiet. The warning from the Pepp in the hall sobers the air. I try not to constantly look over my shoulder like I want to. Chauly had come out of nowhere before. Which means he could be anywhere.

Forcing down the waves of nervousness plaguing me, I pay particular attention to the rock path at my feet. I observe the way the grass crawls between each perfectly placed rock. *Do they have to mow the lawn here?* Probably not. That's something I've never thought about.

Then my eyes glance sideways at Mark. He's wearing attire fit for the Dino Games: a sturdy pair of brown hiking shoes, some old muddied Levi's, and a loose camo-green shirt that shows off way too many muscles. He's standing so close I feel his warmth.

I try to make small talk by asking him about the Dino Games. Then he asks me about the injuries I witnessed, but our efforts at conversation eventually fall flat, and we end up walking in silence. We might have forgiven each other, but there's still an awkwardness tagging along.

A loud commotion catches my attention, and I look ahead. There's a crowd there in the open field. Hundreds of people ... all yelling at each other.

What's going on?

I look at Mark for answers, but he's as confused as I am. The closer we get, the more I can see. Those in the crowd aren't actually yelling at one another. Instead, everyone is shouting at one person in particular: an old man with gray hair who's unsuccessfully trying to calm them down.

Mark leans in close. "They don't have totems on their arms."

My eyes travel from the old man to the rest of the angry people. He's right. None of them have totems ... except for the old man still trying in vain to tranquilize the shouting. Little non-Pepp children run around the angry adults, making their own happy game of tag. That is, until they get yelled at by the adults. Then they slink back to the group.

"You can't just drag us here like this!" A shout travels through the air.

I narrow my eyes. Drag them here? *What's going on?*

But then my eyes land on an old lady.

"Issy?" I whisper the name of the old witch doctor that helped my brother Caleb and me find the Pepps. She's standing on the border of the angry crowd, rolling her eyes.

"Communicators." Mark whispers the word. "They're communicators."

They are, but why are they *here?*

Unlike everyone else, Issy is not talking or yelling but instead standing there with her arms crossed, looking very annoyed.

I walk straight to her and touch her wrinkly arm. "Issy?" *Does she remember who I am?*

Her narrowed eyes move to my face. "Alena," she growls.

Yup. She remembers me

"What are you guys doing here?" I ask, ignoring her piercing stare.

Issy sets her jaw, tightening her already sour face. "Chief brought us here to protect us. Said communicators are getting attacked again. All thanks to you two."

Now I'm the one who's annoyed. If I thought Issy might be nice to me, she's quickly set that straight.

"He brought you here to protect you?" Mark asks, glancing my way briefly. He must be thinking the same thing I am. *Can we protect* anyone *with Chauly here?*

"Well, he says protect," Issy replies, "but you know the chief. He's like a double-edged sword. Says one thing but really means five other things." Issy rubs her temple as if a headache is coming on. "That man over there says the chief wants us to help find Jax. Send out Magbabies to search the deserts, and then keep track of their reports."

Send out Magbabies? I look at Breccia tucked in the band around my arm. That's a good idea. *I* can't leave Petrichor, but maybe I could use Breccia to look in the deserts for me.

"Where will you stay?" Mark asks, and I look around. Good question. Chief didn't just bring the communicators here; he brought their entire families too. Little children.

"That's what everyone's trying to figure out. The chief wants us to stay in the Post, but there's no room there. I say they need to house us in the Burrows. But that man over there is trying to tell us there's no room there either."

Issy's skin is even more wrinkly than I remember, the lines in her face exposed by the bright sunlight, her long gray hair dull.

"How long will you be here?" I ask.

"Until they find Jax. Man, if I had known Jax was working against the Pepps, I would have killed him on the spot when he came to me asking questions after I got attacked by the clan." She kicks a clump of grass on the ground. "I'm sick of being a target because I used to be a Pepp. Chief needs to figure things out so we can all get back to living our lives." Issy looks around. "Where the hell is that man anyway?"

Without another word, Issy stomps off, her tiny body pushing through the crowds to get away from us.

My shoulders slump as I stare at the angry crowd. *The chief brought the communicators here to keep them safe?* He probably arranged that before he knew Chauly was here. But now that we know about Chauly, he should send them back home, right? Nobody is safe in Petrichor right now, especially non-Pepps.

Mark grips my elbow and turns me away from the crowd, rubbing his tired face. "Chief is probably too busy to help us with those messages now."

My tired body sags. He probably is, but maybe it's for the best. I'm tired. And one look at Mark's face with dark circles under his eyes tells me he's tired too.

"Let's go back to GreenGrotto. You need to rest," I say.

Mark shakes his head. "There's no way I can sleep right now. Maybe there's another council member in the Post who could help us listen to those memories again?" He raises an eyebrow in question.

Okay. I nod. It's worth a try.

Just then someone screams behind us. I turn, expecting to find Chauly there attacking the unsuspecting group.

But, instead, I see a familiar baby dinosaur nipping at the non-Pepps.

"Get. It. Away. From me!" a woman growls, pushing into the crowd for protection.

Everyone backs away from the dinosaur, except for one non-Pepp man who's about to kick it. Mark and I yell at the same time, scrambling through the grass to the baby dino. Fortunately, the man doesn't kick it but stands there stunned, until I scoop the dino into my arms.

Mark raises a fist at the man. "You kick the dinosaurs, and I'll beat the crap out of you."

I almost smile. He would too.

The man's jaw twitches, but he doesn't speak. I turn and don't look back, anxious to get away from these people. It isn't until we're out of earshot and Mark touches my arm that I realize that every muscle in my body has tensed.

"It's okay, Alena."

I swallow. *It's okay?* The chief can't keep the communicators safe anymore, so he's brought them here, but Chauly is still lurking around, ready to pounce. We're losing control. How long until the world finds out the state of the Pepps and decides to come attack us while we're weak?

I don't voice my worries, though. I just stare at Mark's warm hand on my arm.

The dinosaur wiggles in my grip, and Mark moves his hand to rub the dino's head. I expect the dinosaur to nip at Mark, but he doesn't. Instead, he leans right into Mark's touch. *Of course.* The dinosaurs all love Mark.

"You need to be more careful, Bud." Mark speaks to the dinosaur as if it's an old friend. "You can't just go around biting everyone."

Bud.

I examine the dinosaur in my arms while trying to calm my anxious heart. Its skin is a darker greenish-brown than last night, and I notice that its eyes have a tiny rim of red around the black irises. Its feet are disproportionally huge, along with its head. It seems like it would fall over from the weight of it. It just might with its tail gone. Surprisingly, my sock is still there, protecting the little stub.

"So its name is Bud?" I ask, loosening my tight grip "I'm guessing Bud is a male based on its name?" How in the world would a person know the gender of these dinosaurs?

"Yeah. He was born only a week ago." Bud nuzzles his head into my neck. Mark traces the movement with his eyes, his gaze warming my body. "He likes you."

I lean into Bud's head. "I met him last night," I say. "He's been following me around since then. He saved me this morning from ..." I swallow, unable to say the horrible man's name.

"Chauly," Mark finishes for me.

I nod. "He summoned another bigger dinosaur—Giggy? Is Giggy his mother?"

Mark stares at me for a long time, his eyes fixated on my bruised face, his jaw twitching. "I'm sorry I wasn't there for you, Alena."

"Don't be sorry," I say.

Mark sighs, then tickles the chin of the baby dino. The gesture lulls Bud's eyes shut while Mark answers my question. "Giggy is not his mother, but she is a relative. Chewy is his mother. Where is she?" He looks around.

Chewy? Hmm. Nice name for a dinosaur who probably likes to ... chew ...

My hand rubs Bud's stub of a tail. "I tried to heal his tail last night, but for some reason I couldn't hear his elements. Something must be wrong with my power." *Or with me.*

"No, nothing's wrong with your power," Mark says. "We just can't heal dinosaurs."

"Why not?"

Mark shrugs. "We're only able to heal things with Peppate in them. Dinosaurs are the one creature on this planet that don't absorb Peppate. At all."

I remember Cody mentioning this a long time ago. She'd said that maybe they would be happier creatures if they absorbed it.

I test my sock to make sure it's still securely fastened. "They don't have Peppate. Just like the serum," I whisper.

When I cast Mark another glance he's staring at me. "Yes, just like the serum."

There's more we need to talk about. Like the serum. Like how I'm sorry for injecting it into him. But Mark just tucks his hands into his pockets and starts walking, signaling with his head that I should follow.

"Can I keep him?" I break the silence after a few minutes of walking.

Mark glances sideways at me. "Keep Bud?"

I nod. "He saved me. With Chauly here in Petrichor, I'd feel safer having him close. Can I keep him?"

Mark stops. Expressions of guilt and anger battle across his features. "Of course, Alena."

"Will his mom miss him though?" I ask, unsure why the mother just lets her baby wander around. It doesn't seem very responsible. But, then, what do I know about dinosaurs?

"No, she's probably enjoying herself in the Dino Games. We can get him back to her in a couple of days."

Good. I have a little protector now.

We walk the rest of the way in silence.

***

It doesn't take us too long to reach the Post. Mark leads us through the busy tunnels filled with guns and protectors until we finally reach the chief's door. Mark is about to knock, when angry voices rise within the room.

"... There has to be a way." Jeter's voice rumbles through the wooden door. I step back, not wanting to eavesdrop, but Jeter's shouted words whip toward me anyway. "We've found our way around the rules before for a good cause. Don't the lives of millions of people—the lives of *children* matter?"

What's Jeter talking about?

"I'm sorry, Jeter," another man says. His voice is calmer, harder to hear. "Even if we could find a way to fight off an entire nation, you know how it would deplete our power. We're barely able to keep ourselves afloat right now. We won't be strong enough to hold our ground. Our people could get hurt. Besides, we have other things to worry about now, like Chauly."

They're talking about the war.

Just like Cody, Jeter has reason to worry about the people in the GreenLands. They're his people. And currently they're getting slaughtered.

"He's watching me all the time, limiting my power," Jeter hisses quietly.

What?

"And you know why. If you aren't guilty, you have nothing to worry about," the other voice responds.

Jeter then bursts through the door, making me jump back. He doesn't even acknowledge us when he fumes past.

Could that be the cause of the tension around his eyes? His worry for his people? I can't say that I would blame him. At least he wants to do something. Change the course of destruction. And he has the power to do it. What is that like? To know you could change things for the better, but forbidden to do so.

What was he talking about at the end, though? Who's watching him? And why?

I'm staring at the empty tunnel Jeter left behind, when Mark knocks softly on the open door to announce our presence.

"Come in."

I pull my mind back to the task at hand and walk into the room after Mark.

I knew the voice I heard wasn't the chief's, but walking into the room now, I see the chief isn't even in here. Instead, it's that man I saw the other night. The one with dark hair speckled with gray. The one who smiled at me. I observe his totem now, which is wrapped in bright blue and camo-green. In his hand is a long gun. He's a protector. I glimpse at the floor. The blood and knives have been all cleaned up, thank goodness.

The man waves us in without a thought, and as if knowing we heard part of the conversation, he tries to explain.

"The war in the GreenLands is getting out of control. Thousands are dying each day. We're doing dropdowns as often as we can, but Jeter thinks we should intervene further by taking out the leaders of Verdure." He rubs his face. "But if we interfere with *this* war, we'll be sought after, hunted down by *anyone* fighting a war. We cannot take sides or we'll get hurt."

Changing the subject now, he says, "Sorry, the chief is busy looking for Chauly at the moment, and we're trying to load our posts, but Chief asked me to sit in for him for a bit. Can I help you with something?"

Then his eyes land on me, and suddenly he's suppressing a smirk.

"How was your night, Alena?" he asks.

His laughing expression reminds me that I look terrible—covered in soot, Doler, and dinosaur blood. I glare at him. Does he know that the chief purposefully sent me on a meaningless errand last night to teach me a lesson? Can he see that it had worked out exactly the way he'd hoped? Here I am with Mark, trying to mend things. I shake my head. *Does the chief always have to get what he wants?*

Mark's eyes glance sideways at me, but he's not laughing like the man. Instead his eyes are warm, running over my body as if he's seeing me for the first time. And regardless of the soot and blood on me, he doesn't seem repulsed. With one step, he's by my side, gently grazing my elbow with his fingers. I glance at his hand. It's such a subtle touch but sends shivers all over the place. It's the way he used to touch me. I gulp past the emotion in my throat.

"Why are you here?" The man clears his voice to recapture our attention, eyeing the dinosaur in my arms while polishing a gun.

Mark's fingers drop away from my skin. "We had an idea, Patrick, about the memories sent by Jax. We think the humming noise in the background might be Gabbro singing a song. A song that's a clue to something. Maybe Danny's location. We were wondering if you'd let us borrow the Magbaby."

The man's name is Patrick, then? Patrick listens quietly, but his expression doesn't change after hearing the idea.

"I think you're right. I'll be honest, though—you weren't the first to think of this. Kapri came by last night after hearing the chief was back. She was asking about Danny. He showed her the memory Jax sent. She's been working on figuring out the clues since then. I'm sure she would love your help. She's here in the Post, down the hall, third door on the right. Why don't you go see how she's doing."

I'm instantly uncomfortable. *Who's Kapri? Why did* she *ask for Danny's memories?*

"We'll head there now," Mark says before lightly placing his hand on the small of my back to guide me out. Just before we exit, though, the man stops us.

"Oh, and, Alena, if you could—the hospital is short-staffed. Do you think you could do a shift tomorrow?"

I almost shake my head, tell Patrick I can't hear the elements, when I remember they're there, ringing ever so slightly.

So I nod instead. He understands my answer and winks a dark-eyebrowed wink. He knows I have power now. Patrick knows a lot about me. I don't know if I like that or not.

"Be careful out there."

This comment has Mark pausing again. "You guys are looking for him, right?" he asks over his shoulder. *Looking for Chauly.*

"Yes," Patrick responds confidently. "If he's still in Petrichor, we'll find him."

Mark wants to be a part of the search. I can tell by the way he's gripping my arm. But I'm grateful he isn't. Chauly doesn't just want me; he wants Mark too. At least I think he does. But if Mark is with me, I know he's safe. We're safe.

After leaving the chief's office, Mark guides me down the hall from behind. He's dropped his arm again since it's too crowded to walk side by side. But he stays close. Finally, when the tunnels are not so loud, I ask a question over my shoulder. "Who's Kapri?"

He doesn't hesitate. "Kapri is the girl Danny danced with at the Dino Dance."

I observe the dirt wall of the tunnel. I recall her. Danny's face had beamed at her request, and her full blonde head of hair had bounced with curls as he held her in his arms. They had both seemed infatuated with each other, but I'm confused. It was a couple of dances. *Did she like that dance so much that she's suddenly trying to find Danny?*

Mark seems to sense the questions I'm too hesitant to ask.

"Kapri and Danny used to like each other a long time ago," he says over my shoulder. "At least that's what I hear. They did initiation together and grew really close. But then Danny disappeared and came back different. Kapri tried to remain friends with Danny, but it just didn't work out."

"Why not?"

I feel Mark shrug against my back. Man, he's close. "Kapri thinks Danny's memory of her was erased, along with what happened the day he disappeared. But Gabbro says Danny remembers her. Personally, I think he was just too insecure to be around Kapri anymore. He didn't think he was good enough for her."

Danny? The person who taught me what I needed to do to be happy again so insecure he would push away such a beautiful girl? Beautiful girl. Why does the thought of a beautiful girl liking Danny make me feel ... jealous?

"That is ..." Mark leans forward, his chest brushing against my back again. "Until you came along. You gave him his confidence back. With someone like you, needing him and being so kind, he regained his courage. Enough to at least accept a dance from her."

We've stopped at a door now, his compliment hanging in the air, his touch making me dizzy. I slowly turn to look at his face.

"Thank you, Mark." That's all I can think to say.

"You ready?" He nods to the door, his hand on the knob, ready to open it.

No. I'm not ready. In fact, I'm really tired and would love to shower then go to sleep right now—if I could actually sleep. The last thing I want to do is hang out with a beautiful *girl.*

"Yes," I say instead.

Placing his hand on my back, he pushes me in.

I squint, allowing my eyes to adjust to the brighter room. Like the chief's office, dust-particled light streams into the room through wooden-framed windows in the ceiling. The room itself is crammed with tables and shelves stuffed with papers. Hundreds of papers.

It doesn't take me long to find Kapri. She's sitting at a table in the middle of the room, her blonde hair highlighted by the sunlight. When her eyes raise to see who's entered, she stands, much too quickly, causing her chair to fall backward. Her cheeks blush pink before she nervously turns to pick up her fallen chair. When it's standing again, she fiddles with one of her long curly strands of hair pulled back in a ponytail.

She looks uncomfortable.

"Hi, Kapri," Mark says, stepping forward. "We're sorry to interrupt you, but Patrick said you could use some help figuring out Danny's clues." Kapri's hazel eyes flicker to Mark briefly, but then they tensely move back to me and Bud.

I'm making her nervous. But why? Does she know how close Danny and I were? Could she be uncomfortable around me for the same reason I'm uncomfortable around her? The idea makes me feel smug, that maybe she knows Danny belongs to me.

But that's wrong.

Sighing deeply, I step forward, needing to put her at ease.

"Hey, Kapri," I say. "I'm sorry we didn't come sooner. It took us a long time to figure out that Danny might be trying to send a message. Longer than it took you."

Kapri relaxes a bit at my words.

"You've been busy," Mark interjects, wandering over to a table full of papers. "What is all this?"

"Songs." Kapri says the word so softly I almost miss it. She points to the tables along the left wall. "These are all the songs that could come from the first Magbaby that was sent." Then she points to the tables along the right wall. "Those are all the songs that could have come from the second Magbaby sent." Now pointing at the back wall, she says, "And those are all the songs that could have come from combining both messages together."

I walk to the back of the room, my eyes wide in disbelief. "Wow, you did this all by yourself? In one night?"

Kapri nods. "This isn't even all of them. My Magbaby says there are more potential songs. I just got tired."

I shake my head. "So, you think Gabbro was humming *different* songs in each memory?"

Kapri nods, plopping down in her chair. "Possibly. But both memories give us so many songs, I'm afraid I'm no closer to knowing where Danny is."

"So, we're supposed to go through each of these songs and figure out what kind of message he's trying to send us?" Mark asks nobody in particular.

It's an impossible time-consuming task. Time. That's something we don't have.

I put Bud down and sit in a chair next to Kapri. "Tell me what to do."

Chapter 10

I rub my head. Kapri instructed me to look through the songs that could combine both messages to see if there's anything that stands out to me. I'm grateful for the distraction from everything, including Mark. I'm also grateful for the chance to finally be working on getting Danny back. But I'm tired. I didn't get much sleep last night, and my body aches from running so much, climbing so many stairs, getting punched in the face. I close my eyes. My ears are also ringing from listening to Breccia play the melodies of the songs written on the papers. I never knew so many songs existed in our world.

A bug drops onto the paper in front of me, and I try not to jump. Wiping it off the table, I shiver. The disgusting little beetles are everywhere here: on the walls, on the ceiling, on me. Ugh. Thankfully, Bud is easily distracted by the little insects and has created his own game of sniffing the bugs into his nose and coughing them out his mouth. Disgusting.

I draw my eyes back to the paper. The songs have been nothing spectacular. Some are about love, and some are about ... not love. The only one that's stood out to me is a commonly known song titled "Memories." But what could it possibly have to do with finding Danny? It sits alone at the side of my large pile. As the hundredth song starts, I sigh, trying to refocus on the words that could give me a clue.

My body freezes when the song reaches the chorus. I pick up the paper and read the words

The Meadow; that's the name of the song.

Where the snow dusts the flowers,

Lies a meadow all ours,

Meet me there before sunset

I'll give you a night you'll never forget.

It's a love song, but I can't deny the irony of the meadow. Grabbing the piece of paper, I stand and practically stumble to Kapri, drawing Mark's attention.

"Can you play me the memories?" I ask urgently.

Kapri, with heavy eyelids, comes to life. "Sure." Her Magbaby has memorized the notes of the hums and sings them out loud. When it stops, I look at Breccia.

"Play me the part of the song that correlates with those exact notes."

Breccia responds quickly, pulsing her beats out loud. I suck in a breath when the notes in the memory play right over the first two lines of the song that speak of the meadow.

Where the snow dusts the flowers,

Lies a meadow all ours.

"What are you thinking, Alena?" Mark asks.

I hand the piece of paper to him. "This song is about a meadow where snow dusts the flowers. It isn't exact, but it sounds a lot like Danny's favorite meadow next to the snowy border."

Mark frowns. "I agree, but why would he be singing a song to lead us to the meadow? He can't be hiding there."

My spirits fall as quickly as they had risen. Mark's right. It doesn't make sense. Perhaps it's not the right song.

"But maybe it's only part of a clue. I found this song." Mark holds out a piece of yellowed paper. I take it and read the words. It mentions an empress named Wintriness.

"Wintriness is a lake out by Danny's meadow," Mark says. I nod, remembering the frozen water I walked past. "It's odd that two different songs would speak of generally the same place. Maybe I'll go check things out."

I nod. "I'll come with you."

Mark smiles thinly and touches my arm. "Alena, I think you should get some rest. I'm going to head back to GreenGrotto myself after. I'm not worth much being so tired."

"Okay." My shoulders slump. He's right.

"You should get some rest too," Mark tells Kapri. "How about we meet back here tomorrow afternoon, after I work with the dinos and after Alena works her shift at the hospital?"

Kapri agrees, but when Mark, Bud, and I leave the room, the girl doesn't budge. I wonder if she'll actually do what she said, or if she'll just stay here all night. I admire her tenacity. Maybe when I'm not so tired, I'll have the same determination.

***

I let my hair air-dry. I still haven't mastered heat yet and haven't had time to practice.

I wonder if Mark found anything.

My eye tingles after finally being healed by me, and the muscles in my body attempt to relax. It feels good to be back in my clean pajamas, in my room. The past few days have been a blur.

Bud is curled up on a blanket over by the body mirror, sound asleep. For being a brand-new baby, he sure doesn't seem to need a lot of nurturing from his mother. He's perfectly content with me, and I'm grateful he's here.

I nervously glance at Cody's bed that curves with the circular branch shape of the room. It's been empty for the past three weeks since Silver-Den.

I haven't had any time to go see Cody since we've been back. Or, rather, I've been so consumed with my own grief that I haven't felt up for it. I wonder how she's doing.

I thought when I saved her from the fire, she'd be happy to see me. But she was exactly the opposite. She fought me, trying to run back into the fire. I haven't taken the time to figure out why.

I need to go see her soon.

But her bed isn't empty now. As soon as I got back from the Post, a girl holding a long gun came knocking on my door. She introduced herself as my protector, otherwise known as Harper. She has dark-red hair slicked back into a bun at the base of her neck, olive skin, and her face is squarish and strong. She said she has to keep watch overnight. There are also two more men stationed outside my door and on the balcony.

I guess that's a good thing. I'm content having my baby dinosaur keep watch over me, but any additional protection is good. Except that Harper, with her staring eyes, makes me a little uncomfortable.

Ignoring her stare, I enter Cody's closet, kneel, and start searching through her small boxes of equipment capsules. So much has happened since I went to the prison, but now that I have a second, I need to find a map.

It's hard going through Cody's stuff without asking her permission. Hopefully she'll forgive me.

It takes me forever to search the boxes, and I'm almost ready to conclude that she doesn't have a map, when I find it. A tiny symbol of a paper engraved on the silver capsule. When I push the releasing button, sure enough it expands into a map of the world. It isn't as large as the one at the prison, and the countries aren't as easy for me to identify, but I am able to see the three barren deserts. Still hiding in the closet, I eye Harper, making sure she isn't being too nosy, then I pull Breccia out and set her on my shoulder. I can't leave Petrichor, not only for my own safety but because I have absolutely no navigation skills. Plus, I can't fly. But Breccia can.

"The chief is searching for Danny in Dakdete," I whisper. "Could you help search in one of the other deserts? Maybe Namib?"

Harper's voice breaks through the quiet. "I heard Chief sent one team to Namib today. You might want to start with the Kalahaki Desert."

Breccia and I look at each other. She heard me?

I clear my throat. "You think it's okay for me to send Breccia out there?" I ask my protector.

Harper shrugs. "Maybe don't send her out there at night because of the whole Morgan issue before. But I don't see anything wrong with her leaving in the morning. Magbabies shouldn't stay away from you too long, though, just in case something happens to you."

Having Harper's permission now has me anxiously looking at the map.

"Where do you want to go first, Breccia?" The Kalahaki Desert is huge. "Do you want to start on the west side and work your way east—?"

Harper interrupts again. "Start at the water sources. I think there are a few there, unlike in Dakdete. If Jax is there, he'll need water."

Of course.

I stare at the map. There are three oases that I can see.

"Start here." I point to the one on the far west side. "Leave in the morning, look around, and then come back to me tomorrow night?"

Breccia nods, her small mouth spreading into a smile.

A knock breaks through the air, and I jump. Harper quickly rises to her feet, cocks her gun, and goes to the door. I hold my breath, peeking out of the closet.

"Chief," Harper says in a low voice.

I exhale.

The old man walks into the room wearing a heavy overcoat.

"Alena, how are you?"

I stand, leaving the map and closet behind. "I'm good."

Chief sits on my bed and pats the space next to him. I sit while Harper stands watch at the door.

"I'm sorry about what Chauly did to you today. We're looking everywhere for him."

"Thank you."

Chief inhales deeply. "Alena, I think I should take your black power. Lock it away with Mark's and keep it safe so Chauly can't get it."

I stare at the chief, his weary face only lit by the two lamps on the nightstands. *He wants to take my black power?* I slowly take my satchel and slide my hand inside. I wrap my fingers around the black sphere, pull it out, and roll it in my fingers.

Handing it over to the chief feels like I'm handing over my big toe. It's a part of me. But the chief is right. For everyone's safety, I need to give it to him. I plop it into his palm.

"I think that's a good idea," I say.

Chief takes the sphere, but his fallen expression doesn't lighten. "Alena, Chauly didn't just want the black power. If he did, he would have left you alone once he had it. He wanted you too. Which makes sense. If Case created a power without Peppate to heal the Mixed Bloods, Jax would only want *you* to use that power because of your Peppate-free totem. Your totem is the only one that won't contaminate the power. I'm worried about you, Alena." He rubs the deep creases in his forehead. "I'm trying to protect you, keep Chauly from getting to you. But, I'll admit, I don't exactly know what we're dealing with here. There's something going on—we should have found Chauly by now." His hand falls into his lap. "Please be careful."

The fact that the chief is worried is not a good sign. "I will," I say.

With my black sphere of power in his hand, he stands to leave. But there's something I need to ask him.

"Chief?"

He pauses.

"Can I help you find Jax?" I ask.

Chief's bushy gray eyebrows rise.

"Your brother at the prison told me that you're looking in the deserts for him," I continue. "Can I send Breccia to look too? Maybe in the Kalahaki Desert?"

His face brightens. "Alena, I'll take all the help I can get. Just promise me *you* won't leave Petrichor."

He's letting me help. I smile. "I won't."

Chief wishes me good night, and I sit on my bed staring at the map still lying in the closet. We will find Danny. We have to find him.

I lie down, my eyes drifting from Harper over to my satchel, where I was keeping my black power. I've hated that power with all my heart, hated what it represents. Death and sorrow. But more than that, I hate it because it came from me. It represents death and sorrow … and me.

I lie on my back to stare at the ceiling.

I removed the black power from my totem the night I came home from SilverDen. I've been so repulsed by it that I've almost tossed it out many times. It deserves to be destroyed. But I can't destroy it for possibly the same reason I don't want to keep it. The cost is too high. Maybe it'll come in handy for something.

I angrily blow out my lamp.

In the dark I still stare at the ceiling. There's something that intrigues me about the power, though. It's different, without Peppate.

Wait.

I sit up.

The power and the serum of the Dilo dinosaur still stuck in Mark's neck have something in common. They both lack Peppate.

My body stiffens. *Could the black power speak to the dino serum? Could it possibly control it?*

Chapter 11

I listen carefully to the hum of broken elements pouring from the injured body in front of me. I've never been so happy to hear the annoying buzzing sounds. I reach out to heal, using the power Jeter gave me this morning. Even though I can't hear the elements perfectly, the sounds are clear enough for me to perform my job. It feels good to heal again.

Breccia left early this morning to go search Kalahaki and should be back later tonight. I'm eager to hear what she finds.

Chauly still hasn't been found, but there have been traces of him seen throughout Petrichor. The red gingham shirt he was wearing when he attacked me, along with his holey jeans, were found at the base of GreenGrotto. He obviously doesn't care to hide the fact that he's still here. I just hope he has other clothes on.

There's an eeriness that's settled on all of Petrichor. How in the world have they not been able to find him? It reminds me of Jax when he disappeared from the chief's office. Is Chauly able to physically disappear? Is that something Pepps can do?

One thing that has eased my worries somewhat is the fact that the Dino Games are still going. The trainers have allowed their dinosaurs to sniff Chauly's clothing, and now they're on extra alert for the man. With the dinosaurs looking for him, Chauly is going to have a much harder time getting around.

I glance at Bud wandering around the room. Thankfully, the medics agreed to let him stay here with me in the clinic. I promised them he would behave, and so far he's been good.

The medics have moved to the hospital now, all Dino-Game-injured patients being sent to them in toboggans. Lying on the bed in front of me is a man with several gruesome gashes across his face, torso, and leg. I can only assume they came from dinosaur claws. Large dinosaur claws.

In this moment, I'm feeling very lucky that Giggy didn't attack me.

I address the more serious wounds on the torso first, trying to stop the blood loss. The man's lungs are punctured, but fortunately those are the only organs needing repair. I pay close attention to the air pockets in the lungs, making sure to get them right.

Blinking my tired eyes, I force myself to focus. I stayed up way too late last night contemplating whether or not I should try to use the black power to extract the serum from Mark. Ultimately, I decided that I shouldn't.

But now I'm extra tired. Maybe I should make this my last case of the day. I need to get to Kapri anyway.

Once I close the muscles and skin on the man's torso, I move to the face. One of the gashes cuts across his eye, something I've never dealt with before.

I'm taking my time healing the retina, when I hear a commotion at the door of the clinic.

My blood instantly runs cold when I see her.

It's Cody.

Her body is thin and frail, and she's leaning heavily on the door frame. But her blue eyes are on fire. Glaring right at me.

"You!" she says through gritted teeth. "You were supposed to leave me there! He promised I wouldn't survive that fire." She pushes away from the door and steps in my direction.

I resist the temptation to bite my lip. To show her how much her words unnerve me.

Why would she want to die in that fire?

I had guessed as much by the way she reacted when I tried to save her, but to hear her admit it so plainly terrifies me. I suddenly see myself in Cody. I see what I've been so close to becoming. Completely broken.

Cody lunges for me, her hands ready to wrap around my throat and strangle me to death. I should move away, but I can't. Maybe I deserve this.

Just before she can reach me, though, Rusty bursts into the room. He immediately wraps his strong arms around her torso, pinning hers to her sides, and lifting her effortlessly into the air. Cody thrashes wildly, kicking her legs, trying to squirm out of his grasp, her long blonde hair tangled around her face. But her efforts are futile. She's too weak.

So she screams instead.

"You should have left me there!"

Rusty drags her from the room, but I continue to hear her screams echoing down the hall.

A heaviness settles on the clinic. I can feel everyone's eyes on me. Again.

"Hey." I quickly gesture to Leinani, thankful she's here. "Can you finish helping this man? I need to go." I point to the patient I was attending to. She willingly takes over.

Then I follow the sounds of Cody's wails.

They lead me down several halls, to a secluded part of the hospital I've never been to before. The walls here are smoother, whiter. I catch up, just in time to see a woman meet Rusty outside a door, her eyebrows drawn down in concern. When she opens the door, Rusty takes Cody inside, then quickly retreats ... alone. Once he's out, the woman shuts the door and locks it from the outside, locking Cody in.

Fortunately, there's a window in the wall next to me that allows me to see Cody.

My heart lurches at the sight of her throwing her body up against the walls. I'm grateful the rock is smoother here. If it was the same rock making up the chief's office, her skin would get torn to pieces.

The woman places her hand on the door window.

Who is she? What is Cody to her?

Her hair, light brown with beautiful red and blonde highlights, stretches in waves down to her waist. But that isn't what captivates me the most. Her totem. It's the most beautiful totem I've ever seen, with several colors wrapped around it: a little red, a little yellow, and a lot of white. But on top of the white ribbon are bright dangling diamonds and pearls tracing the totem for several inches. *Why does she have diamonds on her totem?*

"I think we need to give Cody some time alone in the room for now." The woman says to Rusty, dropping her hand to her side. I'm instantly comforted by her soft voice that moves through the air like a warm autumn breeze. *Who is she?*

"I'm going to go see a couple other patients," she says. "But I'll be back later. Would you mind watching her for a little bit, Rusty?"

Rusty shakes his head. "Of course not."

Then she looks at me. I'm stunned by her green eyes and her smile offered so freely. I attempt to lift my own lips in response but end up just nodding instead. A smile doesn't feel right, right now.

She accepts my gesture before disappearing into another room.

Standing in the middle of the hall, I'm suddenly unsure why I followed Rusty. I shift on my feet hesitantly. Cody obviously doesn't want me here. But maybe there's someone else I came for.

Rusty steps up to my side, staring at Cody through the window. I briefly examine his face towering above me. I've forgotten how muscularly huge he is. But as strong as his body is, something tells me he's breaking inside.

He looks tired and worried, a foreign expression on the boy that was always so mischievous. His blond hair is disheveled, sticking out in odd places, and his unshaven face is shadowed. I haven't seen him since the trip to SilverDen. I've been avoiding both him and Cody for my own reasons, but seeing them now struggling so much, a newfound guilt hits me. I should have come sooner.

"How's she doing?" I whisper, turning my attention back to Cody.

Out of the corner of my eye I see Rusty rub his tired face with his hand.

"I don't know how to help her," he says, his voice hoarse. "She keeps telling me I should have let her die. Sepharine, that woman, is a doctor of the mind and has been working with her, but Cody refuses to talk about what happened." Rusty shakes his head. "Sepharine says the mind can't be controlled with power. That Cody has to make the decision to want help, and until that happens, she won't improve. I can't imagine trying to fix something without being able to use power, especially something like this. It seems so ... impossible."

I watch Cody quietly. She's still thrashing her body, screaming at the top of her lungs with tears running down her cheeks. It's horrible, watching her internal battle rage so wildly that it can't be contained within her tiny body, expressed with such terrible movements and sounds.

To anyone else it might seem scary and monstrous. But watching Cody, I feel a connection to her. In a tiny way, I know what that battle is like. Maybe not to the extent she's experiencing, but I do know.

I reach my hand out and touch the window. Cody flings her body toward me, banging on the glass. I draw back.

"Is she in here all the time?" I ask, looking at the cold, bare room. The walls are all the same. White, smooth. The only difference is the ceiling. It's made of glass that offers a beautiful view of the sky and lets in copious amounts of light.

"It's the only place we can contain her. Until she settles down and stops trying to hurt herself, she has to stay in there."

I pull my attention from Cody and peer at Rusty's exhausted expression.

"How long has it been since you've slept? You look awful," I say.

The tiniest of smirks tugs at the corner of his lips. "I figure I only look as bad as you do."

I almost catch his contagious smile, realizing in this moment how much I've missed him.

"I'm sorry," I say.

His mouth turns down in confusion.

"I'm sorry for dragging you into Gabbro's plan. And I'm sorry that Cody didn't come back the same."

Rusty's look of confusion melts into a look of grief, and he turns back to watch the girl he loves. She's now folded herself into a lump on the floor.

"I'll help watch her if you want, so you can get some rest," I offer.

"Thanks, Alena. Maybe I'll take you up on that soon, but right now I think I'm a little too worried to let her out of my sight. Just going to get some food this morning got me into trouble. Besides, her mom comes to help out too."

Cody's mother. Pam.

My body tenses at the mention of her, guilt immediately pounding me, my head, my heart. I haven't had a chance to talk to her since Tom died, and I don't know that I ever will. It was because of me her Cody was taken, and because of me her Tom is now gone. The dark shadow that had seemed a little thinner the last few days darkens again now. I clench my fists, trying to fight off the tumble of memories threatening again.

I swallow and step back, feeling the sudden need to get away from here. The last thing I want is to run into Pam.

"Okay," I say, then turn to leave. I only make it a couple of steps when I freeze. There she is right in front of me.

Pam.

Her hair is no longer clean cut, and her eyes mirror mine. Swollen, tired, beaten.

I'm so caught off guard that I don't know what to do or say. So I just run past her, down the hall and out of the hospital.

She doesn't try to stop me. I don't know if that makes me feel better or worse.

Chapter 12

My eyes are blurry again, and my chest hurts profoundly. Actually, it's more like my heart hurts profoundly.

I don't want to go back to the clinic, so my feet take me in the direction of the Post. But if I keep running at this pace, I'll get there too quickly, and I'm not ready to face Kapri or Mark right now. So I slow down. Then I kick myself silently, my familiar anger burning.

Why did I have to follow Rusty down that damn hall? Why didn't I just stay in the clinic? If I had stayed away from Cody, I wouldn't have run into Pam. I squeeze my eyes shut, trying to ignore the sting of tears, and stop walking.

Pam. *Why did I run away? Why didn't I just tell her I'm sorry*?

I almost want to go back. Tell her those two words. Not because I want her to forgive me. But because it's the right thing to do. I open my eyes.

Tell her *I'm sorry*? Those words just don't cut it. They don't adequately relay the sorrow I feel from what I've done, and I definitely don't see it making *her* feel any better. It'll probably feel more like a slap in the face.

My feet pace, my guilt still tugging me back. I hate to admit it, but I know deep down inside, regardless of how inadequate those words feel, I need to tell her sometime. Or at least commit myself to doing it soon.

I stand there for a long time, hoping to control the pressure in my body. All I end up doing is crying more. When my head hurts and my neck aches from all the tears, I wipe them away, tired.

I conclude that now is not the time to talk to Pam. I want to formulate an apology in my mind. One that can, in a tiny way, express how remorseful I am for what I did.

For that I need time.

Only now do I realize that Bud is still with me, chin lifted high to get a good look at my face.

I release a heavy sigh and rub his head. It's probably time to go find Kapri. It doesn't matter how long I stand here; I'll never be ready. I blink back my tears and step into the tunnels, my baby dinosaur following close behind.

The Post is more crowded than usual, and it takes me way too long to realize why. The communicators are down here. I guess they finally agreed on where they would be staying. They're angrily carrying bedrolls here and there. Some are transferring metal bed frames from a storage room to their personal assigned room down one very long hallway. Others are complaining about not having electricity for their electronics.

I walk through them, fatigue inching its way back into my body. Unfortunately, my mind is shutting down. I don't know how much I'll be able to help today. Not now.

Finally, I reach the door Mark guided me to yesterday. I knock quietly before entering.

To my disappointment, Kapri is the only one in the room. Mark isn't here.

I thought *I* was running late. Mark must have gotten caught up with something. Confused, I walk toward Kapri past all the piles of paper.

"Is Mark not here yet?" I ask.

Kapri briefly looks up from the paper she's holding before looking back down. "No, I haven't seen him today."

I find my way to the same chair I was sitting in yesterday and begin reading through the papers again. Even though I see the paper, my brain doesn't process what's on it. I'm too distracted by the sight of Pam, too tired from my poor sleep habits, and this makes me angry.

Why am I so worthless?

And where is Mark?

I try to push forward, but after an hour of pointless effort, I slam the papers down on the table and stand, sending my chair to the floor.

"I'm going to find Mark." I storm past Kapri.

I don't allow her to respond before stomping from the room.

I head to MossyHollow first. *Maybe he's with the dino trainers. Or did he head back down to the Dino Games?* I don't know what happened to his dinosaurs, but after yesterday I think it would be stupid for him to go back.

***

Mark isn't at MossyHollow and hasn't been there all day. Something feels off. It could take me forever to look everywhere for him, but I go where I think he might be, hoping that I'm wrong.

I run all the way to GreenGrotto, passing several protectors with guns. Did he ever make it out to the frozen lake Wintriness? Did he find anything?

I burst through the front door of GreenGrotto, and head up the boys' staircase. Once I find his door, I knock. When I get no response, I burst in.

My lungs collapse.

Mark is on his bed, red and sweating profusely. I don't need to touch him to know his body is screaming with infection again, but I hurry to his side and do it anyway. The heat in his skin makes my throat go dry.

I pull a chair in the room next to his bed and immediately start drawing out the infection, paying close attention to the swollen bulge behind his neck. It isn't long before his body begins to cool, but this doesn't ease my panic. It took less than twenty-four hours after Jeter healed him yesterday for his debilitating fever to return. He can't keep going like this. *That stupid serum is going to kill him!*

I pace his room for only a couple of moments, a plan formulating in my mind. I need the black power. But the chief has it now. I reach across to my Magbaby band for Breccia, thinking that she can go get it faster than I can, but of course she's not there. She's searching for Jax.

I need to go find Chief.

With an overwhelming sigh, I leave GreenGrotto, head back to the busy Post, and go to the chief's office. He's in there, thank goodness, standing next to his bookcase, an old leather journal open in his hands.

"Chief?" I knock on his open door.

Unfortunately, he's not alone. Cordelia is in here, along with Patrick, the protector.

Chief looks up. "Yes, Alena?"

I glance at Cordelia. "Can I talk to you alone?"

Cordelia is instantly offended by this request, but I stare at the chief. This is important.

"Yes, Cordelia, Patrick, will you give us a minute?"

Once the door shuts behind them, I step closer. "Can I have the black power back?"

Chief's bushy eyebrows furrow. "Why?"

I take in a deep breath. "Mark is sick again because of the dinosaur serum I injected into him. Jeter can't remove the serum because his power can only speak to things made of Peppate."

Chief closes his book and puts it on his desk. "So you think the black power could speak to the dinosaur serum. You think you could get it out?"

"It's the only solution I have."

The chief rubs his beard. Then walks to the wall to my left. It looks like a regular stone wall, but when he reaches his hand out, the stone melts into metal that then forms into the shape of a small vault door. He opens it and waves me over. When I get close, I see two black spheres of power. Mine and Mark's. But then my eyes rise to something else.

The door opens into a hidden treasury. And in the treasury is power. Thousands and thousands of yellow spheres of power, ready to be pushed into the heart of a totem.

"I've been collecting power the past few months," Chief says, noticing where my attention has gone. He picks up one of the spheres. "I need to be ready for anything."

Eli, Chief's brother, had told me about this. If they're planning to hurt Jax to stop him, they're going to need a lot of power.

"Here." He places one sphere of black power into my hand and shuts the vault. "Please be careful. We still don't know much about this power. I would come with you, but I'm busy. Bring it back, will you? I'd like to examine it closer."

"Yes, thank you."

He shuts the vault, and I run.

***

I shift nervously on my feet back in Mark's room. Using this power goes against everything I decided the night I obtained it. I vowed to hate it forever.

But could it now have a purpose for me? Could it save Mark? The serum in his neck isn't responding to Pepp power. Could it respond to this? Would I be willing to use something so dark to help someone I care so deeply about?

I sigh. Is there a right answer? Chief seems to think this should be okay.

I close my fist around the vial in my hand.

It isn't until I glance at Mark, finding his skin starting to heat up again, that I realize I have to try.

I take the vial of yellow power Scance gave me this morning out of my chest, place it on the nightstand next to Mark, and then, with one last sigh, I insert the black power into the heart of my totem.

I sit in a chair next to Mark and wait. I didn't think this far, but now that I'm here I'm not sure I even know *how* to use this power.

The air is quiet. Unlike with the Peppate power, I don't hear all the elements around me. I hear nothing. My spirits fall slightly, but then I scoot my chair closer to Mark. This power lacks Peppate and so does the serum. Maybe it doesn't hear all the elements around me like the other power, just elements that lack Peppate. Leaning my head closer to Mark's neck, I try to listen for the elements of the serum. I still hear nothing. Nothing like the buzzing and high-pitched notes I'm used to.

But then I notice something. Not necessarily a sound but a dullness. Like something weighs in the air, a heavy presence. I back away and it disappears, only to return when I get closer to it.

Could that be it?

If it is, now what? How do I control it with my totem?

With regular Pepp power, I use the language of the totem to speak to all elements in order to control them. But I don't know if that same language will communicate with the Peppate-free serum.

I don't know what to say, but I simply try within my mind to relay my message.

Extract the element from Mark's neck. I don't use the totem language, like with the other power, but instead use my own words. *Move out of the muscle and through the skin.* My totem should know me well enough to know what I'm asking, right?

Staring intently at Mark's neck, while intermittently glancing up at his face to see if his expression changes, I wait. I repeat my request, then wait some more. I don't know how long I sit there bent over Mark, but my heart skips a beat when the dull sound of serum eases and a collection of white substance forms on his skin, rubbing onto the pillow around his head. I touch it. It's the serum.

With new hope I continue whispering. I'm so focused on the reddened skin now turning pink that I jump when a hand brushes softly against my arm.

I turn my attention to Mark's face that's only inches from mine.

"You're awake. How do you feel?"

Mark thinks before responding. "I feel good." Then confusion flickers across his face. "Better than I have in a long time, Alena. What did you do?"

My relief fades, and I sit up in the chair. I don't want to tell him the truth. I'm ashamed, but I promised myself I would never keep a secret from him again.

"I'm sorry, Mark. I didn't know what else to do."

He raises his arm to my face, gently brushing my cheek, encouraging me to tell him.

I lower the neck of my shirt, revealing the black heart. I remove the black sphere from my totem and hold it in my hand.

Mark's lips drop into a frown, but it doesn't last long.

"It worked?" he whispers.

I shrug, still not sure if I can be happy about my decision.

Before Mark can reply, a shout behind me makes me jump clear out of my seat.

"What have you done?"

I fight to find my balance. It's Jeter, hovering in the doorway, his face red against his blond hair, his hands fisted. Staring at the black power in my hand, he steps forward and rips it from my grasp.

I'm shocked by his reaction and can't think of anything else to do but step back.

"It worked, Jeter. She was able to remove the serum." Mark sits up.

Jeter ignores him. "We don't even know what this is," he growls. "Let alone what it's capable of." Jeter shakes his fist in my face. "Using it on Mark could have severe repercussions. Dammit, Alena! You don't think things through!"

I stare at the floor. His words cut through me like a knife, slicing at my raw wounds. There's no warning for the tears that start to fall.

"Give it back." I hold out my hand while trying to hide my face.

When Jeter refuses, Mark stands, rips the power out of his hand, and places it in mine.

Not wanting Mark or Jeter to see me like this, so weak, I run from the room.

Mark calls out my name, but only the stars know why. It was stupid. Stupid to think I could solve another impossible problem. For all I know I made things worse.

I run down the halls and the stairs and find myself back in my room on my bed. I need to help Kapri with Danny. I need to help Rusty with Cody. I need to be doing a lot of things, but I'm too broken. I wish I could just disappear.

Chapter 13

I must have cried myself to sleep. Now, slowly waking, I realize it's the middle of the night. I toss, trying to remove myself from consciousness again. But I can't. Not when I remember what happened with Jeter.

A dull ache seizes the back of my head. I rub it with my hand before listening for the sounds of the irritated nerves. But then I realize I don't have Pepp power. I left it in Mark's room. The only power I have is the black power still tightly gripped in my hand.

I know I won't be able to sleep, not with this headache or the images of Jeter's fuming face in my head.

Thankfully, Bud somehow made his own way to the room last night. He's snuggled up on his bed. He's a good boy.

I glance at my nightstand. Breccia still isn't back though. I hope she's okay.

Harper stares at me from Cody's bed with that blank look, reminding me that I'm being watched, in a not-so-comforting way. I need to get out of here. Slowly, I put the power in my satchel, put my satchel around my waist, pull on my socks and shoes and open my door. I stare down the empty halls, then with a sigh I step out. Harper tries to follow, but I grit my teeth. I don't want to run into Chauly again, but the thought of Harper following me right now makes me mad.

I go back into the room and wake up Bud. He jumps to life quickly, willing to walk to the moon and back with me. With him awake, I send a silent, stern message with my eyes telling Harper that she needs to stay here. She doesn't obey, though. I show her my knife hidden in my sleeve. Still not enough. Grunting in frustration I finally give in.

"Just give me some space," I demand.

She does ... a little.

Bud follows me down the stairs and into the cold, brisk air that has me rubbing my arms for warmth.

The rocks in the path are painted by the light of the moon. I count ten, fifteen protectors along the way, standing alert, searching the area. Harper's a good twenty feet behind me.

I stop. *How the heck have these protectors not been able to find Chauly?* With this many men, I would think they'd have been able to search every inch of this place by now.

I pass another protector. Chauly has power. Well, I saw the totem on his arm, which means he *potentially* has power. But he didn't use any on me. Why not? He probably didn't feel the need to, knowing how weak I am. One punch to my face disabled me completely.

Weak.

I rub my temples, trying not to replay Jeter's words in my mind from last night. *I never think things through.* Ugh.

I'm weak *and* stupid.

I don't know where I'm going as the events from last night swarm my mind. It isn't until I reach the secluded mental part of the hospital that I wonder if it was such a good idea to be out and about.

The halls are mostly empty with only a few medics on night shifts. I expect to find Rusty outside Cody's room after hearing him earlier, refusing to leave her side, but I sigh in relief when I find the area vacant, lit only by flickering torches on the walls.

Harper is still with me but waits at the end of the hall, giving me some privacy.

Slowly, I walk to Cody's window. It's much darker inside this time, absent of the bright sunlight above, but I'm still able to find my friend. She's lying on the floor, not even a blanket to warm her.

"Cody." I don't know why I whisper her name. I don't want to wake her ... but at the same time I ache to talk. Fortunately, she doesn't budge.

I slide to the floor, grateful the window drops low enough so I can still see her.

Bud curls up next to me.

Why am I here?

I almost cough out a laugh.

This place makes me feel comfortable.

I wonder what it would take to get myself one of *these* rooms. Maybe I could take the one across the hall from Cody. It seems empty and cozy enough.

I sigh again and lean my head against the window. No, that's not why I'm here.

"I'm sorry, Cody," I say to myself, fidgeting with the sleeve of my shirt. The only response is the crackle of the torches.

"I never should have come to Petrichor. Can you imagine how much better things would be if I hadn't?"

My nose starts to run. I wipe it with my sleeve.

"I didn't mean for your friend to get hurt, Cody. For you to get hurt. I didn't mean to make you sad by taking you out of that fire. I was just trying to do what I thought was right." I drop my hand back into my lap, remembering what Jeter told me earlier. "But no matter how hard I try to do what's right, I end up making things worse, making people hate me." My eyes swell. "I don't *want* people to hate me."

A few tears drip into my lap. "Do you ever feel like you're caught in a vicious cycle of mistakes? Like, no matter how hard you try to rise above the water, you're constantly slammed back down?"

Pff, of course she's never felt that way.

"Sometimes I just wish there was a way to know exactly what to do, how to make everything right. Why does it have to be so hard?"

A movement catches my attention, and I almost jump when I see two blue eyes peering at me from behind the dark window.

"Cody," I whisper, "I didn't mean to wake you. I ... uh ...can you hear me?"

She nods slowly. I eye her, expecting her to start screaming frantically like she did earlier. I expect her to bang on the window, demand that I leave. But she doesn't. Instead, she sits there, her expression full of something I've become too familiar with: sadness.

When I realize she isn't going to turn me away, I shift my body so she can see my face better. There's something I need to say before the moment is gone.

"Cody, I'm sorry. So sorry." I wipe my nose again.

She doesn't speak. I don't know how noise works through these windows. Is she only able to hear me, or can I hear her too? Regardless, Cody doesn't seem to have anything to say. At least nothing to say with her mouth.

But I watch her. I feel her sorrow seep through the window. She doesn't need to say anything for me to know how she feels.

I embrace the emotions she pushes through. I want her to know I'm here for her. That I'll do anything to help her.

We sit there for a while, in emotional silence. It isn't until my eyes get heavy and threaten to close that Cody finally speaks.

It's barely a whisper, but her words are crystal clear.

"I don't hate you, Alena."

Then she rests her head back on the glass and closes her eyes.

I stare at her in shock.

How can she say that? After all I've put her through?

Chapter 14

"There's too much at stake. We need access to Cody."

The chief's voice wakes me up. My aching shoulder tells me that I fell asleep on the floor ... in a very awkward position ... in the mental part of the hospital. I rub it slowly and bring my body up to sitting.

The hospital is still dark, the tinge of smoke in the air telling me the torches are still lit. I look up to find the chief towering over me, seemingly unaware of me sitting practically at his feet. He's too focused on something else. Cody.

"I need her trust, Chief." A woman speaks. "I cannot let you access those memories until she's ready." It's the woman I saw here earlier in the hospital, Cody's mind doctor. *What was her name? Sepharine?* She's standing next to the chief, watching Cody as well.

"Do you have any idea the information we could gain from her?" The chief sighs. The torchlight flickers shadows across his face, enhancing the wrinkles around his eyes and the fatigue in his brow.

"Of course, I do," Sepharine says. "You know there's nobody who wants to get Danny back as badly as I do. But stealing Cody's memories will only cripple her progress, possibly freeze it forever. I can't do that her."

I turn my head to the window behind me. Cody is lying in a heap on the floor again, sound asleep. I hope she stays asleep. I don't think she would appreciate this conversation.

I'm grateful that Sepharine is standing up for Cody, refusing to let the chief see her memories. Even if those memories could get us closer to Danny, I know it's wrong. I remember the day when my memories were checked by the chief. I felt betrayed and violated. Cody's been through enough. Her memories should only be checked if she's willing.

Chief rubs his face and beard in fatigue. "You're right. Please let me know the moment she decides to talk."

"Of course."

The chief's eyes now find me sitting at his feet, awake, and he raises an eyebrow.

"What are you doing here, Alena?"

I wrinkle my nose. I don't want to talk about it. Instead, I raise my left hand, the hand with the black power still in it. "Here," I say, then plop the power into his open palm.

"Did it work?"

I shrug. "I hope so."

The air is quiet. He probably wants to know more, but I don't want to tell him.

"Chief?" I'm grateful when the woman draws his attention away from me. "Why can't you find Chauly?"

It's a loaded and complicated question. I can tell by the emotions playing across Chief's face. But it's a good question. After a quick glance at Sepharine, he attempts an answer.

"I can't be completely sure, but I'm beginning to think Chauly is what we call a Jaboacar."

"What's a Jaboacar?" Sepharine asks.

The chief rubs his face again. "A Jaboacar is a rare person who is born without either Peppate or Doler generators. They're what we call a blank slate, swayed by whatever element is around them—Peppate or Doler." The chief stares at the wall. "If a Jaboacar lives among the non-Pepps, they are always filled with Doler. You know what being filled with Doler does, Alena. Makes you care too much about things, clouds your sense of worth." Chief sighs heavily. "But if a Jaboacar becomes a Pepp, with a totem on their arm, they're filled with Peppate. Being filled with Peppate all the time makes them *not* care about things. They lack direction, and because of that they act impulsively. Without the balance of Doler, they become unpredictable and dangerous. If I had known this earlier, I assure you, I never would have given Chauly a totem."

A Jaboacar. *A blank slate?* I recall Danny's explanation of Doler and how it projects our wants, likes, and cares into our minds. I'd never thought about it before, but having Doler is almost like having an internal compass. The cares that sometimes seem so overwhelming actually guide us, keep us from doing terrible things. If there aren't any cares, there isn't any guilt or shame.

"But what does this have to do with you not being able to *find* him?" Sepharine asks.

Chief rubs his face again. "Jaboacars have the very rare ability of blending in with their surroundings *when given power*. We can't find him because we can't see him. He can camouflage."

Blend in? I wondered at one point if Pepps could disappear. I guess blending in is almost disappearing. But Chauly isn't the only Pepp I've encountered disappearing. "Was Jax a Jaboacar too?" I recall how he disappeared that day in the Post.

"No." He rubs his jaw. "But Jaboacars can help others camouflage. I believe Chauly helped Jax disappear that day in my office. I believe that he's been coming and going from Petrichor for a long time, and we didn't even know it."

My knees go weak. *Chauly has been here all along, and nobody knew? Why did he never attack me before? Because I didn't have the black power? Because I was never alone?*

"So how do you find him, if you can't see him?" Sepharine interrupts my frightened thoughts.

Chief sighs. "I don't know. My father's father mentioned in his journal that their Jaboacar only came out of hiding when he was severely hurt, trapped by fire. But I'd have to find him in order to hurt him."

I look down at the chief's dirty shoes. "If being filled with Peppate is the problem, maybe you should just fill him with Doler," I say this almost jokingly remembering how impossible it is for me to hear the elements around me when I'm filled with Doler. If Chauly can't hear the elements, he wouldn't be able to control them and blend in. "You can't hear the elements when you're filled with Doler. He wouldn't be able to use his power and *blend in.* Plus, being filled with Doler might make him care enough about things to come out of hiding."

The air is quiet. When I look up at the chief, his intense stare is trained on my face. I instantly regret my words. It's a good idea. But there's only one way to produce that much Doler at once. A morph by Mark or me.

"A morph?" he whispers in awe. "That might just work. Would you do it, Alena?"

Stupid, stupid, stupid. Why can't I just keep my stupid mouth shut? I back my body into the wall. The last time I morphed, bad things happened. A man died. I vowed that night that I would never do it again.

I shake my head harshly.

"Please." The chief kneels, practically begging. "For the sake of finding Chauly? You wouldn't morph with Mark. You would morph alone. You wouldn't produce lightning."

I sit there frozen. I wouldn't produce lightning, but I would fill everyone with Doler. And that's bad.

Sepharine places her hand on the chief's shoulder, silently holding him back.

The chief sighs and clenches his teeth. "Will you at least think about it? He knows where Jax is, Alena. We find Chauly ... we find Jax."

His proposition is fair. It still doesn't settle right. I only swallow.

"Well, think about it." The chief tries to keep his voice light, but I can tell he's disheartened. With another sigh, he stands, says good night to Sepharine, and disappears down the hall.

"Good night," Sepharine calls.

I watch him walk away, out of sight. Why in the world did I open my big mouth?

"I'm sorry if we woke you, Alena." Sepharine's warm voice drifts through the air. When I glance at her, I find her quietly observing Cody.

"Sorry," I say, scooting away from the glass. She looks at me, confused.

"I shouldn't be here," I clarify and start to stand, but Sepharine stops me.

"Alena, you don't need to go, or be sorry. In fact, I want to thank you. I think you helped Cody tonight." She moves and sits across the hall from me, then pulls out something that looks like dough from her satchel. She stretches it into a long slack string, then balls it up again in her hands.

I try not to look surprised, instantly distracted from the conversation with the chief.

Me? Help Cody? I think it was the other way around. *And how does she know my name?*

Well, that's a stupid question—everyone knows my name.

I settle back against the wall, rubbing my shoulder, then rubbing Bud's head. He's sound asleep in my lap. I try to resist the urge to look at the woman, but I can't avoid her face for long. Thankfully, she's not looking at me anymore but at her ball of dough, her slender fingers skillfully molding it into a long oval shape. The torches light her face in a different way than they did the chief's. Instead of making her look more tired, they make her look more beautiful, her green eyes brighter.

We sit in silence for a while, both of us captivated by her moving fingers. The dough is odd. I'm not sure what she's doing with it, but it calms me, breaks the tension that could be there if she was just staring at me, waiting for me to speak. That's what it feels like—she's waiting for me to speak. And not just to speak but to ask a very specific question. One I've wondered since meeting her yesterday.

Finally, unable to help myself, I open my mouth.

"You're a doctor of the mind," I say, remembering what Rusty had told me.

"Yes," she says without looking up.

"How do you do it?" I whisper. "How do you help someone who's been through so much?"

Sepharine's attention doesn't shift from her dough.

"There are quite a few things I do to help. They're complicated and difficult to explain, but, to put it plainly, I try to help them see that they're safe, and I try to give them hope for the future."

I observe Sepharine's gentle face, her creamy skin, her plush lips. I realize in this moment that I trust her, possibly more than I trust the chief.

"I try to give Cody hope," she continues. "Help her see that even though she's been hurt by terrible people, there are also still very good people out there. Good people like you." Sepharine looks up from her dough now. "You coming here tonight was more important than you know. She needs friends. And based on her reaction to you, *you* are one she needs."

Pff. Good people like me? Sepharine wouldn't even put me close to that category if she knew more about me. Perhaps Jeter could enlighten her a bit.

"I've heard a lot about you, Alena." Her words make me cringe, and I wrinkle my nose. *Everyone's heard a lot about me.*

Sepharine chuckles, a sound that carries softly in the air.

"I've heard a lot about you from *one* very important person."

I stare at her.

"Danny," she whispers. I don't miss the reverent way she says his name. "And Mark," she adds, smiling a little more. "Mark doesn't talk to me much, but he *has* talked to me *about you*. That's saying a lot."

I furrow my eyebrows and shake my head. I don't understand.

"I'm their Pepp mother, Alena."

Ah. Suddenly, everything makes sense. Danny's knowledge about happiness, about Doler and Peppate. He got it all from his Pepp mother. He mentioned her to me once. I'm surprised I've never met her until now.

"I was always closer to Danny than I ever was to Mark. Danny was much younger when he came here, and he needed more care. Mark was very independent and, well, angry when he came here. I didn't help him much directly, but I think Danny has."

I nod, remembering the way Mark praised Danny for his ability to help him. But it was really Sepharine's ideas *through* Danny that helped Mark.

The air grows quiet again, and I turn my attention back to Cody.

"What are you thinking?" Sepharine asks after a couple of minutes.

I stiffen. *What am I thinking? She doesn't want to know what I'm thinking.*

But the simple way Sepharine plays with her dough has my heart calming, has me wondering if maybe I *can* talk to her.

I fiddle with my shirtsleeve again, then open my mouth. "I was just thinking about what Danny taught me. About the Doler, how it makes us feel and what it does to our minds. And how getting rid of it allows the Peppate to come in and help us see the truth." I pause for a moment before proceeding. "I'm wondering how ... the *wiggems*, as Danny calls them, could possibly work for someone like her. Someone who's been through something so terrible."

I don't say it out loud, but what I'm really wondering is how it could possibly work for someone like *me*.

When I look back at Sepharine she's watching me closely.

"Danny was right about the Doler and Peppate. Getting rid of Doler allows us to see truth. As far as the process for those who've been through trauma, it's actually very similar. They need to see truth too. It's just a lot more difficult for them to do so—no fault of their own. The normal wiggems, like work, exercise, listening to music, etc., are helpful but not strong enough. I have other techniques I use repeatedly, and over a long period of time, that tend to help them feel much better. Those dealing with trauma just need a lot more support, patience, and understanding. I do believe that Cody will get there, though. If that's what she wants."

If that's what she wants.

Sepharine's eyes pull away from mine to knead her dough again.

"Maybe you could come visit me sometime. I can only imagine you have battles of your own, considering what you've been through."

The idea of talking to someone about the more vulnerable things going on in my head suddenly makes me feel very uncomfortable. It's embarrassing and almost feels like an invasion of privacy.

Sepharine seems to sense my hesitancy and laughs softly. "Don't worry, Alena. You don't have to. Mark hasn't been too fond of talking to me either." Her eyes flicker to mine. "But I hope you find *someone* to talk to. That's probably the most important thing you can do. Find a friend you can trust."

Friend. I shake my head. That's something I really don't have right now. Danny, Mark, Cody. They're all hurt because of me.

"I'm sorry about Danny," I say, suddenly feeling the need to apologize to Sepharine for losing her Pepp son.

Her smile fades. "You aren't blaming yourself, are you?"

I fist my hands. *Of course I am*.

"Well, it isn't even close to being your fault, so don't. I'm just grateful Kapri has found some leads. She has this idea that the mysterious screams in the Magbaby message are supposed to lead us to a meadow," Sepharine says. "She's thinking that something might be hidden there. But she doesn't know what."

I nod, remembering our finding from two days ago. I never got a chance to ask Mark what he found.

Sepharine continues. "Kapri is very fond of Danny. There was a time when he liked her very much too."

Of course he did.

"I think she's been waiting for him to finally see her again. Personally, I think you've helped Danny do that. Danny needed you, Alena. He still needs you."

I meet her sad expression. I know what she means, and she's right. I need to get over myself and help Kapri find him. He's still out there.

"I have something for you, Alena." I couldn't be more grateful for the change in subject. I really don't want to talk about Kapri anymore.

Sepharine watches me carefully while reaching behind her. She seems hesitant, as if wondering if she should proceed.

"This is a letter." She pauses, bringing an envelope into view. Her eyes bounce from it to me. "A letter from Cody's Pepp mother."

I rip my attention away and shift uncomfortably. I don't want it.

"I've read it, and I think you should too." Her voice stays steady.

I stare at the darkened hall, clenching my teeth, trying to hold back tears.

Sepharine stands and places the letter in my lap.

"I should probably get back to the Burrows and get some sleep. I suggest you stay here tonight. It's too dangerous for you to be out all alone."

I ignore her as she gathers up her dough and walks away. When I'm sure she's gone, I let my tears fall, straining to keep myself from looking at or even touching the envelope. *I shouldn't have come here. I don't want this letter.* But somehow it gets into my hands. I can't control the quiver in my lip or see much in front of me through my tears, but I slowly slide my finger under the tab in the envelope.

I don't want to read it. It's going to say everything I already know. That I ruined her life. That she'll never be happy again. I don't need to read her letter to know how big a mistake I made. I don't want to feel any worse than I already do. But I probably deserve to. So, I read.

Alena,

It's been very difficult for me to write this letter. Expressing my feelings to you seems impossible. But there are some things I think you need to know.

I miss my Tom terribly.

I want to crumple up the paper and shout out loud. *You don't think I know you miss him? You don't think I've been beating myself up every second of every day because of what I've done!?* It takes me a minute to calm my hysterical heart and muster up enough strength to keep reading. I need to finish the letter. I wait for my tears to slow enough to continue.

I've suffered through much grief in my life, and had thought I'd be used to loss by now, but this has left me feeling hollow yet again.

I've found myself wanting to disappear in my sorrows, to place blame on the one everyone else is blaming.

On you.

But as I've reluctantly listened to your story from the chief, I've begun to realize that even though it was you who killed my Tom, you were only capable of doing so because you had been used.

I know what that's like. To be forced into doing something that goes against everything you believe in. To feel like no matter how hard you try to create your life the way you want it, you're trapped in a life you despise.

I guess that's why this loss has been so hard on me. Because for the first time in my life, I had found someone, Tom. Tom never used me. He did just the opposite. He fought for me. He saved me, and when he found out the terrible things I had done, he forgave me.

And now that one person who accepted me is gone.

As much as I want to blame you, Alena, I can't. He taught me better. I know that true healing for both you and me will only come if I do what my dear Tom has done for me.

I forgive you, Alena.

I set you free.

I believe we can both heal, in time. Take care of yourself.

And thank you for bringing my Cody back.

I didn't know I had any more tears left in me, but apparently I do. My body shudders from soul-wrenching sobs that I can't gulp down. Instead of fighting them, I lean my head back and try to catch some air in between. My mind replays Pam's words. I was the one who killed her husband. I cry harder. I've been avoiding that fact. It's just too painful to admit, but with the words so plainly written on the paper, I can't escape them now. Oh, how it hurts to hear her say it.

But then those words melt into the next: *I forgive you, Alena.* Her words are painful at first. They confirm that I need forgiveness ... and that hurts. They confirm that *I* caused significant pain, something I never wanted to cause.

But then a soft feeling enters my heart. Her words aren't meant to act as a twisted thorn in my side, reminding me of everything I've done wrong. Instead, they're meant to set me free. She said so. My lip quivers uncontrollably. I wipe the moisture from my eyes and nose and then pull my knees in. With my eyes cleared, I read her words again. *I forgive you, Alena.*

This time her words reach into my heart, planting love and spreading it throughout my whole body.

I can never fix what I've done. I can never bring Tom back or heal Pam's heart.

But, for a fleeting moment, I wonder if maybe, just maybe, I *can* move forward. Maybe I still have a place. If Pam can believe in me, well, maybe I can survive.

I slowly raise my head and lean it back against the wall.

Then my eyes narrow when they see something in another room down the hall. I sit up.

Both times when I've come to see Cody, or leave her, I've been distracted.

But now, for the first time, I see them.

The prisoners.

The ones I freed. They're in separate rooms down this same hall, and they're all sitting in front of their glass windows, looking at me.

The light quivers across their unmistakable faces. I haven't seen any of them since I got them out of that horrible place, and now I feel guilty for not even having thought to visit. I observe them, the men and women. Their bodies look healthier than when I found them in the mine, thankfully, but they also look hollow, tired, and sad, as if the experience in the mine aged their spirits. Amid the sorrow, though, they each muster a half-smile. A girl actually waves to me. I wave back. A boy is mouthing some words. I can't hear him, but I don't need to hear him to know what he's saying.

Thank you.

Those two simple words woven together trigger another wave of blurring tears.

"You're welcome," I find myself saying before he moves away from the glass.

I may have caused a lot of grief, but maybe there is one thing I did do right.

I got the prisoners out.

Chapter 15

It's still the middle of the night when I begin the walk back to Green-Grotto, Bud and Harper trudging sleepily behind me. Sepharine had encouraged me to stay the night there in the hospital, but I'm tired and want my bed, hopeful for the first time in a while that I'll actually get some sleep. Plus, I have Harper and my baby dinosaur.

As I move through the dark night, my mind replays my conversation with Sepharine again, questions whether she could really help me. Then it moves on to the letter from Pam. A weight has been lifted from my shoulders, replaced with a calm I haven't felt in a long time. My heart still hurts, but it's hurting a little less. And now I'm exhausted after crying so much.

Suddenly, I hear a thump behind me.

"Bud?" I turn. Harper is falling to the grass, her eyes rolling back. "Harper!"

I'm moving to help her, when pain explodes in the side of my face, my bones cracking. The force of the punch upends my feet, and I thud to the ground, landing on my back.

"I can take you to Danny," a gruesome voice says in the dark. "Just come with me."

I gasp for breath. Chauly. *No! Not Chauly!*

I shake the stars from my vision and bring up my throbbing head, aware of my tightening fists ready to fight as hard as they can. Where is he? I can't see him!

The chief's words ring loudly in my head. I scramble to my feet, my eyes frantically searching the grass in front of me, the trees, the rocks. There's nothing! Just the flickering of torches too far away and shadows. Lots of shadows.

Crippling fear grips my body, tensing every muscle, accelerating the blood in every vessel. Where are all the Protectors?

He can see me, but I can't see him. I know I should try to get away from him, but my body freezes as his words repeat in my mind. *He can take me to Danny.* And he can give me answers.

I raise my fists in front of me, ready to put up a fight while trying to get some answers.

"Why do you want *me* so badly?" I ask, still squinting in the darkness.

Then he's there, flickering into view, licking his cracked lips, sliding his sickening eyes over my body. Bud attacks his leg, bites him hard, but Chauly kicks the baby dinosaur away, sending him sliding several feet. Bud doesn't get up.

"Why wouldn't I want you so badly?" He steps closer, and I see that he's naked except for a black loin cloth that blends in with the night. Scars litter his skin, stretched and puckered over his torso and down his arms. "I'll have my fun with you first, if you don't mind. Then I'll send you on to Jax and Danny."

Shivers rack my body, and I scoot back, trying to get away while subtly sliding my knife out of my sleeve into my palm. I don't want to know what this man considers fun.

"Why does Jax want me?" I swallow the bile in my throat, still determined to get more information.

Chauly laughs. *I don't know what's so funny.* "Because of your healing abilities, darling, combined with the black power. His desire for you runs only second to mine."

Without another blink, he's punched my throbbing face again, forcing me onto my back. Then he's on me, straddling my torso like before. I try to move, to fight him off, but something stabs into my side. A knife. My knife. He moved so quick I don't even recall his skin touching my hand to get it.

A strangled cry slips from my lips as the air is pulled from my lungs. I need to scream louder, draw the attention of the protectors. Where are they? But I can't breathe well enough to fill my lungs again.

Chauly pulls the knife out and stabs me again, yanking my flesh, tearing it apart. Warm blood drips down my side into the grass.

"You don't have power ... do you?" Chauly chuckles, discovering that I'm not fighting back like a Pepp with power would. "I admit, things are a little more fun when the fight is even. But whatever."

I wish I had power, if only to help with the pain. It's like fire, so hot, so searing, in my side, my stomach. I reach my hands up to his eyes, try to gouge them out with my fingernails, but my efforts only make him laugh again.

"I sure hope you at least have the black power with you. I'd hate to have to drag you back to GreenGrotto like this."

I don't know whether to be relieved or horrified that I don't have the black power. Should I have given it back to the chief?

Chauly leans down and bites my neck hard, tearing the flesh. This time, the pain pulls more air into my swollen lungs, regardless of the blood filling them, allowing me to scream louder for a moment before blood fills my mouth. *Where are those damn protectors?*

He's like a ravenous, terrifying animal, unlike anything my mind could have ever imagined. His lips red with my blood smile with disgusting joy from his twisted little game.

My legs tremble from the pain that is pulsing everywhere through my body now, tears stinging my eyes. I can't breathe!

Chauly leans down to tear me apart even more, when suddenly he's yanked off. The movement sends more ripples of pain through my body, but I can't scream anymore. I just grit my teeth and gurgle through the blood.

I hear a crack and turn my aching head in the direction of the sound. Mark is there, punching the heck out of Chauly before the despicable man turns and runs away, disappearing in the process. Mark jolts to run after him, but then looks back at me.

Oh, how I've missed that man.

Confusion sweeps over his features. "Alena, do you have power?"

I barely hear his words through my ringing ears. "Go." I try to tell him he needs to go after Chauly, not worry about me, but I can't get any words out. I blink rapidly, when dark spots cloud my vision again. Pain like I've never experience before envelopes my being as if wrapping me in its own type of cruel blanket. My organs, my muscles—everything is dying inside.

Suddenly Mark is hovering over me. "Alena!" He shakes my shoulders. I vaguely feel him pull down the collar of my shirt and press something over my heart. Power. Pain explodes over my stomach. "Alena, heal yourself!"

The ringing sounds of elements faintly tingle through my ears. My body continues to shake, clarity completely wiped from my mind. *I'm supposed to do something. What do I do?*

"Start with your stomach, Alena, please!" Mark's cracking voice tugs me back from the darkness that's beckoning. I focus. The sounds in my stomach. I'm just barely diagnosing my problem, *knife wounds ... too much blood loss,* when arms pick me off the ground, sending more excruciating pain through my body.

"Alena, stay with me." Mark's words are faint. I force my eyes open to see his face one last time.

Thank you, Mark.

***

"Alena."

I listen for the elements around me. My body shifts in its sleep, then I remember. My stomach. I silently reach out for the elements and find my stomach uninjured. Well, mostly uninjured. The cells have been healed, but they're tired. Something that can't be fixed with power.

Man, *I'm* tired. But I open my eyes anyway. The concrete ceiling above me shines in the light of the sun leaking in through the windows. Large sheets hang around me, offering some privacy. I'm in the clinic on one of the beds, a comfortable pillow under my head, a heavy, warm blanket over me. I snuggle into it further, letting my weary eyes fall again.

"Alena."

I sigh and blink my eyes again. The chief is standing off to my right, his gray beard white in the sunlight, his eyes shadowed by fatigue. *Man, this guy needs to get a life.* Yet, I'm so grateful to see him.

"Are you okay?" He grips my hand.

Suddenly the events of last night flood my mind. Chauly. Mark. I look around the room. Where is Mark. Is he okay?

"He's still out looking for Chauly," Chief says, sensing my question.

I lay my head back down, my veins pulsing wildly at the mention of my assailant. He's still out there.

"I'll do it," I say without thinking.

The chief's piercing blue eyes narrow.

"I'll morph. Fill Chauly with Doler," I say, to be as clear as possible. "I want Chauly found. I want him tortured for information on where Danny is. I want Danny back."

Chief squeezes my hand tighter, a relief visibly easing the tension in his shoulders. "Thank you, Alena. I'll let you know when it's time. But don't tell anyone—we don't want Chauly finding out our plan."

"Hurry," I say, unable to contain the desperation in my voice. It makes my skin crawl, knowing that that man is still walking around Petrichor, unseen.

"We will."

It's scary enough knowing that a man is out there waiting to get you. But to know that he's out there, waiting for you, and you can't even see him? That's terrifying. *How long has he been watching me?* What did he plan on doing to me out there? If he was going to take me to Jax, why did he push me so close to death? I have the sudden urge to vomit.

The chief kneels on the ground and holds out his hand. There in his palm is my Magbaby.

"Breccia!" I sit up and take her. "Did you find anything?"

Breccia glances at the chief then at me. "I'm not sure. I did what you said. Went to the water source on the far west side of Kalahaki. I searched all over for footprints, people, shelters. I found nothing. The only thing that stood out to me was the water seemed a little low."

The chief nods as if he's already heard her report. He knows what she's going to say.

"But it's in the desert. I don't know what's normal out there and what isn't. I'll go back out tomorrow."

I look at the chief. "Have you found anything in Dakdete?"

Chief shakes his head. "No. Nothing yet. If Jax is there, he would need a water source, but unlike Kalahaki, there aren't any at all there. That doesn't necessarily mean anything, though. We're pretty sure Jax has Pepps working for him, and if that's the case those Pepps can quickly fly to the next country and get water whenever they need it."

My body sags under the weight of disappointment.

"It's okay, Alena," Chief says. "We'll get Chauly and use him to find Danny." He stands now. "Now get some rest."

"Wait," I say. "Harper. Is she okay?"

Chief nods wearily. "We almost lost her too, but, yes, she'll be fine."

"And Bud?" My eyes look around my small space.

"He's in the corner over there. Sound asleep." Chief gestures at my tiny protector.

I'm relieved. *Thank you.*

Then he walks down the hall out of sight. I lay my head back down, trying to do what he suggested. Get some rest.

Yeah, right.

Chapter 16

I lean my head in, listening for the sounds of the injury. The girl sitting in front of me was knocked out of a tree by a dinosaur in the game. She's conscious but feels like her head is going to explode.

Not that I want others to be in pain, but I'm grateful for the distraction of the injury. I haven't left the clinic since Chauly attacked me three days ago except to shower, change my clothes, and go to the library. The fact that he's still out there and I haven't seen Mark at all has my nerves frazzled to bits. I'm worried about Mark, about what Chauly could do to him.

It takes me only seconds to identify the culprit of the girl's problem. I start speaking to the totem in my mind, fixing what appears to be a burst vessel. The totem acts quickly, and soon the bleeding stops.

I frown. That was too easy. Much easier than healing a brain bleed without power would be, and now I need to find someone else to heal.

The girl sighs in relief, touches her head, and then grins widely.

"Thank you."

I help her off the bed, and then she's gone, leaving me alone in the clinic with Bud, who is chewing on a bone Chief gave him.

Looking out the door, I find the hall sadly empty.

The Dino Games are still going, but apparently the dinosaurs are getting less aggressive and just enjoying their time free. Making less work for me. Hopefully they'll be fully aggressive if they see Chauly.

At the end of the week, the end of the Dino Games, they hold what they call the Festival, where the trainers get to show off their dinosaurs and allow them to get out any last bits of energy before they're shrunk again. I think I'll just stay here.

Sighing, I kneel next to the table the girl was just lying on and pull out a stack of books from underneath it.

I needed another distraction yesterday after clinic. My hands tend to shake when I think about what happened with Chauly, so I went to the library to get some books with Harper. She told me that Chauly hit her in the head with a rock when she was following me home. Knocked her out and caused some major brain bleeding. I'm glad she's okay.

I found some books about totems at the library and brought them back here where I feel safe. I also found one book on infectious agents. After being so blindsided by the flesh-eating bug that killed Mitch and the prisoners, I've been determined to learn as much as I can about every virus, every infection, and every bug out there.

Today, though, during this quiet time, I pick up a book about totems. I scan through the pages until I find a section of images. Images of everything relating to the totem.

First, I see a picture of a totem extracted from the totem tree. It's only about four or five inches long in its *unattached* state, almost looking like a pencil. It stays that way until it's touched by live skin. Then it burrows into the vessels and stretches throughout the entire body.

A diagram shows the external part of the vine on a Pepp and explains that thousands of tiny Peppate generators reside in each totem.

Peppate generators.

I move through more pages until I reach a picture titled *Peppate generators.* I stop and examine the generator carefully.

The first thing my brain relates the generator to is a tadpole. It has a perfectly circular "head" with a swirly indentation in the middle and a long translucent tail that funnels out at the end. At the connecting point of the head and tail sits a small circular sac.

I read the descriptors. The swirling circle, "or head", is where the Peppate is produced. It then passes through the channel, or "tail," where the Peppate is taken outside the skin into the air. The sac that sits at the joint of the head and tail creates—and holds—the *power* generated as the Peppate passes through.

PEPPATE GENERATOR

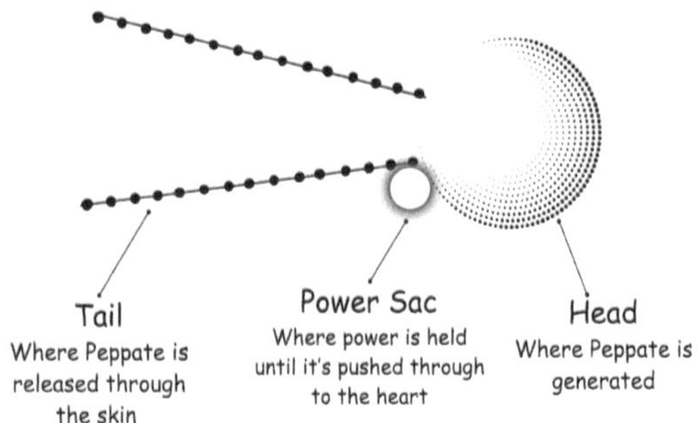

When a Pepp morphs into an eagle, by pounding their chest once, the Peppate generators are activated, *making* Peppate and in return producing power. When the power sac gets full, the power is pushed out into the totem, where it travels to the heart. The heart of the totem is a hole just over the chest the size of a large coin, where a glass sphere sits to collect the yellowish power. Once the glass sphere is full, it can easily be popped out and transferred to other Pepps if needed. Putting a full sphere of power into the totem's hole reminds me of pushing a marble halfway into hardened clay. It's easy and painless, and the feeling of power immediately surges through your veins. Taking it out is just as simple. Squeezing the totem makes the sphere pop out.

The diagrams go on for pages, identifying and describing the parts further, but I don't bother reading on. Slowly, my eyes move from the book over to my totem.

My totem is very different than the normal Pepp totem. The biggest difference being that mine isn't even a full one. It's half a totem. Whoever created it broke it into two different pieces for some unknown reason. One piece is in my skin and the other in Mark's.

Whoever made the totem wanted Mark to attach both to him the day his dad died. But when he went to attach the second one just outside his old cabin, a bear came and interfered. The second half got lost in the hot spring. The same hot spring I went swimming in.

The morph is different for Mark and me too. In order for the power to be generated like it is in Pepp generators, Mark and I *both* have to morph. Together.

Unfortunately, when that happens, lightning is produced. Powerful lightning that destroys everything within miles, turns it to dust. Without the lightning, there is no black power.

Which is why I have such conflicted feelings about the black power. I won't ever create that lightning again, which means the black power we have ... is all the black power we're ever going to get.

The black power.

It's different too. Unlike normal Pepp power, it lacks Peppate and can control non-Peppate things. Like Dilo's serum.

I close my eyes. I don't know exactly what *my* generators look like, but I picture them in my head looking like the picture of Peppate generators in front of me, just black. The head produces Doler. Then after a combined morph, black power is generated in the power sac. Once it's full, the power is pushed through to the heart of the totem.

My totem may produce a different type of power, but it was constructed using the same framework of a normal totem, right? Where did my generators come from? I wish I could cut out a section of my totem so I could examine it, but that's already been tried. My dad and Dr. Brown had experimented on it in the beginning. It turned to dust as soon as it left my skin. I open my eyes and rub my neck. There has to be a way to see what my generators look like. And what they sound like.

I've totally forgotten about trying to listen for the sound of Peppate generators like Bapoto suggested. Maybe the next time I'm around a Pepp, I'll pay closer attention. But after healing Mark, I'm pretty sure listening for the Doler generators is going to be a whole different project to tackle.

I skim through the pages of the book, feeling the air as they flutter. I wonder if there's anything in here about the defected totems. I flip to the index to check.

"Hey."

I draw a shallow breath, hearing the voice of the man I've been so worried about the past few days.

I look up. Mark is there, more worn and ragged than I've ever seen him, his hair tousled, his clothes wrinkled and dirty. There's even blood on his shirt. *Is that my blood? Has he not changed since our run-in with Chauly?*

"Mark."

"I couldn't find him." Mark shoves his hands into his pockets and leans his back against the wall, discouragement leaking from every pore of his body.

I can't help myself. I walk to him, quickly closing the distance between us. Wrapping my arms around his waist, I bury my face in his chest.

"You're okay," I say, feeling as though I'm finally able to breathe after days of drowning in worry. Chauly didn't hurt Mark.

But then my heart sinks. It's weird that Chauly would go out of his way to follow me, get me alone, attack me, and leave Mark completely untouched. Is it because Mark could probably beat the crap out of him? No, Chauly had mentioned needing my *healing* power. That's probably the reason. I'm a medic, and Mark is not.

"Thank you," I whisper. "For saving me. I don't know why you were there, but I'm sure glad you were."

Mark speaks into my hair, his arms embracing me. "I'm sorry he even got to you. I've been sleeping on your balcony ever since I found out he attacked you. Dacite, my Magbaby, took shifts with me, keeping his eyes open when I couldn't. When we saw you leave your room, we followed. But I didn't want you to see me. I was too far behind when Chauly attacked you. I'm sorry."

He's been sleeping on my balcony? He followed me, and I didn't even know it? Was he there in the hospital that night? Did he hear my conversation with Sepharine? Man, I need to be more aware of my surroundings.

"Thank you, Mark." Emotions rise within me now, catching me off guard. If he hadn't been there for me, I don't know where I'd be right now.

Mark drops one of his hands to my stomach. His thumb, hot through my white shirt, fingers the spot where Chauly stabbed me. "Are you okay?"

I bury my face further into his shirt. "Yes, thanks to you."

"You almost died in my arms." His voice cracks.

I swallow, gripping the back of his shirt. "But I didn't, thanks to you," I repeat stupidly, unable to think of anything else to say. I listen to his heart beating, smell the mixture of metallic blood and dirt on him.

"It's probably a good thing I didn't find him. I think I would have killed him, which wouldn't be very helpful in finding Danny." His voice rumbles deep.

I shiver. The idea of the awful man still lurking out there makes the hair on my neck stand up. But he's right. Chauly is our key to finding Danny.

I try to change the subject, think of something else to talk about, but the only thing my mind can focus on is his thumb still brushing my stomach.

"By the way, I've been meaning to tell you that Jeter had no right to yell at you the other night. What you did helped me a lot."

I realize for the first time that I've been so upset about what happened with Jeter and Chauly, I haven't even inquired to see if Mark's neck was really healed. I pull away to get a better look.

"It's better," he mutters. "Thank you."

I drop my gaze to the floor, his words drawing out unexpected emotions from the night with Jeter. Jeter's harsh words ring loudly in my head and suddenly that heavy awkwardness is back. I'm embarrassed. Embarrassed that I tried something so stupid ... again. That Mark heard Jeter's angry words.

"Also," he continues, lowering his voice. "I looked through the meadow, around the lake Wintriness. I didn't find anything."

I sigh deeply, my shoulders sagging. "I guess I didn't really expect you to find anything there." But now we're back at square one.

Well not really. My sluggish brains finally starts working, remembering what I'm going to do to find Chauly. I swallow. I should tell Mark.

"Hey, um," I start. I don't really want to talk about this. I don't see Mark liking this plan. But I need to tell him.

Mark winds his arm tightly around my waist and pulls me back against his warm body. I melt into him, leaning my forehead against his chin.

"Mark, did the chief tell you what Chauly is?" I murmur.

"Chauly? Well, Chief said he's a ... what did he call it? A Jaboacar?"

I can see Mark's heart beat pulsing in his neck. I resist the sudden urge to kiss him there.

"Yes. Did he tell you about his ability? How Jaboacars can camouflage with power?"

Mark nods.

"Well, I had an idea."

I pull my head back so I can see his face. *He's not going to like this.*

"We have to cripple his ability. And the best way to do that is to fill him with Doler. When he's filled with Doler, he won't be able to hear the elements around him; hence, he won't be able to control them. He won't be able to camouflage." I let my voice trail off.

Mark stares down at me with a conflicted expression. I feel his fist tighten against my back—in fact, all of his muscles have tightened. He knows where I'm going with this. I take in a deep breath. "I told the chief I would morph."

Mark's nostrils flare, and his teeth grind against each other. I brace myself for his anger, expect him to demand that I not do it, the way he demanded I not go into the silver mine. But those demands never come. He closes his eyes, takes a deep breath, and then speaks through gritted teeth. "That's ... a ... good idea, Alena."

I almost laugh. That sounded painful.

But then my body warms. As difficult as it was for him to say those words, he's not going to *forbid* me from morphing like I thought he might. Instead, he tightens his grip around my waist and silently begs me with his look.

Please let me do it instead.

I bring my fingers to his face, trace the line of his jaw.

I could let him do it. Morph. A part of me wants him to, just so I don't ever have to morph again. But this is my chance to hurt Chauly, the way my blood begs to do to that inhumane animal. Take away his power and then let the chief take him away.

Still, one look at Mark's pleading face reminds me that he means more to me than revenge.

"Would you want to morph instead?"

Mark closes his eyes and lets out a heavy sigh, his muscles visibly releasing their tension.

"Yes, please."

I continue touching his scruff with my fingers, sudden stupid tears threatening my eyes. I don't deserve this good man who has saved me countless times and forgiven my many mistakes so easily. It's both painful and exhilarating at the same time, knowing that regardless of my shortfalls and weaknesses, this man still might want me.

Someone at the door clears their throat loudly.

I peek sideways and find Rusty standing there, his hands in his pockets.

A sudden new tension strikes the room, and my neck tightens. Mark and Rusty weren't the best of friends before Rusty and I freed the prisoners, but any friendship that did exist before was quickly extinguished after. Mark's jaw tightens when he sees Rusty and I step back.

But before speaking, Mark takes in a deep breath, releasing the anger with it.

"I need to talk to Alena, and then she's all yours," Mark says. I'm surprised by the control in his voice.

"Actually," Rusty says, "I was hoping to speak with you, Mark, but I can come back later."

Mark blinks, his dirty, tired face going slack with surprise. I find my own mouth gaping open. *What could Rusty possibly need to talk to Mark about?*

Rusty turns to leave, but before he can escape, Mark drops his arm from around me and says, "I'm sorry, Rusty. I ... What did you need to talk to *me* about?"

Rusty swallows uneasily. "It's about Cody. I remember when you first came here, you were angry, like she is now. I was wondering if you could tell me how you got past that. Or what I can do to help her. Thankfully, she's actually talking to Sepharine now. But I still feel helpless. What do *I* do?"

Mark's face softens a bit. I didn't even think about Mark being able to understand Cody's grief, but of course he does. He lost his father and blamed himself for his death. Just like Cody probably blames herself for what happened to her friend we never found.

"Well, I wouldn't have ever gotten better without the help of Danny," Mark says.

"*How* did Danny help you? What did he do?" Rusty asks, earnestly wanting to know the answer.

A thoughtful look sweeps over Mark's face. After thinking for a couple of moments, he speaks.

"There were two things he did for me that stand out in my mind. First, he was always there. He didn't talk much, obviously, but he was always physically there with me, no judgments, no disparagements, just there. He made me feel as though I was important to him."

Mark pauses, an amused look sliding across his face.

"The second thing Danny did was he forced me to do things that made me feel like myself again." Mark snickers, recalling a memory. "I love hunting. Somehow Danny found that out and invited me to go hunting with him, but I refused. I was hunting the day my dad died. It seemed too painful to try again.

"But one day Danny drove me mysteriously out to a meadow." Mark signals to me, silently telling me that I know the meadow he's talking about. "And when we got out there, he pulled out some shotguns. As soon as I saw them, I started to leave, but Danny pointed the gun at me and told me that if I didn't hit every target he'd set out for me, he would shoot me."

Mark shakes his head and chuckles. "I didn't believe he would do it. After he shot me in the leg, he made me sit there on the ground, practically bleeding to death, and forced me to shoot every target. When I did, he loaded me onto the four-wheeler and took me to the hospital."

Mark's smile fades now. "He took me out there every day after that for weeks. I resisted so much at first, but it wasn't long until I realized how much I had missed shooting. I didn't know it, but rejecting hunting was almost like rejecting a big part of me. Without it, I felt completely lost. Danny helped me find that part of me again."

Mark looks seriously at Rusty now. "Perhaps Cody needs to find a piece of herself again. A lot has been taken from her, but maybe you can give her something back. Help her feel like herself, even if in a small way."

Rusty rubs the stubble on his face, nodding with a new hopeful look. "I don't think I could ever shoot Cody in the leg, but maybe I can figure something else out. Thanks, Mark. That was exactly what I needed."

Rusty steps further into the room and pounds Mark on the shoulder. Mark only grunts in return. I watch them both. It feels right, their talking to each other.

Rusty turns to leave the room, but before he gets far, Mark stops him.

"Hey, Rusty, one more thing. There's something Danny *never* did. Something I've since learned the importance of."

Rusty nods again, encouraging Mark to proceed.

Mark hesitates. I examine his face closely, eager to hear what he has to say. He briefly meets my gaze before turning back to Rusty.

"Danny never made my happiness his responsibility."

Rusty's eyebrows furrow in confusion, as do mine.

"You can't make Cody happy, Rusty. You can love her, support her, and hope that she'll find herself, find her happiness again. That will help immensely. But true happiness requires action from the person. They have to choose it. The moment you absorb full responsibility for her happiness *without expecting action on her part* is the moment you head down a dark path that will be harmful for both you and her. She has to choose happiness for herself."

Mark's words pierce my heart.

My mind is instantly taken back to when I first obtained my totem. The time I spent at home, and the severe moods I experienced. I think about Caleb. How he withdrew from school to stay with me. How his relationship with Jess was more strained because he felt like he needed to take care of me. I suddenly realize the challenge I must have placed on my brother's shoulders. I didn't realize it then, but Caleb absorbed responsibility for my happiness. And I let him.

But then I recall how he practically dragged me out of the house the day we learned about Issy. He didn't make me very happy that day. But that's just what I needed. That was love. It must have been difficult for him, wondering if it was the right thing to do ... wondering if it would work.

My mind shifts. Happiness? From an outside perspective, of course I would say that each person has to choose for themselves whether or not they want to be happy. But looking inside myself now, I can't help but wonder: Do I really have that much control? To *just choose* to be happy? *How do I do that?* I replay Mark's words in my mind.

Maybe it's not so much a choice to be happy but more of a choice to take responsibility for my happiness. That portrays happiness as more of an effort. An effort I make.

I must have been deep in thought, because when I look up, Rusty is gone and Mark is staring at me.

I want to busy myself with something: put my books away, clean another table, heal another patient. Anything to escape his gaze. But, instead, I stand there.

Have I expected Mark to make me happy? Because it seemed impossible to make myself happy, have I hoped he would take on that responsibility? Probably.

And now I've been corrected. Whether Mark intentionally meant to lecture me or not, that's how it felt.

Mark turns toward me. "Alena." Warmth radiates from his body. I don't speak, but I do meet his eyes. I want him to know that I acknowledge him. That I understand what he's said, regardless of how hard it was to hear.

"Alena," he says again, softer. I search his face, his strong jaw, his dirty stubbled cheeks. I want to reach up and touch his face. Touch him.

"I'm going to go help Kapri after I shower," he whispers. "I need a break from looking for Chauly. I was wondering if you wanted to come."

I want to say no. The thought of sitting there with Mark and Kapri for the rest of the night looking over songs does not appeal to me at all. Plus, I won't be much help, considering how foggy my brain is. But then I look up and see hope in Mark's face.

This is a chance. *No, a choice*. Not just to help Kapri, but to prove ... to Mark that I care about him.

"Okay." I finally say.

Chapter 17

I grab my plate from the long buffet table loaded with food. I don't feel very hungry tonight. Again. But I know I need to eat. Picking at some of the fruit, I load a couple of strawberries onto my plate, but then I just stand there, staring, my mind distracted.

Breccia came back again this morning. She went to another water source in Kalahaki and found the same thing as the first. Water was a little low. She's concluding that it's just a normal thing. She'll go out again tomorrow, though.

I worked with Mark and Kapri last night and again today. We worked through more songs Kapri wrote down, and we reviewed the ones from before. The three songs about Wintriness, memories, and the meadow still stick out in my mind, but after hours of trying to figure out how they fit in the puzzle, I came up with nothing but frustration.

We're never going to find Danny. Not without capturing Chauly.

I haven't heard anything from the chief yet, when he wants me to morph.

Other Pepps anxiously skirt around me, grabbing their food, leaving Bud and me behind.

I'm glad I went with Mark. As hard as it was to swallow my pride, it eased some of the guilt I've hung on to. Unfortunately, there's still a heaviness between us. *How do I get rid of that?* I've thought a lot about the night he took me out of Petrichor to see the snowy pine trees. The night he kissed me. It was just him and me, and we talked.

Maybe that's what we need. Some time alone, to really talk.

I take a step further down the table.

There's something else that's been bothering me today. What Mark said about happiness, about how we sometimes have to find the things that are missing, be reminded of the things we love.

Since he said that, it's been surprisingly hard for me to recognize what it is *I'm* missing. What it is I *want*.

I have to admit that being able to work as a medic again has helped me a lot. I've appreciated staying busy and having a job to do.

I *want* to find Danny. I'm trying to find Danny, but we're not getting anywhere with that.

"Hey, Alena."

I purse my lips, irritated that someone has interrupted my deep thoughts. I quickly decide to ignore them, but then I realize it's Rusty. I can't ignore *him*. I give him an acknowledging nod as he grabs a plate and steps beside me.

"How's Cody?" I ask softly, pulling my mind from its thoughts.

When Rusty doesn't speak right away, I turn to search his face. His hazel eyes are bright, emitting hope. Hope I haven't seen in a long time.

"She's doing better," he says with a crooked grin. "It's almost as though a friend was able to reach her in a very special way. Thanks, Alena." He winks at me before turning back to the table. My lips twitch. It's good to see Rusty's playful side again. "She actually let me talk to her today," he says. "She didn't talk about her experience, or what happened, but she asked about what was going on around here, and about you."

I add another strawberry to my plate.

"I've been thinking a lot about what Mark said," Rusty says. "About helping someone get back on their feet. About reminding them of the things they enjoy. I had a thought and wanted to run it by you."

I reach the end of the table with barely any food on my plate but give up trying. Instead, I wait for Rusty to finish collecting his dinner.

"Cody loves going on runs," he says, adding a large piece of meat to his overflowing pile. "She also loves her homeland. More than anyone I've ever known. She talks about the beauty of the hills her home sat in. She's loyal to her people, and I think she misses them a great deal, which is what got her into all this." Rusty pauses, sighing deeply before proceeding. "I want to take her on a dropdown. I want to take her home."

I stare at him. He's serious, I'm pretty sure, but he can't be.

"Rusty, there's a war going on over there. And everyone she loves is gone—her family, her friends. Don't you think it will bring back too many bad memories?"

Rusty nods while guiding me to a bonfire close by. The spot offers a perfect view of the setting sun.

"She feels guilty about leaving, about being saved while the rest of her people were not. I talked to her about it today and asked her if she'd like to go back. She didn't respond right away, but when she did, she surprised me too. She wants to go, Alena, to help. I wouldn't take her to the heart of the war, but I figure I could take her to one of the safe towns on the outskirts that hasn't been affected yet. She could help pass out food and clothing." Rusty shoves a forkful of steak into his mouth, not bothering to swallow before speaking again. "Maybe if she helped in a direct way it would ease her conscience."

I shake my head. "I don't know. Is it safe to leave?"

"I talked to the chief. I expected him to shut the idea down too, but he said it would actually solve a few problems for us if we made it more of a humanitarian dropdown/Peppate run at the same time."

I peer at him, trying to understand.

Rusty's expression turns serious. "Chief wants to collect as much power as he can to brace for whatever is coming. The best way to collect power is spread Peppate."

I nod, remembering his already large stash of power.

"I hope he warned you to be careful," I say. Rusty's muscles and combat experience might make him the best candidate to leave Petrichor, but we still don't know exactly what we're up against or how much information our enemies have. I hope the chief has chastised Rusty thoroughly.

"Yes. He made me promise to be careful."

Looking down at my plate and pushing my berries around, I say, "Well, if Cody wants to go back and the chief says it's okay, then I think you have your answer. I hope it helps her."

Rusty swallows deeply before clearing his throat. When he speaks, his voice is barely a whisper. "There's one condition." I push a strawberry in my mouth. "Chief won't let me go unless I take you."

I cough, sure that I misheard. "What?"

"He wants you to morph tomorrow night during the festival." His voice has lowered even more. "With everyone at the bottom of Training Mountain, Petrichor will be empty. You morph, fill Chauly with Doler so he can't camouflage, help us find him, and then I'm to take you and Mark far away from here while the chief gets information from Chauly. Once he has the location for Jax, he'll send it to us. We'll already be out and about. We'll find Danny." Rusty straightens then raises his voice to normal. "Plus, Cody wants you there on the run as well. I told her everything that happened that night, how you were betrayed by Gabbro and Trevor. How you lost Danny. She seemed to soften. I think she's decided to be your friend."

Rusty winks again. I gawk at him before rolling my eyes. *Decided* to be my friend? How nice.

My gaze finds the fire again.

Morph? Tomorrow night? And find Danny? Could our plan really work? My spirits rise then fall. Tomorrow. Morph tomorrow. I have to admit that I'm relieved I won't be the one morphing. But my stomach burns anyway. Will Mark be safe?

My mind then flips to what Rusty just told me. He wants me to go with him after the morph?

"Rusty, what if Jax finds out we left Petrichor and comes after us. As terrible as it is with Chauly here, at least we have hundreds of men and women protecting us. Hundreds of men looking for him. I'm sorry, but I think I should stay here." I lower my voice now. "By the way, Mark is the one that's going to morph. Not me."

Then, I look down at my plate of scant strawberries, feeling my mood slip with my words. Which confuses me. It was the right thing to say, that I shouldn't go along, so why does it hurt so much?

That's when I realize how much I've longed to leave Petrichor. To get away from the glaring faces of the Pepps. I can't leave, I know that, but now that Rusty has offered the chance, I can't help my body from reacting to something it wants so badly.

I sit up straight, noticing the feeling growing. *Is that what I'm wanting? Freedom?*

No, not freedom but the chance to be me without constantly worrying about being watched or making a stupid mistake. To just experience. That's what I miss. Petrichor holds too many bad memories and constantly reminds me of what I've done. *Would leaving Petrichor with Rusty give me some freedom from my own mind? If it did, would it be hard to come back here?*

"We're going to find Danny." Rusty knows just how to tempt me.

I stare at him, watch him toss a large chunk of meat to Bud, who swallows it whole. "I guess what I'm trying to say is that the chief has given me permission to take you. We'll have to be careful, but it might be good for all of us to get away."

A seed of excitement grows within me. Leave Petrichor?

But then I remember Mark. Would he be okay to come along even if Rusty is there?

"Well?" Rusty says.

Gripping my fork, I stab at another strawberry. Smiling as I push it into my mouth. "I'll talk to Mark tomorrow, then let you know."

The wide grin on Rusty's face brightens the night. We both turn to the fire and quietly watch the sunset, before I take out Breccia and send a message to Mark.

He'll have to morph tomorrow night.

I'm gonna try not to think about it.

Chapter 18

Breccia was going to leave again this morning, but I held her back. If I'm leaving Petrichor tonight after the morph, I want her with me.

I'm standing in front of the mirror, my hair still messy from another restless night of sleep.

I promised Rusty I would talk to Mark today about going on the dropdown. He had made the run sound so important and exciting, made me excited to ask Mark. But that excitement is now gone.

What if Mark doesn't want to go? What if he's still angry with Rusty and doesn't want me going either?

I stare at my figure in the mirror. My clothes hang off my body more than they used to, and my eyes are permanently swollen, but for the first time in a long time I have the sudden urge to get myself ready. If I'm going to see Mark today and ask him something so important, I should try to at least look a little better.

I tug on my best pair of Levi's and a loose light-blue shirt. Then I pull my dark-brown hair into high ponytail with a ribbon. Loose strands brush against my temples, but I push them aside.

After placing some darkening makeup on my eyelashes, eyeshadow that brings out the auburn color in my eyes, and olive-colored smoothing powder on my cheeks, I step back. It's been a long time since I've gotten myself ready for the day. It feels good.

Unfortunately, I have to work my morning shift at the hospital before I go see Mark. Maybe by then, though, I'll have formulated an effective way of asking him to go with me.

I make my way to the hospital and work through the first hour slowly. It's one of the last days of the Dino Games, and the injuries have completely stopped. I try not to think about the dino festival going on later, what will potentially happen before they officially shrink the dinosaurs.

I'm a little worried about having the dinosaurs shrunk. What if our morph doesn't draw Chauly out like we want it to? Couldn't we keep the dinosaurs out for a little longer?

I push that thought away.

With no patients coming in, I open my book about viruses and bacteria to distract my heavy mind.

I'm immersed in the book, when a soft humming sound enters the room. It's a Magbaby—one I would know anywhere. Dacite. Mark's Magbaby.

"Dacite?" He lands in the middle of my book. "Is something wrong?" I ask, instantly worried.

He quickly shakes his head. "Nothing's wrong. Mark was just wondering if you'd help him with something today, if you aren't too busy. He's in one of the MossyHollow dino training rooms."

I let out a relieved breath. "Of course." I close my book and stand. The clinic is dead anyway.

I follow Dacite out of the hospital and through the green fields toward MossyHollow.

I wonder what Mark needs my help with. My mood falls slightly when I remember that I need to talk to him about the run, but then I shake my head. It'll be okay.

Dacite enters the large hall of MossyHollow, taking us past all the clothes, the stairs, and the waterfall, to the back of the room. Instead of entering the Dino Covert, though, like I've stupidly done before, Dacite shows me to a door off to the side. "He's in there."

With sweaty hands, I hesitate briefly before pushing the door open. The room looks a lot like the middle of MossyHollow with wooden walls and a tall ceiling of green foliage. It also has the same opening on the far side that's only separated from the dino covert by thick bars crisscrossing up and down. The large gate in the middle must allow passage for dinosaurs, in and out.

I look around and find Dilo first, stomping close to the bars. The fact that her orange frills are slicked back and that she ignores my entrance means she's in a good mood. Maybe she's getting used to me. Bud, who hasn't left my side since my run-in with Chauly, runs to her now.

I feel a soft brush at my right hand, and my body warms. My skin would know that touch anywhere.

But when my eyes find Mark's face my blood runs cold.

He's there leaning heavily against a table, his skin clammy and pale. Something's wrong.

"Hey, Alena." He tugs me into the room, letting the door shut behind me.

"Mark?" I furrow my eyebrows before looking down at the leg he's obviously favoring. I don't have to ask him what's wrong. I know the answer; I can hear it. The infection is back. *But why? Didn't I heal him? Why is it now in his leg?*

My heart sinks further. My plan to include him in Rusty's run won't work. There's no way he could go in this condition. Would Mark let me go without him? Do I even want to go without him?

And why is the infection back?

Mark interrupts my thoughts, a gentle smile creasing his fevered cheeks. "Please don't worry about my leg, Alena. There's something else I wanted your help with."

My eyebrows won't unfurrow. I don't understand. I listen for his elements, quietly observing his vitals.

"I need to take Dilo for a run today," he says. "She's getting antsy, but I can't drive the four-wheeler like this. Would you mind helping me drive?"

He pulls me closer in between his legs. I raise my hand and finger his hot, scruffy cheek. He looks exhausted.

"What's going on, Mark?" I whisper. "Was the serum always in your leg?"

He sighs when I place the palm of my hand over his forehead. I help his fever first.

"No. I just woke up with it this morning." Then he changes the subject again. "Will you go with me?"

He's waiting for my answer, but I focus on the ailment.

When the ringing sounds of infection fade, I gently rub the sweat off his temples. His cool temperature doesn't reassure me. The fever will just come back. I want to try to heal him again with the black power, but Jeter's warnings are fresh in my head. I don't think I should.

"Yes, I'll help you Mark," I finally whisper.

He closes his eyes. "Thank you, Lena."

Dilo approaches now, rubbing her snout against my head, pushing me to the side.

I push back at her. "She seems like she needs a good run."

Bud comes to me too, begging for attention, his head barely reaching my knees. Compared to Dilo, he's tiny.

Mark struggles to stand. I gauge how limited he is at first, if he can walk. It doesn't take long for me to see that he's in pain.

I move my body to his side and wrap my arm around his waist, very aware of the back muscles hard through his shirt. He gazes down at me, slowly draping his arm over my shoulder.

"Thanks Lena."

I nod. When he takes a step forward, he pulls me easily along. I don't know if I'm actually helping him at all, but I grip his shirt tight, too selfish to let him go.

When we step outside, Mark stops. Finding his balance on his good leg, he leans away from me to reach into his pocket for a capsule.

After pushing the button on the end of it, the capsule expands into a four-wheeler. Mark leans onto the vehicle, lifting his body into the seat, then using his arms he drapes his bad leg over to the other side. When he's seated properly, he scoots back as far as he can go, then looks at me and pats the space in front of him.

I remember the last time we sat on this four-wheeler together. Times were better for us then. They weren't stained by bad choices or experiences. I'm saddened slightly. But then things can get better between us, can't they? The crooked grin on Mark's face urges me forward. He must think so.

I step up to the four-wheeler and grip the handle, trying to drape my leg over the seat and sit without touching Mark. It proves to be very difficult. When I'm seated, Mark leans forward and grips the handles, then yanks the throttle and kicks the wheeler into gear. At least I think that's what he's doing. My mind can only focus on his breath close to my ear, his chest pressed against me.

Bud jumps onto the back, and Mark strains to tie him down somehow so he doesn't go flying off. I guess Bud doesn't really need a run. Just an outing.

When he's ready, Mark leans forward and rests his hand on my leg. "Let's go," he whispers in my ear. I glance down at his hand, feeling his warmth, his closeness. I gulp.

Shaking my head to clear my mind, I grip the handles. "Where are we going?"

Mark points at Dilo. "Just follow her."

Dilo is already well ahead of us, so I speed up to catch her. We roll through the fields of grass away from MossyHollow in a direction I've never been. Dilo speeds up, and so do I. The wind blows through my hair, through my shirt, and across my skin. It draws out a smile, one that's been absent a long time. I breathe in the beautiful scene and the freedom I feel in this moment.

Mark eventually moves his hand to hold onto the bars in the back, but his warmth never leaves.

We follow Dilo for over an hour, letting her run until she slows and enters a grove of trees. She finds a large river and stomps through it, gulping up water before collapsing on the shore.

"Let's stop here for a minute," Mark says, tapping my leg again.

Killing the engine, I get off the four-wheeler first and then help Mark, allowing him to lean on my body. He's heavier this time, tired.

I walk him to a nearby tree next to the river and help him sit against it. His breathing is strained, but I try not to worry. His elements sound okay.

I drop down next to him, making sure to leave a little space between us. We sit in silence for a while listening to the quiet gurgling of water flowing over the smooth rocks of the river.

My thoughts return to Rusty's request, but in this perfect moment with Mark, I quietly decide that I'll stay with him. He needs someone to monitor his fevers. That someone should be me.

I pick up a leaf lying in the dirt. I study the lines in it, suddenly realizing that the pestering awkwardness between Mark and me has lessened. At least for now.

I pluck the stem off the leaf. As much as I wish it wouldn't, though, I know the awkwardness will return. There's still too much we haven't talked about, like what happened at SilverDen.

But this moment right here seems too good for that.

So when I speak, I ask him about something else, something safe. Something I've wanted to ask him for a long time.

"Mark?"

He picks up some rocks next to him and throws one in the river. "Yes, Lena."

I fidget with the leaf a moment, trying to gather my thoughts. "Have you learned to accept your totem?"

I feel his gaze on me, but I don't face him. Instead, thinking he might need further clarification, I continue. "When I first got to Petrichor, Danny told me that I needed to learn to accept my totem as a part of me. He said it would make me feel better. But ... I hate it." Meeting his gaze now, I ask my question again, "Have *you* learned to accept your totem?"

Mark nods his head slowly.

"How?"

He grins mischievously and raises his hand to my neck.

"I just think of how it looks on you." His finger traces the vine across my skin. "I can't help but love my totem when I know the other half of it lives in *your* skin."

I shiver at his touch, feeling my lips inch upward. Trying to hide the heat suddenly rising in my cheeks, I look back to my leaf. But when Mark doesn't say anything else, the silence becomes heavy and I have to look back up.

When I do, his jovial expression is gone, and his eyebrows are pressed down hard over his eyes.

"What?" I ask, suddenly worried.

His gaze drops to my lips.

"You smiled," he whispers.

His comment triggers something inside me, opening the door for my stupid emotions. *Blast it!* I clamp my jaw shut, trying to hold everything back, but Mark scoots closer.

I crumple the leaf in my hands and look down in the dirt.

"Why are you still so nice to me, after all I've done to you?" The words spill out.

Mark braces himself on his arm and leans toward me. He doesn't respond for several minutes. Only the rise and fall of his chest and the occasional brush of his breath keeps my frustration at bay. I want to lean into him, listen to his heart beat, smell his black shirt. *Why does he have to look so good in black?*

When he finally speaks, his voice is low.

"You know after that first night we met, at the rendezvous point," he murmurs, his breath brushing against my hair. "I couldn't stop thinking about you. It drove me crazy. I didn't understand it. I knew so little about you. Then I saw you that first time with Danny. I didn't find out until later that you'd been treated so cruelly in Petrichor, practically kept as a prisoner, forced to train for initiation and then physically hurt by Flint. You had every right to hate every single Pepp in Petrichor, and yet, when you saw Danny, you chose to be kind."

My bottom lip trembles and my eyes blur. Mark scoots closer.

"And then when I asked for your help that night with Danny, you came, calmed him down, and talked to me about my dad, giving me more peace about his death than I had felt the entire year since losing him."

Mark's fingers brush against my jaw, gently wiping at my stupid tears.

"You were kind, and I loved you for it." Mark pulls my face upward. I look at him, trying to see him through my blurry eyes.

"Gabbro, Jax, whoever is behind everything, unfortunately, knew about that part of you, and they used it against you. I hate them for that. It wasn't fair. But *I* can't be angry with you. I can't be angry with you for wanting to free those prisoners. I can't be angry with you for doing something kind. Not when that's the reason I fell in love with you in the first place."

Mark's words reach into my heart. It feels as though he's punctured an infectious tumor within me. One that has tormented and pained me for so long ... and now he's letting it bleed out.

I wipe my nose and my face in vain, trying to get myself under control.

"I've missed you, Alena."

My heart rate picks up at his words. I'm grateful I took the time to get ready today, even though I've turned into a blubbery mess already. I bring my eyes to his face and allow them to graze over it. The love for Mark I've been trying to hide because of my own insecurities, since losing Tom and Danny, moves inside me, willing to be set free. His kindness is more than I deserve, but could he think differently?

"Oh, how I've missed you," he murmurs again, his face inching closer.

He hovers there. It's agonizing, feeling his breath, being so ... near.

Then he closes the painful distance between us, his lips brushing gently against my mouth. He's so warm, so achingly warm. His fingers move from my face to my neck, sending tingles down my spine.

And, of course, I cry more.

He pushes his love through me. It tugs on my heart, begging me to let it through. I don't want to fight it anymore. Accepting my totem and everything that's happened might still seem like a daunting task, but perhaps I can rely on Mark's love for me until I find enough strength to love the totem myself.

"Mark," I wrap my hand around his neck.

"Hmm." The sound comes from the back of his throat, but he doesn't give me a chance to respond, moving his lips over mine.

"I've missed you too." My words spill out.

Unable to hold back now, he grips my waist, crushing my body to him. His warmth is everywhere, breaking through the barrier in my heart, washing away the anger and frustration that's been my constant companion since I obtained the vine. My tears fall more. His love is like overwhelming light, sweeping the dirtiness away.

When he pulls his mouth free to kiss the tears on my cheeks and my chin, I swallow hard, trying to catch my breath. Then he's back.

I move my lips with his, finger his jaw, feel the muscles there move as he kisses me. Then I sweep my touch across his scruff, to the back of his neck and into his hair. When I gently pull him closer, a groan escapes his throat and he presses down harder.

My body trembles at his every touch. *Oh how I've missed this good man.*

When his kisses gradually slow, I pull away for air and lean my forehead against his, breathing heavily against him. I let my hands move from his jaw to his chest, where I grip his shirt.

"I love you too, Mark."

I feel so amazingly light that I want to weep even more. *Why can't I ever stop crying?* I'm sure my body is covered in Doler, thick and dirty. But I feel cleaner than I have in weeks.

We sit there a long time, just Mark and me, the feel of his heart beating against my hands.

It isn't until the familiar sounds of infection ring too loudly to ignore that I realize that Mark must be terribly uncomfortable with his leg in this position. Even my bum is going numb.

"It sounds like your infection is coming back," I murmur. "Can I look at your leg?"

He doesn't answer my question, doesn't release me from his arms.

"Please."

He sighs. "Okay."

Breathing him in one last time, I pull away and help him scoot back to the tree so he can lean against it. Then I kneel beside his right lower leg. Carefully, I pull his loose Levi's up past his knee.

I bite the inside of my cheek when I see it.

"Oh, Mark."

Every blood vessel woven through his skin is bulging and swollen. Fluid is pooling around his ankle, puffing it up to twice its size. *How did he even get his shoe on*? I touch the vessels softly, letting my fingertips glide over the abnormality.

"Does that hurt?" I ask.

"No."

I follow the vessels up and around to the back of his knee. I search for the deeper vessels, the arteries. Leaning over, I push harder.

"Does that hurt?"

"No."

He's lying. I can hear the strain in his voice, but I'm grateful he lets me examine him. The vessels are thick and dangerously hard, and they continue that way past the knee. There's also a big knotty bulge just behind his calf, a vessel almost bursting. The skin is swollen, hot, and disturbingly tight.

I need to see his toes. With how swollen he is, his circulation could very well be cut off. I unlace his shoe and remove it without any protests from Mark. When I free his sock, I gasp.

His toes are a deep blue.

"Mark!"

When I glance at him, he's staring at his foot ... unsurprised. *He knew it was like this! And he still insisted we come out here?*

"Mark, I need to get you back. I need to try to recirculate your vessels. I might need help. You could lose your toes, possibly even your foot."

I move to stand, but Mark pulls me back down.

"Please, Alena. I don't want to go just yet. My toes are fine."

No, your toes are not fine!

But Mark's eyes are pleading, desperate. *What do I do?*

Facing him, I slowly sit and tuck one leg beneath me. Then look him right in the eye.

"Can I at least examine your arm to see if there's any serum lodged in it?"

Mark's eyes turn mischievous. "Sure."

Settling right in front of him, I grab his right arm and run my fingers over his skin, searching his deep vessels. Most of them are still soft, but I find a hard one that trails up his shoulder into his sleeve.

"Can I see your chest?"

Mark stifles a smirk, raising a seductive, teasing eyebrow. "Of course, Alena."

I roll my eyes. This isn't funny.

Curling my fingers under the hem of his shirt, I lift it to expose his heart. Then I swallow hard.

Oh.

Maybe this is a bad idea.

Shaking my head, I ignore the abundance of muscles there and focus on the vessels. I press the skin around his totem.

Out of the corner of my eye, I see Mark suppressing a grin.

"Anywhere else you'd like to examine, dearest?"

I roll my eyes again, then look closer. The skin here isn't necessarily swollen, and it's hard to feel the vessels, but there is a wound, tiny, like a pinprick. It's just over the artery leaving the heart.

Mark's warm hand moves to my thigh, pulling at my attention. I gulp. Then his nose brushes against mine, and I fight to breathe amid his gentle touch.

"Mark."

All I see now is his mouth, all I feel is his breath. I was just kissing this man, but it obviously wasn't nearly enough. I itch ... for more.

"Mark," I say again.

Then his lips meet mine, immediately moving in distracting patterns. A groan escapes my own throat, and every lucid thought escapes me.

Fine. The leg can wait.

Still gripping his shirt with one hand, I weave my fingers into his hair and pull him to me.

He willingly responds, gripping my thigh tighter, biting my lower lip.

Oh boy.

It's amazing. How lost and unbalanced I've felt without Mark, but how complete he makes me now.

Mark weaves his fingers into my hair, possessively bringing me closer, kissing me so deeply that every inch of my body responds to him. I melt as his fingers send trails of fire up my back, into my hair, down my thigh.

As worried as I am about Mark's toes, I know I need this. *We* need this.

I can't harness my hands either. They find their way behind his neck, down his biceps, across his stomach.

I don't know how long Mark's lips work through mine, or how long my fingers are lost in his hair, but when our kisses slow and I rest my forehead against his, I realize there's something I need to say. And for my sake more than anything, I need him to hear it.

"I'm sorry, Mark," I whisper. "For injecting you with the serum, and ..." He opens his mouth, but before he can interrupt me, I rush on. "And for keeping so many secrets from you."

His body tenses.

Do I finally have his attention?

I examine his face. His bright expression is gone, replaced by a look of deep hurt. Hurt from not being trusted.

"Thanks, Lena," he whispers.

I know he has more to say. And I need him to say it. I need to know what's in his heart. I patiently wait.

"Can I ask *you* something?" His words rumble through his chest.

"Of course."

"Your muscles." His fingers trail up my arm, sending familiar shivers through my body. "They got more defined before you left for SilverDen. Were you training with Rusty?"

"Yes."

"Did you enjoy it?"

My heart aches painfully. *He thinks I enjoyed it?* Thinks I enjoyed being with Rusty?

I pull away so he can see my face clearly.

"No, Mark. I hated every moment of it. The only reason I survived was I had something to look forward to—seeing you."

Mark's expression relaxes, and the corner of his lip lifts in relief. I lean forward and gently kiss him. I feel terrible that I made him wonder about that. That he thought I would enjoy being with Rusty the way I enjoy being with him. I have a lot of work to do, to prove to Mark just how much he means to me.

Touching his face, I whisper, "You're my favorite person in this whole world, Mark."

There couldn't be a truer statement.

"Thanks, Lena."

Of course, it's in this exact moment the ground vibrates beneath us—two dinosaurs stomping our way. I don't even have time to brace myself before my head gets pushed to the side by Dilo.

Mark chuckles. "I think she's ready to go back."

He's right. We should probably get back so I can heal him.

I'm about to stand, when Mark grabs my hand. I'm surprised at the serious look on his face.

"Alena, to answer your question honestly, about learning to accept the totem, I need to tell you that overall, yes, I have learned to accept it for what it is, but that acceptance didn't come right away. It's required a lot of time. Time has a way of providing new perspective ... through new experiences. Unfortunately, trudging on in the dark until you reach those experiences is hard." Rubbing my hand, he pauses. "Just keep going, Alena. That's all I can tell you. Keep trying. It may take a while, but eventually you'll see light. Even in your totem."

His honesty touches me. This is probably something I'll struggle with for a long time. But if Mark can keep going, so can I, right?

"Thanks, Mark."

He squeezes my hand before letting it go to try to get up.

I help his tired body back onto the four-wheeler, then shift into my spot. Instead of leaning back this time, though, Mark slides his arms around my waist and pulls me close. "Don't buck me off," he mutters low into my ear.

A new energy pulses between us, warm and tender, and I cling to it, never wanting to lose it again.

I start the engine. Dilo is slower this time, which I'm grateful for. If I had to drive any faster, Mark might have to hold on to the four-wheeler instead of me. Plus, this gives us more time together.

Mark's body begins to sag, though, halfway there, and I can tell he's getting weaker. I don't bother asking where he wants me to take him. I head straight for GreenGrotto, where he can get some rest. I park the four-wheeler next to the front door of the mountain, help Mark get off, and then collapse it before assisting Mark inside. He tells me how to tie up Dilo and Bud for now.

We're just steps inside the front doors when we hear it.

A man screaming.

Then we see him, his skin slicked with blood. I scan the room. *Where is everybody?*

Mark removes my grip around him and pushes me toward the Pepp who so obviously needs help. I run to him, listening for the elements, trying not to notice how closely his wounds resemble mine from several days ago, torn skin chunks with curved edges. He was bitten.

I don't even need to ask the man who did this to him. I already know.

"Breccia. Go get the chief."

Chapter 19

Jeter comes running in with the chief. I've healed most of the damaged skin, and I'm almost done restoring the man's blood count. Even though I'm grateful Jeter's here to better my efforts, I'm still afraid of him, of the way he shouted at me before. I jump back to Mark when he approaches and takes over for me.

"Chauly," the chief says. "I knew it was only a matter of time before he started hurting others." Chief turns now, revealing another man behind him—Patrick, the protector who was in the chief's office polishing his guns that one day. "Get your men ready."

Patrick doesn't hesitate. He bolts from the room to carry out his new orders.

Chief kneels next to the man who's still trembling, as if his repaired cells are still recovering from the horror of what just happened.

The chief's eyes slowly rise to look at Mark. I know what's coming, and I hate it.

"It's time."

Time to morph.

"Mark, maybe I should do it," I say, worried about how heavily he's leaning on me. If he can't even stand, then ...

"I'll be okay."

The chief scans Mark, not oblivious to his serious condition. But he doesn't push to agree with me. Instead, he says, "I'll take Alena with me. Give us some time to get to the festival, then go ahead and morph. Circle Petrichor several times, keeping your eyes open for Chauly. If you see him, signal to Patrick and his men if you can."

The festival. That's why GreenGrotto is empty. Everyone is down below Training Mountain.

"What if I *don't* see Chauly," Mark asks, wiping sweat off his forehead, looking like he's going to fall over.

"Come down to the festival. We'll figure things out there."

I stare at Mark. I had agreed to this, agreed to morph, agreed to let him morph for me, but now that it's time, with Mark looking so terribly ill, suddenly I'm not sure.

"It'll be okay," Mark whispers again.

"What if Chauly hurts you?" I point to the man still trembling before us.

"Chauly is trying to *capture* you and me, not kill us. I'll be okay."

That doesn't ease my worries at all. Chauly attacked and almost killed me.

"What if he takes you away? I can't lose you." My voice is rising, but Mark grips my arm and pushes me toward the chief.

"I'll be fine, Alena. Just promise me you'll stay with the chief."

He seems so sure. So stupidly damn sure. I want to tell him I've changed my mind, that I'm going instead. That he needs to rest. But there's something in his eyes. A pleading, begging me to let him do this so I don't have to. The last time I refused his help we were at SilverDen, and things didn't go very well. I need to let him go.

"Fine. I promise."

The chief drags me to the door.

I don't look away from Mark.

"Please be safe." I beg. *Please.*

***

I wave to Dilo and Bud stomping around outside. They should be fine, right? The morph won't affect them, will it?

Chief morphs into the largest, most beautiful eagle I've seen yet. In daylight he's blinding with almost pure white feathers and huge. After lifting into the air, he grips me in his claw and carries me down the mountain. I close my eyes, not wanting to fight against the stinging wind.

I know when we're close to the festival because I hear noise. Lots of noise. Music, with guitars and twang drifting through the air, roaring dinosaurs, clattering metal grinding against itself. I open my eyes.

There in the same open field where Leinani and I stationed ourselves as medics during the Dino Games, is a wide stadium, with bleachers being stacked high. There are dozens of food stands, and Pepps. Thousands and thousands of Pepps. It's absolute chaos as everyone pieces the festival together bit by bit.

Even Issy the communicator has come to enjoy the festival, moving from stand to stand, getting food, and observing the dinosaurs. I wonder if any of the communicators miss Petrichor.

Gates sit to the right of the stadium, breaking off into dozens of compartments where the dinosaurs now wait to be shown off, more at ease than I've ever seen them. Perhaps they're worn out from roaming free this week.

Chief sets me down gently on the green grass, morphs back into his human form, then grips my arm, still pulling me along like a little child.

"Stay with me until we find Chauly."

He hurries around the area to deliver messages to the announcers: that no morphing will be allowed while we're down here, that nobody is allowed to go back to Petrichor until they have *his* permission, and that everybody needs to be on alert for suspicious activity. When the announcers ask him questions, he keeps his answers very cryptic. I think I know why. We don't want Chauly knowing what we're doing if he's lurking around here.

I stumble beside him, looking over my shoulder for Mark. All I see up the canyon are trees. No sign of Mark.

We walk around, my arm getting sore from being pulled to and fro. Time is quickly ticking by, and my worries are deepening. *What if this doesn't work?*

The festival comes together, and soon Pepps are gathering in the stadium. Chief drags me to the other side, which takes forever since the stadium is huge. Then he drags me through the crowds, up the steps, and across the bleachers, until he urgently shoos away Pepps from the seat he wants at the very top. Then we finally sit in the tight space. I just now realize why he chose these seats. They offer a perfect view of the path toward Petrichor.

The crowd roars around us when the festival begins. I watch as the trainers show off the skills of the dinosaurs, some riding on their backs. Others have their dinosaurs sniff out hidden animals. The trainers of the meat-eaters seem particularly proud when they show off the restraint of their assigned carnivore, as chickens, goats, and other live animals prance right in front of their faces. Even I'm impressed when the dinosaurs don't budge an inch. That is, until their trainers say a certain word. Then they swallow an animal in one bite, feathers, hair, and all.

I gulp. Impressive as long as the trainer keeps the dino on the right track.

The air moves around me. The smell of food drifts past my nostrils. The sounds of dinosaurs jumping around and people cheering ring in my ears. Dust floats up from the arena before me, coating my skin and making my nose itch. But I keep looking for Mark.

I don't know how much time passes, maybe another hour.

A large group of eagles comes flying down the canyon. My heart beats rapidly in anticipation, only to drop in frustration when I realize that these are probably the last of the Pepps coming down to the festival. Perhaps those working at the hospital. They morph into their normal forms before joining the crowds of Pepps.

No sign of Mark for a while. We go through about ten dinosaur trainers, all surviving the erratic movements of their dinosaurs, showing off in different ways. The sun drifts behind me, cooling the air and offering shade to those on the bleachers below us.

Then I feel it. The change in the air. The cheers die down. I look around at the confused, somber expressions on the Pepps' faces. They aren't used to the feeling Doler causes. The feeling of sad tar sucking the life out of every cell in your body.

Mark has morphed, and now we're suffering from the effects of the Doler, even from this distance.

I didn't realize how good I've felt lately until this moment of stark contrast. It's like a light quickly being turned off inside, or like a smile sadly fading away. All of a sudden, my mind crashes with memories, bombarding me with the same self-depreciating thoughts I've been fighting so hard to push through.

Chauly is here for the black power. Why haven't I just given it to him? Why didn't I just let him take me? It's my fault Jax took Danny. I don't deserve to be safe when Danny is not.

Everything is my fault. Cody, Mitch ... Tom. All. My. Fault.

Even though I know I felt completely different only a few moments ago, this feeling is so real, so profoundly debilitating, that I want to cry. *It's all true. I am a horrible person.*

And yet, as real as the emotions are, I bite them back, refusing to let them drag me down now. I need to look for Mark. We need to find Chauly so we can then find Danny.

One look around the arena tells me that I'm not the only one feeling these things. But I might be the only one who fully understands what's actually happening. Which gives me an advantage. I know what's going on, so I can fight it.

The only thing the Doler doesn't seem to affect is the dinosaurs. They're naturally full of Doler, so they keep kicking away at their trainers, gaining some ground over the confused Pepps.

Mark must be close. I squint to distract my mind, ready to spot him.

Protectors have created a circular barrier around the bleachers to keep anyone from coming in or out, their long guns perched against their shoulders. The excitement of the games has been snuffed away, and those around us stare angrily in my direction, knowing darn well why they suddenly feel so depressed. Even though *I* haven't morphed, they know the same capability flows in my veins.

I ignore their glares. *Where is Mark?*

A man in front of us spills his dark drink, accidentally drenching the shirt of a woman. I only blink once before the woman is at the man's throat, making irrational dark threats. The man huffs in frustration and moves to morph, when the chief grips his shoulder.

"Nobody morphs!" I clap my hands over my ears at his suddenly amplified voice that thunders through the entire arena.

I wring my hands. *Come on, Chauly … and Mark. Where are you?*

The sun drops more, sending out more shadows that match the dark mood of the arena.

In an attempt to recapture everyone's attention again, two dino trainers come out, chanting something. Another dino trainer opens a gate to a cage holding a medium-sized dinosaur with wild eerie-looking eyes and jerky moving limbs. It's a creepy dinosaur, unlike Dilo, who suddenly seems docile compared to this wild animal.

The stadium goes quiet when one man pulls out a long metal chain.

"Go, White Eye," someone shouts. *White Eye? Is that the name of the trainer or the dinosaur?* I'm going to guess the dinosaur, based on the white color drenching its skin.

I watch White Eye lazily enter the arena, completely ignoring the trainers in front of him. Looking off to the side, he suddenly takes off at full speed, pouncing into the bleachers. He's ready to take a bite out of a girl's arm, when a chain wraps around his neck and pulls back with an incredible force. The dinosaur doesn't hesitate though, using the force of the chain to pull itself closer to the trainer. I gasp when it turns and heads right for the man who held it back, mouth wide open.

I watch the man jump into the air, do a flip over the dinosaur, and land on its back.

Holy crap. The crowd roars in approval, regardless of being filled with Doler. The man tightens his grip on the chain now acting as reins for the dinosaur that's bucking like crazy. This performance is different from the others. The dinosaur isn't controlled, which means the trainer isn't showing off the dinosaur's ability to restrain itself but instead the trainer's own ability to be quicker than the dino. It's a pure show. And it definitely has my attention.

The whole scene reminds me of rodeos I've seen on TV. Men trying to stay on the backs of bulls for more than ten seconds. Riding a bull, though, seems like nothing compared to this dinosaur with its sloped, slippery back. *How in the world is he staying on?*

I bet Mark would be down there doing this same thing. If I hadn't injected that stupid serum into his neck.

I shake the thought away.

Just then a gut-wrenching, agonized scream breaks through the air. Chief immediately stands next to me and scurries across the bleachers. I stand too, my eyes searching for the source of the sound. It's not coming from the man on the dinosaur, who, thankfully, is holding on tight to a jumpy White Eye, regardless of the horrible sound.

My eyes sweep the area. *Where is it coming from?*

Then I find him. There, in the middle of the arena, is a man, running around completely naked. Chauly.

He's here. And he has a metal box in his hand with wires going all different directions. I cringe at the sickening crunching sound that echoes against my eardrums when he hits the metal box to his head over and over again, then screams. Blood drips down his temples onto his cheeks. White Eye's attention turns to him, ready to attack, when I hear the chief's booming voice.

"I need him alive!"

Where is the chief? Where are the protectors?

Dozens of dino trainers swarm the arena, pulling out chains to halt the dinosaur's progression. It takes all of them to get the dinosaur to stop just barely short of Chauly.

Chauly looks up and around for the first time, his face pulled into a horrible grimace, his neck muscles tight, his teeth exposed by a snarl. *What's he doing?* He looks around the arena until his eyes fall on me high in the bleachers.

"What did you do!" He screams, then bangs his head again with the box before shaking it in a sickening way as if he's being tormented into madness. What's wrong with him? Is it the Doler? He's not used to it, and the stark difference in emotion is enough to drive any person completely mad.

Why hasn't the chief captured him?

"Is that a bomb?" someone whispers behind me.

My body chills. Of course. Chauly is obsessive about bombs. And the metal box in his hands looks very much like one.

The chief finally comes into view down in the arena, stepping closer and closer to Chauly. "Please. Put the box down."

Chauly stops banging his head and steps back with wide-eyes, a finger purposefully posed over some button.

"Stop right there," Chauly screams.

The chief stops, but Chauly doesn't remove his finger. Instead, closing his eyes, he presses it down further.

"Everyone get out ...!" the chief shouts, but it's too late.

The ground explodes all around us, blowing up the bleachers down below and sucking the air from my lungs. I bring my hands to my ears and drop down as low as I can into the unsteady bleachers crammed with other Pepps. Flames and smoke engulf us, boiling our skin. I grit my teeth, trying to hold in my scream, but it's pulled from my lungs anyway, joining those all around us. Through the crackles of the flames, whooshing sounds pop through the air. I don't understand what they are until I hear a sucking sound and open my eyes to find a knife imbedded deep into the shoulder of the Pepp next to me.

Knives. It's a bomb loaded with knives just like the one used in the attack on the chief.

I scream again and crumple weakly forward, when one lands in my lower back. I cough through the pain, then focus on breathing one breath at a time while chaos pursues around us.

"I need a medic!" someone shouts, only to be met with the reply, "I can't hear the elements! Why can't I hear the elements?"

My throat is suddenly dry. The goal was to morph and fill Chauly with Doler so that he couldn't hear the elements and would come out of hiding. But in the process, we've crippled the entire Pepp community. Nobody can use power, a phenomenon that's rare and completely disturbing.

A simple Pepp morph would probably solve the problem for the Pepps, but nobody can morph until Chauly is captured. I slide my eyes around the arena, squinting against the smoke. I cough with everyone else, waving my hands in the air, hoping to help the smoke clear. It takes way too long, but eventually I can see enough. There in the middle where Chauly was standing before is a large crowd of protectors, gathered around something. *Please tell me they got Chauly. Please tell me he's alive.*

"I don't have power!" a girl wails next to me.

With my eyes still pinned on the chief, I wait, ignoring the girl.

Then I see him. Chauly, standing on his own two feet, totem removed, naked body tattered to bits, but wrapped in chains. I almost cry out in relief.

It worked! They got Chauly. For once in my miserable Pepp life something went right!

Well, almost. I still need to find Mark. But, first, I need to heal this knife wound.

Everyone should be safe to morph now, right? Chauly doesn't have a totem anymore.

"Morph," I whisper to the crying girl next to me. "Morph, and when you fill up with Peppate again, you'll be able to hear the elements. You'll be able to use your power. Once you have power, will you heal me?"

Her body straightens, and she sniffles back her tears. "Okay. Yeah."

She morphs into her golden eagle form, lifts off the bleachers, and flies through the sky. Others follow suit when they see her. Before I know it, she's back down with me, extending her hands to heal. But her face pales.

"I still can't hear."

Dammit.

She might have morphed and produced Peppate, but until she gets the Doler out of her body, she still won't hear the elements. I inhale deeply.

"You have to get rid of the Doler," I say, forcing my painful body to stand.

"How?"

"Go for a run." That's all I tell her before forcing my way through the crowds. I don't have time for this. I need to find Mark.

Man, I wish *I* could morph and fly. I would cover way more ground that way. I search the crowds for a familiar face, someone willing to help me find Mark, but the area is chaos, smoke, fire, frantic injured Pepps screaming. Precious seconds are ticking by. The muscles pull angrily in my back against the knife, sending shots of pain everywhere. At least the knife didn't hit something important. I squint at the crowds around me.

Where is Mark?!

"Alena!"

I spin on my heel to find Rusty running toward me, his blond hair disheveled, his face covered in dirt. I bend over and rest my hands on my knees in relief. *Oh, thank you, Rusty!*

"Alena, Chief wants us to leave Petrichor now, go on a dropdown, and be ready to look for Danny. Are you ready?"

"No." I shake my head. "I need to find Mark."

Rusty's face cringes when he finally sees my condition. "Alena, you have a knife in your back."

You think I don't know that!

He grips my arm to support me. "Do you have power? Can you heal yourself?"

"I can't hear the elements." I pant. "I can't heal."

Rusty's face falls. "I can't hear them either. It's okay." Rusty purses his lips, then before I can stop him, his hand reaches out and yanks the knife out of my back.

Pain ripples through my back, up to my shoulder, into my head, drawing a scream from my lungs.

I clench my fists. "Rusty! You could have warned me!"

Rusty takes a bandage from his satchel and starts wrapping it around my torso. "It's best to just get it over with. Here. I'll bandage you up for now, and then we'll go find Mark."

Rusty wraps the bandage around and around, but the blood quickly leaks through the fabric, sticky and warm.

"It'll have to do for now," he says, then morphs into his large eagle form, rises off the ground, and picks me up with his claws. The movement and confinement send all sorts of pain through my body, but I force myself to breathe.

Before long, we're flying toward Petrichor. This time, I force my watery eyes to stay open, searching the ground beneath me for any signs of

Mark. He was supposed to join the festival if he never found Chauly. And since I know he never found Chauly, I can't help but feel that something is terribly wrong.

It only takes a few minutes of flying before I see the shadow of a black shirt peeking through the trees.

"There!" I shout to Rusty. He hears me and instantly redirects his wings. I plop to the ground the moment Rusty's claws release me and stumble toward Mark.

My body slows when I see him, trembling uncontrollably. I swallow.

"Oh, Mark." He's holding his shaking, bleeding leg.

"Sorry ..." The word squeezes out through his clenched teeth. "I couldn't quite make it all the way."

I gingerly drop down next to him, my eyes trained on his pants soaked with blood.

Taking a knife out of my sleeve, I quickly cut the tough fabric of his pants up to his shaking thigh. The air leaves my lungs. I've never seen anything like it. His entire leg is swollen to more than double its normal size, with deep striations digging into the swelling, oozing blood that now pools in the dirt below. The vessels that were hard and bulging before are shredded and bleeding as if stretched beyond their limit. They must have resisted the morph because of the serum pulsing within them.

His leg is shredded to bits, and he's bleeding to death.

I need to heal him. But I can't hear the elements!

I clench my fists and close my eyes. *Please! I need to hear the elements!*

Mark's bloodied hand reaches for mine, and I open my eyes.

"Just breathe, Alena. Slowly, in through your nose and out through your mouth. Allow yourself to relax."

Relax! I search his brown eyes. How the heck am I supposed to relax?

But I do as he says. I close my eyes and breathe. It's agonizingly hard—with Mark bleeding to death in front of me. I want to scream at the Doler, tense my muscles so much that it'll just be forced out of my body.

But that's not how it works.

In and out. Mark trembles; his breath shudders in pain.

I stand and move away, to a tree where I can't hear him suffering. I lean my forehead into the bark, my bottom lip trembling. *Please!*

In through my nose, out through my mouth.

"You're welcome to take off my shirt again if that helps you ..." Mark strains to get the words out. It's not funny. And yet a smile tugs at my lips, remembering the feel of his warm skin beneath my fingertips, the feel of his lips pressed against mine.

I'm looking back at Mark, shaking my head, when I feel it. Fresh Doler pushing through my skin, littering my arms with black dust.

No way. That worked?

The sounds are light but there. *I can hear!* I full-on smile and run back to Mark. I take in an even deeper breath now with new purpose, filling my lungs to their max and then releasing it slowly. The sounds get stronger.

I immediately get to work repairing what I can, grateful I still have some power left.

"That did the trick, did it?" Mark teases, his leg still shaking. "I'll have to remember that."

I ignore him and repair the vessels first, to stop him from bleeding out. Then I redirect the blood so it doesn't pool in his leg. I work around the serum, healing, calming, and pushing the skin back together. Then I restore the blood supply.

When I've done as much as I can, I dig the heels of my hands into my eyes.

"I'm guessing he probably shouldn't go with us?" Rusty says next to me. I almost forgot about him.

"Go with you where?" Mark's body is slumping against the tree now, his tired voice grinding against itself.

I clench my teeth. I already made my decision to stay behind, but I should have explained things to Mark. I clear my throat. "Chief got Chauly. Now he wants us to leave Petrichor, go on a run. Once the chief gets the information on Danny's location from Chauly's memories, he wants us to go find him." I turn to Rusty. "But I've decided we're not going. Mark is sick, and I need to be here with him, to help his fevers."

Warm fingers brush my jaw, silencing everything around me, slowing my thumping heart. I look at Mark.

"You should go," he whispers, his fingers brushing against my cheeks.

I draw back. "No, Mark, I need to stay here with you. I ..."

Mark doesn't bother hearing what I have to say. Looking at Rusty, he says, "Take her, please."

I don't know whether to be offended by Mark's gesture or grateful. "Why ...?" I try to ask, but he looks at Rusty again. With a tip of his head, he sends a silent message asking for some privacy. Rusty nods and takes a walk into the trees.

Mark sits up and takes my hand, rubbing the inside of my wrist.

"I don't want you to go, Alena. But this place isn't good for you. You need to *get out of here.* Since I can't take you myself, I guess Rusty is the best option I have." He cups my cheek with his other hand. "Go find Danny." I try to interject, but Mark hushes me. "Please. Just promise me you'll be safe?"

"Mark, I really don't want to go."

Mark shakes his head impatiently. "You *need* to go."

My chin trembles. I just found him again. I don't think I can leave. I breathe in his smell.

What do I do?

I lean into his hand still cupping my cheek. "Will you at least let me try to heal your leg? Will you let me try the black power again? If it doesn't work, I'll need to mess with your vessels."

I look at his face.

That teasing twitch in his lips has returned. "Alena, you can do whatever you want to my body."

I scoff, failing to hide the blush in my neck.

"Come on. Let's get back to Petrichor," he says, trying to get up. I jump to my feet and help him. Once we're standing, he drapes his arm around my shoulder and kisses my head.

"Rusty, you can come out now," he says. When Rusty steps through the trees, Mark asks. "Can you carry both of us?"

Chapter 20

I hate this.

I grip my seat tightly. The last time I was in an aircraft was when I was coming back from SilverDen. I don't remember much of the ride home; I was too distracted by the events of the night. But I do remember how I felt, and those feelings are surfacing plentifully now. For some reason going on a run, in my mind, did not involve getting on one of these horrible aircrafts. Rusty had to explain to me that we have a long journey before us, and getting a head start with the aircraft is smart.

I try to relax and let go of my seat, gripping my satchel instead. It's bulkier than normal, the electric belt stuffed inside. The knot in my stomach tightens even more. I never want to use it again, but it's the best weapon I have. So I brought it just in case—and the knives I've carefully planted under my sleeves.

I glance sideways at Cody sitting next to me. Instead of nervously gripping her seat like me, she's practically chewing her lip off.

She looks much better than she did when we first found her. Even though her cheekbones still stick out oddly, a light-pink color has returned to her face, and her blonde hair is brighter and thicker than it was.

She's even applied brown eyeshadow and black eyelash cream to enhance her bright-blue eyes. Once again, she's stunning.

She leans back into her seat now and takes in a measured breath.

Rusty, who's sitting on the other side of her, looks my way. For a moment, I can see within his eyes the same relief I feel knowing that Cody is doing well enough to leave her room at the hospital. But then it's replaced with worry. She's doing better, but she still has a long way to go.

Sepharine advised Rusty to keep a close eye on her. Going to her homeland could do her good, but it could also trigger her in a way that we might not be prepared for. Before I got on the aircraft, Sepharine gave me a shortcut phrase to use on Cody in case of an emergency. It's supposed to shut down the overactive parts of the brain. It would help her relax in the event of uncontrollable emotions. She said Cody won't even know I'm doing it.

I lean my head back now too. Over the loud screech of the pieced-together aircraft, I can hear the faint ring of power in my ears, thanks to the full vial of power Rusty gave me moments ago.

I sigh inwardly. With the chief's permission, I used the rest of my black power to heal Mark's leg. I got a lot of serum out, more than seemed reasonable, but that hasn't eased the heavy brick of worry sitting in my gut. It was odd, the serum. This time it seemed to be lodged in Mark's blood vessels instead of the muscles. I was able to extract it easily, but I have a feeling the serum will return, bringing with it the fevers and infections. And I won't be there to help him. I probably should have asked Jeter to keep an eye on him, but I'm still afraid of the man. So, I asked Scance instead.

Suddenly, in the middle of the aircraft, an animal appears out of nowhere. I jump at the appearance of it, drawing my legs up instinctively.

The walrus plops around on its belly, making the aircraft bounce in the air. When it starts rocking the airplane sideways, the pilot shouts back, "Stop it, Sef!"

I should be used to Pepp surprises by now, but I can't seem to slow my racing pulse.

Our Pepp team sitting against the walls of the craft start throwing shoes, pens, and food at it. Finally, the walrus changes back into a young man.

"Okay, Okay!" he shouts, holding up his hands in surrender. The Pepps stop firing and let him get up.

"He's a morpher," Rusty whispers over Cody, seeing my nervous look. "They're very convenient to have on runs. Morphing into an eagle is obviously easy for most Pepps, but to morph into other animals, you have to have an extensive knowledge of the makeup of each species and all their predators, not to mention the languages they have to learn to speak. They're pretty skilled."

Sef hears Rusty's compliment and puffs out his chest in response.

Cody rolls her eyes. "They might be skilled, but every morpher is always extremely immature."

I laugh. Then observe the man. He's not too tall and has brown hair and dark skin. It isn't as dark as Bapoto's but still a dark-chestnut color. His nose is a little longer, and he speaks with a different accent that hosts a lot of *D* sounds in place of the *T*'s. He's different, maybe immature, but also polarizing. I find myself drawn to him. He reminds me a little of Caleb.

"Anybody want to air ski?" Sef asks, walking toward the back cabinets. I'm reminded of my first experience on one of the Pepps' aircrafts, when the boys tied themselves to the floor and jumped out the back hatch. I thought they were going to die.

"No," Cody shouts at him.

Thankfully, the pilot intervenes. "You can't. We're almost there."

I turn my head at the sound of the pilot's voice, and my body stiffens. It's the first time I've really looked at him. He looks sickly. But his body is filling out. Even his eyebrows and eyelashes look like they're in the state of repairing themselves.

"Cody," I whisper. "Is he—?" I don't point, but I let Cody follow my look.

"Yes, Alena. He's one of the prisoners you got out. His name is Luis."

The man turns around to speak again, but his eyes catch mine. He smiles at me quickly, and then says what he has to say. "Five minutes."

I turn away. He's the man I saw in the room just down the hall from Cody. The one who took the time to say thank you. I swallow. He's okay. That comforts me. A lot.

The team comes to life. I look around at the six other Pepps asked to participate in this run. Other than Rusty and Cody, there are two more I know.

Kapri.

Rusty must have asked her to come along. I'm sure she easily agreed, especially if he told her we'd be looking for Danny.

And then there's Harper. Our protector.

Standing now, Kapri places her satchel around her waist, preparing for the drop. Her curly, golden hair is pulled away from her face in a tidy ponytail. She moves gracefully but quietly. I don't think she's said a single word on this aircraft, and watching her hazel eyes bounce nervously off mine, I would say she still doesn't love being around me.

"Everyone, listen up," Rusty demands. The space quiets—at least as much as it can with the loud shuddering of metal. "We're gonna drop down here and fly for the rest of the day. The chief wants us to spread as much Peppate as possible as we head to the GreenLands, while he gathers information from Chauly. It'll be tiring, but if you can all be strong, our reward tonight will be to sleep at a rendezvous point instead of in our own tents."

Several Pepps shout their approval at this news.

A young man with lots of freckles on his face looks particularly excited.

"I'll carry you on my back," Cody whispers to me, holding out a rope. "When we're in the air, tie yourself to my torso."

I eye Rusty, silently asking him if that's a good idea, but Rusty simply nods. "When you're tired, Cody, let me know, and I'll take her."

I'm surprised he's allowing it. But then I take the rope, recalling the first time I met Cody. She had such a strong spirit. Maybe I need to let her feel strong again.

The back hatch suddenly opens, and wind whips through the aircraft. Everyone moves toward it and gets ready to jump.

Suddenly, my hands feel very sweaty. I've never done this before. Even though I know the chances of me actually getting hurt with so many Pepps around are slim, I still feel nervous.

"Here, get on my back," Cody says. It's awkward piggy-backing her tiny frame. We both laugh nervously when we wobble, but then, before I know it, Cody has jumped into the air after the others.

I tighten my arms around her neck, burying my face in her back. I try to force my stomach down my throat while Cody lets us freefall, but then her skin changes into something soft, feathery, and wide. Afraid of losing my grip and falling off, I grasp at Cody's feathers, but she looks back. I'd say she doesn't like that. Remembering what she said about the rope, I force my sweaty fingers to wrap the rope around us.

Her torso is huge, though, in bird form, and it takes me a minute to grab the rope with my other hand with the wind blowing it around. When I finally get it, I tie it around me, instantly feeling more secure. I pull my head up and look around, the wind drawing tears from my eyes. The scene below steals my breath away, with snow-covered mountains, white clouds, and tall pine trees for as far as I can see.

Why are we in mountains? I look around the land. Weren't we supposed to head in the direction of the GreenLands? This definitely isn't what I expected the *GreenLands* to look like.

I search the group, examining each of their bird forms. I recognize Rusty's golden-feathered figure in the front, leading the way. The others range from blond-feathered, to brown-feathered to speckled-feathered. Kapri is probably the blonde one. The freckled boy is probably the speckled one.

I wonder what I looked like in my bird form.

We fly for hours, spread out, my teammates morphed into the creature that was designed to spread Peppate most effectively. Unlike Doler, I can't see the Peppate, but I can definitely feel it. It seeps into my tired body, replacing the worries that have plagued me so much lately with a sort of peace. The only thing missing—the only thing that would make this better would be to have Mark here.

Eventually, the sun drops until it hovers over the horizon in front of us. It sends out blasts of flaming orange and red colors that reach far into the sky. They paint the clouds, trees, and even the Pepps beautiful sunset shades.

As soon as the sun slips out of sight, though, the air grows cold and dark. Flying at night isn't nearly as entertaining, so I lay my head on Cody's back to rest. I can feel her speed slowing, her flying becoming more strained. I hope for her sake we land soon.

Thankfully, we do. Rusty starts dropping toward the trees, and soon I'm covering my face with my arms, trying not to get scratched by the branches.

Seeing the dark ground approaching, I brace myself for landing, but it does no good. Cody thuds down, and my head jerks forward, falling into cold snow.

Snow?

I untie myself from the ropes and roll off Cody before looking around. We've landed in a clearing, and in front of us I see a dark building waiting silently. It takes a couple of moments for my tingling legs to cooperate, but when I finally get them to work, I stand and take a step toward the building behind the others.

But then I stop.

I know this place.

The rendezvous point where I first met the Pepps, where I first met Mark. It's where I last saw my brother, Caleb. It's the rendezvous point closest to my home. Weren't we supposed to be headed toward the GreenLands? The other direction?

Almost everyone is inside, when I see him. My twin brother, Caleb, squeezing through the crowd, coming out of the building toward me. A surge of emotion explodes in my heart without warning, and I begin to sob. With a face-splitting grin, he finds his way to where I stand.

"Hey, Alena." I hear emotion catch in his throat as he wraps me in his arms. I cling to him. Others call out my name, and my heart swells more. Mom and Dad. I can't even pull away in time to look at them before their arms embrace both Caleb and me.

I stand there encircled by the ones I love, the ones I've missed so terribly. I both laugh and cry. Oh, how I'd forgotten what it feels like to be loved by family.

"Let's get you inside, Alena, before we all freeze," Dad says. Wrapping his arm around me, he guides me to the front door of the cabin. I stare at it as we walk through. Mark brought me through here. He took me to the large gathering room in the back where I first saw the Pepps, and where I was first exposed to their healing power. I remember Caleb lying on the couch with a broken leg. He was so easily healed ... by Scance.

Laughter echoes down the hall now, from that gathering room. My team must be back there, maybe getting some much-needed food. But that isn't where my family takes me. Instead, they guide me down a different hall, up some stairs, and into another, smaller gathering room with velvet carpet and log walls.

A kitchen lit with lanterns emits the smell of a familiar home-cooked meal. Enchiladas. My favorite. A fire blazes to my left, immediately warming my cold skin. I quickly search the room, finding more friendly faces.

"Jess?" And her family, including Rick. I didn't know there was so much light left within me. So much happiness. But, sure enough, it comes up now, filling me to the brim. *My friends!*

Jess comes to me and pulls me into her arms. "Oh, I've missed you, Alena."

Rick comes to me too but stands awkwardly before settling for a hard pound on the back instead of a hug. I laugh before wrapping my arms around him. I can't let him get away without a hug. Even if it is *Rick.*

When I pull back, I find everyone looking at me. It's been a little over five months since I've seen them all. They look as though a day hasn't even passed. Yet my mind frantically soaks in every feature. It's been too long.

"I don't understand," I say.

Retrieving a piece of paper from his pocket, Caleb walks to me.

"We received this message earlier today."

I take the paper and read the words.

Alena will be there later tonight. It'll be a surprise for her. She won't be able to stay long, but she needs to see you guys.

Mark.

I stare at the words through my blurry eyes. *He set this up? For me?* He must have talked to Rusty when I was packing my stuff. I glance at Caleb for more of an explanation, but he doesn't speak.

"I have so many questions," I whisper to them.

"So do we," Mom says before ushering us over to the dinner table.

"Why are you all still here?" I ask, taking a seat at the table. "I know the chief wanted to keep you safe after initiation, but I guess I thought you would have been able to go home by now." Suddenly I feel guilty. I haven't communicated with my family at all. I should know this.

Dad speaks for the group, "No, the chief still believes we're in danger, and since the Brown family was aware of your condition, he advised they come here too."

I hang my head. "I'm sorry. I didn't realize you'd all have to stay couped up here because of me."

"Alena, don't be sorry," Mom says, moving the food from the kitchen to the table. "We've actually really enjoyed our time here. And the chief has kept us busy with some fascinating things."

"Like what?"

So much for sitting at the table and eating. Dad stands and signals for me to follow. He opens the door to a room beside the fireplace and walks inside, then lights a tall candle. I slowly enter. The room is tiny and crammed full of stuff. I see papers, lots of papers, pinned on the walls and scattered on a wide table sitting in the middle of the room. A small refrigerator has been shoved into the shadowy corner, and a glass box sits on the far side of the table next to a well-used microscope.

"Your chief has asked us to study totems to see if we can figure some things out."

Totems? What things?

Stepping closer, I look at the glass box. Sure enough, there's a totem inside.

But something next to the totem catches my eye.

Two wide glass vials filled with an eerie chunky red substance sit there.

"What is that?" I ask.

Dad clears his throat and looks hesitantly at my mother before responding. "Those are blood vessels from a Mixed Blood."

"What?" *Mixed Blood? Those born sick from Pepp-Human relationships*? Dozens of questions flood my mind. *Why are they studying vessels of a Mixed Blood? Did they hurt a Mixed Blood to get them? Have they found anything relevant?*

Dad runs his hand through his hair, a nervous tic I've sorely missed. "You probably already know this, but totems were created by taking Peppate generators from the blood vessels of a pure-blood Pepp and putting them into the branches of a totem tree. The tree where all totems come from."

I nod. I do know this.

"Well," Dad continues. "Your totem is different. Instead of Peppate generators, your totem is full of Doler generators. Question is: Where did they come from? A human?" Dad shakes his head. "Your chief doesn't think so. He thinks they came from the blood vessels of a Mixed Blood. He's asked us to study the Peppate generators found in a normal totem to see if there's something similar in the vessels of the Mixed Bloods."

I furrow my eyebrows. "A link between the Mixed Bloods and *my* totem? And he wants *you* to figure it out?" I don't say it out loud, but isn't this something that should be handled by the Pepps, not my dad? The Pepps have power and more understanding.

Dad senses this question as well. His eyes pass to the doorway where Dr. Brown is now standing. Lowering his voice, he says, "The chief believes there are some in Petrichor he cannot trust. Mainly the medic? But I guess he trusts us enough to ask for our help."

I furrow my eyebrows. *The chief is doubting Jeter.* I remember overhearing Jeter's conversation with Patrick in the chief's office. He had said someone was watching him. Did he mean the chief? And why?

"We've just barely been able to grasp how the normal totems work," Dr. Brown says, pulling a paper off the wall. "The generators, which are located throughout the totem, generate the Peppate."

I analyze the diagram drawn on the paper in his hands. It strongly resembles the pictures I found in the library book. The tadpole-like structure.

"This is where Peppate is made," he says, pointing to the head. "And this is the channel that extends through the skin and takes the Peppate into the air." He moves his finger to the sac that sits next to the joint of the generator and channel. "This is where the power is created and stored until it's pushed through to the heart of the totem."

I nod, impressed that they've already learned so much. Then I observe the vessels sitting on the table.

"So, have you found anything in the vessels of the Mixed Blood?"

Dad runs his hands through his hair again.

"Yes, we found generators. *Doler* generators."

I furrow my eyebrows. "Mixed Bloods have *Doler* generators too? Like humans?"

"Humans have Doler generators, but their generators don't have a power sac. Hence no power in humans," he says, pulling out another paper with a diagram on it. "But." He points to a new diagram in his hand. At first, it looks like a normal Peppate generator, but when I look closer, I realize there's one difference. "The Mixed Bloods not only have one power sac, they have two," Dad whispers.

I draw back. So, whoever created my totem took the Doler generators from a Mixed Blood and put them into a new totem. And they did it for power. I'm sure of it. But then I have a new question.

"Why did they need to take the generators *out* of a Mixed Blood and put them into a totem? If these generators are truly inside the vessels of a Mixed Blood, can't they just morph or something, activate that power, and use it for whatever they need it for?" My mind goes back to the purebloods in Petrichor. The Pepps who don't need a totem. The Mixed Bloods sound similar to them.

Dad shakes his head. "The Mixed Bloods don't have *access* to their own power." He sighs, and my confusion deepens. "We think it has to do with the extra sac on their generator. We're not sure what's inside that sac, but whatever it is, it's somehow deactivating the power the Mixed Bloods are capable of."

I sit, trying to process what he's telling me.

"I wish we could examine your totem further," Dad says. "If we could just see how many sacs are attached to your generators, we could confirm our theory. See, we believe that whoever created your totem knew the potential of the Mixed Bloods' power, and in order to take advantage of that potential they removed the second sac from Mixed Bloods generators, and then placed them into a blank totem. Your totem."

I scrutinize my totem. Is that true?

The room is quiet until another thought enters my mind.

"So, the Mixed Bloods are potentially like me." The thought makes me kind of sick. "Does that mean they have the same type of power as me? The ability to create lightning?"

"We think they do have the same ability, but they *can't* right now," Dad says. "Probably because of that extra sac." Dad rubs his face. "Then there's the question of why the totem was split in two. Every other normal totem is only one piece. Why was Mark told to put one on first and then the other? Was it dangerous to put them on together?" Dad puts his hand on my shoulder. "We're working hard to figure it out."

I study the room, the papers, the totem, the Mixed Blood Vessels. Then I step forward and wrap my arms around Dad's broad torso. "Thank you." He's doing all this ... for me. I don't know of a smarter person that could be assigned this task.

He's holding me, resting his chin on my head, when my eyes land on the small refrigerator in the corner flickering in the candle light.

"What's that?" I ask, pulling away.

"Oh, that's where the Pepps keep their memory bugs." He walks to it and opens it up, letting out a puff of white mist. When it clears, I see four black bugs sitting on the frozen shelf.

I shiver. "Why do you have memory bugs here?"

"There used to be a lot of Clan spies that came around the rendezvous point. I guess the Pepps would capture them. Then when Jeter could make it down, he'd use these memory bugs to extract what he could from the men. He hasn't bothered to come pick them up." Dad shuts the fridge. "There aren't many men that come around now, though. It's been pretty quiet."

Probably because I killed them all.

The cramped room grows quiet, and I study everyone's faces. Dad, Caleb, Dr. Brown. "So, you basically all work for the Pepps now?"

They nod, but instead of seeing disappointment on their faces, which is what I would have expected to see, I see a great deal of pride. They enjoy it.

"You would be great Pepps." I sigh.

"Yes, we would," Mom says behind everyone. Then, gently pushing Caleb and Jess to the table, she adds, "Why don't we eat some dinner. I'm guessing you're hungry after your long flight."

We make our way back to the table and quickly catch up on everything that's gone on the past few months. At first the conversation is lighthearted, until Mom asks me what happened at SilverDen. Then the room draws quiet. I don't want to tell them. I've enjoyed having conversations with people who are unaware of my mistakes. They've treated me like a normal human being, and I don't want to lose that.

But they should know the truth.

So, I put my fork down and explain what happened. Every detail, before, during, and after SilverDen. It's crushing to relive everything again, to put memories into words. I stare at my hands tightly wound in my lap, hoping to keep my emotions in check. But when I get to the part about Mitch dying, I can't hold my tears back. They just leak out. And so do the words. I couldn't stop them now even if I wanted to.

My family listens. Nobody says a single word.

When I have nothing else to say, I blink my eyes, wipe my nose, and stare at the salad on my plate.

The room is silent. And the silence stretches on. Mom reaches over the table and rests her hand on mine. I know it's a gesture of love, but right now it stings. Once again, I feel unworthy. I can't bring myself to see the disappointment on their faces.

I don't know what I expected. *Isn't this why I never wrote them?* I knew how it would make me feel. I knew it would possibly change the way they see me forever. It was stupid to share. Stupid to think it would be okay. Why couldn't I have kept it simple—just told them some of the things that happened, not everything?

They still don't speak, and my hands start shaking. Why don't they say something?

I'm almost ready to pull my hand back and leave the room, when Caleb pounds the table.

"Dammit, Alena!"

I jump at his unexpected outburst.

"Why do you get to have *all* the power?" He throws his hands into the air. "Man, after letting you go that day, I've done nothing but dream about how cool it would be to become a Pepp like you. But now I would never settle for just *normal* Pepp power. You can create lightning? And survive it?" He looks at Jess, who's sitting next to him. "Do you remember Colton Joe in fifth grade? He played that prank on me by wrapping my school chair with wire, then placing it in the outlet nearby?"

Jess chuckles, showing off her pretty teeth. "Yes. You should have seen your hair. It stood straight up. And then you made these weird gurgling noises until Mrs. Wood could get the maintenance guy in there."

Caleb stares at Jess with wide eyes. "It's not funny, Jess. I could have died."

Dad shoves a forkful of salad into his mouth. "From what I remember, you deserved it, Caleb. Didn't you tie him to the train track down the canyon?"

Caleb waves his hand. "That was hardly a prank. There wasn't a train for hours. I finally had to let him go because we had to get home for dinner."

Mom snorts across the table and removes her hand from mine. I look up to see her smiling as she pushes a forkful of food into her mouth.

"Besides, I was grounded for a week after that. That was punishment enough."

"Colton obviously didn't think so." Mom picks up the bowl of rice and hands it to Caleb and Jess.

"All I'm saying," Caleb says, taking the food, "is that with Alena's powers I could finally get back at him for what he did to me."

"By killing him?" I mutter.

"I wouldn't kill him," Caleb says, dishing food for himself, "I would take him back down to that train track. I'd tie him to the rail, and then fly miles away. You said that the power only reached a certain distance, right? Well, I would travel that distance. Then I would produce electricity and let it travel down the metal of the train track, giving him little zaps. When the train came, he would have a chance to say he was sorry for what he did to me. If he chose to, I'd let him go."

"How would you know when the train came, or whether he was saying sorry if you were so far away?" Jess asks.

Caleb thinks for a moment. "That's a good point. I guess I'd just have to zap him until I felt restitution had been made."

Dad scoffs. "Hopefully, he doesn't get hit by a train."

Caleb passes the enchiladas to me, and I take them, my hands freezing midair. I look around the table at each of the faces there. Jess punches Caleb's arm for telling such a grotesque story, and Rick starts backing Caleb up, adding new ideas. Dad inhales his food and talks to Dr. Brown about the totem's electricity. Mom and Mrs. Brown continue passing the food.

And just like that, they've forgiven me and moved on.

My bottom lip trembles, and I stare at the enchiladas in my hands, biting back new tears. They heard what I did, what I've become. They had the chance to reject or chastise me. But, instead, in a very direct way, they've shown that they still accept me for who I am. That my mistakes haven't changed the way they feel about me.

My eyes get blurry.

I didn't know how much I needed that until this very moment. I just needed to feel loved.

The conversation lightens quite a bit after that. I answer their questions about Petrichor, but mostly I just sit and breathe in the scene, trying to soak in every feature of my family's faces, the sounds of their laughs, the colors of their eyes. I want to hold on to this moment.

Silently, I thank Mark. I can feel a part of my heart beginning to heal. He knew I needed this. I needed something familiar, something hopeful.

We stay around the table well into the night, and even though I'm tired, I don't want the time to ever end. Unfortunately, it does, and before I'm ready, everyone is retiring to their rooms. Mom shows me to mine.

Standing outside the door, she turns to me. I observe her bright auburn eyes that shimmer in the candlelight. Gripping my face, she softly says, "I love you, Alena, so very much."

Of course I start crying. I don't deserve those words, but they soften my heart all the same. I recall all the times my mother comforted me throughout my life. The times she simply listened when I needed someone to listen. I suddenly feel vulnerable, wishing to share my true feelings with her.

Looking down at my left arm, I whisper, "You love me, even with this defected totem on my arm?"

Mom seems shocked at my comment, but then understanding dawns. Staring me straight in the eyes, she says, "Alena, your totem does not define who you are. You are just the same beautiful, fun, and loving girl I had the chance of knowing from the time you were a baby. The totem on your arm didn't change you, it just made life harder for you, but I believe you'll find a way to manage that." Rubbing my cheek, she lets her words settle. "I'm glad you have someone in Petrichor who's taking care of you. I have a feeling Mark will help you remember who you are."

When I glance at my mom's face again, the light in her eyes is gone, replaced with tears.

Oh no, Mom, don't cry.

"It's hard to let you go, you know," she says. "To let you go out there where I know you'll get hurt. I don't want to let you go back to Petrichor where so many bad things have happened to you." Her tears fall down her cheeks. "You do know that you can stay with us, right?"

I nod. I do know that. There was a time when that was all I wanted, to return to my family. But she's right. There's more I need to do.

"I need to find Danny."

I pull Mom into an embrace. It's odd, after going through so much, seeing so much death, I've realized how fragile life is. I find myself questioning if I'll ever see her again. See any of my family again. It's sad that dark experiences can do that to you.

All too soon, she pulls away.

"Thank you, Mom. I love you."

Wiping the last of the tears from my face, she tells me she loves me one last time before disappearing down the hall into her room.

***

Opening the door to my room, I find Caleb on a pile of blankets stretched out on the floor. "Hey, Lenny, because I love you, and because I've missed you, and because Dad told me I had to, I'm going to let you sleep on my bed tonight."

I roll my eyes. Caleb has his own room, with his own bed. Dad told me so, but I wouldn't send Caleb away for anything. Somehow, he knows I need him here tonight.

"Thanks, Caleb."

I take off my satchel, lay it on the bedstand, and climb into the blankets. I should go to sleep, but my mind is still spinning. Looking down at Caleb, who's staring back at me, I find that he's not so tired either.

"So, you and Jess are still a thing?" I say, propping my head on my hand.

Caleb looks up at the ceiling, putting his hands behind his head. "Oh yeah. She's just great. It didn't take much for her to agree to come live here with me." Caleb winks. Then a little more serious, he adds, "Mark seems pretty great too."

I sigh. "Yeah. He is." Then I narrow my eyes at him. "How often does he write you?"

"Well, if I don't hear from him at least once a week, I send him threatening messages. He's gotten pretty good at keeping me updated. It's just been the past couple weeks that I haven't heard much. You know, after the silver mine thing." Caleb eyes me seriously. "Are you doing okay?"

I lie back on my bed, observing the wooden ceiling above me. "I wasn't. But thanks to Mark and you guys, I think I will be." I pause before saying, "I want to do something for him, Caleb. He's done so many thoughtful things for me. But I don't know what to do."

Caleb yawns. "He loves hunting. Didn't he used to live in the cabin at Falling Rock? I wonder if there's something there that you could retrieve for him."

That's actually a good idea. Go visit his cabin. It's not too far. I lie there in the quiet until I hear Caleb snoring. The corner of my lip inches upward. He was more tired than I thought. I turn to my side and try to sleep, but my mind still won't slow down, especially now that I have the sudden desire to go to Mark's old cabin. *Would Rusty take me there before we leave in the morning?*

Soon my thoughts turn from Mark to my family and their new purpose here at the rendezvous point. I think about the totem on the table, the diagrams on the walls. Then the refrigerator in the corner.

Suddenly I sit up. The refrigerator in the corner.

Cold.

It's what keeps memory bugs alive, what keeps the *memories* themselves alive inside the frozen bug.

My mind starts buzzing as I recall the songs in the room with Kapri, the songs that connected with Danny's, or Gabbro's, or whoever's pitched screams. Three songs. One about memories, one about Wintriness the frozen lake, and one about the meadow.

Waking Breccia up, I pull her out of her harness. After finding a piece of paper, I frantically scribble my message to Mark. What if the songs from the screams aren't pointing us to where Danny is but instead to where his memories lie? The memories of what happened to him that day a long time ago when he suddenly left Petrichor and came back unable to speak. Mark had said once that Danny's memories were checked for what happened. Nothing was found. He said it was as if the memories themselves were completely missing.

What if someone had used a memory bug to physically remove Danny's memories from his brain? Then hid them in the frozen lake Wintriness?

Is that possible? To remove a memory altogether from someone's brain? If they were removed, who removed them? Jeter? He's the only one who knows how to command memory bugs. Why would he do that?

It doesn't necessarily make sense. Danny didn't know where the memories were hidden before, so why would he suddenly be pointing us in that direction? Maybe he's learned something since SilverDen.

It's worth looking into.

When I'm done with my message, I place the paper in Breccia's message pocket. "Please get this to Mark quickly, then come back to me, and let me know what he finds."

I walk to the only window in the room, then open it and flip the switch on the bottom of Breccia. Whipping out of my hand, she disappears into the dark night.

"Come back quickly."

Chapter 21

I walk through the trees toward the cabin, pine needles and snow crunching beneath my shoes. The place is even more unsettling now than it was last time I was here. Cold and gloomy.

I step up to the cabin's open door hanging on its hinge and go inside. It takes a moment for my eyes to adjust to the darkness, but when I can finally see, disappointment churns in my chest. I don't know what I was expecting to find, but with the piles of leaves and dust-covered furniture, I'm not sure I'll find anything here that'll be meaningful to Mark.

We had to leave the rendezvous point early this morning to get on our way, but Rusty agreed to bring me here first before we began our journey to the GreenLands. The rest of the team is standing within the trees waiting patiently. We still haven't heard anything from the chief.

I walk through the mess, picking up pillows and lifting fallen shelves. There's no food left, no furniture that can be salvaged. It's just a mess. I walk into the two bedrooms, the first completely empty and the second with torn-up floorboards. I'm about to leave the room, when a piece of white paper catches my eye, hidden in a hole in the floor.

I bend down and pick it up. It's a photo. Or, at least, part of a photo, of an old man with a heavy beard and a young teenage boy with brown eyes. It's Mark ... with his father.

On the left edge of the photo next to Mark's father, the paper is torn and a piece missing. I furrow my eyebrows. *The part with Mark's mother? Why would it have been torn off?*

I look closer at the eyes of the man. They've been scratched out.

That's creepy.

"Hey, Alena," I hear Rusty in the other room. "Look at this."

Walking out to the main room while tucking the photo into my satchel, I see him holding an old shotgun. "Could this have been Mark's?"

I take the gun from Rusty, running my fingers over the barrel. It's dusty, old, and smells faintly of sulfur. But on the end of the barrel three letters have been scratched into the metal.

Dee.

"It's probably his dad's. Thank you. This is perfect." *It would be a good gift, right?* Returning his father's gun to him? I hope so. Draping the gun over my torso, I look around the cabin one more time.

"I think we can go now," I say.

***

We fly for hours, covering more ground than I thought was possible for birds, even if they are very large. I watch the terrain change from mountains to flatlands in half the day. We stop only once for a lunch break. I've never been so grateful for a lunch break in my life. I'm not exerting myself at all like the rest of the group flying, but sitting on the back of a large bird isn't necessarily comfortable, especially with the wind constantly blowing my eyes out. Not to mention the fact that I didn't get much sleep last night. I'm tired.

The Pepps pull out their food and rest on rocks and logs while I stretch out my back.

As I'm rubbing a sore spot, I see Harper with her dark-red hair tightly pulled back into a bun walking around the group, holding her large gun in her hands. She's not one for talking to.

Rusty and Cody are quietly talking together. I don't want to interrupt them. So, I look around for the only other person I kind of know.

Kapri.

I find her sitting alone on a rock, eating in the sunlight. I need to tell her about the idea I had last night. Speaking of, where in the world is Breccia? Was she able to get the message to Mark? Maybe it's taking time for him to look for the memories. Or maybe Breccia's having a hard time finding me since we're moving so fast.

I take a sandwich from the stack the freckled boy prepared for lunch and walk to Kapri. Plopping on the ground next to her, I rub my tingly legs.

"Hey," I say.

She only offers a polite nod before taking a bite of her sandwich.

"Kapri." I lower my voice. "I had a thought last night. It was the middle of the night and maybe it's nothing, but remember those three songs you wrote out—the three songs we reviewed in Petrichor?"

"Which ones?" I've piqued her interest.

"The one that talked about memories, the one about an empress Wintriness, and the one about a meadow dusted with snow." Kapri nods.

"Last night my dad showed me a refrigerator of frozen memory bugs they keep there at the rendezvous point. He told me they have to be frozen to be preserved." I look down at my sandwich. "What if the sounds within Danny's screams aren't leading us to where he is physically but instead to where his memories are hidden? The memories of what happened to him? They would provide answers to so many questions and could maybe even guide us to him."

Kapri's body freezes. "You think the memories are hidden in Lake Wintriness?"

I nod slowly.

Her hands begin to tremble with urgency. "You could be right." Stuffing her sandwich into her mess kit, she stands and reaches for her satchel. "We need to get back."

I grab her arm, stopping her. "Kapri, wait. I sent a message to Mark last night. I asked him to check it out, to see if there really are memories there."

Kapri's eyes brighten. "Have you heard back?"

"No, but I think we should give him more time. He might still be looking."

Kapri clasps her shaking hands together and looks around the area.

She can't leave. Not yet. Hoping to distract her, I pull her back down. "Tell me about Danny. How did you meet him?" Maybe this will help ease the awkwardness between us.

Biting her lip, Kapri remains quiet for a moment. When she opens her mouth to answer, Rusty shouts out to the group, demanding our attention. I eye Kapri apologetically before we both turn to listen to Rusty.

"The GreenLands are only a couple hours away. For those of you who haven't been there, it is a war zone and may be unlike anything you've ever experienced. We're going to stay on the west side of the country as far away from ground zero as we can. We want to help out in little ways, but even though it's far away, there's a chance you will see death and pain. Prepare yourselves." Rusty pauses for a moment while sending a side glance at Cody. I watch her too. A nervousness has crept into her features.

"We'll stay there no more than three days. If we need to leave sooner, we will. Our goal is to help find the lost and injured and provide food and water. We don't want to be recognized, so be sure to cover your totems with these." Rusty hands each of us a black shirt. With its long sleeves and tall collar, it completely covers my totem.

"Please wear them the whole time we're there. The last thing we need is for people to attack us because we're Pepps.

"Before we head more inland to help, though, there's something else we're going to do." Rusty smirks contagiously at Cody. "Something fun."

Cody looks quizzically at Rusty, but he doesn't reveal his plan. He just collects his supplies and shouts out his last demand. "Lunch is over. Let's move out."

Facing Kapri, I pat her arm, "I'll let you know if I hear anything from Mark, okay?"

Without looking me in the eye, she nods and busies herself with her stuff.

I scarf down the rest of my sandwich, silently hoping I get a message from Mark soon.

Chapter 22

This time Rusty asks the freckled-face boy, Benjy, to carry me on his back—probably to give Cody a break and to free himself in case Cody needs help. Benjy's torso is wider than Cody's, and his feathers aren't nearly as soft. They scratch at my skin. But he's strong and steady. We fly through the day, the dry lands changing into ocean. Lots of ocean, until we finally see the outline of cliffs ahead. Rusty signals for us to land.

I'm getting anxious to search for Danny. I hope we can get to him soon. Has the chief been able to extract any information from Chauly?

Harper immediately stands guard again, raising her gun and marching through our rest site with a determined look, while the rest of us stretch our tired bodies. I take Mark's shotgun off my back and roll my shoulders.

The brilliance of the green mountains in the distance immediately tells me that we've reached the GreenLands. I quietly watch Cody's reaction, observing how her blue eyes reverently graze over the hilly terrain. The first thing she says is that the green is fading. Rusty explains that it's because of the lack of Peppate, since the Pepps have only been spreading Peppate close to Petrichor.

I scan the vibrant color of green stretched across every inch of the land. To me it's outstanding. *And it's faded?* I can't even imagine what it would look like in its healthiest condition. No wonder she loves this place.

I sit on the side of the cliff, listening to the waves crashing hundreds of feet below us. The strong wind blows in my face, and the heavy fog threatens to wet my clothes. But I don't mind.

I watch a flock of little birds find their way past the cliffs, over the water. Their tiny wings strain against the wind, carrying them farther than I would think they have the strength for. But then they pause, wings outstretched, to rest. Caught in the current of the wind, that simple brief pause sends them all the way back to the coast. Undoes all their efforts. But then they start pumping their wings again, inching their way out. They reach the same distance before pausing again, getting pushed back.

They aren't trying to make progress. They're out there having fun. Enjoying the wind. I watch them float in the air so peacefully. *How would it be to fly?*

"They're Bearded Reedlings."

I turn, finding Sef standing there enjoying the same scene. "They're beautiful birds." He sits beside me, letting his legs hang off the steep cliff.

"My mom was fond of birds but especially of these. They have a special call."

The reverent way Sef looks at the birds makes me think he's not as immature as Cody indicated. I also like the unique sound of his accent. I wonder where he's from.

"My mom told me a story once, of how she got lost in the Torry Desert alone. She lived close to the desert, and one day when she was angry with her parents she ran away. Not very smart." Sef looks at me and huffs. "By the time she decided to head back home, she was lost." Sef's eyes turn serious. "She was out there for two days. No food or water. She said she eventually just laid down to die. She was too dizzy and sick to walk. She probably *would* have died too, if she hadn't heard the call of a bird. It was unfamiliar and woke her up enough to get her moving again. She knew if she followed the bird, it might lead her to someplace with water. So she followed it, and it let her, maintaining a slow enough pace for a dehydrated little girl to keep up."

The sun starts peeking through the clouds in the sky, brightening Sef's golden skin. Based on how his brown eyes glimmer, I can tell he loves his mother very much.

"It led her to a water well. And people. After she drank her fill and became more lucid, she observed the bird perched beside her. It had an orange belly, a long brown tail, and a blue head. She'd barely looked at it before it flew away.

"She spent years after that, researching birds, trying to identify the one that had saved her life."

Why's he telling me this personal story?

"She eventually found it. The Bearded Reedling. They live on the coasts here and in Verdure. But definitely not in the desert."

Sef pauses for a moment before looking down at his hands. "I thought my mom was crazy—or lying—when she told me this story. Then several years later she died. I was devastated. She was all I had."

My heart squeezes at the mention of her death. Sometimes I forget that every Pepp orphan has lost both parents. I don't know why I assumed Sef would be any different. Maybe because of how happy he seems. But, of course, he's experienced loss.

"We lived beside Lake Ausie at the time, not quite in the desert but close. She had told me about the totem, how I was supposed to take her extra totem and go looking for the Pepps should she ever die. When I didn't attach it, I wondered if the chief would physically come for me. Regardless, I had vowed to myself that I would never leave her grave. He could try to drag me away, but I would refuse to go. I laid on that rocky headstone for two days. My skin was covered in blisters from the sun. And then the chief came. I gripped Mom's grave, ready to hang on for dear life, when this little bird came and sat in front of me. It had an orange belly, a blue head, and a long brown tail. It was so out of place against the sands of the desert, but I immediately recognized it from her story. Then the bird flew up to on the chief's shoulder and perched there."

My body warms at Sef's words, at the miracle he experienced. He shakes his head, and his eyes get misty.

"I could not, for the life of me, explain that little bird away. I knew with every fiber of my being that it was somehow a sign. My mother telling me not only that she was okay but that I needed to go with the chief." Sef wipes his nose with his hand. "So I went. And I did what my mom did. I studied the Bearded Reedling. Learned everything about it, and then when I got power for the first time as a Pepp, I morphed into one." Sef points to the flock of birds still flying in the wind. "Those birds. They give me hope."

Sef stands now, tosses me one last full grin, then jumps into the air, morphing into the tiny bird. I watch his little wings take him to the flock, where he joins them in their game.

And then his story replays in my mind, his last word echoing.

Hope.

What does that word even mean? Hope? I watch Sef drift back and forth in the wind.

I used to think having hope was believing that somehow life would go the way I wanted it to. I've hoped to remove my totem so I could go home, so I could be happy like I used to be. But that hope hasn't gotten me anywhere. It's only left me more frustrated.

Suddenly the birds are blurry.

Sef has hope even though his mother is dead? What does he have hope *in*?

I blink, trying to clear my eyes. Even if I was able to remove my totem now, I will still have many scars. Scars that'll be a part of me forever. My family showed me that I can feel peace again, but there's a heaviness in my heart that I don't think will go away anytime soon. So, if I can't have hope that my life will return to the way it was, what can I hope in?

I think about Sef. He doesn't seem to believe his mother will come back to life, but maybe he believes that there's more to life than what we can see.

Maybe having hope doesn't mean you believe everything will turn out the way you want it to. Instead, maybe it's believing that someday all things will be made right.

Tears spill onto my cheeks now, and I swallow.

What do *I* hope for then?

My lip trembles.

I hope ... that someday Pam will be reunited with Tom.

My tears drip off my chin into my lap.

I hope that someday Mitch will be rewarded for his courage, that Cody's mind will be freed.

That *my* mind will be freed.

I watch the blurry waves crashing below. I hope that someday, somehow, our fight, our efforts, our endurance through the struggles of life will all somehow be acknowledged ... that everything will be made right.

I hope there's a day like that. Goodness, if there is, I definitely have something to look forward to.

I wipe my tears. In the meantime, I guess I have to do what Mark told me to do. Just keep going through the darkness, reminding myself what I thought back in Danny's meadow.

That I'm worthy of living a good life.

I cringe. Why do I still hate those words? Why can't I just believe them? Maybe if I keep trying, one day they'll stick.

I look up at Sef flying in the sky again. I *will* keep trying, and I will keep looking for the beauty in life, because there really is a lot of beauty in it.

Much too soon Rusty interrupts my thoughts and calls us all back in. I reluctantly pull myself away from the cliff edge, saying good-bye to the waves below and the birds in the sky.

When we've all gathered around Rusty, he holds out several golden equipment capsules glistening in the sunlight.

"There's a town about ten miles east of here. We're going to pay them a little visit. I thought we could enjoy the scenery a little more by traveling on land instead of in the sky. So each of you take a bike, and we'll bike our way there." The look on Cody's face is hard to miss. She looks stunned, frozen as if she's just been hit by something pleasant and terrifying at the same time. When she doesn't take her bike from Rusty, he opens her hand and places the capsule in her palm.

"I used to bike," she says mainly to herself, "all the time. I loved it."

Rusty closes her fingers over the capsule. "I hope you *still* love it."

Cody eyes the capsule in her hand before stepping back. She gently pushes the button and expands the bike. Holding onto the handles, she drapes her leg over and sits on the seat. With one foot on a pedal and the other on the ground, her lips twitch upward.

And then she takes off.

Rusty doesn't hesitate. He's off with her.

I'm next in line. I fling the shotgun over my shoulder and expand my bike. Once on, I pedal slowly. Sef, who's behind me on the thin trail, seems put out by my slowness. It looks like he's back to being his annoying self, but I ignore him, allowing Cody and Rusty to get well ahead on the thin path. Not that they need my help with that. They're both ridiculously fast.

I push the pedals, feeling the strain in my legs. It feels good to ride a bike. I'm instantly grateful for Rusty's insight. Traveling in the sky offers a different kind of beauty, seeing the twists and rises of the land in full view. But down here next to the earth, with the ability to see each patch of moss, each strand of grass, each insect perched on a plant, I'm offered a new, more intimate perspective of the place.

I enjoy my leisurely ride, until Rusty and Cody get so far ahead that I almost can't see them. I try to catch up, but no matter how fast I move my legs, I can't. It isn't until they both stop at the top of a hill that I'm able to reach them.

I can't even hide the struggle of catching my breath.

When I can finally breathe again, I scope out what's below us, what Cody and the rest of the team are staring at.

A beautiful quaint town tucked in the green hills below. Its white buildings, bordered with brown and tan scaffolding, glimmer in the bright sunlight.

"Make sure your totems are covered," Rusty says. I tug at the collar of my shirt, ensuring my jaw is hidden.

Then we walk our bikes down, following a tiny dirt path. Kapri walks her bike behind me.

We eventually stop just outside the town. We don't collapse the bikes. That would give us away with too many people in sight. So, instead, we lean them against a tree close by. Harper leaves her large gun with the cycles and encourages me to do the same. I hope nobody takes Mark's gun, and I hope she has another hidden weapon just in case.

When we approach the first building, the dirt path turns into a wide shiny cobblestone road, occasionally splattered with bits of moss. Ivy, bright green in the intense sun light, crawls up the buildings, carefully trimmed around the windows. Flowers of pinks and purples are crammed into every spare pot available and carefully placed beside pathways and apartment doors. A stone bridge arches over a shimmering brook off to the left, and church bells chime in the distance. I look around, easily able to spot the steeple rising above the town. Where there isn't a building, there are trees of all different variations.

If it wasn't for the occasional boarded-up window, men dressed in dark-blue uniforms, and the untrusting eyes of those we pass, I wouldn't believe this quiet, beautiful town was part of a war.

"Are these weapons?" Cody's question interrupts my observations of the town. She and Rusty are standing next to a large wooden box outside an apartment building. Stepping toward them, I find the box loaded with chilling weapons.

Growing up in the high mountains, I saw my fair share of guns. They're part of every household much like a fireplace or a couch. Used for hunting, the guns are the livelihood for lots of families. They provide skins, furs, and meat for the people to sell.

But these guns are bigger, scarier. Guns that I've only ever seen in pictures or on TV. They're not used for hunting bears or animals. They're too big for that. No, they're used for killing people. Lots of people.

Rusty holds up a large-barreled contraption. "Where did they get these? They haven't had weapons like these before? Are they able to make them now?"

"Maybe they stole them," Cody says quietly. But as she says it, I can hear the doubt in her voice.

Rusty stops a boy with bright, almost white hair, probably no more than twelve-years-old, who is passing by.

"Where did these come from?" Rusty asks.

The boy shrugs, but then says in the same accent as Rusty and Cody, "We don't know for sure, but some say they're from a mysterious Pepp." The boy brings his finger to his lips as if what he's told us is a big secret. "Isn't it great, though? To finally be able to fight back?" The boy punches the air.

Rusty doesn't look nearly as happy as the boy.

"When did they arrive?" Rusty asks. He probably didn't mean for his voice to sound so hard, but it did. And now the boy is backing up nervously.

"A couple weeks ago, I think." Rusty drops the gun in the box, angrily. The boy jumps, obviously confused by the response. Then he turns and runs away.

"A Pepp?" Cody's face looks both heartbroken and hopeful. And I know why. These weapons are giving a country that's been constantly pounded for the past five years a chance to fight back. A chance to win.

But, if a Pepp truly did send these, the laws of Petrichor have been broken. Who knows what consequences will follow.

Rusty's tight expression softens the moment it lands on Cody's torn face. He wraps his arm around her shoulder and leads her down the street.

"We'll worry about that later. For now, there's someplace I want to take you. I just hope it's open."

I follow Rusty down the road, eyeing each wooden box of weapons I pass. *Who could have sent them? Jeter?* Shouldn't they hide them so their own enemy doesn't get their hands on them?

I ignore the glowering looks of the people. Unfortunately, even the beauty of this place can't mask the tension rolling through the town in waves.

Rusty finally stops in front of a corner store tucked inside a large apartment building. The windows are boarded up, and I wonder if it's been shut down, but when I step through the door behind Cody, I breathe in the most wonderful smell.

"Chocolate." Cody sighs deeply next to me, as if the smell of the candy is somehow the very breath of life. We walk to the counter and look into the glass case. I immediately bite back a frown. The case is huge but almost empty. Only a few pieces of chocolate sit in the corner.

A large man quickly appears from a room in the back, wiping his hands on his stained apron. His thinning black hair is slicked to the side, and his pale-green eyes are beady, narrowing at the sight of us.

"What can I do for you?" His words are nice enough, but his eyes are not. They wander suspiciously over each of us, landing purposefully on our necks that are covered by the black shirts. I resist the urge to bring my hand up to my neck now. Looking at the group out of the corner of my eye, I realize these shirts don't make us inconspicuous at all. We stand out like a sore thumb.

"We'd like to purchase all the chocolate you have here," Rusty says lightly, ignoring the man's unnerving glare.

I decide to ignore him too and instead observe Cody, who's practically drooling over the glass case.

"You like chocolate," I whisper.

She chuckles softly. "Not just any chocolate. This chocolate. It's made with the best milk in the world. Milk that comes from the Holstein cow."

Cody's eyes water. "We owned one of those cows when I was growing up. Her name was Nellie. Mom would take her milk and make this chocolate every Christmas. I've missed it."

A tear spills onto her cheek, but she quickly wipes it away when the man hands her a large chunk of creamy chestnut-colored chocolate.

She takes it carefully, as if handling a precious gem that could disappear with the slightest movement. Then bringing it to her nose, she closes her eyes and smells it deeply. Just watching her is making my mouth water. Thankfully, Rusty hands the rest of us a tiny little piece.

With how small the morsel is, I don't bother saving it. I put it into my mouth, where it melts into the smoothest, richest piece of chocolate I've ever had. I grieve slightly when the chocolate slides down my throat. *I wish there was more.*

"You have our accent," the man says to Rusty while ringing him up for payment. "But you're not from around here."

My body tenses at the statement. There's something in his tone that makes the hair on the back of my neck rise. But Rusty doesn't seem bothered.

"We're just passing through, on our way further inland. I couldn't go any further, though, without stopping here for some chocolate. I came here a couple of years back and promised myself I'd return." Rusty smiles genuinely at the man. The man does not smile in return.

"You're Pepps."

Now Rusty tenses. And Harper, who's standing behind him. She slips her hand behind her back as if reaching for a hidden weapon. Kapri has stepped up beside me, standing close.

"He knows who we are," she whispers. "Be prepared to disable him if he becomes dangerous."

I'm grateful for Kapri. I've heard about Pepps being attacked on runs, but to be standing here in a potentially dangerous situation, I'm frozen. And if it wasn't for Kapri, I probably would have stayed that way. But now I simply picture what I could do to the man's brain to make him temporarily unconscious. If needed.

Rusty doesn't bother denying the man's accusation, but he doesn't turn to leave either.

"Did you come to bring more weapons?" the man asks.

Rusty clenches his jaw, and the man sees it, immediately interpreting the reaction.

"No, not you, huh. You're not here to bring us weapons. There's only one Pepp who cares about us. The rest of you are scum."

"One Pepp?" Rusty asks ignoring the insult. "Who is this Pepp?"

The man shakes his head and draws his lips back into a snarl. "I'm not gonna tell you."

Rusty steps forward. *What's he going to do? Attack the man? Take him with us? Somehow get him to talk?*

Before I can step up to intervene, another group of men walks into the store, dressed in black uniforms.

"We need to go," both Harper and Cody say, pulling on Rusty's arm.

But Rusty's gaze stays pinned on the man. Harper's and Cody's pulls are nothing against Rusty's large frame. If he wants to hit the man, he could, and none of us could stop him. Thankfully, Rusty knows better. Without taking his eyes off the man, he lays a pile of green currency on the counter. I don't know much about the money here, but I'd say Rusty is giving him more than enough.

"Thank you for the chocolate," he says slowly, then adds, "Be careful who you trust."

The man's surly expression deepens. "Oh, I am careful," he says, clearly indicating that Rusty is not among those he considers trustworthy.

Finally, Rusty steps back, nods to the other men in uniform, then signals for the rest of us to follow him outside. We don't speak at all on the way back to the bikes, but Kapri walks beside me. She gently meets the gaze of those staring at us, but I choose to hang my head low.

I'm surprised they aren't attacking us.

Once we reach the bikes, we quickly load up and travel up the hill without looking back.

By the time we reach isolation beyond the top of the hill, I'm winded and irritable. And so is everyone else.

"What's going on?" Kapri asks quietly.

Rusty doesn't respond but busies himself with writing a letter I can only assume is to the chief.

Thankfully, Cody doesn't seem too fazed by everything. She sits down and sniffs her chocolate again and again.

"Who do you think it is?" Kapri asks beside me. I examine her soft face, her hair golden in the setting sun.

Is she finally warming up to me? She doesn't seem to bother conversing with the others.

"I don't know," I whisper, but then I remember overhearing Jeter's conversation again. He was upset about what was going on in his homeland and angry that the chief wouldn't intercept.

"Could it be Jeter?" I say out loud.

"That's exactly who I think it is. And based on how much those town people hate us, I'm guessing Jeter has promised them more than just weapons," Rusty answers.

"Have you heard from Mark yet?" Kapri asks, interrupting my thoughts.

My eyebrows furrow. "No." I search the sky for my missing Magbaby. *Is something wrong?*

The whistle of Rusty's Magbaby flies through the air, and he stands. He's more serious than before, but he tries to lighten his mood for Cody's sake.

"Okay. Now the real fun begins. We're going further inland until I hear from the chief." Rusty eyes Cody carefully. "I'm not sure how much things have progressed since I last came here, but as far as I know, the outlying towns haven't been hit; they just need food and supplies. Your power capsules should be full from flying, so when we get there, we'll do as much as we can. Benjy—" Rusty addresses the freckled-faced kid. "You create as much food as you can. Cody and Alena, you look for anyone who's injured or sick. And Sef, just stay out of trouble."

I glance at Sef, who's not even paying attention but looking at some insect crawling in the dirt.

"We're going to fly until it gets dark. I think we should probably stay as hidden as possible." Rusty looks back in the direction of the town. "Those people didn't trust us. I have a feeling that distrust will only intensify the further inland we get. Be careful."

And just like that, the mood of the trip has turned. I grip my hands anxiously, wishing Mark was here.

Chapter 23

We fly, me on Benjy again. The green hills eventually turn into magnificent mountains with waterfall after waterfall cascading down their sides. A beautiful bushy moss stretches across the landscape, the color deepening when the sun lowers to the horizon.

We pass a couple of towns. Their windows, shimmering in the last bits of sunlight, tell us they've remained untouched by the war. But we don't stop. Rusty apparently wants to get even further inland.

The day is drawing to a close, and I find myself wishing night wouldn't come. I enjoy seeing the green. But the humid air grows instantly colder the moment the sun is gone, and dark shadows cascade over the mountains.

But we keep flying. I'm starting to doze off when I hear something break the peaceful night air. A deep thrumming sound hums in the distance. Squinting, I look ahead, searching for the source. There in the darkness, miles ahead in the sky, are lights. Like flashing lights on an airplane. But the loud sound echoing off the mountains tells me these aren't normal airplanes. They sound like jets. And they're flying toward us. *What are jets doing out in the middle of nowhere?*

But then I look down and find that we're not in the middle of nowhere. We're approaching another town. No, more like a city, perched on the side of a dark mountain. Twinkling lights flicker cozily out of each window.

My mouth instantly goes dry. Something's wrong.

A whistling sound slices through the air followed by a large explosion. I draw back at the bright dome of flames that rises from the city and consumes dozens of peaceful homes within seconds.

No!

The people! The children. My trembling hands cover my mouth in horror.

We weren't supposed to get close to the war!

Benjy reacts without hesitation, flying straight for the houses.

I hear it first—the cry of a human. It floats on the wind, whistling by so quickly that I question if I really heard it at all.

But Benjy seems to have heard it too. His body pauses and stiffens. Then it comes again, another scream, and then another. Benjy dives low, quickly, competing with other bombs dropping at the same time. My heart plummets to my stomach. If it wasn't for Benjy, who had the smart sense to keep moving forward, I would still be frozen in the sky.

The fire burns bright against the darkness, and the flames reach out, quickly swallowing more and more. Before we land, I try to foresee the possible injuries that'll be found. Burns, of course. I close my eyes. I hate burns. I look around and find the other Pepps all diving in the same direction we are, determined to provide help. Cody is in the lead with Rusty, who's already commanding waves of water over the flames.

We land and quickly disperse, each Pepp doing what they've been trained to do on dropdowns like this. I don't bother to see where each of them has gone but follow the screams I can hear that are coming from almost every direction. I finally focus on one high-pitched scream. There in the rubble of what used to be a home, surrounded by flames, I find a young girl.

I curse. Why haven't I learned how to create water? That would come in real handy right now. Stepping into the fire, I move quickly, throwing off burning pieces of wood to get to the girl. I want to scream in pain now too, with the fire eating at my skin, hungrily burning through the soles of my shoes, my clothes, melting everything it touches. The smoke bites at my eyes, obstructing my vision. But I bite back the pain and follow the sounds until my hands finally land on the girl. She thrashes wildly in pain at my touch, making everything so much harder.

Holding on as tightly as I can, I stumble from the flames, then roll with her through the dirt to put out the fire on our clothes. The town is in chaos now—people running in all directions, shouting. Tears sting my eyes from the painful burns, but I pull my body up and focus on the sounds of the elements coming from the girl. The burns bring back memories of Mitch, but I push them aside, commanding her body to heal.

Kneeling next to her, I don't get far before a hand lands on my shoulder and throws me to the side, ripping me away from the girl. I land on my burned right arm, gritting my teeth to hold back a scream from the pain that erupts.

When I look back, I find a man hovering protectively over the young girl. I expect him to call out for help now that he's found her, but he doesn't. He's focused on me, potently full of hate.

"Stay away from her," he growls.

"I can help her," I shout over the loud crackle of flames.

But the man ignores me, trying to lift the girl who's now passed out from pain. I calmly touch his arm. "Please. Let me help her."

"Get away from me!" he shouts. But then his eyes trail to my collar and his hate deepens darkly.

I take a step back.

"You're a Pepp, aren't you?" His voice is cold. *Why in the world did we wear these stupid shirts if they just give us away?* I stand in shock as he puts down his severely injured daughter to deal with me. I should probably run.

"Take it off and let me see who you really are," he says. But I ignore him, silently reaching past him, to the girl's elements, commanding them to heal her faster. I *have* to heal her.

I get farther this time. Out of the corner of my eye, I can see the redness and blistering in her cheeks fading, the sloughing skin filling out, but then the man's hand pulls down the collar of my shirt, exposing my totem.

Now I jump back. "Please, we're just here to help. I really can heal the girl."

"*We're*? Of course, there are more of you," he says. Grabbing the front of my shirt, he brings me within inches of his terrifying face.

"You'll regret coming here," he says. "You've ignored our pleas too long. Thankfully someone else will be coming. Someone *better* than your people, someone stronger than all of you combined." With his free hand, the man reaches down to grab a flaming piece of wood and hits me with it. Pain ripples through my head, and my ears start ringing. I raise my arms to protect myself, but he hits again.

It'll only take a few more hits before I become unconscious, if not dead.

I need to do something. Many things flash through my mind. I have power. I could hurt him, disable his brain, cause him to collapse, or command his heart to stop.

But thinking of what to tell my totem with a brain that's getting hammered is impossible. I can't remember the shortcuts.

That's when I remember the knives. As quickly as my slow limbs will move, I slide the knife out of my right sleeve. I don't know where the man is. I don't know where I am, so I stab the air blindly and almost cry in relief when it finds him. Finally, he stops crushing my head and lets me fall to the ground. But the pain pounds on. I grip my head in my hands.

I think the man falls to the ground next to me. I wish I could see! I wish I could move. But even breathing is sending crippling pains through my head.

"Alena!"

I've never been so happy to hear Rusty's voice. Before I can comprehend what's going on, an arm around my waist hoists me into the air onto the back of an eagle. I can't hold back the screams now. We obviously need to get out of here, but I wish I could just stop moving my head!

But then the pain subsides quickly, turning to a faint ringing. I open my eyes.

Did Rusty just heal me? I can see now.

But maybe I don't want to see.

I'm on Benjy's back again, with a clear view of the city burning below. It'll be wiped out within minutes.

And we're flying away? Why? It's still on fire! There's so much help that's needed.

I take a silent count in my head. I see Kapri, Harper, Sef, and Rusty flying with us.

But no Cody. I frantically look back at the village, but then stop. There's no way Rusty would've left without her.

That's when I hear the screaming.

I look down at Rusty's claws.

Cody is thrashing wildly in his grip. And she's begging him to go back.

Oh no.

Chapter 24

I cling to Benjy's feathers. Man, I really wish I could fly. It would probably distract me from replaying the horrible events in my mind. The explosions, the fire, the burns, the screams that still ring loudly in my ears. I wasn't prepared for that.

And then there was the man. Why was he so angry? And what did he say? That they were getting help from someone more powerful than we'll ever be? Was he talking about a Pepp? Jeter?

Somehow, I don't think he was.

And that scares me.

I grit my teeth. That stupid man!

Things were supposed to go differently in that town. I could have saved that girl. But instead of accepting my help, that man beat me. Rejected me in the harshest way. And now I feel like I did in Petrichor. My only consolation is that I wasn't the only one rejected. Every Pepp flying in the sky with me now was unwanted down there.

When Rusty finally lands in an open space surrounded by tall trees and thick bushes, I'm shivering in shock. I get off Benjy and silently watch the group set up camp, putting up the protective fog first. It'll at least keep angry humans away.

Rusty immediately takes Cody into his arms and tries to calm her. It's not working though. After wrestling with her for several minutes, he finally sends me a painful, pleading look.

I don't get close. I don't think she'll appreciate being besieged mentally. I know I wouldn't. So I stand where I am and whisper the shortcut Sepharine gave me.

It works quickly. Cody thrashes only a few more times before her body stills. Her fiery eyes turn confused. Then they whip around the area until they land on me. I shiver. She knows what I just did.

Clasping my trembling hands, I ignore her and busy myself with setting up my tent. Thankfully, Cody doesn't come after me but sobs into Rusty's chest.

Once my tent has been fully expanded, I step inside, zip the door behind me, and quickly get dressed into something warmer. I pull out the coat Mark gave me the night of initiation. It calmed my trembling then. Wrapping it around my shoulders, I push my arms through. Maybe it can calm me now.

Once I'm dressed, I take a deep breath and step outside. A fire, crackling wildly, has already been started.

I'm guessing Benjy is a very good cook based on the smell of the food over the fire. After flipping several tinfoil-covered dinners, he sits on a log and attends to a burn on Harper's leg.

He can heal? Why didn't I realize it before? His totem is wound with a red ribbon. He's a medic. He must have been the one to heal my head as we flew away.

I breathe in the smell of food and grab my mess kit, ready to use it for dinner, avoiding eye contact with Cody. I search the logs around the fire and find a spot next to Kapri.

I have so many questions about what just happened. I try to keep them to myself, sure that everyone is shaken in their own way. Maybe we all just need time to process things, but soon I find myself unable to hold my questions in.

"What happened out there?" I whisper to Kapri, trying to keep my voice down so nobody else hears. But from the way everyone shifts uncomfortably, I can tell they heard.

It's Rusty who responds. "They're angry," he says.

"Why?"

I'm surprised when it's Cody who answers this question. "No, they're afraid. Verdure has taken so much from them, and even though those people might not have been bombed until tonight, they've seen the horrors of what Verdure has done. They were afraid we would take their children away." Cody stops, her bottom lip trembling. She knows firsthand what it's like to be ripped away from family.

Putting an arm around her shoulder, Rusty continues. "That's not the only reason they acted the way they did. A lot of it is our fault. We haven't been spreading Peppate here like we used to. We've been staying closer to Petrichor. Even if they wanted to react better, they couldn't. Peppate has been absent from their lives for too long. They can't trust or love. They're just filled with fear. The GreenLands isn't the only place this has happened. It's happening all over the world."

Suddenly the magnitude of what Pepps do hits me. *Is that what we turn into without Peppate?*

I compare that man's behavior to Chauly's. His judgment was clouded by fear and protectiveness, and it made him dangerous. Chauly, on the other hand, acted dangerously because he had no fear, no care. I swallow, the importance of balancing Peppate and Doler hitting me now. We need both.

"The man who attacked me mentioned that they're getting help from someone," I say. "Someone more powerful than we'll ever be. I got the feeling he wasn't talking about a Pepp. At least not a normal Pepp. Who could he have been talking about?"

The air hushes, everyone thinking. It's Cody who eventually breaks the silence.

"He promised me freedom for my people," she whispers, her voice catching in her throat.

I glance at Rusty. *What?* But he's focused on Cody's face.

"The man, who tortured me and my friend," she clarifies.

Suddenly she has everyone's attention. Especially Rusty's. She hasn't talked about her time as a prisoner at all.

Cody studies her fingers, tears spilling onto her cheeks. "He cut her tongue off right in front of me and then her fingers. He told me it would all end if I would help him capture Mark and Alena." She closes her eyes, "He promised me that if I helped him capture you both, he would take care of Verdure himself. He would end the awful things being done to my people."

"*Who* promised you that?" Rusty asks carefully. "Case? Jax?"

Cody shakes her head. "No. I don't know who he was. But he wasn't Case or Jax. He wore a black cloth over his face every time he came to me. His voice was different. Raspy."

My spine straightens. *There's another man involved?* Could he be the one behind everything, the one Case was working for? There are many other questions I should probably ask, but I'm suddenly stuck on one thing. This man tortured Cody and her friend to get to me.

"Why didn't you do it?" I stare at her. "Why didn't you do what he asked?" It would have ended everything. Made everything easier for her ... and for me.

As if sensing the fragile moment, Benjy, Harper, Sef, and Kapri all leave the circle and make another campfire out of sight.

I ask my question again when they're gone, softer this time. Dark shadows of guilt and shame swim heavily in her expression.

"I did." Her tears turn to sobs, and she covers her face, trying to hold them back. "They tortured her over and over again. Eventually I gave in. I told the man everything he wanted to know, what your tendencies are, how you're soft, kind. Your attachment to Danny. I even told him everything I knew about your family. I'm just grateful I didn't know exactly where they lived. I'm sorry, Alena, I wanted him to stop hurting my friend. And he did, for a little while ..." Cody's heart-wrenching sobs deepen, thick with sorrow, breaking up her words.

"The night you came to SilverDen, he killed her right in front of me, stabbed her in the heart. Then he dragged me from that cave he kept us both in. He took me out in the woods and tied me to a stump. Told me if I wanted to prevent anyone else from dying, I would stay there." Cody cradles her head in her hands. "It was all part of his plan. He knew that by killing her, I would lose all my fight. He knew I would want to die in that fire. As soon as I saw it, I felt hope for the first time in a long time. Hope that the pain would all end soon."

The air is silent except for the crackling fire. Rusty holds Cody tight.

"And then I came," I whisper. "And pulled you from the fire, removing what little hope you had left."

"I'm sorry, Alena." Cody says, burying her face in her hands.

Standing, I walk to her and kneel at her feet. There's something very important she needs to know.

"Don't you ever be sorry, Cody." Now tears threaten my eyes. "I can't even begin to imagine what you've been through. And it all happened because of me and my totem. I'm sorry that being my friend led to Abby's death and put you through such horrible things. I wish I could return everything you've lost. But I can't. I just hope you know I will do anything for you, Cody." I reach for her hand. "Anything. And maybe someday, even though I don't deserve it, you can find a way to forgive me."

Cody's eyes lighten at my words, and the corner of her lip lifts. "I've already forgiven you, Alena."

I didn't realize how much I needed to hear those words until now. *She's forgiven me?* The one who caused the death of her friend? The one who caused her so much pain? My heart aches to accept that forgiveness, let it sooth its sorrow.

Rusty gives Cody a kiss on her forehead, then quietly slips away, leaving us alone. I rise to the empty spot he just freed and sit. A calmness slips through the air. It pulls at the burden I've carried for so long—the guilt from hurting Cody—and takes it away, rising with the ashes.

Cody breaks the silence. "You used the Ataractic on me."

I tilt my head. "What?"

"To calm me down."

"Oh." I stare at my hands. "I'm sorry. Sepharine told me to. I thought I could do it without you knowing."

Cody scoffs. "Actually, I have a confession to make."

I glance sideways at her, seeing her swollen pink eyes. "I used it on you once," she says.

I try not to be offended. *Me?* Cody scrunches her nose apologetically. "I'm sorry. It was the day after your memories had been checked. I found you in the room after you'd written to your family. You were so angry,

I felt like you might explode. So I helped you calm down a little. It might help you feel better to know that you didn't need too much of the Ataractic. It turns out just letting you talk helped."

I look back at the fire. I remember that day. I remember being angry that Cody was talking to me and even angrier that I was listening. Whatever she had done had worked. But I had felt much better afterward. It feels like an invasion of privacy, though, knowing she messed with my mood without letting me know. But I can't be mad, since I just did the same thing to her.

"Thanks, Cody." I tease her. "I guess I can let it slide as long as it was only once."

Cody scrunches her nose. "It might have been twice. I don't really remember."

Now I laugh out loud. *Oh well.*

Then I bite my lip. I have one more question I hope she'll be willing to answer.

"Cody, why were you tied to that stump, away from all the other prisoners? With a totem on your arm."

The fire's reflection flickers in her eyes. She stares at the flames quietly for a moment before responding. "I'm not exactly sure. I think it had something to do with the morph. Something about your power not filling up unless a Pepp died by the lightning. That's why they attached the totem to me."

My blood runs cold. *A Pepp had to die from the lightning for the power to fill our totems from the morph?* Cody was supposed to be that Pepp, but I got her out.

Unfortunately, there was still another Pepp down there.

"Tom." My shoulders droop. He's the Pepp who died instead and filled my power holster.

"I'm sorry, Cody. I'm sorry about Tom."

Cody places her hand on my knee. "I know." I stare at her hand. It's starting to shake. And so is mine.

Perhaps that's enough talking for one night

"You want to join the others?" I ask.

She nods, and we find our way to the other fire.

Cody sits next to a tired but relieved-looking Rusty.

I find Kapri, who's staring intently at me. I immediately sense her question when I drop onto the log next to her.

"No, I haven't heard from Mark," I whisper, then take a plate of food from Benjy.

I should have heard from him by now, shouldn't I have? I search the sky, as if Breccia will just magically appear now, but the sky is empty except for the ashes floating from the fire.

"Something's wrong," Kapri whispers. "I might ask Rusty if I can go back to Petrichor tomorrow. I know the run isn't over, and we're not supposed to split up, but I can't really stay here any longer. Not without knowing what Mark found."

I nod, waving away smoke from the fire. Then cough. "I agree. If Rusty says you can go, will you take me with you? Do you think you could carry me all the way back?"

For the first time since I've known her, a mischievous grin slides across Kapri's mouth. "You don't think I'm strong enough?"

I pause, caught off guard by her direct question. "No, I just ... I know you're strong enough; it's just a long way. That's all."

Kapri smiles a full smile. "I can carry you. I won't disturb Rusty right now, but when he's less occupied, I'll see what he says."

Kapri's daring mood has me realizing there's more to her than the eye can see. I decide I want her to be my friend. As we eat our food, Kapri opens up to me, sharing how she was born in Petrichor. I hadn't thought about it before, but I guess two Pepps can choose to have children. Her parents had to remove their totems, so Kapri is technically human, but she's been raised solely by Pepps. Her mom is a *mother* who takes in new orphan Pepps that come to Petrichor, and her father is a protector. Kapri met Danny when she was sixteen, during initiation training. She loves the beach, dancing, and music. Maybe that's why she and Danny liked each other so much. They both love music.

A sadness creeps in as I talk to Kapri. When we find Danny, things will never be the same between us. Kapri was made for him, I know it—which means I'm going to have to stop encouraging a relationship between us. Help him find Kapri again. I look forward to seeing the two of them together again. And maybe if Danny has Kapri, I don't have to hide my feelings for Mark from Danny anymore.

After a while, the air grows cold. The fire is almost out, and the group has retired to bed. Except for Rusty and Cody.

I cough when more black smoke and embers rise up from the smothering fire. I'm waving my hand across my face, trying to escape them, when a whistling sound reaches my ears. A Magbaby. I jump to my feet, move away from the fire, and stare up at the sky.

"We should probably get some rest," Rusty says, rising to his feet and pulling Cody with him. "We have a big day tomorrow."

The shadow of a rock comes into view above the fire, and Rusty freezes.

Kapri straightens.

My muscles tighten. *Breccia?*

I open my palm, waiting for Breccia to fly down, but the Magbaby doesn't come to me. It goes to Rusty.

Cold worry floods my body as I search the night sky. *Something's wrong.*

"What is it?" Cody asks.

Rusty opens the paper hidden in his Magbaby and reads silently before clearing his throat. A smile spreads on his face.

"It looks like Chief was finally able to get through to Chauly. Jax is hiding with Danny in Dakdete."

"The red mountains?" Cody whispers.

"Yeah. The driest place on earth." Rusty's eyes roll in annoyance. "I hate Dakdete, but now we know where to go." Then his eyes continue skimming the paper. "Wait, there's more." He reads in silence for a moment. I watch his fingers tighten, curl around the paper, I see the muscle in his jaw twitch.

What's going on?

His next words barely make it through clenched teeth. "Jeter is missing."

Before I can blink, the paper is crumpled and in the fire. "Shit." Rusty spins on his heel, throwing his hands into his hair. "I told him to do it months ago!" he yells. "I told the chief to remove Jeter's totem after that memory bug was found in your head, Alena. I knew Jeter had to be working with Jax somehow. Jeter's the only one who can control those damn bugs. But Chief didn't listen to me. Said Jeter is too valuable to just speculate. He had to be sure."

"Wait, what?" I shake my head in confusion. "You think Jeter put that memory bug in my head?" The memory bug. I had thought I was only having weird dreams of Cody being tortured when she disappeared. But after several nights of having the exact same dream, I finally went to the chief. Jeter looked in my head and found a memory bug there, acted completely innocent as if he didn't know.

After SilverDen, after Gabbro did what he did, I thought he was the one responsible for all the weird things that happened in Petrichor: the Morgans, the location missing from the threats. Everything was explainable with Gabbro behind it.

Well, everything except for one thing. The memory bugs. *How had I forgotten about that?* Jeter is the only one who can control the memory bugs.

My brain urgently replays the events in my mind, filling in the holes with this new bit of information, as if I can see Jax's plan clearly for the first time.

Jax took Cody and tortured her. Then he snuck into Petrichor and allowed himself to be caught and brought to the chief's office. I remember that day in the chief's office, standing there with Mark and Danny.

Just after Jax delivered his cryptic message, he disappeared into an explosion of smoke.

It all makes sense.

Everyone ran from the room to look for Jax, but the smoke was just a distraction. It allowed Chauly, who was probably there camouflaged in the same room, just enough time to make Jax disappear.

Jeter was in that room too. He had come in late, and then when everyone else left to look for Jax, he stayed there.

Because he knew Jax was still there.

I shiver as an eerie feeling creeps through my skin.

From there, Jeter took a memory bug and collected the memory of Cody being tortured from Jax's awful brain. Once he had it, he somehow put it in my head. When I was sleeping?

I want to throw up.

They did all that to manipulate me into turning myself over to them. All for the black power.

And Jeter was working with them all along? Why?

Rusty and Cody are urgently talking about the GreenLands now, about the weapons, answering my question.

Jeter wants to help his homeland. That's why he sent all those weapons. But he wants more. He wants the black power.

But I look down at my totem. How would this totem's power help his homeland? I don't understand.

Then my hands begin to tremble.

I had sent Mark on an errand to possibly find memory bugs. Did he find them? Did he take them to Jeter?

Oh no.

"Rusty." I don't say his name very loud, but there's a horrified edge to it that makes Rusty pause.

"I sent a message to Mark when we were at the rendezvous point." I gulp past the bile in my throat. "I think something's wrong."

I quickly explain what I think might have happened. Kapri moves to stand next to me. When I'm done, Rusty pulls out another piece of paper and starts scribbling a new message.

Did Jeter take Mark? Is that why he hasn't responded?

I rub my temples and close my eyes. *Please tell me he didn't.*

"I'll have Chief look into it."

His words hang in the cold air. I stare at the ground, pressure building inside my head.

"Hey." Rusty steps forward and places his hand on my shoulder. "It'll be okay. We'll leave for Dakdete first thing in the morning. We'll find Danny. Then we'll get you back to Mark."

He makes everything sound so simple. I just wish it made me feel better.

"Try to get some rest, Alena. We have a big day ahead of us."

He and Cody disappear into their tents while I battle with the knots in my gut. I'm being torn painfully in half. We know where Danny is now. We need to go find him.

But now Mark could be missing? Ugh! Why can't my friends just be left alone? I wring my hands.

"Come sleep in my tent tonight," Kapri says.

Before I know it, she's helping me gather my sleeping bag and pulling me to her tent.

Once inside I slip into my bag, covering my head.

I won't be sleeping much tonight.

Chapter 25

I don't know how Pepps get any sleep on runs. Of course, my mind wouldn't rest, with so many worries. I was tempted to use the Ataractic on myself, to calm down, but then I remember Sepharine telling me it's only to be used in emergencies. So, I fight to find sleep—in vain.

When Rusty starts waking everyone up, I groan in fatigue but only for a moment. Danny. We need to find Danny so I can go find Mark. *Please be okay, Mark.*

I pack up my stuff quickly, an acidic bile churning in my belly. I pick at the egg and bacon breakfast prepared by Benjy but ultimately throw away my food. I can't stomach the stuff right now. Once I'm ready, I stand by Kapri, waiting for the rest of the team. I wish they would hurry.

When the team is all packed up, each team member morphs into eagles, and with Rusty in the lead, we head out.

I'm not sure which direction we're heading, but the change of land suggests it's south. The land is getting dryer.

We fly all day, only needing one break. Eventually, the dry, flat land changes again, giving rise to bright red-rock mountains, barren but magnificent. I've never seen such a deep color in rock.

When Rusty dips down into a valley at the base of a large canyon, he demands we take another break.

I take advantage of the stop, stretching out my body, then I sit on a large red rock and eat some of the granola I brought in my satchel.

I stare at the vast red mountain range before us. Some of the mountains look like the ones back home with peaks at the top and canyons below. But off to my left there's a tall mountainside that goes straight up at least a couple hundred feet, with a perfectly smooth surface. I can't picture even the most skilled rock climber being able to find a toehold in that rock. There's nothing to grab hold of. I get dizzy looking up it, imagining it falling over and squishing us all. I shake my head. And it's bright red, such a profound contrast to the blue sky beyond it.

I smack my lips and swallow, then look around. It's unbelievably dry here. And hot. I bring my hand up to shade my eyes while they search for plant life: a tree, a bush, even a cactus. Nothing. There's not a single leaf within the miles I can see. It looks like it hasn't rained here in years. Possibly ever.

"Everyone, ration your water," Rusty says. "This is Dakdete. It never rains here. Even making water here with our power is difficult."

Hmm. I was right.

A scuffle behind me interrupts my thoughts. Turning around, I find Sef and Benjy holding Kapri in a cradle, threatening to throw her into a pit below. She frantically squeals and thrashes her limbs.

"Hey!" I shout dryly.

Sef and Benjy obviously aren't serious about throwing her in, because they set her down. But based on her expression, they succeeded at scaring her. When she's free, Kapri kicks Sef and pushes Benjy, threatening them with words I can't hear. Which makes me laugh a little.

When she's done requiting them, she turns back to look into the pit, a hand rising to her mouth, her eyes widening.

What's down there?

My feet scuffle across the red sand. I barely reach the edge of the pit, when I see it and stumble back.

Hundreds of large snakes, gray with black stripes, lie woven on top of one another in a disgusting hissing heap.

"Rattlesnakes," Sef says. "Can you hear the rattles? You don't want to get bitten by one of those."

I shiver at the sight and slowly back away.

We don't really have snakes where I come from, in the high mountains. But even in the high mountains we've heard of these kinds of snakes.

"Watch your step around here," Sef adds. "They're everywhere—under rocks and in holes."

Suddenly I'm scared to even move.

I stand there in the sun, feeling it suck the energy from my body. My mouth already parched. I agree with Rusty. I hate Dakdete.

I swallow, trying to wet my tongue in vain, then look back at Rusty and Cody, who are still staring at the mountains. What's Rusty doing? I tiptoe across the ground, jumping at any unexpected moving sand, searching for holes. When I reach Rusty, I examine his face.

"What's wrong?" I ask, my face contorting in response to his obvious worry.

Rusty continues to study the red mountains towering high above us on both sides.

"Something doesn't feel right."

Sef joins us quietly on Cody's other side. "It's a trap."

Rusty nods in agreement. "I have a feeling Danny is right through that canyon, but if we walk down there, we'll be easily spotted. Jax is probably waiting for us in those rocks. He could shoot us down before we even reach him."

My heart pounds wildly. Rusty thinks Danny's *here*? I hope more than anything that he is. *But this could be another trap?* I'm not good with traps.

Clearing his throat and rubbing his hands together, Sef says, "Let me go in." A grin spreads wide on his face.

I expect Rusty to immediately reject the idea, but he nods. "A lizard should do it." Before I can even blink, Sef morphs into a reptile and quickly scampers over the rocks into the canyon.

"Jax knows the Pepp eagle form," Rusty quietly explains. "He also knows too much about Magbabies. We need something a little less conspicuous to go in there and look around. Lizards are a normal presence around here, so Jax won't suspect too much. Hopefully."

I understand now why Rusty said morphers are convenient. There's no way to tell if an animal is real or a Pepp.

We wait.

Man. It feels like the hot sun is only inches from my already sun-burnt skin. I sit on a rock to rest for a moment, but the heat of it hurts even through my clothes, so I stand back up. Then I glance down at my shirt. I'm sure I'm sweating, but the air must be so dry it's frantically stealing away any sweat I have to offer. There's not a single drop on my clothing.

Kapri fans her face frantically before pulling a straw hat out of her satchel. Benjy goes a step further and pulls out a white sheet to cover his entire body. Smart. Wish I had something like that.

Needless to say, I'm almost a raisin by the time Sef gets back.

Morphing back into himself, he leans over to catch his breath. The seven of us quickly gather around, waiting for his news. Finally, he stands tall, showing off the fullest of grins.

"Danny's in there."

Danny's here? My body trembles in anticipation.

"Trevor, and Gabbro are in there too. They're tied to posts, sitting out in the middle of the canyon." Looking to Rusty now, his excitement fades. "You were right—it is a trap. Jax is hiding in a cave close by, ready to attack when we get there. But he isn't alone. He has the help of three other Pepp men." Sef emphasizes the word *Pepp*. "Well, three that I could see."

Three Pepp men?

"Is Jeter with them?" Rusty asks.

"I didn't see Jeter."

"Do they have power?" Cody pipes in. "The other Pepps?"

"They have totems, so probably," Sef answers. "We should go in there expecting it."

"Is Danny okay?" Kapri interjects quietly.

Sef's face grows grim. "He's alive. But he might not be for long. We need to get him home."

"What do we do?" Cody asks.

Sef's smirk returns, and he points to the pit of rattlesnakes. "I have a plan."

***

I crouch behind a rock, waiting for everyone else to get into position. I can still see the disgusting den of snakes weaving their way up the side of the mountain with Sef—morphed as a snake—at the lead. The rest of the Pepps, though, are out of my sight.

Bait. That's how Rusty is using me in his plan. I'm the bait. I turn my gaze to the canyon ahead of me. My hands are shaking, but I'm more alive than I've been in weeks. I hope this works.

Finally, after waiting the allotted time, I slide out of my hiding place and walk down the middle of the two towering mountains. The sound of rocks crunching beneath my feet bounces through the air, but that's okay. I want Jax to hear me. I roll the glass power container in my hand. Rusty reminded me of the number one thing Jax wants: the power created in my totem. If he finds out right away that I don't have it, there's a good chance he'll kill me on the spot. Or take me as a prisoner. That's why Rusty insisted we create a fake copy.

Rusty also gave me a full vial of power. Mine was completely empty this morning, which confused me since I'd hardly used it yesterday. But then I remembered stabbing the man with the knife. Did that deplete my power?

Before I left, I gave Harper Mark's gun and my satchel, asking her to keep them safe.

The only thing that would make me feel more comfortable is having Breccia with me.

That, and if I didn't have to wear this electric belt. I try not to fiddle with my shirt hiding it. I hate the way it sticks to my hot skin. I was hoping I would never have to use this thing again. But Rusty refused to let me go in without it. It's probably for the best.

The mountain shadows drift over me the deeper I go. I'm supposed to go straight to Danny. Sef told me to just follow the base of the canyon. He'll be in plain view on the right, tied to an old piece of wood. He's confident that once I find Danny, Jax will find me.

I take in a deep breath and focus on the path, moving quickly. Sef tried to prepare me for finding Danny. *He's not in good condition*, he had said.

I anxiously search the rocks on the right, looking for any signs of life.

Finally, I think I see something. Two long posts pounded into the ground with two darkened figures slumping forward at their bases. The moment I recognize Danny's distinct profile, I start to run. I can't help it. I run up the hill, through the red sand, until I slide on the dirt next to him and kneel. I inhale sharply when I see him in full view.

He's thin, as if he hasn't eaten in weeks. His hair, which had been neatly cut the day of the dance, is thin. The rest of his exposed skin is bruised to a dark-blue color or burned purple by the hot sun. On his leg is a gaping wound filled with insects eating away at his blackened flesh.

Trevor the bear is there too, tied to the other post, a wound on his arm filled with the same insects. And then Gabbro, encaged by metal and tied to Trevor's arm. He might be a rock, but he's a very sick rock, unresponsive and soft. *What happened to him?*

And why is he caged? I thought he was working for Jax.

"Danny." I whisper his name but get no response. I reach out to touch his face, listening for the sounds of his wound. I need to heal him, but the moment I touch his face, I hear a click right next to my ear.

"Don't move." A gruff voice says behind me, the metal barrel of a gun tapping my ear.

I freeze, holding my breath, trying to quiet my heart.

"It took you long enough. Where's the rest of your team?" Jax's voice hasn't changed at all. It terrifies me now just as much as it did on the day I first met him, leaving me speechless. *Where did he come from?*

Cursing under his breath, Jax moves around me, and before I realize what he's doing with the gun in his hands, I hear a shot ring out through the rocks. It only takes a moment before the shock wears off enough for me to feel the pain in my leg. I gasp at first and then scream. Excruciating pain radiates up my thigh, to my torso. I look down at my already blood-soaked pants.

I wasn't expecting that!

Before I can react, Jax reaches down, grabbing the power out of my totem just like Rusty said he would, fortunately, not seeing the electric belt. Taking my Pepp power, he looks at it before throwing it to the ground and crushing it beneath his shoe.

"Do you have the black power?" Jax asks, impatience pulsing through his face.

The pain in my leg is consuming my thoughts. I can't think. That is, until Jax slaps me across the face. The power. I shake my fuzzy head. He wants the power. Raising my hand with the fake power in it, I show him the vial of black liquid.

Jax rips it out of my hand and looks at it closely. *He won't know it's a fake, will he?*

After placing the vial in his pocket, Jax grabs me by my arm and drags me to my feet. Blood drips down my leg, spilling into my shoe. I bite my lip in pain, dragging my dead leg along.

"I know your team is out there. They're free to take Danny ... If they can get him." I almost hear the laughter in Jax's voice, and it makes me sick. He's enjoying this.

Shouting out to the air around him, he says, "Don't leave your posts until you have them all."

His Pepp men.

I resist Jax's pull, but he tightens his grip and draws his face close to mine. "You might not be able to help your friends, but you can help yourself. The best thing you can do right now is exactly what I say."

Tears sting my eyes, which amuses Jax. This wasn't quite what I had planned, but it'll be okay, right? I just need to go along with it until my team can get Danny and Trevor out.

Through my blurred eyes, I look ahead. Jax is pulling me to a large hole in the red rock. I stumble several times, dragging my leg, but Jax doesn't loosen his grip. We enter a dark tunnel that winds back and forth, going down and then up again. At least I think it does. I've lost too much blood, and my vision is pulsing with the little blood I have left.

Through the ringing in my ears, I almost miss it. A gunshot, echoing through the tunnels.

"Sounds like your friends got a little too close to Danny," Jax says.

I hope he's wrong. I hope the gunshots were his men shooting at the snakes. Well, at any snake except Sef.

Finally, we reach a room dimly lit with torches. Jax throws me against the wall. I scream at the contact and then slump to the floor, trying to cradle my leg, new tears seeping down.

"Look up." Jax's voice is gruff.

Mustering as much strength as I can, I force my head up.

We're in a dark red cave, no windows, stuffy air, with several lit candles dripping onto a wooden table against the far wall. There are shelves full of liquid ointments and wraps, as well as odd-smelling dried leaves. Another table shoved into the corner is topped with weird-looking roots and food. A basin of water sits on the floor. *Where did they get water?*

My gaze wanders back to Jax, who is pointing to a bed behind him. I blink, trying to see through the pain. Someone is lying on the bed. A girl, with stringy light-brown hair plastered to her skin. She's lying down, but she isn't asleep. Her face mirrors mine, creased with pain. On her skin I see several swollen, oozing lesions, some red and some black, all mixed with sweat.

"You will heal her, with this power," Jax says, holding out the fake vial he took from me. His voice cracks with emotion. I examine his face for the first time. He's still old and worn. He still has that disgusting scar extending from the side of his mouth to his ear. But underneath all the age and anger, I sense something else.

Pain. Not physical but emotional pain.

My leg pulses again. "What's wrong with her?" I murmur. I need to stall as long as I can so Rusty can do his work. I slowly bring my body to standing, gritting my teeth in the process.

"She's sick, and the only power that can heal her is this power."

Jax confirms what I've suspected.

"She's a Mixed Blood," I calmly state.

Jax's nostrils flare. "Yes."

I find my way to the side of the young girl. I remember my conversation with Eli at the prison. How he had extracted one small piece of information from the memories of the clan man there. And that information was that Jax had a daughter. This must be her.

Regardless of all that's happened, all that's been done to me to create black power, I feel bad for her. She's pale, yet reddened with swollen, broken skin. She's depleted like a balloon stretched too far then deflated. She's sweating. Which is really saying something in this dry-as-heck place. Just looking at her I know that her condition reaches down to her very bones, her very cells. She can't eat, can't sleep, and is only just barely surviving.

And she can't be healed. I've heard little about the Mixed Bloods, but what I have heard is that regardless of the Pepps' desire to help them, they can't.

I hate seeing others in pain. I've gained a great deal of satisfaction being a Pepp and being able to eliminate suffering. Standing here now, though, I'm completely helpless, just like Jax. And I hate it.

It's like I've been walking around in complete darkness, until this very moment. *Is this why he's gone through such great lengths to get the black power?* Would the black power really be able to help a Mixed Blood like this girl?

Holding out his hand, Jax hands me the fake vial of power. I take it, cringing when my fingers brush against his clammy palm.

Hurry, Rusty, please, before he finds out.

Popping it into my totem, I lie through my teeth, stalling more. "This power is different, Jax. It sounds different. I haven't been able to figure out why. It'll take me time before I'm able to use it."

Grabbing the collar of my shirt, Jax yanks me forward. I flinch, frightened by his palpable emotion.

"You *will* heal her. I don't care how long you have to stay here. But you will do it!"

I'm about to nod, when someone enters the room.

"Jax."

Without releasing my shirt, Jax turns his head in irritation to the entrance.

"I thought I told you not to leave your posts!" Jax yells so loud it makes my ears ring. Following his gaze, I see two men there, barely standing, trying to hold each other up.

"We've been bitten by rattlesnakes."

I stifle a grin. If there are two of them in here, that means there might only be one left outside. The plan is running its course, which means I need to get ready for my next attack. Jax's gun. He had propped it up against the bed so he could grab me by the collar. I need to get it.

"Well, heal yourself!"

I almost feel bad for Jax. He's not going to get his way.

"We can't." One of the men slides down against the wall until he collapses on the floor. His totem is wrapped in red. He must be a medic, and he's been bitten several times. I study the other man who is now unconscious.

"The snake swallowed my power," the medic says through labored gasps.

Sef. He wanted to make sure their power was gone.

Jax spins his head back to me. He knows we've played him. He reaches for his gun, but I'm there first, screaming in the process, pain stretching up my wounded leg. Gripping the gun with all my strength, I slam the barrel into his stomach and push myself away from him. Once I'm far enough away, I keep it pointed in his direction as best as I can through my weakness.

And then I pull my shirt up.

"Don't move," I say. His gaze wanders down to my exposed waist, where I've activated my electric belt. "One touch and you'll be dead."

Now all I need to do is hold this pose until I hear the signal. I grit my teeth. The strain on my body is agonizing. Blood pours down my leg, muscles weakening with every second, pain pulsing stronger and stronger. I grip the gun tightly, channeling the pain into it. *Hurry, Rusty.*

When I finally hear Rusty's yell echoing through the tunnel, I sigh in relief and force my sluggish eyes open. Danny and Trevor should be free now.

"I'm in here!" I shout as loud as I can, then I drop to my knees. I hope that was enough noise for Rusty and the others to find their way through the tunnels.

Jax bends down. *What is he doing?* Something screams in my mind that I should move, should raise the gun in my hands, but I'm way too dizzy.

Before I realize it, he's picked up a heavy red rock. The rock slams into my head, sending my body to the floor.

My vision blacks, and my lungs stop working. The gun clatters out of my hands, and Jax is now scrambling to get it. I lift my chin high, willing my pained lungs to inhale. I need to warn Rusty. But it's too late.

"Alena!"

Jax's gun goes off.

"Dammit!" I hear Rusty curse, followed by a lot of shuffling and shouting.

I'm just seeing stars. *Man!*

Then Cody is there.

"Deactivate your belt, Alena," she shouts above the chaos.

I reach my hand into my shirt and flip the switch as quickly as my sluggish body will allow.

"Cody." I sigh, grateful to have a medic at my side.

I feel her power in my leg first, feel the muscles tugging and pulling as they mend, then the skin stretching itself back into place. Then my body inflates, a certain strength returning as she restores my blood count. Finally, she heals my head, restoring my vision. The room finally comes back into focus.

Sef and Benjy are at the tunnel entrance, tying the hands of the two unconscious snakebitten men.

Rusty has pinned Jax facedown on the floor and is tying his hands behind his back.

"Where's Harper?" Rusty asks.

"Harper was right behind me with the last one," Sef says.

Benjy shifts on his feet, then runs out the door to look for Harper.

Rusty rips Jax off the floor and grips the front of his shirt fiercely. "Where's Jeter?" he shouts, spit flying from his face.

Jax sneers. "Jeter? I don't know, but when I find him, I'm gonna kill him. Traitor."

I blink twice.

"What?" My voice grinds dryly against my throat. "Jeter isn't working for you?"

Jax's jaw tightens. "We used to all work together. Until SilverDen. Then everything fell apart thanks to Case. Jeter hasn't helped me at all since then. Bastard."

Just then Harper and Benjy enter the room carrying a large unconscious man. My stomach churns at the sight of blood seeping through several spots on the man's gray shirt. He's been shot ... multiple times.

"The idiot decided to take flight when he saw me. It took five shots to get him to stop," Harper says, dropping the man's body on the floor. She glares at him with irritation, blowing a strand of auburn hair out of her face.

"The chief will be happy to know we found three of his missing Pepps." Rusty points to all three unconscious men lying on the rocky floor. "And Chauly. Looks like things are finally turning in our favor."

I remember the pictures of missing Pepps displayed on the wall at the prison. These men must be some of those that ran away so they wouldn't have to go to Algor.

A gruesome smirk spreads Jax's bloodied lip. "Where is that son of a bitch? Chauly was supposed to bring Alena here."

Rusty, Cody, and I all exchange a glance at one another. When Rusty doesn't bother to explain what we did to find Chauly, I bite my tongue too. Perhaps Jax doesn't need to know.

Instead, Rusty says, "Algor seems to be a good place to put them."

Jax mumbles at Rusty's comment. "Yeah, I'm sure they'll love it."

Bending down on one knee, Rusty puts his face close to Jax's. "You're going to jail too. Tell me, was it worth it? Doing all this for what— a vial of mysterious power?"

Jax spits in Rusty's face. "You don't know anything."

Rusty's neck reddens, and his hands clamp up, but he takes in a deep breath and wipes the spit off his face.

"Well, maybe we can change that by taking you back to Petrichor."

This humors Jax. "Ha, is someone going to torture me? Who? The chief? He was always too soft for things like that. He couldn't even discipline his own brother when he was caught doing the same things we did."

This catches my attention. *What's he talking about? Eli, the man at the prison?*

I don't know why Jax looks at me after saying this, but he does and observes the confusion on my face.

"That's right, Alena. The chief's own brother was our leader when we all went off the deep end. He committed the same crimes we committed. The same crimes those in the prison committed, but instead of throwing his brother in with the rest of them, the chief made him the prison warden. He didn't even get a slap on the wrist."

I rip my eyes away from Jax and glance at Rusty. *Is it true?* I want to ask him, but his eyes avoid my gaze. *Would he really throw everyone in prison except his own brother?* I shudder silently when I think about the awful, angry man, Eli.

"Your chief isn't all he's cracked up to be," Jax says. "He's just like the rest of us, wandering and stupid."

"That's enough," Rusty shouts. "We're taking you to Petrichor. The chief will decide what to do with you there."

Jax's face darkens. "You will not take *her*." He gestures to the table with the girl on it. "You know it'll kill her. And you know she can't take care of herself. If you take me with you, she'll die."

Rusty's anger doesn't waver. "I don't have a choice, Jax."

Jax screams, the sounds jumping off the walls.

But Rusty ties up the girl and places her in a toboggan, making Jax scream louder. It's somewhat heart-wrenching. *He loves his daughter.*

I sigh in relief when Cody disables Jax somehow. Knocks him unconscious with power.

Thank you. But then I hear the girl groaning in pain. Unfortunately, none of us can help her.

Harper makes her way to me and hands me Mark's gun and my satchel.

"Thank you," I say.

"This is our last toboggan," Rusty says to the team. "We'll need to carry Jax and his men back to Petrichor ourselves."

"The last toboggan?" I whisper.

Cody hears me. "We sent Danny and Kapri back in one and Trevor and Gabbro back in the other."

"Are they okay?" My chest swells, remembering they're the reason we came here.

"They look like they're in rough condition," Cody says, "but they're alive. They'll make it." Cody says this brightly to reassure me. Suddenly the reality of the events hit me.

Danny—he's alive! And almost home.

A crushing weight of worry finally lifts from my chest, replaced with a cleansing relief that melts into my bones. I fall to my knees. Danny's alive!

I can't wait to see him again!

It doesn't take long for the Pepps to clear the room, each of them dragging an unconscious prisoner. I follow them out, quickly taking off my electric belt before it hurts someone I care about. Without a break, we're in the air flying back to Petrichor.

Chapter 26

I still can't believe it. The wind whips in my face. *Danny is safe!*

Chauly has been captured and now Jax!

The joy this brings me is quickly snuffed out.

Mark.

I still need to make sure Mark is okay. Rusty still hasn't received a reply from the chief. I wish we could take a break long enough for Rusty's Magbaby to catch up with us.

Carrying Jax and his men back to Petrichor slows our trip immensely. I rotate flying on the backs of my teammates, allowing them to take turns carrying the men. We've taken several breaks to rest, and right now we're back in the sky, and I'm sitting on Sef. I expect Rusty to instruct us to make camp after the sun sets, but during our last break he demanded that we move on, stating that we need to get back to Petrichor as quickly as possible. I don't know how far we have to go, but after all the flying we did earlier today, we probably still have a long way.

To darken the night even more, clouds loom ahead, stretching across the horizon. I can only guess there's rain somewhere in the midst of those clouds. Rusty doesn't change course, though. Instead, he whistles something out to the fellow eagles, who understand what he's saying. We don't stop, and it looks like we're heading straight into the storm. It doesn't appear too dangerous, though. No signs of lightning, just a little rain.

Sef heaves beneath me, just like the other Pepps are heaving.

Then rain hits us, starting out as light pattering. But then the rain drops pelt my face, making it sting with cold. I hide in Sef's slippery feathers, holding on as tightly as I can. The sky blackens around us, and soon we're surrounded by nothing but dark. *How does Rusty know which direction to go?*

Soon I'm cold and shivering. My hands are going numb, and my body is starting to slip. Raising my head, I look for some sign of clear sky, when suddenly Sef falls limp beneath me.

My stomach rises to my throat as we plunge in the sky. I try to scream, but the air whipping around me steals my breath away. My body detaches from Sef's back, and I lose sight of him in the blackness. I can't tell which way is up or down. I try to draw on the elements around me, hoping to get my bearings, when I remember Jax stole my power. I don't have anything. Trying not to panic, still unable to see the ground, I brace for impact. *Where's Sef? I don't see him anywhere.*

Then I belly flop into ice-cold water, pain rippling across my limbs, stomach, and face. Am I dead? No, but the water grabs hold of me and takes me under. Kicking my feet, I try to rise above the surface, but my limbs are in such shock that I can't seem to move them. Miraculously, I break the surface, gasping for breath, but I can't hold myself up for long before I start sinking again.

It's so cold!

As I fight to hold on, something wraps around my stomach. *What the ...?* When I grab at it, I almost cry out in relief. It's a rope. Sef must be saving me. The rope tugs me forward, slowly at first, but then the pull draws me across the water.

Skidding across the surface at such a fast speed doesn't help me catch my breath. Coughing and sputtering, I wrap my fingers around the rope and hold on tight.

The rope eventually loosens and my speed slows until finally my knees scrape against rocks beneath me. I fall to all fours and cough my lungs out.

"Alena?"

The voice is familiar but not one I was expecting to hear out here. Goose bumps rise on my skin. With a shaking body, I fight to lift my head enough to see if it's really who I think it is.

"Jeter?" I whisper.

Kneeling on one knee, with a lantern on the ground next to him, Jeter unties the rope and grips my arm to help me stand.

"Alena, are you alright?"

My legs shake under my weight.

Why in the world is Jeter out here?

"Sef," I whisper through chattering teeth. "He's out there somewhere. He fell with me."

Jeter looks out into the blackness over what is probably a lake. "I saw him fall. I'll get someone to help him. He'll be fine, I'm sure."

Will he?

Looking around, I see a cabin ahead, a light twinkling in the only window.

We walk to it, my body shivering uncontrollably. When we reach the door, Jeter opens it and gestures me inside.

I look back into the darkness behind me. "I'll wait for Sef."

Jeter grips my arm and pulls me in. "He'll be here in a minute. Come get dry."

My heart thrashes wildly in my chest. *No.*

I cast my eyes frantically around the room. The cabin is small. The wooden walls fresh. Two sets of bunk beds are pushed against the far wall, and a fireplace crackles to my left. Then my eyes land in the middle of the floor. I step back into Jeter.

There's a man lying there, covered in a gray holey blanket.

Jeter gently pushes me forward and shuts the door while my eyes quickly skim over the man's sickly body. The exposed skin on his face is covered in large sores, some of them oozing yellow liquid onto the white pillowcase under his head. In addition to how scary he looks, there's a putrid smell of dead flesh mixed with infection.

His condition looks oddly similar to that of the girl with Jax but much worse. From natural instinct, I reach out for the elements of his body ready to control them. But I don't have power.

A hand lands on my shoulder.

"Our power won't work on him," Jeter says, somehow knowing I was trying to heal him. Then pointing to the only other door in the room, he says, "Go in there and change. When you're warm, you can join me out here. I think I could use your help."

Suddenly, my foggy mind clears, and I freeze.

Was it coincidence that Jeter just happened to be here when I fell out of the sky? How did he know I was drowning in the lake? My gut churns. It's not a coincidence, which means he's the one who made Sef fall. To get to me. To help him with this man.

With difficulty, I pull my eyes away from the man and lift my gaze to Jeter. *What do I do?* Every cell in my body tells me I should run. That whatever Jeter needs my help with shouldn't be done. But I know better than to try to escape. I wouldn't get far, not with Jeter, especially since I don't have power. No, I better play along and hope that somehow I'll come up with an idea.

I obey his commands and head to the room, which seems to be some sort of bathroom. In the back of my mind, I find the cabin odd. It seems too clean, the wood too new, too out of place in the middle of nowhere. It doesn't even have a kitchen.

It must be from a capsule, brought to this specific spot by Jeter. He must have known we would be flying right over this place. *But how?*

I quickly change my clothes, using dry clothing capsules from my satchel. I observe the windowless walls. No way to get out. Reluctantly, I return to the room.

"Alena, come here," Jeter says, still standing over the man.

Putting my wet clothes on one of the bunk beds, along with Mark's gun that is soaked, I walk to his side.

"What's wrong with him?" I ask. If I get a better understanding of what's really going on, maybe I'll get a better idea of what I need to stop.

"He's a Mixed Blood," Jeter says.

I never saw a Mixed Blood in my life until earlier today. And now I'm seeing a second?

Furrowing my eyebrows, I step closer, observing the man's painfully swollen skin. He has light hair—at least what's left of his hair is light. In addition to the open wounds on his skin I see scars. Lots of scars from previous wounds that healed very poorly.

Jeter taps my arm.

"If you try to heal him with your power, you'll only make it worse. I have an idea of how to help him, but I need you to trust me. Please give me your power."

But as he says this his face turns thoughtful. "Wait, you don't have any power." It's not a question. Jeter must be able to hear the lack of Peppate in my totem.

"No," I say, "It was taken by Jax when we saved Danny. I never got it back."

A dark shadow crosses Jeter's brow, and he clenches his jaw.

"You saw Jax?"

"Yes," I say. *Did he even hear the part about how we saved Danny?* "But don't worry, Jax is on his way back to Petrichor now, where he'll be put in prison." I watch his face, curious to see his reaction. If he's happy about that, that means he and Jax aren't working together. At least not now.

The man on the floor coughs, muttering something under his breath. I don't quite understand his words, but Jeter does, and he finds them amusing.

"Yes, it's about time," Jeter says, then, stepping toward me, he holds out his hand. "Now put this in, Alena."

Interesting. *I guess they're not friends with Jax anymore?*

I look down. There, resting in his palm, is a full vial of real black power. It can't be mine. I used all my power on Mark's leg. Which means this vial ... is Mark's.

"Where did you get that?" I whisper, suddenly very concerned. The last time I saw this power it was hidden in the vault.

"Mark gave it to me. I think it could help us here."

"That's a lie. The power was hidden away."

Jeter raises his eyebrows at my accusation. "Chief gave it back to Mark after Chauly was captured."

I set my jaw. I don't believe him. "Is Mark okay?" I don't know why I ask this. It doesn't matter what Jeter says. I won't trust a word out of his mouth.

"Of course he's okay. Why?"

"He's in Petrichor?"

"Yes, Mark is in Petrichor. I spoke with him just yesterday." I watch his face, looking for any twitch, any broken eye contact, any sign that he's lying. But I find none.

Still, my stomach plummets. Deep down, I know he's lying. But what does that mean? *Is Mark in danger?*

"Here, put this in." Jeter is anxious to move on, pushing the dark power closer to me. "I think you'll be able to help this man. I would do it myself, but my totem has Peppate in it. This man needs to be treated with something one-hundred percent Peppate-free."

My totem.

I move to obey Jeter, silently hounding my mind to think of a way out.

I pop the power in, immediately recognizing the difference in sound.

"I've been studying this man for many years," Jeter says. "Trying to figure out what is ailing him and why he can't be healed."

Opening up a book, Jeter reveals diagrams I'm familiar with.

"Peppate generators," I whisper, recalling the spiral tadpole-like diagram.

Jeter glances my way, surprised I would know what a generator looks like. I curse under my breath. I should have played dumb. He wouldn't expect me to heal what I don't understand, right?

"Yes, that's correct," he says. "This is a Peppate generator in a normal totem." Sliding his finger to a diagram drawn on a piece of paper tucked in the book, he adds, "Even though the Mixed Bloods don't have totems, they seem to have properties similar to those of the Pepps, such as generators."

I examine the hand-drawn picture. It looks identical to the one my dad showed me. The generator with the extra sac.

"It looks like they have generators, but instead of producing Peppate, the generators in their blood vessels produce Doler, just like yours. It spirals around and then is released through the skin." Jeter pauses, letting this information sink in. He doesn't realize I already know this.

"Why is he so sick, though?" I ask. "I produce Doler just like he does, but it doesn't make me sick like this."

Jeter nods. "He's sick because he's allergic to Peppate."

Allergic to Peppate? Eli at the prison had thought the Mixed Bloods were allergic to plants. I guess he was almost right. Plants are loaded with Peppate. So is water, air. In fact everything has Peppate, except for dinosaurs, which explains why this man looks so terribly sick.

"Something," Jeter continues, "about being born to a human and a Pepp makes every Mixed Blood allergic to Peppate. The sores are a reaction to any Peppate that touches their skin. But that isn't all."

Pointing to the second, smaller sac in the second picture, Jeter explains further. "The worst part is that they produce Peppate themselves, here, in this second sac. Many Mixed Bloods live their lives hiding in rocks to escape what makes them sick, but the truth is they will never fully escape it."

Dad had wondered what was in the second sac. The second sac doesn't hold power. It's a Peppate generator. Mixed Bloods produce both Peppate and Doler.

I eye the man who looks like he's suffered a lot of pain in his life. I feel bad for him, amazed that a person could survive such terrible circumstances. To be allergic to himself. Nobody deserves to live like that.

"So how do we heal him?" I ask, still unsure of what I should really be doing.

Jeter seems pleased with this question. "With the black power, we need to find a way to keep his body from producing Peppate."

Suddenly my dad's voice rings loud and clear. I hear his theory about how the Mixed Bloods harness the same properties in their bodies that Mark and I harness in our totem, including the power to produce lightning. He believes the second sac, or Peppate generator, is somehow not only disabling the power but also disabling the lightning that comes from any morph. If I disable the Peppate generator, could this man create lightning, become dangerous, just like Mark and me?

I wonder if Jeter knows.

I point to the other sac. "What is this sac for, if the other is a Peppate generator?"

"It doesn't matter!" Jeter yells, making me jump. Then he takes in a deep breath.

That's when I know. He thinks the same thing my dad does. That it's a power sac. A power sac that has never worked because of the Peppate generator. Which means if I heal this man, I could possibly make another horrible weapon. A weapon like Mark and me.

But why would he want that?

Just then another man enters the room from outside, soaked from head to toe. He starts whispering something to Jeter, giving me the opportunity to think things through. That is, until I hear Sef's name. I glare at the man now, noticing his arm lacking a totem. He's a non-Pepp.

Did he find Sef? If he did, is he going to hurt Sef?

I'm unable to contain the panic that rises within me now, like a boiling pot ready to spill over.

I can't do what Jeter is asking me to do.

I try to calm my beating heart. I have to compose myself. Maybe I can think of some way to crutch the process—maybe do what he's asking but in a way that can be reversed easily? I shut my eyes. *Think, Alena, think.*

"Alena?" Jeter clears his throat. I raise my head to find him staring at me intently, the other man gone.

I rub my temple, trying to wave off my pounding heart. "I'm sorry, Jeter, I'm just trying to think. I don't know what these generators sound like or what to say to disable them." I stall. "I'm also worried about the amount of power I have. I don't think it'll be enough to disable every single generator in his body. There have to be thousands of them."

The man on the floor suddenly grabs my ankle with his scabby hand, making me jump.

"You have to do this tonight. Tonight!" His croaky voice frightens me. Wide-eyed, I stumble backward. He releases me and starts coughing wildly. "You brought me out here, Jeter, made me sicker than I've been in years. No more waiting. Tonight!"

"Okay." Jeter holds up his hands in surrender, then scowls at me. "If you hadn't wasted the rest of your power on Mark's leg, perhaps we *would* have enough."

I glare at Jeter. *How does he know I used the rest of my power on Mark? Did Mark tell him?*

Jeter waves his hand. "But never mind that. I thought this might be a problem, so I thought up an alternative." He pulls a box off one of the bunk beds, then reveals several syringes full of white fluid.

"Dilo's serum," I say, my worry for Mark now uncontainable. "Where did you get that?"

Jeter's losing his patience with me.

"You know where I got it. Mark, of course. Now, I've learned this serum is also Peppate-free and has some paralyzing properties. I figure if we inject this serum right into the blood vessel leaving his heart, the heart will pump it through his entire body. Once it's everywhere, you command the serum from the vessels into the Peppate generators."

"What about the infection?" I say, frantically trying to stop his plan. "Mark's body didn't respond well to the foreign substance."

"True," he says. "But the Peppate generators are so small we won't need much serum. I'm hoping with the scant amount we use, it won't cause infection. Regardless, it's a risk we're willing to take at this point."

I stare at the serum. Everything is starting to make sense. I recall Mark's leg. I'd found it odd that after I had cleared the serum from his neck it had returned only a day later. The distribution of it was different too, only in the blood vessels instead of the tissues. How would Jeter know the serum traveled so evenly through the blood vessels if he hadn't tried it on someone first? Mark.

This is why Jeter was so angry with me when I used the power on Mark the first time. Because he wanted the power for himself to heal this man.

"Who is he?" My voice is deep and demanding when I point to the man. Jeter turns his body, sensing my sudden change in tone. He knows I suspect him.

"Alena, just do as I ask. You won't get hurt."

"Who is he?" I repeat. "Why is he so important?"

The man on the floor stirs angrily, but Jeter ignores him, his hard eyes never leaving mine.

"Alena, your little friend, Sef, has been captured by my men. If you don't do what I say, he'll die."

I feel as though the wind has been knocked out of me. I somehow knew this was coming but could never fully believe it. Not even now.

"Or it might just be easier to take out Mark." The man on the floor says dryly. "He's half-dead anyway."

"You have Mark." *I knew it.* I clench my fists, suddenly wanting to strangle the man on the floor. And Jeter.

"Oh, and I have your little Magbaby too," Jeter adds. "She helped me locate you flying back to Petrichor."

I stare at him, fighting the trembling in my legs. He could be bluffing. But I don't think he is. And now he's forcing me to do something I know will be harmful. Is he really making me choose between creating a potentially dangerous being and saving the people I care about? How do you choose between something like that?

Jeter grabs one of the syringes and without warning jabs it into the chest of the man, just above the heart. The man jumps slightly but allows the needle to sink in. Once he's satisfied with the amount of serum injected, Jeter turns to me.

"Do it for your friend, Sef." Jeter leans closer to my ear. "Or the man you love. I don't care. Just do it."

"Why?" I whisper.

Jeter's brows drop heavily over his fuming eyes. "Why?"

"Why are you doing this?"

"You're not the only one who's seen death and pain, Alena." Jeter's neck vessels bulge as he tries to contain his anger. "I'm doing what I have to do, to save those I love. Now move the serum!"

I try to think. I have power now. I can feel it moving through the branches of my totem. I could try to stop Jeter's heart. If he dies, I won't know where to find Mark or Sef, but maybe I could use the man on the floor for that information. He doesn't seem very strong.

I pretend like I'm listening to the serum in the man, but I really listen for the sounds in Jeter's heart with the black power. They're different because the black power is different. I curse. I can't figure it out, and I don't have time to play around. So, I guess, using the same shortcut I would use with the other power, command the elements in his heart to die. But the heart doesn't respond.

Without batting an eye, Jeter throws me up against the wall, a rope tight around my throat, my feet hanging above the floor.

Where the heck did that rope come from? Did he really make it that fast with his power?

I kick my legs, searching for some footing, but only find air. I couldn't disable his heart, but somehow he knew I was trying.

It hurts—the strangling, the sudden panic of my lungs. I stare at the ceiling, trying to command the elements of the rope to loosen, but they're not listening. Jeter must have a tighter grip on them than me.

"How dare you," Jeter growls. I claw at the rope, trying to break free, get away from the pain, but I'm stuck. I've been threatened like this before, with Scance, the first time I went to the rendezvous point. But I didn't feel even remotely as terrified then. Jeter's angry scowl is only inches from my face. He *will* kill me if I don't cooperate. Or, worse, he'll kill Mark.

How did I end up so trapped?

"Okay." I try to whisper the word, but I barely get out any air.

"What?" Jeter needs more reassurance.

"I'll do it," I say, squeezing the air out as forcefully as I can.

Jeter gets even closer, pointing a finger in my face. "You try something like that again, I will kill Mark. Do you understand?"

I nod my head emphatically, tears squeezing from my eyes.

He waits two more excruciating seconds before releasing me. I fall to the floor in a heap, gasping for breath. Grabbing the back of my shirt, he forces me to my feet and drags me back to the man.

"Now heal him!" Jeter shouts in my ear.

I try to keep my lip from quivering. Oh, how I wish Mark or Rusty were here. They would know what to do. Jeter knew that I would be completely helpless, which is why he worked to get me alone. It feels terrible knowing that Jeter knows how weak I am. How utterly weak.

The only hope I have is knowing that if we use the serum, this process can be reversed. With black power.

I kneel next to the man and listen for the dullness I first heard in Mark. It's slowly moving through the body. I isolate the sounds in my head to the serum in the man's arms first. Then I remember how Bapoto described the sound of Peppate generators. It's like listening to someone turn the pages of a book. Slow and steady.

I listen. That's how they sound with normal power. Will it be the same?

My head aches as I open my ears and focus. Then, I think I hear it. It sounds almost like the pages of a book turning, but muffled, like it's underwater? That has to be them.

I talk silently to my totem. This is different than what I did with Mark. Instead of commanding the serum out of the body, I have to redirect it, into and around the Peppate generators. Which requires me to hear the sound of the generators.

But I do it. Through my tears, I figure it out. I redirect the serum, I listen and then redirect some more. My totem responds and so does the serum. I work my way from the top of the man's body down to his toes.

While I work, my mind briefly wanders to Jeter.

How long has he been against the Pepps? Did he really try to heal Danny, or was he just trying to keep Danny quiet by hiding his memories?

When I'm finally done moving the serum, I shift on my sore knees and stand. When I look out the window, I notice daylight shining through. *How long did this take?*

In pure defeat, I turn to Jeter, who is still standing beside me.

"It's done."

"Wonderful," Jeter exclaims.

I hear scuffing boots on the wooden floor behind me, and then something hits the back of my head. I see stars briefly before slipping into unconsciousness.

Chapter 27

The thick murky air is driving me crazy. The bugs stick to the sweat drenching my forehead, the only skin on my body that's exposed. I've long since given up trying to swat them away. Two days of walking through this muck has made me too tired. Hopefully we get to the place soon.

I analyze the man leading me. Mom told me to go with him. Right before she died. To help him figure out what's wrong with us. And I would do anything for her, even if that means suffering more pain to learn about our condition. At least I think I'm okay to suffer more pain.

Pain. It's there all the time, all over my body inside and out. I haven't lived as long as some, but the older I get, the worse I feel. Most days I just want to die.

"We're almost there." The man calls back. I look through the scarf covering my face and see a large mansion peeking through the trees ahead. I almost smile in relief. My body hurts, and nothing sounds better than stopping this hot, painful journey.

The trees break into a clearing where the mansion sits, and we walk up to the front door. The man doesn't bother knocking. This is his house. I walk in and look around. It's nice, made of shiny materials I've never seen before.

Very different from the rock home I grew up in. Halfway down the hall we're greeted by a young boy. My age with dark hair and a thin face.

But we don't stop. The man guides me past the boy to a dark room downstairs. The walls are made of cold stone and no windows. A candle is the only source of light in the room, sitting on a table in the corner next to a small cot.

This is my kind of place. Room of stone where I can rest.

And I do rest.

Days pass, eating good food from the dark-haired man. My stomach still hurts, but the wounds on my skin start to heal more than they ever have before. For the first time I feel good.

It doesn't last for long, though. Eventually he has to start his experiments. Even though he apologizes, he still carries on with them. He takes me to a room full of weird-looking bottles. The man lays me down on a bed, then ties my arms and legs, telling me it's best if I don't move. I don't like it.

Then the man touches my skin. Over and over again with different objects and chemicals. They instantly burn. Everything burns ... like fire. The dark-haired man hates my screams but doesn't stop.

Then the man forces me to drink something, making my insides boil. I can't even scream; the pain is so bad. Time becomes an incomprehensible thing. I don't know how long he pesters me—hours or days? I don't know. All I know is that I wish more than anything I could just slip away.

Then it stops. I'm taken to my room to recover. To sleep and eat. Then he comes again.

That's when I realize that coming here was a big mistake.

***

I open my eyes slowly.

Ugh.

My head pounds. Jeter must have had someone knock me out from behind. I raise a hand to the back of my head. Sure enough, there's a large bump there. When I pull my fingers away, I don't see blood on them, but they're tangled with globs of hair.

Wonderful.

Just then a sharp pain ripples through my stomach, stealing the attention from my head. It spasms over and over again, deepening relentlessly.

I groan. Rolling onto my side, I look around. I'm in a dark red-rock cave. The only opening is in front of me, covered by heavy metal bars. Just on the outside of the bars is a torch perched in the wall, providing a tiny bit of light.

Rolling onto my knees, I gasp, my stomach spasming again. The pain draws sweat from every part of my body, and I grip at my pants, needing something to hold on to. I hold perfectly still until it passes, and then find my way to one of the cold rock walls. The movement steals my energy, and I gasp for breath, leaning my head back.

My mind tries to make sense of the dream I just had. At least it seemed like a dream. But the pain in my stomach is too distracting. I need to go to the bathroom. I search around the cave and find nothing to act as a toilet. Tears sting my eyes, and I curse under my breath.

To make things worse, I hear something pattering around the floor of my cell. Rats. I gulp. In the faint torchlight, I see them, scurrying from one end to the other. And smell them. The strong stench of rodent feces reaches my nose, and I close my eyes.

Have they tried to eat me yet? I should check my skin to see if I have any marks, but my energy continues to deplete. All I can do is pull my legs in close.

That's not good enough, though. One of the rats approaches my side. All I can do is stare at it. But then I lift my head. It's just sitting there, looking at me with … familiar eyes. Without warning, the rat starts to grow and transform. I gasp, scooting frantically back into the wall.

"Shhh." The transformed animal puts his hand across my mouth to keep me from screaming. I instantly recognize his voice and burst into tears.

"Sef," I whisper into his hand.

"Are you okay, Alena?" He lets me go. "Are you hurt?"

I shake my head. "I don't feel well. But I'm not too hurt."

Then my head clears enough to realize he shouldn't be here.

"How'd you get in here? Jeter said he captured you. Doesn't he know you're a morpher?"

If Jeter knew that, wouldn't he have taken more precautionary measures to keep him imprisoned?

Sef's brows furrow. "Jeter never captured me. His men looked for me, but I knew something was wrong when I got shot down. I morphed into another animal. They couldn't find me."

I recall the man who had come to Jeter to report. He must have been telling Jeter they couldn't find Sef, but knowing my concern for him, Jeter lied to me to get me to do what he wanted me to do.

I groan, my hands shaking from chills.

"Did he lie about Mark too?" I ask, my mouth feeling dry.

"No." Sef's voice lowers. "Jeter really does have Mark, and he's torturing him. Listen, Alena, I don't have much time. I need your help."

Sef takes my cold, shaking hand and places something inside. I would recognize the shape of the object anywhere.

"Alena, you need to somehow get into Mark's cell. It's down the hall to the left. Here's a full vial of power. Use it to get out of here and then into his cell. Once inside, you'll need to heal him. He's in terrible condition. I would do it, but I can't heal. Please don't use a lot of the power on him, though. You're going to need most of it to break through the wall furthest from the cell bars. It leads outside. Tell Mark to blow it up. Alena?" Sef pauses and waits, forcing me to open my heavy eyelids. "You need to get out. The chief is coming, and he can't afford to hold back."

I nod my head in understanding, but then a red flag flickers in the back of my mind. I grab Sef's hand.

"Sef, the chief needs to be careful." I grit my teeth as another spasm racks my body.

"What's wrong with you?" Concern radiates from him, but I shake my head.

"Jeter forced me to do something to a man, a Mixed Blood. I have a feeling that whatever I did released something dangerous in the man. You need to tell the chief that the man can probably produce lightning, exactly like Mark and me." I grip his hand tighter, fighting to tell him everything. "He's allergic to Peppate though. Terribly allergic."

Sef nods. "Okay, I'll let him know."

Footsteps echo off the walls of the tunnel. Someone's coming. Sef looks nervously behind him. "I need to go, but please get out as soon as possible. We're all waiting on you."

Sef quietly slips back into his rodent form.

Laying my head back against the wall, I try to relax the spasms in my stomach. The footsteps get closer until a burly man appears in the torchlight. He sits in a wooden chair just outside my cell. With a cruel sneer he stares at me. I moan.

Great.

Chapter 28

I wait as long as I can for the man to leave so I can attend to the diarrhea plaguing me. But when I can't hold it back any longer, I make my way to the corner, where I relieve myself. I should be terribly embarrassed, but I'm not. Just too sick.

The smell quickly permeates the entire cell. When it reaches the man, he stands and leaves.

Finally.

That's when I collapse on the floor. Chills shake my body profoundly, and my bones ache. I can't think. I need to find a way out of here, but I can't. I know I need to save the power, but if I can't even get myself to stand, there's no way I'm getting Mark out. *Should I heal myself?*

A squeaking noise pulls me from my fogginess. Another rat. Its whiskers tickle my forehead and I cringe, but it continues to pester me. I'm pretty sure this one isn't a Pepp.

"Frustrating, isn't it." A voice croaks from the dark tunnel after a while. I raise my weak head. I didn't even know anyone was here. I must have fallen asleep.

"It's frustrating when your body doesn't work the way it should. When simple things become impossible to do. The gate here has been unlocked the whole time. You could have left the cell. But your body wouldn't even allow you that freedom." The voice stops, allowing the silence of the tunnel to weigh heavily in the air.

I turn my head until I see his face. I grit my teeth. It's the man Jeter made me heal, the torchlight enhancing his terrifying scars. I squint when my stomach cramps again. There are two men behind him. One of them looks like a leftover clan man. Apparently he wasn't at SilverDen when I morphed and killed all the other clan men. And the other is ... Jeter. I tighten my grip on the power and curse under my breath.

Can he hear the power?

"Pain removes light from life, doesn't it?" The man starts talking again, drawing my attention back to him. "It takes away any desire to move, to think. To live."

Is this what he feels like? All the time? I want to deny it, tell myself there's no way he could survive daily pain like this, but I've seen his skin. I've touched his vessels with power. I've seen how broken down, how tired, every cell in his body is. That kind of aging could only come through extensive damage. Extensive pain. Sympathy rises within me, like a string of smoke needing to fill the air, but I quickly snuff it out. I can't afford to feel sorry for him, no matter what he's suffered.

"You're the boy?" I manage to say before another cramp cripples my body.

My question is vague, but he understands. "From your dream? You saw me? Yes. That was me. Jeter said the memory bug would work. My name is Aitin."

A wave of chills swarms my body, and sweat continues to pour from my skin.

Why is my head spinning when I'm lying on the ground? I take in a deep breath, trying to push the conversation. There has to be something important about this man, right? Some information I should try to collect? I recall the dream. The man who was experimenting on the boy looked familiar with his dark hair. He almost looked like ... I groan. He looked like Danny, or an older version of Danny. Which means he was probably Danny's father, Jose.

I raise my head. "You're a Mixed Blood. The boy Danny's father was asked to heal. Everyone thinks you're dead." That's all I manage to whisper. I want to say more about the boy who answered the door. His resemblance to Danny was also unmistakable. Case.

"Yes, I'm a Mixed Blood that was tortured by two of your old Pepps."

"Jose," I whisper, dropping my head back to the floor. That's one person I know of that tortured the boy. But who is the other?

"Yes, Jose and *Jax*," Aitin whispers back. Then, opening the cell door, he enters my space. I recoil. My cell stinks. I hurt. I don't want anyone close to me.

But the man doesn't approach. Instead, he crouches a good distance away.

"My mother died during what we call the Black Month, the peak of summer, when all the flowers and plants thrive. We thought it was the plants making us sick, but it turns out it was really Peppate. The flourishing plants held so much Peppate that our people just died, dozens at a time." His voice drips with unmistakable bitterness.

"But before she died, she made me promise to go with Jose. He was the Pepp communicator who had repeatedly visited our community asking for volunteers to go with him and help him figure out what was wrong with us. He was honest. Told us plainly that it would cause more pain. Which is why nobody went with him."

I finish for him. "Until your mother died."

Aitin nods. "Dealing with Jose was almost bearable. His experiments with different elements always ended quickly. He couldn't stand seeing my pain. But then Jax joined him. Jax was anxious to figure out the truth behind my condition. He didn't see me as a boy like Jose but as a lab rat. His experiments weren't controlled and lasted too long. I could never stay conscious for his visits." Aitin shakes his head. "But slowly they found answers. First, they learned my condition was an allergy. Then they learned I was allergic to Peppate. Jose and Case created a way to remove Peppate from food and water. That, along with keeping me in the cellar away from the elements, helped a lot. But I still struggled, and Jose couldn't figure out why. Then after several years, the experiments suddenly stopped. It wasn't until I read Jose's journal that I understood why. He had finally discovered that Peppate is created inside me, that I'm essentially allergic to myself.

"That's when I killed Jose. He shouldn't have kept the truth from me. I really wanted to kill Jax too, but Jax was still determined to find a way. Jose was giving up."

I nod, the story getting clearer. "So, with Jose dead, Danny and Trevor left for Petrichor and Case stayed behind. To help you find a way to get better."

"Yes, and he did. He found a way to take the generators from my body and implant them into a blank totem, of course removing the Peppate generators in the process. He's the brilliant mind that created *your* totem. It's required so much painful patience on my part. To wait for him to create it. Then wait for you and Mark to morph together, to create the black power. You and your friends haven't been very cooperative." He sounds more than annoyed, but then a foreign softness enters his expression. "But you eventually came through. I owe you my life, Alena.

I probably shouldn't have given you that stomach bug, but I always enjoy seeing people suffer. It helps me feel better. That being said, for the first time since the day I was born, there's very little pain, and that's because of you."

I want to roll my eyes. He says all this as if I willingly decided to heal him. As if he wasn't the one who threatened Mark's life to get me to do what he wanted. I should kill him. I have power in my hand. I could easily destroy him right here. Based on what he's telling me, I finally know who's behind everything, who started everything. And I could end it.

But what about the other man standing outside the cell? Jeter. His ability to counter my attempt at stopping his heart still baffles me. *How was he able to sense that?*

He can sense power. Can he sense the power I hold in my hand? Then, my mind pauses and clears for just a second. *What if Jeter doesn't have his power in?* He still seems totally oblivious to what I hold in my hand.

Now that I think about it, it kind of makes sense. Aitin's allergic to Peppate, so anytime Jeter doesn't need his power, he would probably remove it. He doesn't want to make Aitin sick. And now would be one of those times power would seem unnecessary. I'm in prison, stripped of my weapons, and sick as a dog. Why would he need it?

I roll my face into the floor, the clarity of my mind gone, focusing on fighting off another cramp.

Can I really take any chances, though? One misstep and Jeter will not only end me, he'll know I somehow got power. He would take it from me, I would never get to Mark, and we would never get out.

No, If I kill Aitin, they kill me. Mark doesn't get out, Jeter carries things on, and the Pepps still don't win.

"I've heard you don't really fit in with the Pepps." Aitin breaks my bruised train of thought. "That's probably because of the totem on your arm. Sorry about that."

I almost snort at his pathetic apology. But then his words sink in, stinging more than I would like them to. *How does he know I don't fit in with the Pepps?*

"I doubt your precious Pepps will be eager to have you back after they learn what you've done to me. But I do know a place where you would fit in beautifully. Here. Together we can free the world of Peppate. We can heal all those who are hurt by it."

Aitin's eyes were probably blue once, but now they've faded to a sickly gray that could easily blend into the white part of his eye if the white part wasn't so bloodshot.

His words replay in my mind. They couldn't be truer. I've never fit in with the Pepps, and going back will be harder than before once they realize what I've created. They won't take the time to understand how I was manipulated. All they'll see is that I was weak. And they'll despise me for it.

I hate how tempted I am by Aitin's words. To have a place where I'm not feared or hated. To be able to heal people who've suffered so long. *How many other Mixed Bloods are there?*

Even as I think it, though, I know it would never work. Aitin may not fear me, but I would fear him, forever. I don't want to live like that.

And then the gravity of his plan hits me.

"Free the world of Peppate? You're going to kill the Pepps."

Aitin nods his bald head reverently, as if he's doing the world a service. "As soon as I'm fully well. Jeter wants me to wait until I recover, to make sure the procedure worked before I activate the power, but once I can, I will."

I shake my head. "I'm sorry. I'm sorry for what you've been through, but I can't help you do that." I've personally seen what a lack of Peppate does to human beings. Killing the Pepps would create a world I would rather not live in.

My comment doesn't seem to surprise him.

"I assumed as much. Maybe if you'd suffered your entire life, you wouldn't be so quick to reject my plan. Even so, I am indebted to you. You know the coolest thing about what you did to me?" Aitin leans closer. "Even cooler than healing me? By disabling the Peppate generators, you activated my power sac. You gave me power. I can feel it flowing through my body, and soon I'll be able to use it. You're the one person who finally gave me what I want, and I would like to repay you somehow. What do you want? Do you want me to let you go?"

He must be joking. He would never let me go, would he? After all he's done to get ahold of me? Unfortunately, I don't know what game he's playing at, so I try to feel him out.

"You want to repay me? You've captured Mark, haven't you? Let *him* go."

For the first time, Aitin's temperate composure cracks.

"You would stay here then? You would sacrifice your life for his?" I don't need to acknowledge his questions. He knows the answers.

"I'm sorry, Alena. I'm willing to give you lots of things, but that I cannot give you. By the way, I found this in your clothing." Aitin pulls out the picture of Mark and his dad. The picture I found at the cabin. Weary anger slowly grows within me.

"I remember seeing this picture once." Aitin sneers. "At Mark's old cabin?"

My vision is blacking out. "Please give it back," I whisper with no strength, realizing now that the gun is probably long gone.

Shaking his head, Aitin slowly rips the picture. "I don't think I'll do that either." With the picture now scattered in tiny pieces, I lay my head back down.

"Why do you hate him?"

Aitin's mouth twists into a strange grimace. "If you only knew."

I can feel myself slipping away. I need to hurry.

"Fine. If you won't let Mark go, then at least let me see him one last time. That's what I request."

The air is quiet, and I'm cringing in pain.

"You think I'm stupid?" A suspicion has entered his tone. My eyes feel like heavy lead at this point, but I force them open now. It was a simple request. *What is he suspicious of?* Does he know about the power?

"One simple morph with him, and you'll destroy us all."

I groan. "I hadn't thought of that." I hadn't either. Tears tug at my eyes. *How am I supposed to get out of here with Mark, when my brain is so worthless?*

Then I have one idea. It's probably terrible. But it's all I've got.

"Fine." I pant through my words. "I request a bucket or some sort of toilet so I can go to the bathroom."

This makes Aitin laugh out loud.

"I'll do you one better. I'll have Jeter heal you."

"No!" My shout is louder than I thought I had the strength for, and now Jeter, the clan man, and Aitin are all looking at me puzzled. Dammit. Now I need to explain myself without telling them the truth—that I don't want Jeter to put his power in to heal me, because I don't want him hearing that I have power. Fortunately, what I say isn't a lie either.

"I don't want him touching me." I grind out the words as hatefully as I can.

Aitin raises a hairless eyebrow, looking between Jeter and me.

"Okay," he finally says. "For now, we'll get you a bucket. But if you start dying, I'm having him heal you. You're too important to let go of."

Aitin groans softly when he stands to leave, the movement semi-painful for him. He's still weak.

But just before he exits through the bars, I hear him stomp down hard. A panicked squeak bounces off the wall before silence falls.

"Filthy creatures."

He just stomped on a rat.

I really hope that wasn't Sef.

Then I breathe in deeply through my nose. I don't have much time left. I need to hurry.

Chapter 29

It takes all my energy just to keep my eyes open, but I grit my teeth and clasp my hands together. *Just hang on.*

Aitin exits my cell, signals to the Clan man to go get me a bucket, says one last good-bye, and then disappears down the hall.

It's just Jeter and me.

Dark shadows chase each other across his features, making his face look sterner and more serious. The only thing that brightens him in the torchlight is his hair, which stands as a golden halo around his head. He's handsome. And I used to think he was kind, but I was terribly wrong.

I take in one last deep breath. I have one chance at this. If I blow it, or if I'm wrong about Jeter not having power in, then the chief will have to be smart enough to come anyway, even when Mark and I don't come out.

In one swift movement, I pop the power into the heart of my totem. Elements ring loudly all around, the most prominent ones being the viruses in my stomach. *What did he do to me?*

But I ignore everything else and focus intently on Jeter. His body has stiffened, seeing my movement, but in a split second I reach out to every neuron in his brain, commanding them to rest.

Jeter's eyes double in size the moment he realizes I have power, but his body collapses to the ground before he can respond.

The moment his head hits the floor, I sense it. Power depletion. My heart pounds fearfully. I had forgotten about power depletion! It feels like a swollen water balloon with a hole. I still have power, but it's draining. I just hope there will be enough left!

I roll onto my stomach. The man will be back soon, and I don't know how long Jeter will be knocked out. I need to move fast.

Unfortunately, my legs and arms feel like noodles, and my stomach twists painfully, making me double over.

It takes forever, but eventually I get up and work my way to the bars. Aitin didn't lock the cell again.

Big mistake.

But the door squeaks loudly enough that someone could surely hear. I stumble as quickly as I can down the tunnel. *Where did Sef say Mark was? Down the hall to the left?*

I stop. He's probably in another cell, but that cell might be locked. I want to cry now. The idea of going back just a few steps to search Jeter for keys seems like an impossible feat. I drop to my knees and crawl on my hands.

I exhale loudly in relief when I find keys in Jeter's pant pocket. Sometimes it feels like the universe is against me, like nothing I do ever works out the way I hope, but here in this moment, finding these keys on Jeter, ready to assist me in my weak plan, it's as though all the stars have aligned in the sky. Just for me.

Using the bars, I try to pull myself up, but I can't. I have no more energy, and I'm wasting time.

I have to heal myself, at least a little. Reaching out to the viruses in my gut I command a few of them to go away, then I ease my symptoms only enough to give me energy. Unfortunately, with the pain eased in my stomach, the pounding in my head gets louder.

I rise quickly to my feet, ignoring the pulsing in my head, and shuffle down the tunnel until I hit a split in the paths. Voices are approaching, but I can't tell which tunnel they're coming from. I don't have time to figure it out either. I have to go left. Being as careful as I can. I edge myself along, trying to look for signs of Aitin's men. They must have been down the other tunnel because the sounds are growing fainter.

Then I see him.

Mark, sitting inside a dark cell. He's chained to the wall, his arms anchored above his head. Shirtless, his chest is exposed with entire patches of skin missing, the muscles beneath uncovered and terribly swollen.

No.

"Mark," I whisper his name but get no response. Sure enough, his cell bars are locked. Fiddling with the keys, I try each one. *Man, why is it so hard to put a key in the lock?* My fingers won't cooperate. And now my stomach is starting to cramp again, the viruses reactivating. I really wish I had that bucket!

It's the seventh key I try that opens the cell. I push it open too quickly, drawing out a heavy squeak that echoes down the tunnel. Stupid bars! I don't risk closing it behind me but make my way to Mark, quickly speaking to his elements.

He's alive, but I hear burns. Lots of burns, and they're not from heat. The sharp smell of acid reaches my nostrils along with his rotting flesh.

What did Aitin do to him? I drop to my knees. I want to pull him into my arms, tell him it's okay, that we're getting out of here, but that would only hurt him and waste our time.

"Oh, Mark," I say again, still healing him. Thankfully, his skin is already starting to change, from red and black to light pink. Now, I reach out and touch his face. He stirs.

"Lena?" He heaves my name in an eerily raspy way. My heart drops through my toes. The worst burns weren't even on the outside. I reach out again, listening to the deeper sounds of his respiratory tract. He's been burned on the inside. I cringe deeply. The acid. He was forced to drink it. I can't even imagine what that felt like. A picture of Mark screaming in horrific pain forces its way into my mind, and my shoulders shudder. I need to get him out of here.

"I'm sorry, Mark." I bite back the tugging tears. Focus. "Where do you hurt the worst?" I whisper, now forcing myself to address his almost dissolved throat. I don't know how much I need to heal him before he'll be strong enough to get us out of here.

"Lena," he repeats again, this time less painfully.

Just then, someone yells down the hall, and I know my time is up. Trying to keep my voice as calm as possible, hoping my healing was enough, I tear the power out of my totem and push it into his.

"Mark, listen. I've put power in your totem. I need to you to loosen your chains and then destroy the wall on your left. It's supposed to lead outside ..."

I inhale sharply when Mark finally opens his eyes. Several blood vessels have burst within them, making them horribly red. *Oh, Mark.*

"Okay," he says, already moving through his shaking muscles and ragged breathing. I wish I could heal him more!

Sure enough, the chains melt off his raw wrists. I extend my hand to him, triggering another more painful stomach cramp.

"What's wrong, Alena?" His voice drips with concern, tugging on my heart. *He's in horrible pain, and he's asking* me *what's wrong?*

I brush him off, pointing at the rock wall I think he's supposed to destroy.

"Blow it up."

Mark hears the shouts getting closer now and acts quickly.

I don't know how he does it—commands an explosion so effortlessly and controls it in such a way that makes it go outward, not inward. The only thing I don't like is the sound. It blasts through my ears, erupting into an agonizing headache. I drop to my knees, stripped of energy once again.

A bright light has entered the cave, which only intensifies the pain in my head. Someone tugs on my arm, but I just want to lie down and sleep.

Squinting, I see Mark there, terribly worried. He's talking. No, shouting at me. But all I hear is a loud ringing. Then I realize he's pointing at something. Turning around, I see Aitin's face.

He's standing there at the entrance to Mark's prison cell, his pale eyes bulging in anger.

My body starts to move. Ignoring the pain, I allow Mark to pull me over the rubble, through the opening. I stumble, ready to be grabbed from behind at any moment, but Aitin seems to be having a hard time too.

Then I see him pull something out of his pocket.

A gun.

I move faster, but it's not fast enough. I was shot in the leg only yesterday. At least I think it was yesterday. The pain now isn't nearly as bad as it was then, though. Probably because my head feels like it's going to explode or because my body is too tired to pounce on the pain. Or maybe it's because of the encroaching darkness. Everything is going dark.

I collapse forward.

Chapter 30

I can't make sense of what's going on around me.

Is someone carrying me? I open my eyes, able to make out only the faint line of a profile I would know anywhere. I groan in pain. No, nobody's carrying me because my legs are moving, running as fast as they can, with Mark's arm around my waist. Man, my body hurts.

But Mark doesn't slow or let me go. He just keeps running, glancing behind us several times.

It's not until I practically fall to the ground that Mark lets me lie down, swiping at the sweat pouring from my face. My body is freezing cold, although in the back of my mind I know that doesn't make sense. The air is unnaturally hot.

Mark pulls down the neck of my shirt and pops power back into my totem.

"Heal yourself, Alena, please."

I immediately hear my body's ailments: the virus in my stomach, a bleed in my brain, and a gunshot wound in my shoulder. But that's all the power allows me to do, diagnose myself, before fizzling out.

It's gone.

My gut spasms in response, and I groan.

"The power's gone," I whisper to Mark, then close my eyes. I tell myself I just need to lie there for a second, rest, but the moment my eyes close I know it was a mistake. Getting up is going to be excruciatingly hard.

"Alena, let's at least ... get behind a rock so we're not sitting out in the open." Mark's voice grinds against his throat. It's a grueling, painful sound, but he talks anyway. If he can talk, I can move.

Rolling onto my stomach, I push myself up again, with blood dripping down my arm. Mark tries to help me as best as he can, and together we find our way behind a large rock. It's better protection than nothing. I don't hear anyone behind us. Nobody is yelling or shooting, but, then again, I can't trust my ears. They're still ringing. Once behind the rock, Mark stops, heaving painfully.

I double over, brushing his arm gently. "You okay?"

He nods, his eyes meeting mine for the first time. "Yeah, you?"

He's not okay. I can still hear the crackling sounds in his breathing and the raspy break in his voice.

"I'm sorry, Mark. I wish I had more power. I should have healed you more." I can't stand up all the way. So, I lean against the large red rock and slide to the ground, careful not to hit my shot shoulder.

"What did he do to you?" Mark crouches, wiping more sweat off my face.

I smack my lips and try to swallow, my tongue feeling like sandpaper.

"Nothing compared to what he did to you." I see Mark's burned skin in my mind, smell the acid, sense the shredded tissue in his esophagus. *How could Aitin do that to him?*

I change the subject. "Are they following us?"

Mark peeks around the edge of the rock.

"It doesn't seem like it, but that doesn't make sense. Why wouldn't they come after us?"

Thoughts swirl in my mind for a moment before I know the answer. They aren't going to follow us for the same reason Aitin refused to let me say good-bye to Mark.

"They're afraid of us. One morph, and they know we could destroy them." Maybe we should. But then I remember Sef's warning. The chief is coming. He might be close. We would kill him if we morphed.

Mark's shoulders tense, and he continues to search the rocks for Aitin, but I reach for his hand and gently pull him down. He needs to rest too, based on how he's breathing.

Thankfully, he concedes and slides down next to me. With my heavy head leaning on the rock behind, I stare at him.

"How did he get you?" I ask weakly.

Mark gently winds my arm through his and pulls me close, holding my hand tightly. His skin feels so warm.

"I went to Wintriness to test out your idea." Mark tries unsuccessfully to clear his throat. When he realizes he can't, he proceeds. "Sure enough, I found a memory bug hidden in the ice there. I took it to Jeter, knowing he's the only one who could command it." Mark shakes his head. "He took one look at the bug and knew. I don't remember anything after that. I just woke up in that cell. With that ... man."

Mark clamps his mouth shut, and his hands begin to shake. He must be talking about Aitin. Of course, it was Aitin that tortured him. He'd said he enjoys seeing people suffer. *But why Mark?* I want to ask Mark about the man, about why he would hate Mark so much, but he's struggling to keep himself composed.

"Are you okay, Mark?"

Mark coughs. "I'm fine. How did he get you?"

I stare at my hand clasped in his. I'm so tired. All I really want to do is sleep. But I can't sleep. Not now. So, I tell Mark how we found Danny, realizing just now that Mark didn't know. His eyes lighten when I tell him Danny's alive. That he's safe. But then I proceed to tell him about flying back to Petrichor on Sef. How Sef was shot from the sky, how Jeter got me out of the lake.

Then I clamp my mouth shut. I don't want to talk about this anymore. The gravity of what I've done presses down on me, crushing me with a newfound guilt. *Did I really liberate a Mixed Blood? Create another weapon?*

I press my free hand to my head. Crying will only make my head worse. I can't cry.

"Alena, what's wrong?" Mark turns his body toward me. "What did Jeter do to you?" Mark's raspy voice catches when my bottom lip trembles.

I fist my hands. "It isn't what he did to me, Mark," I whisper. "It's what *I* did ... to that man."

My vision is starting to pulse from the pain in my head. "Do you remember how Danny's father, Jose, had spent many years trying to heal a Mixed Blood boy?" Mark nods. "The chief was told that that boy eventually died. But he never died, Mark. That boy is now a man and very much alive. He was in there. He's the one Case was working for and now the one Jeter is helping out. His name is Aitin. Jeter told me to heal him, using Dilo's serum. It worked. I still don't fully understand it. But by healing him, I activated his powers." I look down at my hands. "Mark, he was born with the same properties our totems possess. I essentially created another one of us."

I bury my face in my hands, trying to hide my tears, but Mark gently pulls my head to his shoulder.

"He used you, Alena. You did nothing wrong."

I shake my head. "I didn't think I had a choice. He told me he would kill you if I didn't do it. But there had to have been another way. If I was better. Smarter. A true Pepp." I bring my hand to my temple. "You should have left me behind in there. I can't go back to the Pepps. Not now." I drop my hand into my lap. "Why couldn't I have just been a real Pepp?" I whisper. "None of this would have happened if I was a ... normal Pepp."

Mark moves to face me, grips my chin in his fingers, meeting my eyes. The movement forces me to hold my head up, sending a painful flash of light through my vision. When it clears, I search his brown eyes. They're so swollen, so red.

"Alena, I think there's something you need to hear," he whispers, wiping the tears from my cheeks. I lower my eyebrows, observing him in the silence. When he finally speaks, his voice is barely audible. "Alena, you will *never* be a true Pepp."

Mark's words strike a chord inside me, a chord I didn't even know was there. I stare at him. I want to pull away, be offended. I want to fight back with some sort of retort, even in my fatigue.

But I can't.

What he's telling me is the truth. The truth I'm supposed to see. The truth I've fought ever since getting my defected totem.

"But, Alena," he continues, his bloodshot eyes burning with conviction, "just because you'll never be a true Pepp, doesn't mean you're worthless."

My tired body stills. It's as though something has just clocked me upside the head.

That phrase. It's oddly similar to the one I committed to telling myself that night in Danny's meadow. I lean my head back on the rock and close my eyes.

I've tried to get that truth to stick over and over again, but it never has.

Why hasn't it stuck?

Then, as if summoned by my thoughts, all the faces of those who've ever hurt me since obtaining the totem flash through my tired mind. First Scance, then the chief, Cody, Flint. Case, the Clan men. Even Mark distrusted me the first time he saw my totem. Those who haven't physically hurt me have hurt me in other ways—by fearing me, hating me, not giving me a chance.

I rub my eyes. Those people—their actions have told me over and over again that I'm not worthy of living a good life as long as this totem is on my arm.

How could I *not* hate myself when everyone else so clearly despises me?

Then, suddenly, I see it. The Doler projection in my mind for what it is. The icky beliefs of others that have kept me from accepting my totem, accepting me. It's like an overgrown weed filling the free space of my mind, strangling any other hopeful thought.

It's gotten big, and I've let it, but how could the weed inside my head *not* grow when there's so much dislike to feed on?

Tears threaten behind my eyelids.

Hearing the truth now from Mark's lips, I think I finally understand Danny's words from so long ago.

I could sit here and choose to believe the projection, allow it to continue growing, grasping on to everything everyone else believes about me. *That I will never be worthy of living a good life as long as I have this defected totem.*

If I choose to dwell on that, then that is all I'll ever be, and all everyone else will ever see. An unworthy, defected Pepp.

Or I could choose to accept the truth. *That I will never be a true Pepp ... but that doesn't make me worthless.*

Believing that truth means I will stand alone. That I'll have to build myself up from the inside out. That I'll have to continue ignoring the hateful stares from others and remember the rare kindness I've been shown instead. It means I'll have to focus, hard, on the good parts of me.

I want to see the truth, to help it grow again, but the moment I realize that's what I want, the discouragement returns. I'm so tired. So tired of fighting. It's an uphill battle, one I'm not sure I have the strength for.

Can I fight anyway?

For the first time since obtaining my totem, I allow Mark's words to sink into my tired heart. I allow myself to feel the aching sadness the truth triggers. I allow myself to grieve the loss of something I'll never be.

I will never be a true Pepp.

That's when it happens. Just when the sorrow has fully enveloped my broken being, the other words finally sink in. And for the first time, they fit.

But I still have worth.

My throat catches with emotion, and a warmth flows through my body, filling me with peace.

Peace. It's like the perfect calm of glassy water after an ocean storm. Or a magnificent orange and blue sunrise after a long dark night. I've never truly understood its power until now, and even though I know this moment will be fleeting, I don't think I'll forget the feeling. Ever.

"I'm sorry, Alena." Mark's voice croaks as he gently caresses my jaw. "I didn't mean to hurt you. It's just that the man, Aitin, told me he'd get you to join his side. That he'd convince you this was the only place you belonged. I'm glad you didn't choose to stay. I just don't ever want you to think this is what you deserve. There's no way I would ever leave you here, Alena. You deserve happiness too."

More tears spill from my eyes. I reach out weakly for his face.

"I love you, Mark. Thank you." Unable to hold it up any longer, my hand falls into my lap. "Did he try to collect you too? Tell you this is where you belong?"

It's a simple question. I'm not sure why I asked it, but it elicits a darkness in Mark I've never seen in him, an unspoken fear.

"What's wrong?"

He rests his forehead on mine but doesn't speak. I intently study his face. *What did Aitin do to him?*

I pull him close.

I don't know how long we sit there. All I know is that my concern for what happened to Mark and his ragged breathing is the only thing that keeps me from slipping into a very tempting sleep.

When Mark straightens, I force my eyes open.

He's gazing up at the sky.

What's he looking at?

It takes way too long for me to understand what he's suddenly so interested in. But when I do find it, my jaw drops.

A large black cloud is sliding through the sky, blocking the light. It seems to be heading impossibly fast toward the mountain we just emerged from.

My body freezes.

The mountain we just emerged from. It's enormous! I instantly get dizzy looking at its peak. I expect to find snow capping the top like large mountains where I come from, but it's much too hot here for snow. Even at that altitude.

And the mountain is so red!

Red mountain? I look around the area, seeing it for the first time. Red rocks everywhere, red dust caking my skin, lodging in the wrinkles of my hands.

"Dakdete?" Mark whispers as if he's seeing it for the first time too.

Jeter brought me back here? It doesn't seem to be quite the same area Jax was hiding in. But if it is indeed Dakdete, why are there clouds? Didn't Rusty say it never rains here?

"Look." Mark points at the sky.

Following his finger, I see what he sees. Dozens of large birds at the front of the clouds.

"The Pepps. They're bringing the clouds with them." Mark voice is barely a whisper. He should probably stop talking.

Wanting to see what's going on, I struggle to my feet with Mark's help. I'm reminded again of how weak I feel without power. Oh, how I wish I had something. Even my knives or that blasted electric belt would be helpful now.

I slide my feet, move around the rock, wanting to get closer, but Mark stops me.

"We're not strong enough, Alena. We'll only get in the way."

He's right. He's leaning heavily on the boulder, and so am I, barely able to stand.

I watch the Pepps flying in the sky from my spot here on the ground. They're all different colors, darkened by the heavy clouds they're bringing. There's no way for me to know if Rusty or Kapri or Cody are up there. But one dark Pepp makes eye contact with me. It stares at me for a long time before nodding its head.

They know we're here. They've seen us. We've done our part, now we need to let them do theirs.

I grip the rock anxiously, watching the cloud extend past the mountain, growing and spreading like expanding foam until it's smothered all the blue in the sky. Strong gusts of wind come out of nowhere, tossing red dust around that pelts our skin and eyes. The strong smell of rain weighs heavily in the air. It smells like Petrichor.

The storm reminds me of one we got back home in the high mountains several years ago. Eerie clouds that came on so suddenly with so much wind. Caleb and I went outside to feel the power of it for ourselves. We watched the trees bend and twist wildly. Caleb's eyes got really big when we heard the loud cracks of breaking tree branches. We were stupid to challenge nature that year. We could've gotten hurt.

Fortunately, there are no trees here, but something tells me that won't make this storm any less dangerous.

Soon, the clouds in the sky all start moving in one direction, around and around like a whirlpool over the mountain. I gawk at its magnificence, swiping my hair out of my face. *What are they doing?*

Just then a tiny bulge extends out the middle of the swirl. It hovers in the air for a split second before popping out into a fully extended funnel that reaches to the opening of the mountain we just emerged from. At first I think it's a tornado, but the wind quickly carries the contents of the funnel to my face.

Water. It splatters my body, soaking me in seconds. It's a waterspout.

Suddenly it all makes sense. Dakdete is a forsaken land with no water and no plant life. That's why Jax and Aitin chose to live here. Without water and plants, there is no Peppate.

In this moment, though, the Pepps are changing that, bringing water here—water full of Peppate, to flush Aitin out. My lips twitch. Chief got my message.

I focus on the drowning opening. *Is Aitin still in there?*

Water starts spilling out, creating a gushing river. At first it flows past us, but then the borders widen, spilling into the rocks where we stand. My feet are soaked within seconds.

I anxiously watch the water for bodies—Jeter, Aitin, Clan men—anyone who might have escaped. But I only find a river thick with red sand.

"Look," Mark croaks over the gushing water. I follow his finger back to the opening in the mountain. The funnel spout has now retreated halfway into the sky, exposing a water dome bubbled over the opening.

Inside the dome is a body. No, two bodies.

A Pepp drops from the sky and lands on a tall rock several yards in front us. My body wants to cry out in relief when the white bird morphs into human form.

It's the chief.

The wind swirls around his body, whipping at his loose shirt and gray hair. Sand pelts his skin and lodges in his beard, but his blue eyes stay piercingly focused on the water. The way he's controlling the elements makes me wonder if he's an enviro. Like Mark.

I shield my face from the flying sand and look back at the dome. There inside the water is Jeter, frantically trying to gain control of his flipping body. I gucss what I did to Jeter's brain didn't kill him.

It's an odd feeling, being both relieved and disappointed that he didn't die. If I had killed Jeter, chief wouldn't have to, but his death might have depleted all my power. Mark and I might not have gotten out. I just hope the chief can contain him now.

I squint in the darkness, looking for the other body. I see it. It's Aitin, but he's not moving. His skin is bloody red inside the dome. The extensive damage done to his skin in such a short amount of time is terrifying. *Is he still alive?*

Suddenly, the dome explodes, sending a forceful wave of water flying in our direction. The wave sends me back into the rock behind us. Pain ripples through my shoulder up to my head. I grit my teeth, water pouring over me. I need to get out of the water.

"Where's the chief?" Mark shouts over the noise as I stand on wobbly feet. The rock where the chief was standing is now empty. Trudging through the water, holding onto boulders to keep from getting swept away, I search. Thankfully, I find him getting up a from a muddy mess a couple of yards away.

"I took you in, Jeter," the chief shouts.

Jeter is now standing on his own feet, soaked, angry, and terrifyingly uncontained.

"Even after what you did with your mother's lab," the chief says, "I was sure it was just a mistake. That you were a young boy messing around with something you didn't understand."

With hands extended, fingers shaking, the chief's power slams Jeter against the red mountain, bringing up vines that tie him down.

"It *was* a mistake," Jeter roars angrily, burning the vines imprisoning him. "That agent was only supposed to hurt the boys who beat me because of my deformed face. I never imagined it would spread all over the town and kill my own ..." The muscles in his jaw bulge as he grits his teeth, unable to finish.

Under the chief's control, the vines wind tightly around Jeter's neck.

It's hard to watch, yet I can't pull my gaze away. Chief is going to kill him.

Just then a sound comes from the bloody body lying on the ground close by. Aitin. I gape at him. *He's still alive?* His limbs move, his hands grasping at the sand, scooting his horrible body closer to Jeter.

He's alive, but ignorable for now, right?

Five large birds fly down from the sky, their skin shifting from feathers to human skin. I recognize only one of them, Scance, with her dreadlocks bundled carefully atop her head. The other four older Pepps have the same red mark of a medic and the blue mark of council members. Simultaneously they reach out to Jeter. I look his way; he's arching his back in pain, gripping his heart.

How in the world does he do it? They're all working together, using their power to kill him, but he's able to resist them.

"It was a *big* mistake," Chief continues, using his hands to tighten the invisible force behind the vines. "A big mistake that I thought you would have learned from. But, instead, you've continued your research to further learn how to control things. The memory bugs. The Morgans. The flesh-eating bug that killed the prisoners. I can't believe you had that in you."

That was all Jeter?

Jeter grunts weakly. Big red boulders start flying in the air, crashing into his body. I'm just thinking there's no way he could survive that, when an explosion of fire from Jeter sends us all flying back again and breaks his binds.

I don't think I can get up again. The pain in my shoulder is sucking my energy, and my head explodes with each movement. I sit there in the water, trying to process what's going on from where I am, wishing I could help.

Free of the vines, Jeter sits perched on all fours catching his breath. When Scance finds her footing again, she focuses her attention on Jeter. A vein in her temple bulges. I'm not sure what she's trying to do, but she's concentrating hard. Unfortunately, Jeter seems totally unaffected.

"Of course, I've continued my research," Jeter says, standing, then walking toward the chief, who's trying to get up. "After what happened to my mother, I vowed I would learn how to control them. She told me there was nothing more powerful in this world than the microscopic killers." Jeter's face darkens, his eyes swimming in hate. "I've learned that by giving them exactly what they want, a host to feed on, they're just as predictable and controllable as human beings."

Jeter stretches out his hand toward the chief.

The chief grabs his head and screams.

It chills my bones, a man howling in pain.

No!

I lean forward, my hands perched in the water, silently hoping the chief has the same deflection ability Jeter has when it comes to the body. *Get out of his grip!* When Scance and the other medics realize they have no power over Jeter now, they focus on the chief, trying to liberate him, but soon they're grabbing their own throats, cut off from air.

Out of the corner of my eye, I see another bird sneak down from the sky. It lands on the rocks just behind Jeter and morphs into human form.

It's Cordelia. Flint's mother.

I'm surprised at how happy I am to see her. Perhaps a hateful, bitter Pepp is exactly what we need right now. Someone who won't hold back.

"You should have helped me when I asked." Jeter growls low, straining to keep a solid grip on the chief and others. "None of this would have happened if you had agreed to save my people."

Jeter still doesn't see Cordelia, but all it would take is a shout from Aitin for Jeter to know who's behind him.

I find my way to my knees, sinking into the wet sand. Maybe I can be a distraction. Keep Jeter's attention forward, give him one more body to command so he's stretched thinner. My arms shake relentlessly. If I can just get closer to the chief.

"Alena?" Mark whispers. But then he understands what I'm doing and follows.

Cordelia has a knife in her hand. She takes another step toward Jeter, then releases the knife into the air. Using power, she lets it float closer.

"Jeter!" The groan from Aitin is barely audible, but he's trying to get Jeter's attention.

I push myself harder, gritting my teeth. I can't lean on my left hand because of the wound in my shoulder. My head is heavy, and my stomach is still cramping. Crawling with only one arm is terribly hard and slow, but with Mark's help, we eventually make our way to the chief. Thankfully, Jeter is still looking forward.

He sees me and Mark.

The vessels in his neck are bulging profoundly. It must be hard for him to control so many Pepps.

An invisible force immediately blocks my airway as he dominates my body. It takes all my strength to stay on all fours, unable to breathe. I count the seconds. *Five, ten, fifteen. Please hurry, Cordelia!* My body is frantically grasping for oxygen. I search the water next to me for Mark's hand. When I find it, I grip it tightly. *Hang on, Mark!*

Then I fix my gaze on Jeter, watching Cordelia's knife get closer and closer, until in one swift movement it slams into Jeter's neck. He cries out, grabbing for the knife, releasing the force on our airways. I inhale sharply, my lungs sucking in every bit of oxygen they can. I hear Mark do the same.

Blood is gushing from Jeter's wound. The five medics, who've been released from his hold, now seem to have some hold on him.

Mark crawls next to me and pulls me into his side. It was just enough of a distraction. Just enough.

Another explosion throws Cordelia and everyone back to the ground ... except Mark and me. We're already there. I grip my head that feels like it weighs a hundred pounds. *Why does he have to keep using so many loud explosions?*

Mark cradles my head against his body, relieving some of the pulsing pain.

The Pepps have lost their hold on Jeter again, but this time, instead of using this to his advantage, Jeter runs back to Aitin. In one hasty movement he pulls out a toboggan, lifts Aitin, and puts him inside.

Then he pauses.

I expect nothing less than for him to kill us all.

But Jeter doesn't kill us. Perhaps he can't. Perhaps his power has run out.

Pulling himself inside the toboggan, he shuts the lid, and, just like that, he's gone.

Pepp birds in the air fly in the direction he disappeared, including Cordelia, but even I know they're no match for a toboggan.

My body sags against Mark.

He got away.

Someone shouts out to the chief. I turn myself just enough to see him lying in a heap of mud.

"My power's leaked," Scance says urgently. "Does anyone else have anything left?" The others shake their heads. One of the older council members shouts up at the remaining birds in the sky.

"We need power!" I gasp at the sharp pain his shout triggers in my head, then watch several birds drop down. Soon all five medics have full vials of power.

I close my eyes. *Chief should be okay, right?*

"He's alive," Scance whispers. "But why won't he wake up?" The dry air is quiet for a moment.

"Nothing seems to be wrong with him," another Pepps whispers. He's older, reminds me of Tom, with a handsome face and a bit of gray highlighting his black hair. Based on his facial expression, he's listening for ailments of the body, but then shakes his head.

"Something's missing."

"A piece of his brain ..." Scance's voice goes up in pitch with the last word, as if she's questioning her own diagnosis.

What does that mean? Why would Jeter remove a piece of the chief's brain?

"Can you replace it?" someone asks.

"I don't know," the man says. "Brain regeneration is tricky, especially with such a large piece. Let's get him back to Petrichor. I'll try there."

Fear punches into my gut. We *can't* lose the chief.

After pulling out a toboggan, the council member carefully loads the chief and sends it to Petrichor.

Handing another toboggan to Mark, he says, "We'll meet you back at Petrichor."

He doesn't bother to heal us. There are too many other matters to attend to. Instead, he morphs into eagle form with the others and disappears into the sky.

Resting my head gently against the boulder behind me, Mark moves to expand the toboggan. I can't make him do all the work. Gritting my teeth again, I muster up enough energy to slide over to the contraption. Mark helps me inside before scooting in next to me. As he shuts the lid, I shiver violently and bury my face in his chest.

Petrichor.

It's the last place I want to go.

Chapter 31

In the deep of sleep, someone pulls on me. With my mind slowly awakening, I silently assess the condition of my body. The cramping in my stomach is gone, my shoulder doesn't feel like it's been blown off anymore, and my head feels pounds lighter. Either I'm dead or I've been healed.

"Alena." It's a woman's voice. Familiar, but my mind is still too foggy to place it.

Who's pulling on me?

I wake further. I'm warm, comfortable, tucked against someone's body. I breathe him in. Mark. Amid the acidic scent still clinging to his skin, I pick up his original musky scent. I'm not dead. I immediately listen to his breathing.

He's been healed too, thank goodness.

Burying myself further in him, his strong arms embrace my body, holding me tight. We must be in the hospital, still in the toboggan. I can feel the itchy red dust still caked on my skin.

Someone pulls on me from behind again, but I can't let go of Mark. I'm not ready to face the Pepps again.

"Alena, it's Danny," Mark whispers into my ear. My eyes fling open, and I pull back to look at Mark's face before turning around. Sure enough, Danny's standing there, his beautiful brown eyes peering down at me. I stumble out of the toboggan and fling my body into his warm embrace.

"Danny," I whisper into his neck. I breathe him in, my bottom lip trembling. *My dear, sweet Danny*! I listen to his heartbeat, feel his muscles beneath my grip, relish the way his arms wrap around me. *Oh, how I've missed my Danny.*

Then, remembering his condition down in Dakdete, I pull back and search his body, his arms, his leg. "Are you alright?"

Mark is now out of the toboggan, giving Danny an embrace of his own.

"Yes, thanks to you." The answer doesn't come from Danny's smiling face. I turn to the side to find Kapri there, with Danny's spokesperson perched on her shoulder ...

Gabbro. My body stills.

"You." I can't keep the distaste from my voice.

"I know," he says, already holding his hands up in surrender. "We have a lot to talk about."

As long as he knows that, I'll ignore him for now. My eyes raise to the top of his head, where his usually black tendrils are wound into a large purplish bun almost twice the size of his head. Odd. Their different color almost makes them look hurt. But rocks can't hurt, can they?

I move on to Kapri, who has Danny's arm wrapped around her shoulder. "Are you okay?"

She nods, but then concern etches her expression. "We're okay, but we heard the chief might not be. What happened to him?"

The glass honeycomb room stills. I look at Mark, who shakes his head. "We don't know."

***

I quietly walk to the Post, my hands in the warm pockets of Mark's large, comforting coat.

After briefly catching up with Danny and Kapri, we were ordered by a council member to get showered and changed. There's going to be a big meeting. And Mark and I are supposed to be there.

I stare at the stone path in front of me, observing the little blades of grass that have popped up between the rocks.

The warmth of the shower felt good. Being clean for the first time in a week feels good. But even though my body is clean and healed from its wounds, I can tell it still needs to recover. With sleep. I'm so tired, I wish I could just go to bed. It doesn't help that I know I'll have to face the Pepps soon, tell them what I've done. I keep thinking it might go over better if I was more rested.

But, then again, maybe not.

I push myself forward, reaching the Post and making my way into its tunnels. It's buzzing with life again, but when I reach the chief's room, I find it empty ... except for Mark. He's sitting on the floor against the stone wall, his expression blank. I let the door shut behind me and slowly walk to him.

My heart twists in my chest. His eyes are so different. Swimming with that same hollowness I've seen in Cody, an unspoken darkness resting just beneath the surface.

And, just like Cody, he tries to hide it.

Patting the ground next to him, he beckons to me. I slink close to him, winding my arm through his and resting my hand on his thigh. Thankfully, he's no longer hot with infection. What I did to him last time with the black power must have worked. Now he's plagued with something else.

As we sit in silence, I stare at his hand in mine. There's so much I want to ask him, about what Aitin did to him, about what happened, but it doesn't feel right. I don't know how to explain it. It feels as though he's silently begging me not to ask. So I don't. Instead, I say something else.

"Thank you, Mark, for convincing Rusty to take me to see my family. I really needed that."

Mark attempts a weak smile. "Of course, Lena. It was time for you to go back."

I run my fingertips along his forearm, enjoying the feel of his arm hair.

"Before we left the rendezvous point, I attempted to go to your old cabin." I watch Mark's face, measuring his emotions. The only thing I sense is curiosity.

"I wanted to see if there was anything there I could return to you. Something maybe you would want back. The only things I found were a picture of you and your dad and a shotgun with *Dee* carved into the barrel."

Mark squeezes my hand. "Dee was my dad."

I rest my cheek on his upper arm.

"I tried to bring the gun back to you. I carried it to the GreenLands, to Dakdete, but Jeter took it from me when he captured me. I'm sorry."

Bringing my hand to his lips, Mark kisses my fingers. "It's okay, Lena. Thanks for thinking of me."

My spirits fall. If there was any moment when Mark needed a token of love it would be now. But my attempt at doing something kind for him failed miserably. I have nothing to show for it, and now I'm out of ideas.

Mark leans his head back against the wall. "He took Dilo too. Probably to extract more serum."

My body stiffens. *Jeter took Dilo? Why would he need more serum? Was he worried it wouldn't work the first time? Or is he going to heal other Mixed Bloods? He can't do that without our power, can he?*

"What about Bud?" My voice cracks with worry.

"Bud is fine. He's back with his mother in the dino tubes at Mossy-Hollow."

Oh good. I lean my head against the wall too, staring at him. "I'm sorry about Dilo."

Mark nods solemnly. The air is quiet before I add, "He has Breccia too."

Mark closes his eyes. "Yes, I had her with me when I took the memory bug to Jeter. He must have taken her when he knocked me out."

Mark keeps his eyes closed. I study him. He's clean now—no more acid or red sand lodged into his skin. But he didn't shave, as evidenced by a shadow across his cheeks. His hair is longer than I've ever seen it, wavy on the top. Burying my body further into his side, I kiss his shoulder, just when the door opens.

Kapri enters with Danny.

I'm instantly torn. Do I pull away from Mark for Danny's sake, like I used to? No, that doesn't feel right. Not now with Mark so obviously struggling. I glance at Danny's face to scope out his reaction. He notices our closeness but doesn't seem to mind, probably since his own fingers are woven through Kapri's.

"Guess what, Alena," Kapri kneels in front of us, bringing Danny with her, her hazel eyes sparkling in the candlelight. "Danny got his memories back."

My jaw drops. "What?" I turn to Mark. "I thought Jeter took them,"

Mark nods, straightening a little, looking as confused. "He did."

Just then Sef enters the room, with Gabbro on his shoulder and Trevor the bear stomping behind.

"Sef, tell them what happened," Kapri says avidly.

Sef's mischievous grin slides into place. "I was hoping you'd be here," he says. "There's a lot to catch up on before the council arrives."

Kapri tries to sit next to me, but Trevor manages to wiggle his large, hairy body between us. Kapri scoffs before scooting into Danny.

Sef settles on the ground across from Mark.

I look at Danny. If he got his memories back, does that mean he can speak now? As if recognizing the question in my expression, Danny shakes his head.

No?

I turn my attention to Sef along with the rest of the group. He says, "So, you know the night we were flying back from Dakdete in the dark ... I was shot in the shoulder. It hurt like hell, and I knew right away it was a targeted attack." Sef looks mostly at me while he talks. "It took me a moment to realize we were above a lake, but when I did, I decided to let you fall into the water so I could see what was really going on. Sorry." Sef cocks his head to the side apologetically. I shrug, trying not to take offense that he just left me out there.

"I did slow you down in the sky, though, so your contact with the water wouldn't kill you."

I hold back a snort. "Well, thank you, Sef."

"Anyway," he continues, "I morphed into a smaller type of bird and regained my bearings. Then I followed you through the water and found Jeter at the end of the lake." Sef shakes his head. "It seemed odd. Him being out there. I suspected him right away and re-morphed into a smaller bug to slip inside the cabin where he took you. I had a hard time understanding what it was he was trying to accomplish and who that other man was. I kept thinking that maybe I should hurt Jeter, but then I saw him strangle you when you tried."

Mark's hand tightens around my fingers. I glance at him and see his jaw is twitching.

"He tried to strangle you?" Mark's teeth are clenched.

He knew I'd been hurt. This shouldn't be news to him, but obviously hearing it so plainly is different from guessing. I open my mouth to reassure him, but Sef doesn't give me a chance to speak.

"Oh yeah. I don't know what Alena tried to do, but the moment he realized what she was doing, he strangled her, pinned her to the wall. Demanded that she do exactly what he said or else he would kill you, Mark."

Mark's breathing is too shallow. Maybe we shouldn't talk about what happened to me right now.

"It's okay, Mark." I attempt to ease his worries by rubbing his forearm, but I don't think it works.

Sef keeps talking. "After watching what he did to Alena, I knew I didn't stand any chance against Jeter, so I slipped into his satchel and waited. That's where I met another little guy."

Sef exchanges a look with Danny. I'm confused.

"A memory bug." Sef looks back at me, and suddenly it makes sense.

"You found Danny's memory bug in Jeter's bag," I say.

Sef's favorite smirk pops onto his face. "Oh yeah. I didn't know it was Danny's, but I knew it might be important. It took me a little bit to figure out its language, but by the time Jeter knocked you out and dragged you back to Dakdete, it had been almost a day, which was plenty of time."

Mark's grip tightens. Sef better be more delicate in how he talks about what happened to me or else I might lose my fingers.

"When we got to Dakdete, I snuck out of the satchel, commanding the bug to follow. The dark tunnels helped keep us hidden. Then I took him back to Petrichor, told the chief what happened, and came back for you, Alena, to tell you to get the hell out of there."

I wiggle my fingers and force some blood back into them.

"Sef is the one who gave me power so we could get out," I say to Mark. I need to tranquilize his emotions somehow. My comment helps only a little.

"Anyway, with Jeter gone, we didn't really have anyone to command the memory bug, so I gave it a go. I put it in my own head. Man, those things are crazy, able to connect with the brain like they do. It wasn't too long before I realized whose memories they were."

Sef nods in Danny's direction. I let my own eyes follow, meeting Danny's eyes halfway.

"So, you remember what happened now? The night you left Petrichor those years ago?" I ask, allowing my gaze to flow over every inch of his familiar face, his brown eyes, strong nose, and crooked smile. I still can't believe he's here and alive.

Danny nods.

"But you still can't speak," I whisper.

Danny's nose scrunches at this, and he shakes his head.

So his speech problem had nothing to do with the missing memories and everything to do with the fact that he has two totems crammed into his brain, interfering with his communication.

I realize only now that Gabbro isn't sitting on Danny's shoulder. I look around and notice him sitting gloomily on Trevor's. He senses my glare and meets it.

"Can *you* tell us what's in those memories?" I ask Gabbro. "Along with everything else you need to tell us?" I should try to harness the annoyance in my voice, but I don't. I have too many questions, and Gabbro needs to answer them.

Gabbro's black eyes move to each member of our group before they land on mine. I see the tiny Adam's apple in his throat bob up and down as he swallows. He seems to be contemplating what he should say but finally clears his throat.

"First of all, Alena. I need to tell you I'm sorry. Sorry for not sharing the truth about my plan. I'm sorry for tricking you into morphing. I'm sorry."

I don't want an apology; I want to know the truth. Perhaps I can forgive him if I get it. I only raise an eyebrow, encouraging him to keep talking. He does.

"I guess I should start at the beginning. The night Trevor and Danny got a message in Petrichor. A message from Lilly."

It's nice knowing Gabbro owes me big because that gives me full control of this conversation. I stop him already.

"Who the heck is Lilly?"

Gabbro sighs, knowing it's going to be a long night.

"Lilly is the woman you saved the night at SilverDen. The woman hidden in the wall behind the generator. She's the woman Case loves. Everything he's done, he's done to save her."

"Save her from what?"

Gabbro rubs a hand over his face. "I'll get to that."

I think for a moment. Then, satisfied with his answer, I tell him to proceed.

"Trevor got a message here in Petrichor from Lilly one night. She told him she was worried about Case. That he was creating something dangerous. So Danny and Trevor left Petrichor, traveling to their old home, where Case, Lilly and Aitin lived. When they got there, they found Case tampering with a totem. They learned that it had the ability to create a Peppate-free power, but it was dangerous, able to destroy Pepps with lightning. Danny and Trevor immediately attempted to destroy the two-part totem with their power, but Case fought them off. Desperate, Danny and Trevor each grabbed a totem, hoping to personally break them with their hands. But as soon as they touched the totems, the totems attached to their bodies, crippling them, as you know. Trevor can't morph back into his human form, and Danny can't speak."

Trevor grunts loudly at the word *crippled*, then stretches out his furry legs, pushing Kapri, Danny, and Sef away before leaning his heavy body into me.

"Unfortunately," Gabbro says, "when Aitin saw the precious totem disappear into Trevor and Danny, he panicked. The totem was gone, and Case was second-guessing everything, talking about quitting. So Aitin did the only thing he could think of doing—he kidnapped Lilly. He took her away and hid her in a place Case didn't know about. When he came back, he told Case that if he ever wanted Lilly back, he would do whatever it took to heal him.

"Case was heartbroken. With Lilly hidden from him, he had no choice but to follow Aitin's commands. He re-created the totem and helped

Aitin come up with a plan to force Mark into attaching the new totem to himself."

Gabbro shakes his head. "But Trevor and I didn't know about Lilly. All we knew is that Case was creating a totem that could hurt the Pepps. We didn't know he was being forced to do it. Trevor intervened when Mark tried to attach the totem, then he intervened again when Case tried to capture Alena at initiation. It wasn't until after initiation that Case came looking for Trevor and begged him to stop messing things up. He told him about Lilly, about how Aitin was hiding her from him. He told him the only way to get Lilly back was if he got the totem back.

"Trevor and I felt awful when we learned the truth. That's when we came up with a plan."

Gabbro straightens his body and rubs his neck.

"Aitin needed to be healed, and the only way he could be healed was with the black power created from your morph." Gabbro points to Mark and me. "So, we thought we would get you to morph by trapping you in a fire where the only way out would be up. Then we would take you, Alena, have you heal Aitin with the new power, then let you go. With Aitin healed, Lilly would be returned to Case, and Case could move on with his life.

"But we didn't want any other Pepps getting hurt, so I had to figure out how to get you *away* from Petrichor, *alone*, without other Pepps. Luring you with the Pepp prisoners seemed like a perfect option." Gabbro hangs his head in shame. "I'm sorry."

I purse my lips. I can't dwell on how I feel about that now. I still have questions.

"What about Aitin? Did he know about this plan?"

Gabbro takes in a deep breath. "Yes. He knew that Case was going to send messages to try to get you down to SilverDen to save the prisoners.

Case assured Aitin that you had a soft heart and you would be easily persuaded. And Mark would surely follow."

It hurts knowing they knew exactly how to get to me.

"Aitin agreed and took part in sending the messages, but he was convinced he had to make it more personal. At first he tried to capture your family, but when he found out they were at the rendezvous point, he knew it would be too hard to get through there. Even if Case did have a totem, he would be outnumbered by Pepps with power. That's when he told Jax to go looking for Cody's friend. And then Cody."

The room is quiet for a moment, allowing all the memories to flood back.

"Aitin was sure that once he had Cody it would be easier to capture you. He kept sending those pictures of Cody to you with the location of SilverDen."

My head snaps up. "The location," I say. "I never got a location. It was always removed before the message got to me."

Gabbro nods his head knowingly. "That was me. I knew that if you saw the location, you'd leave before it was time. So, I removed it from every message I could."

It was Gabbro who removed the location?

"Why? *Leave before it was time*?" I say, "What were we waiting for? Not my strength?"

Gabbro sighs. "No, we weren't waiting for your strength. Case was building a hideout, a place he and Lilly could escape to once she was free from Aitin. He begged me to give him a little more time to finish it before everything happened. Aitin, of course, couldn't understand what was taking you so long to come down and grew impatient. With Jeter's help, he took some of the prisoners and sent them back to Petrichor in toboggans with the Corpuscites. That was not part of our plan."

I shiver, remembering that night. The night with the flesh-eating bug. Gabbro couldn't remove the mysterious location then, not when it was glowing from the sides of every burning toboggan. No, that message was altogether too hard to ignore.

"I felt sick when I realized the chief and council members were now involved," Gabbro says. "It complicated everything. But, looking back, it couldn't have worked out better. They got the prisoners out and got away, and then you found Lilly in SilverDen. You finding Lilly changed everything, you know. Case was outside in a mound of rocks, waiting for you to morph. Once it was done, he was going to collect you and your power, take you to Aitin, force you to heal him, and then leave the moment he got Lilly back. But then you came out of SilverDen with Lilly in tow. He saw his chance to escape with her and took it. That allowed you and Mark to get away."

I lean my head back against the wall. Maybe *we* were able to get away, but Aitin still eventually got me. Got what he wanted. And, unlike what Gabbro said, I think things at SilverDen could have gone better. Tom could have been saved.

Then there was Jax, who obviously worked with Aitin for his own selfish reasons. When he saw his chance of getting the black power slipping away, he took Danny, Trevor, and Gabbro to try to get to me.

I look at Danny and Trevor now. "Jax hurt you," I say, my sorrow and guilt etched in each word. "I'm sorry. I'm sorry you were there that night. I'm sorry Jax got you."

Danny smiles, exposing his charming crooked front tooth, and shakes his head, dismissing my words immediately.

A grimace crosses Trevor's bear expression. *Is that a smile too or a frown?* I can't tell. But then he messes my hair up with his rough paw. I swipe it out of my face. I'll take that as a smile then.

"I have another question. Who changed Mark's clothes after the fire started?" I had found it odd that his clothes were different.

Trevor raises his hand, and Gabbro speaks. "That was Trevor. Mark's clothes were full of Peppate. We knew they would be destroyed the moment he morphed, so we tried to make things a little less awkward."

Kapri's face blushes bright red, and I swallow. Yes, that would have been awkward. I glance at Mark, who has thankfully softened his grip on my hand. A smile is even tugging at the corner of his lip.

I shake away the heat in my body. When I look back at the group, I avoid looking at Danny and let my eyes drift to Kapri.

Clearing the embarrassment from my throat, I continue. "There's something else I want to know," I say to Gabbro. "The hums in the messages Jax sent us—were they from you, Gabbro? Were you leading us to Danny's memory bug? Did you know about it all along, before Danny was captured?"

"Yes it was me humming, but, no, I didn't know about it all along," he says. "Danny was having a hard time after Jax captured him. I think he recognized Jax, but without the memories, he was running into dead ends that left him frustrated, throwing more tantrums. Then one night Jax's tongue slipped. He asked Danny what it felt like to have part of his memories missing. I had always wondered if the memories of that experience had somehow been physically removed.

"So, one night, when Jax was asleep, I slipped my tendrils across the room into his brain. It hurt stretching them that far, but I was able to quietly search through his memories like I did with Danny. I'm not able to do it as efficiently as the memory bugs do, but after about a week of searching every night, I found memories of conversations with Jeter. Jeter had assured Jax that Danny wouldn't talk about what had happened the night he disappeared. He told Jax that he had physically removed the memories from Danny. Then he explained how he froze the bug containing those memories in the lake.

"Now, I'm pretty sure it was because of the gaps in his memories that made Danny have those tantrums. Looking back, it was always when we were talking about things related to Case and that night, or even the defected totem, that Danny acted up. It was as if he knew that he knew something but couldn't quite figure it out and then couldn't control his frustration. Even that day he met you in GreenGrotto, Alena. I think he saw your defective totem and knew that somehow he was a part of that.

"Anyway, after I realized that Jeter had not only removed part of Danny's memories but had kept them hidden in a lake, we thought it would be helpful for everyone else to know. That's when Danny thought of the screams."

The room stays quiet for several minutes. I recall the screams and the hum in the background. Searching for answers with Kapri. It's amazing that it worked. But then I look atop Gabbro's head. His tendrils are still purple, still stretched out. They'll never be the same. None of us will ever be the same.

"How does Jeter fit in to all this?"

Gabbro sighs. "Danny's father, Jose, worked for a long time to figure out what was wrong with Aitin. When he couldn't, he called on Jeter, a medic, for help. Of course, Jeter quickly learned that his power made the boy worse and backed off. It wasn't until Jose died and Case created the new totem that Jeter saw Aitin's potential, especially with the lightning. I guess you could say that things have just evolved over the years. The war in the GreenLands hasn't helped."

I lower my eyes to my lap. No, it hasn't. Jeter wants Aitin to use his new power and destroy Verdure, I'm sure of it. And now, because of what I've done, that is a possibility.

I tighten my fists. "Unfortunately, even after all that's been sacrificed, Aitin still got his way."

"Yes, he did." An angry voice echoes through the door, making me jump. Cordelia enters the room, bringing with her the same haughty air she carries everywhere. I quickly kick myself for appreciating her earlier. *How could I have been happy to see someone like her?* Even if she did stab Jeter in the neck, possibly saving me and everyone else who was seized by Jeter's grip.

Several other council members follow behind her, her bright reddish hair bouncing against her back. Our little group stands, including Mark, who pulls me up.

Here we go.

"Aitin got away, because of you," Cordelia says, pointing a long-painted fingernail at me. Her green eyes are piercing, but so are Mark's.

"Don't you dare blame Alena for all this." Mark lowers his voice and steps in front of me, protectively. "I recall you being there today too. You didn't seem to capture him either. This is bigger than Alena, and you know that." I grip his shirt.

"You're right." She sneers. "You deserve some blame too. All of you, actually." Cordelia waves to include the rest of our group. "You're a bunch of teenagers who meddle in things that are none of your business."

"That's enough!" A gruff voice from the doorway silences the room. I turn to see who it is, but then immediately turn away. It's Eli, the chief's older brother, with Rusty standing tall behind him. Neither of them looks happy.

"Leave Alena alone," Eli says.

I blink twice. *Did he just defend me?*

Eli steps further into the room. His graying hair and beard are longer, whiter, and greasier than the chief's, and he stands an intimidating few inches taller than the chief ever did, but his eyes are the same piercing blue. And he seems sober tonight.

"My brother goes down," Eli says, "and this is what happens to the council? We all fall apart? Start pointing meaningless fingers?"

It isn't so much his accusation that sobers the room but the mention of the chief, who still hasn't recovered.

Eli glares hateful daggers at Cordelia across the room. Her eyes rage against his, but she doesn't say anything. Only when she finally breaks eye contact and crosses her arms in annoyance does Eli finally turn to Rusty.

"You're the one who called us all here. Can we get this over with?"

The usually confident Rusty gulps loudly before stepping around the large man into the middle of the room.

"There are a couple of important things we need to discuss," Rusty says. "Before the chief left Petrichor to approach Aitin, he asked me to deliver a message to all of you, should things not go well." He draws in a long slow breath. "The chief is turning his post over to his brother, Eli, who will not only become the new chief of Petrichor but also the leader on our new mission as Pepps."

"What?" I don't know who shouts this louder, Eli or Cordelia. The word echoes off the walls like a ping-pong ball.

Eli stares at Rusty for a long second before turning to leave.

Before he can disappear, though, Rusty hurriedly finishes what he has to say.

"He said that you have to go to *her*. And if you refuse, I am to personally get her and bring her here to Petrichor."

Who is her? *What is Rusty talking about?* I lean around Mark to get a better view.

Spinning on his heel, Eli turns to Rusty. "You wouldn't dare." I wonder if Eli could take Rusty down. He sure is big enough.

Rusty's gaze doesn't waver, though. "I promised the chief."

Eli clenches his fist and steps forward. I gasp. He's about to take a swing at Rusty, but at the last second, he twists and pounds the wall instead with a force that makes me jump. The vibration of his contact ripples through the floor, and I hear the loud crack of his bones. *Ouch.*

Then he leans against the wall, cradling his broken hand.

"Why did he leave?" Eli asks Rusty in an almost desperate voice.

"He had to try," Rusty says gently. "While Aitin was still weak, he had to try. He would have won, too, if it hadn't been for Jeter."

With the room now quiet, Cordelia, finds her opportunity to speak.

"You can't expect us to follow this man, who should really be in jail. There's no way I'll ever support him as chief."

I watch the expressions of the other council members. Some seem ready to disagree with Cordelia, while others seem torn.

Rusty's eyes become instantly weary, much like the chief's always seemed to be. But he ignores her comment for the moment, still speaking to Eli.

"Alena has found a way to make their life more bearable. With her help, maybe we can convince more of the Mixed Bloods to join our cause."

My heart drops. *Heal more Mixed Bloods?* Does Rusty realize I can't do that without serum, without more black power?

Eli shakes his head. "It's too dangerous. I can't risk their lives like that."

"You mean risk her life?" Rusty says with a raised eyebrow. "We'll never be able to get back to being Pepps unless we defeat Aitin. And now, with his power, there's no way we can even *attempt* to fight him. We need help."

It's apparent that they already know what I've done. The chief must have explained it, after receiving Sef's message from me.

Eli remains silent for a moment, providing the perfect opportunity for Cordelia to speak again.

"Is anyone listening to me? There's no way I'm going to serve a man like Eli!" Her voice is annoyingly high-pitched.

Straightening his body, Eli turns to her, his eyes on fire. "You think I want this, old hag? I'd rather die than be on a council with someone like you!"

I try to follow the yells and accusations that follow, but it's hard. Finally, another yell rises above them all.

"Stop!"

I look around the room, trying to find the source of the strange voice, when my eyes land on Kapri standing next to Danny.

Did that really come from her?

I purse my lips. Amazingly, she has everyone's attention.

"May I make a suggestion?" Her voice returns to its quiet nature but with a new authority I didn't realize she had. Without waiting for permission to speak, Kapri faces Eli. "The chief has handed his post over to you. Now that it's yours, you have the authority to pass it on."

I watch Cordelia's face brighten, her body straightening as if she should be the one to receive the new title. Eli scowls deeply at her. "Who? Give it to someone like her? She'll destroy us even faster than Aitin could," Eli says.

Before Cordelia can start another yelling match, Kapri rushes to speak. "No, my suggestion would be Rusty."

The air is silent. Nobody moves.

"He's been working alongside the chief for years now. He's trustworthy, and everyone in Petrichor respects him. While he runs Petrichor, Eli can help us defeat Aitin."

It's a good idea. When I look around the room, I see many others nodding in agreement. All except Cordelia.

"I don't want to be chief," Rusty says.

For the first time, Eli grins, pounding Rusty heavily on his back. "Now *that's* a great plan."

Kapri rolls her eyes at Eli before stepping forward.

"You'll have the council behind you, Rusty. They'll help you." As she says this, she eyes each council member closely. "Won't you?"

Cordelia refuses to make eye contact and stares at the wall, shaking her head. I ignore her and look at the others. They slowly nod.

Rusty's shoulders sag. "I'll accept, for now, but you all need to be searching for another way. Or ..." He turns to Eli. "Maybe you could just step up and do what you're supposed to do."

"No, I think you're perfect," Eli says.

"Will you at least agree to go see Mia?" Rusty asks, folding his arms across his broad chest. Eli takes in a deep breath, running his non-broken wrinkly hand through his white greasy hair. Before he can decline, Rusty changes his question into a demand.

"If I'm taking over as chief for you, you *will* go see Mia."

Turning to the rest of those in the room, he says, "Now, will the rest of you help me come up with a plan to defeat Aitin?"

Chapter 32

Tiny drops of water fall from the middle of MossyHollow to the brook running beneath the bridge. It's still night, but the drops collect light from the torches around the room, making them twinkle softly. It's beautiful like it's always been, but even amid the water I can sense the change in Petrichor. MossyHollow is quieter, its shelves almost empty. Petrichor itself is more solemn.

I look around the large room inside the tree. Everything has changed. It's scary not knowing what the future will look like, whether MossyHollow will always stand or if it could be destroyed one day. Whether the Pepps will be destroyed. Whether the chief will die. I try not to let the guilt lodge in me now but instead focus on what I have to do to fix things.

After searching for some basic equipment capsules, Mark finds his way to me on the bridge. His fingers rest at my elbow, touching it softly, sending warmth up my arm.

After our conversations in the Post, Mark made me promise to tell him every little thing Jeter and Aitin did to me. Of course I will tell him, but I wanted to offer some sort of trade: I'll tell *him*, if he tells *me* everything.

Somehow, I don't think that will go over very well. I step into his side and wrap my arms around his waist.

It doesn't matter. I'll be here, ready to listen whenever he's ready.

Until then, we just have to hope we survive what comes next.

Acknowledgements

My goodness! Thank you all for your support! It's not easy releasing a book and allowing others to judge what goes on in my head. Your time, kindness and enthusiasm towards The Vine means a lot to me!

Thank you to my four boys. As much as I try to hide the struggles of writing from them, they still see it and are more supportive than I imagined young boys could be. They celebrated with me when I got my first book in the mail, helped me with the book covers, and have encouraged me repeatedly. I sure love you!

To my husband, again. Your patience and constant encouragement baffles me. Thank you for all you do!

I would like to thank Charles Alderton, the inventor of Dr. Pepper. I assure you this book would not exist without that very helpful, caffeinated drink. Thank you!

To the first reader of The Black Heart. Carrie England. You were the first to experience this book and I appreciate your feedback, time, and kind words!

To those who first read the entire series, Abbie Conley, and Kymbree Mitchell. Your continued enthusiasm and support means the world to me!

To my emotional support system: Mom, Dad, Kristi Farnsworth, Jessica Arch, Tess DiPiero, and Rich. You listened and lifted me when I needed it.

A special thank you to my silent supporters, Dalene Teichert and others. I'm always surprised when I learn that you're rooting for me on my journey. Thank you!

Another special thank you to my vocal supporters who are willing to share my book with others: Adrie Thomson, Christa Weaver, Amber Beckenholdt, Lindsay Welling, Amber Rex, Brenna Berry, Tess DiPiero, Heather Johnson, and more! You make writing a book worth it!

Thank you to my amazing editor C.S. Lakin, for your critiques. Your specific comments were like guiding lights that allowed me to clearly see what I needed to do to make the book better. And thank you for your time and encouragement. I appreciate all you do for me!

Lastly, I want to thank my Heavenly Father and Savior, Jesus Christ, for always being there for me. It's amazing how much this difficult process has drawn me closer to my Savior. I know He lives. I know He loves each one of us. And I'm grateful for His constant love, support and comfort. He is truly the brightest hope in my life.

www.ingramcontent.com/pod-product-compliance
Lightning Source LLC
Chambersburg PA
CBHW020601310726
48979CB00008B/1295/J

* 9 7 9 8 9 9 0 3 8 0 2 4 0 *